BiG BONED

BiG BONED

JO WATSON

wattpad books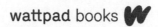

wattpad books **W**

Content Warning: alcoholism, anxiety and panic attacks, bullying, divorce, fat shaming, infidelity, mental health, neurodivergence, underage drinking

Published in Canada by Wattpad Books, a division of Wattpad Corp.
36 Wellington Street E., Toronto, ON M5E 1C7

www.wattpad.com

First Wattpad Books edition: September 2021
ISBN 978-1-98936-529-8 (Hardcover original)
ISBN 978-1-98936-530-4 (eBook edition)

Library and Archives Canada Cataloguing in Publication information is available upon request.

Printed and bound in Canada

1 3 5 7 9 10 8 6 4 2

Cover design by Kyle Light and Diané Pretorius
Interior images © Gleb via Abobe Stock
Typesetting by Sarah Salomon

To Jack. Whose brilliant brain astounds me every single day.

1

Leonardo da Vinci once said that when you looked at your work in a mirror and saw it reversed, it would look like some other painter's work, and then you'd be a better judge of its faults.

I stood, feet anchored to the ground like they were sprouting roots into the carpet beneath me, and glared at the mirror in front of me. It glared back. Flat, shiny, and unrelenting. So utterly bloody unrelenting that I wanted to toss something at it just to break its icy stare. Shatter it, like it was so fond of shattering me.

When I couldn't take it a second longer, I turned my back on the thing, pulled yet another T-shirt off, and tossed it to the floor. My previous school was easy; I'd wake up each morning and slip on our black and white uniform, no mirror needed. But everything was different now, and it wasn't just the lack of a school uniform that made it that way. In fact, it couldn't be more different if my mother had decided to uproot the family and move us to one of Jupiter's far-flung moons.

I'm a city girl. Born and bred. And up until seven days ago, we'd lived in a penthouse in one of Johannesburg's cool, newly renovated downtown areas. My school, the Art School, where I was studying fine art, was only a few blocks away. After class, my friends and I would walk the streets lined with coffee shops, art galleries, and vintage clothing and record stores, and hang out in our favorite place, the smoky, laid-back jazz café, Maggie's.

At night, I'd sit at my window and watch the city below spring to life. I loved listening to the frantic symphony of the city. A soundscape of honking taxis, shrieking police sirens, rushing, shouting, pushing people. Everything so alive. Everything pounding, blaring, screaming, and growling at you.

I'd gaze at the brightly colored lights of the Nelson Mandela Bridge that took you right into the thumping heart of the city. Johannesburg. Joburg. Jozi. It's called many things. But my favorite name is its isiZulu one: Egoli, Place of Gold. Which is exactly what it is when the sun dips down and the city lights flicker on, casting that warm, molten glow across the tops and sides of the skyscrapers.

Gold's my favorite color, by the way. But there's no gold here. Looking out of my bedroom window all I could see now was blue, the massive sea stretching to the horizon, reaching up into a never-ending cloudless sky. An infinity of it.

Blue . . . it's such a simple color, really. A primary color.

Gold, however, well, that's another story. It's complex. Layered. Much harder to create, and it's also so much more than *just* a color. Gold contains a certain magic, an extravagance, a mystique.

JO WATSON

I tried to sigh but the breath got caught in my esophagus. I turned my back on the window now too. I've never liked the sea. Too much water. Too much sand. Besides, I'm not exactly a bikini kinda gal. I haven't been beach-body ready since, well, forever. How ironic then that I've landed here, in the middle of bikini-Barbie, thigh-chafing hell.

Clifton, Cape Town. A place where you're either wearing activewear because you've just left your early morning gym sesh—green smoothie in hand—or you're in swimwear 'cause you're headed to the beach, green smoothie in hand. And don't even get me started on what it's like when the sun goes down. Let's just say you won't find a moody jazz club on these streets. It's more upscale eateries, shucked oysters, and cham-bloody-pagne.

Currently, I'm staging a silent protest against my mother for uprooting my life and dragging me here. But what's new? My mother and I have been locked in a kind of protest for the last four years now.

I do, however, understand *why* we came here. I just can't help feeling that I wasn't consulted. Which I wasn't. The closest thing to a consultation came when she'd walked into my bedroom three weeks ago and declared, *We're moving to Cape Town.* She might as well have detonated an atomic bomb—that's how it felt as I sat on my bed and saw my entire life explode into a million pieces.

We came here for my brother, Zac. I'm not blaming him for this, how could I—I love him more than I can probably describe. He's nine. He's also *specially abled*, as my mother prefers to say. She enjoys upbeat euphemisms, but between you and me, he's on the autism spectrum.

Over the last few years, his symptoms had gotten worse, until his school had finally "suggested" that he attend a facility "better aligned with his unique needs." (Everyone likes euphemisms, it seems.) So, after a quick google search by my mother, the best assisted learning school in the country was located, and now here we are. Sunny, beachy, activewear central—*with green smoothie in hand.*

"Crap!" I pulled yet another outfit off and tossed it to the floor, adding to the massive patchwork of clothes that lay twisted at my feet. My floor was starting to look like a Hannah Höch artwork, my favorite collage artist, and I swear, if you looked hard enough, you could see a galloping horse desperately trying to break free of the tangled mess.

But nothing I owned seemed right. And you need to wear the right thing on your first day. Something that gives off the vibe that you didn't try *too* hard, but that you tried *just* hard enough.

"Hurry." My mother's voice raced up the stairs and burst into my room like an unwanted guest. I'd already told her she didn't need to take me to school—I had my own car—but she was insistent. "I'm going to be late for my meeting!" She sounded rushed and angry, which had been her general vibe for a while now, certainly since that fateful day four years ago—the day the doves cried, as I've come to call it in my head.

"Late, late, late," my brother echoed. Zac often repeats words. I try not to swear in front of him, not since the unfortunate *crap, crap, crap* incident.

I forced myself to face the mirror again. On some days, I can look at myself for longer than a few seconds; today was *not* one of those days. My pale, flabby thighs that touched, my stomach that oozed over the top of my very unsexy panties, and worse, my "hellos and good-byes"—those flappy bits of fat on your arms that jiggle when you wave at people. I try not to wave.

"Aaargh." I covered my face and turned away from the evil

thing again. I've long suspected that mirrors were invented by some gorgeous, stick-thin, yet completely sinister, creature for the sole purpose of tormenting girls like me.

I reached for the nearest outfit I could find: my most comfortable pair of worn jeans and a cute, vintage, button-up blouse I'd found at a little secondhand shop with the boys—my BFFs—Andile and Guy. At art school there were four distinct groups: art kids, drama kids, music kids, and dance kids. For some reason, I'd made friends with the ballet guys pretty early on. We'd just found each other, like attracting magnets, and since then we'd moved around school like a little impenetrable team. I missed them so much . . . and we'd been separated for only seven days.

I tugged my jeans on. They felt a little tighter than usual, probably from all the stress eating I'd been doing lately: *carbs really are from the devil* (perhaps also invented by the same person who gave us mirrors?). I pulled them up, trying to cover the muffin top, but not pulling them so high that I was now sporting a gigantic camel toe. The black, collared blouse also felt like it was straining across my bust. I adjusted my bra, trying to flatten the ladies, but clearly they were also protesting today, because they weren't going anywhere.

And then there was my hair, the massive mop of curls that I'd long given up on trying to wrangle with a straightener.

I slipped a pair of comfy, old sneakers on and gave myself an extra spray of deo; it was hot today, and the last thing I needed was to be the smelly girl too.

I inspected myself. I looked fine. *Sort of.* I looked like me, like I always did. But today I wasn't so sure how well Me was going to go down at my new school.

Bay Water High, where surfing and bodyboarding were

extracurricular activities because the school backed onto the beach. I'd gone to the school's Facebook page a few days ago and scoured their photos, hoping to find someone, *anyone*, who looked vaguely like me. But nothing.

Because it seemed that being gorgeous and thigh-gap thin were prerequisites for being a student at BWH. I was *not* gorgeous. My hair was red and frizzy. My skin erred on the pasty, pale side, with a smattering of cellulite for added texture, and the only gap I had was the one between my front teeth.

She's just big boned, I'd once overheard my mom say to another mother. *It's probably puppy fat, she'll grow out of it*, the other mother had offered up with a look that resembled pity, as if thinking, *Thank heavens she's not mine.* But I was seventeen now, turning eighteen in two months, and I wasn't growing out of it. If anything, I was growing into it more than ever. My phone gave a sudden beep and I looked down at it. A message from my dad lit up the screen and my stomach dropped.

DAD: Good luck on your first day. Thinking of you!

I stared at the message and then left my dad on Read.

"Loooooriiii!" My mother's shrill voice came at me again, like a sharp-beaked bird dive-bombing you because you'd stumbled upon its nest.

Oh, that's the other thing you should know about me—my name is Lori Patty Palmer. Of course, when the elementary school bullies got wind of my middle name, which I got courtesy of my great aunt Patty, they had a field day with it.

Move out the way, here comes Lori Fatty Palmer. I could still hear their taunts. My old therapist, Dr. Finkelstein—whose name I always thought conjured up images of impassioned, academic debates in smoky, wood-paneled rooms—said that much of my anxiety stems from the bullying. From the time I'd had food thrown in my face, the time someone wrote "Kill yourself fat bitch" on my locker, and of course, there was the pool . . .

I took a deep breath; just thinking about the pool was making my insides quiver. I'd been so relieved when all of that was over and I'd gone to art school, but now, today, I felt like that person all over again.

Lori Fatty Palmer.

I inhaled deeply and then tried to breathe out all the negativity, like that meditation app I'd downloaded told me to. Breathe in positivity, breath out negativity. *Or was it the other way around?*

Maybe this wouldn't be as bad as I thought. Maybe I was just projecting my own fears and anxieties onto the situation. Maybe I would love it at BWH. Maybe everything would be okay. *Maybe.*

I took another deep breath and the buttons on my blouse strained. (Note to self, no deep breathing today for fear that buttons might pop open.) I walked out of my room, grabbing my pill as I went and throwing it back with a sip of now-cold coffee. I grimaced at the taste. Prozac. I've never gotten used to that melt-in-your-mouth, spearmint flavor even though I've been taking it for years. Why even bother with a flavor? It's not like the taste can disguise what it really is.

2

I arrived at BWH and surveyed my surroundings.

Gorgeous girls with oversized beverages in hand walked past me, sucking on long straws. These were probably the same girls who made those blue, smoothie bowls for breakfast with those cute, star-shaped cutouts of dragon fruit.

Boys with rippling muscles also walked past, oversized beverages in one hand, protein bars in the other. And they all seemed so perky. Smiles, bright eyes, and bushy tails, and I wasn't even inside the building yet. I was walking past a row of perfectly polished SUVs that had uniformly ramped the pavement to drop off the kids. Moms in activewear, gossiping to each other in hushed tones. Dads in suits, looking busy and talking on their phones as they climbed out of their overcompensating midlife crisis Maseratis—*Kinda like my own dad, I guess.* I'd made my mother drop me off a block away from school. I didn't need her causing a spectacle, adding to the overall nail-biting stress of this day.

I pulled the finger from my lips, thrust my head into the air, and tried to look as unfazed as humanly possible. Cool, calm, confident. Breathing in negativity, breathing out positivity, looking for silver linings . . . *or something like that.* I made my way past the cars and found myself at the school entrance, and just as I'd suspected, the cool kids were all standing outside waiting, talking, laughing. Have you noticed how they always seem to move in packs? Like little meerkats. Hyenas. Swarms of bees. I lowered my head again and resisted the urge to bite my cuticle.

A steep flight of stairs rose up in front of me, and I sighed. My body and stairs aren't exactly friends, and the last thing I needed was to be out of breath when I reached the top. That would draw even more attention to me, and I hated attention. At that moment, a girl and a guy walked past me, arm in arm, laughing, looking like a pair of Insta models and taking the stairs two at a time: #couplegoals.

Despite my previous silver lining–laced thoughts, I was beginning to get the distinct impression that I wasn't going to like it here, nor was I going to fit in. I hoped this was going to be worth it. But judging by my brother's first day at school yesterday, it was unlikely. As my mom and I had been leaving the school, he'd burst out of the classroom, thrown himself onto the gate, and tried to climb over it while screaming at the top of his lungs. Let's hope day two would be better.

I made it to the top of the stairs, impressed that my breathing hadn't even kicked up a notch—probably due to all the nervous adrenaline surging through my veins.

"Hey!" someone called, but I didn't look up. Surely they weren't talking to me?

But when a foot entered my field of vision, and a body blocked my path to the entrance, I was forced to look up.

Small, cut-off denim shorts. White crop top, exposed flat stomach. Dewy complexion, impossibly long, blond hair. Conditioner-commercial hair.

"Hey, are you the new girl?" conditioner commercial asked, her blue eyes and hair actually glinting in the morning light.

"Uh . . . yes. Lori," I stuttered, averting my gaze.

"Hi! I'm Amber Long-Innes, and this is Teagan." She sounded so perky, as if she was high on the sunbeams themselves. I looked from her to Teagan, who in contrast to Amber was olive-skinned and dark-eyed, with the poutiest lips I'd ever seen. Then her lips parted, and she smiled at me. I was almost knocked off my feet, it was so big and luminous.

Okay, okay. I have a confession to make. A big one. As much as I like to mentally slag off girls like this, silently judge and mock, I'm jealous as hell of them. *There, I said it!* Not to mention truly and utterly intimidated. My acerbic, inner sarcasm is just a defense for my outward fears and insecurities. Dr. Finkelstein once explained that defense mechanisms were essential to survival, that many creatures had them. Well, at least I wasn't a Malaysian exploding ant.

"I'm president of the BWH SRC," Amber chirped.

"SRC?" I was unfamiliar with this acronym.

"Student Representative Council," she cooed.

"And I'm VP," Teagan added.

"My portfolio is HOSS," Amber continued, tucking a stray strand of hair behind her perfectly shaped ear. She reminded me of Goldilocks, except you could see she didn't eat bowls of porridge.

"And mine's PPC," Teagan jumped in. They talked as if they'd rehearsed this speech many times before, expertly jumping from line to line, like actors on a stage.

"HOSS and PPC?" I asked, when it looked like they'd finally finished the scene.

"Head of School Spirit and Primary Peer Counselor," Amber qualified.

I'd suspected this school was overflowing with teen spirit. Still, I hadn't expected "Spirit" to be an actual thing. The only teen spirit I had was that old Nirvana vinyl that I'd found in a vintage store in Joburg.

"It's our job to show new students around and introduce them to the school."

"Introduce?" I looked into Amber's ridiculously clear blue eyes as panic slid a cold finger down my spine. I tried to push the panic down. I've learned that showing the enemy how you *really* feel is not a good idea. They can, and will, prey on it.

But then Teagan did something unexpected; she pulled me into a hug. "Welcome to BWH, Lori."

"Uh . . . thanks!" I was surprised by what seemed like a genuine show of friendliness. Maybe I'd judged everyone here too soon? *Maybe.*

"Great! We'll do the introduction in assembly first period," Amber said casually, and then they both turned, flipped their hair at the same time (had they rehearsed this move too?), and walked away. I stood there, unable to move, as if the rubber soles of my shoes had melted into the hot concrete. Which was conceivable, since it was scorching today.

"Aren't you coming?" Amber turned, tilting her head and looking at me from a different angle. I wondered if she was thinking, *Nah, still fat from this angle.* I sucked my stomach in quickly in an attempt to appear more streamlined.

"Uh . . . I . . ." Dammit. I exhaled when I realized that the stomach-sucking had caused my voice to rise two unnatural-sounding octaves. "Suuuure." I tried to sound casual even though every cell, nerve, fiber, and muscle in my body wanted to turn around and *run, run, run*!

3

I was seated in the front row of the lecture hall. Amber and Teagan had placed me there and told me to stay. *I didn't want to stay.* And I certainly didn't want to be introduced to the entire school. The repetitive motion of picking at my cuticles was somewhat comforting, but it wasn't enough to quell the anxiety, especially when a bell rang and people began streaming into the auditorium.

My eyes swept the crowd, hoping to find at least one of *my kind*, but the more I looked, the more I realized that no one here was like me. I was officially the biggest person at school.

Big. It's a euphemism, isn't it? I should just call it what it is—I was the fattest person at school. This wasn't a foreign concept to me; I was usually the fattest person everywhere I went. Except for that time my mother enrolled me in Weight Watchers. I'd felt bad for feeling so damn overjoyed when I'd discovered a girl my age who was actually fatter than me.

"But you have such a pretty face . . ." If I had a rand for every time someone said that to me, I'd be rich. But it's not like I want to be like this and haven't tried to lose it—trust me, I have. I'm not one of those body positive people who embraces their curves. Sometimes I look at their Instagram accounts and envy them so much it hurts. The way they flaunt their bodies and look so damn good doing it. I could never be like that.

I turned my attention back to the hall. Everyone was seated now, including Amber and Teagan, who were perched on the edge of their chairs with their knees together. A red-hot bolt of envy made me clench my jaw when I realized I could see all the way through their nontouching thighs to the floor below.

The general chatter around me finally stopped as the principal walked onto the stage and took up position behind the podium. Even the principal here, Mr. Du Preez, was good-looking—a George Clooney type with perfect gray hair, wrinkles that made him look distinguished, and a killer white smile.

I was too beside myself with nerves, too busy obsessing about what Amber and Teagan were about to do, to listen to him. Mr. Du Preez continued talking and I tried to grab on to some of his words, but they blurred together into gibberish. And then he stopped, and someone else walked onto the stage.

A man. Muscular and wearing head-to-toe Adidas, he stood there for a few moments before he thrust his hand into the air.

"Go Dolphins!" he yelled.

Chaos broke out around me. Everyone jumped out of their chairs, and like those mind-controlled people from cults who drank the Kool-Aid, they, too, raised their fists in the air and shouted, "We are the Dolphins, and no one could be prouder and if you cannot hear us, we'll shout a little louder!"

What the blessed-be-the-fruit hell was going on here?

"Woo-hoo!" The man, who I was now assuming was the sports coach, clapped his hands together and gave a loud whistle. "Just a few sports announcements for the week. As you all know, the BWH Dolphins *crushed* the Sun Valley Seals at the water polo match last week."

"Crushed!! Crushed!! Crushed!!" everyone echoed.

"All thanks to our star center, Jake Jones-Evans!" The coach gave a totally lame salute and I paused. I wanted to take a second and allow this moment to sink in. This was the kind of place that had actual sports stars, who were *not* fictional characters in American teen movies. This was the kind of place that *crushed* and had teams named after marine animals and sang war cries in assembly. We didn't even *have* sports at art school! A freezing Jupertonian moon might actually be preferable to this place. At least it would have been more familiar.

"Stand up, Jake!" the man shouted, and this time, I turned to look. I had to see this Jake, who had another double-barrel surname. This jock of jock legends who crushed mere mortals with his thumb and was probably . . .

H . . . ooo . . . ttt!

My mouth fell open. He was leaning against the wall, not seated like everyone else, arms folded, legs crossed, oozing this kind of nonchalance that was strangely attractive. He was so *not* my type—*allow me to make this very clear*. And yet, he was stupidly good-looking. The kind of good-looking that should not be allowed to exist in nature. It was almost unnatural. As if he was the product of some secret CRISPR experiment. All

the good genes in the world had been spliced together to form
. . . *him.*

A shaft of light streamed through a window, illuminating just one side of his face, and plunging the other side into a dramatic shadow. Usually this kind of play of light and shadow, called chiaroscuro, has to be painstakingly created with the deft strokes of an artist's paintbrush, but his was totally natural.

But then Jake fist-pumped the air a few times (which quickly made him a lot less attractive to me).

"I don't think I have to remind you that it's regional finals next Friday!" the sports coach said. "We'll be playing the Blue Bay Marlins"— (what the hell was with all these animal names)—"and as you know, it's compulsory to support the team!"

Compulsory?! To support the water polo team?! The mind *boggled.*

"Also, some great phys ed news—now that the new shark nets are up, surfing can start again."

A massive cheer rose up from the crowd and reverberated around the room, building and amplifying. *What the hell?* There were just so many things wrong with that statement I didn't even know where to begin. Sharks, surfing, bathing suits . . . *on the beach*! The last time I'd worn a bathing suit in front of my classmates it had ended very badly. I really, *really* hoped surfing wasn't also compulsory. The thought made my heart bang against my rib cage so hard that it felt like it was attempting an escape. I tried to take a deep breath but my lungs weren't pulling enough air into them and suddenly, *I'm drowning again.* The sports coach left the stage and two more gorgeous girls walked up carrying a velvet-draped stand.

"Hi, everyone," one of them gushed, and smiled. Again, it was massive. *Did they all go to the same dentist here at BWH?*

"I know you're dying to know what the theme of this year's summer dance is going to be."

Another cheer rose up from the crowd. This couldn't get any worse if it tried. Not only had I arrived at this strange, alien place, but I'd arrived at this strange alien place in the middle of dance season, which was possibly the worst time of the year for girls like me.

"So, without further ado, the theme is . . ." She paused, and a collective inhalation was taken by every single person in the room—except me. The only inhalation I would ever be taking when it came to the dance was the massive in-breath I'd need in order to squeeze myself into a dress. If I was going. Which I wouldn't be.

"The theme . . . is . . ." She dragged the words out, building a tension in the air that was palpable. "*Royal Wedding!*" She whisked the cloth off the stand to reveal a kissing photo of Kate and William. The whole hall burst into applause. "So, guys, think morning suits, ballgowns, and tiaras."

Amber walked onto the stage, clutching her hand to her heart as if genuinely touched by the brilliance of this magical, amazing idea. *Where on earth was I?*

"I think I can safely say, on behalf of everyone here at BWH, that you guys, Katlego and Nina-M and everyone else on the dance committee, have totally outdone yourselves," Amber said, and they all fell into a group hug.

I blinked, trying to make sense of everything. I felt so uncomfortable that I wanted to crawl out of my skin, and then, when it couldn't possibly get any worse, Amber turned and looked straight at me.

Her lip-glossed lips were moving but I couldn't hear any

words. My brain buzzed and raced a million miles an hour, and my ears filled with a static that drowned out everything around me. *Throat expanding, hands clammy . . .* I couldn't move.

"Lori! Don't you want to come up here and introduce yourself?" She flashed me a massive smile.

My head started shaking all by itself. I wasn't even aware of the shake until I noticed the shapes of the world blurring in front of me.

"I know everyone is dying to meet you!" she said, but I was still frozen to my seat.

"Lori!" This time I could see her smile was forced, and when I still didn't move, she shook her head and marched off the stage. I breathed a massive sign of relief—*not so massive as to pop my buttons, though.* But then, to my horror, she veered toward me with the most determined-looking face I'd ever seen before. And before I could register what was happening, I was on my feet, being dragged to the stage, her hand digging into mine. My head spun, my lips and fingers tingled, cold sweat prickled on my forehead, and that was when I knew I was in the grip of full-blown panic. My inner mantra kicked in. It was something that Dr. Finkelstein had taught me, phrases I needed to repeat in order to ground myself.

My name is Lori Patty Palmer.

I'm seventeen years old.

My birthday is on the fourteenth of November, and I live at 101 The Exchange Stree—wait! I didn't live there anymore. Wait! What the hell was my new address?

"Wait!" I didn't realize I'd opened my mouth and said it until I heard Amber gasp.

"Wait, what?" She stopped pulling me.

JO WATSON

"Wa . . . uh . . . uh . . ." My tongue tripped over the words as I tried to break free of her grip, but for someone with such delicate-looking wrists, she was surprisingly strong.

"You're embarrassing me," she hissed through a clenched jaw. "I get extra credits for this."

My heartbeat felt like it was getting more and more irregular. My breathing more labored. I put my free hand on my diaphragm, *In for three, hold for four, out for three. In for three, hold for four, out for three* . . . but it wasn't working. *Please, please, please*, don't let this happen. Not here. Not now.

And then . . . a bloody miracle!

"*Fire alarm!*" someone screamed as the sound of an alarm ripped through the room and everyone scrambled to their feet again. I seized the opportunity and pulled my hand away from Amber's. But I pulled so hard and fast, using all my weight, that Amber tumbled to the floor.

"Sorry." I stepped forward apologetically, only to be met with an angry glare. I tried to dissipate the tension with a smile, but it didn't work. And then her eyes trailed down to her hand. I followed them and saw three snapped, false nail tips lying on the floor next to her.

"Crap," I whispered when her eyes came back up to mine. I could see what she was thinking. She made no attempt to hide it. *Great, day one and I'd already pissed off a girl like her.*

4

On a scale of *worst first days ever,* I would say that my first day at BWH was right up there with the best of them. After the fire alarm, the day had kind of deteriorated. The fire alarm had actually been a false alarm. Don't get me wrong, I was ever so grateful it had gone off when it had, but what followed was almost equally awful. The entire school was made to stand in the blazing sun at the bottom of the field, while Tasandra (yes, that was her name—with a *T*) and other members of the evacuation squad ran around clearing each room, one by one. For most students, this didn't seem to be a problem. In fact, they seemed to be having the time of their lives. A few now-shirtless guys were playing an impromptu game of rugby. Some of the girls, Amber and her gang, were lying in the sun, skirts hiked up catching a tan. *Me?* I was wearing black and sweating like a pig. I could feel the moisture gathering in all my folds: stomach folds, neck fold, and worst of all, big under-boob fold. I was hot, and wet, and uncomfortable, and I wished I'd put on more deodorant.

After being finally allowed back into school, the next unpleas-ant thing happened. And it happened in isiZulu class. I'd quickly discovered that the only available seat in class was in front of Tasandra, Teagan, and Thembi (now known as the Three Ts in my head), and behind water polo Jake and his two friends. And this, I soon learned, was a special kind of hell. Because every five minutes I was tapped on the shoulder and given a note to pass. This went on for the entire class, and by the end of it, I was sure I had whiplash and seriously wished that Mrs. Ndlovo hadn't forced us to put our phones in a box at the start of class. Old-school messaging was hard work; a carrier pigeon would have been preferable.

But this still wasn't the worst part of the whole experience. During one of the routine passes, I stretched my arm too far, too hard, and heard a familiar noise. I looked down just in time to see one of my shirt buttons bounce on the floor and then skid under a desk. After this unfortunate mishap, I was forced to fig-ure out a way of hiding my bra, which was now on full display. And it wasn't a pretty bra either, *oh no*. It was one of those dou-ble strength sports bras with extra wire and thick straps that desperately attempts, yet dismally fails, to defy the inevitable pull of gravity. So, for the rest of the day I had to walk around awkwardly clutching a book to my chest. Which might not have been so bad if I hadn't then proceeded to do ten thousand steps with Teagan, who insisted on showing me around the entire school: ". . . toilets, janitors' closet, you can make out there . . . storeroom, you can also make out there . . . gym, science lab, bleachers, also make out, but be careful—last month Amber and Jake were caught by the hockey coach. But Jake's not really into Amber anymore because she kind of went ballistic when she caught him DMing Nina-M, 'only as friends!'" She threw some dramatic air quotes around, and I wasn't sure I got their meaning. *Were they just friends, weren't they just friends?* The social structure of this habitat was so foreign to me, I wished this was a National Geographic documentary and David Attenborough was narrating the ins and outs of it all, so I could better understand it. "I think Jake made out with her because she's number one on the Hot List, though . . ." she said. "He kind of makes his way down the list. Mind you, Amber is the one who publishes the list on our WhatsApp group, so she could have put herself at one, since no one knows who makes the list every year." The Hot List, I discovered, was a list that came out once a year, rating all the girls from hot to not. Thank goodness I wasn't going to be around next year.

The tour, and Teagan's enthusiasm, seemed never ending, and it was boiling, especially with a book pressed to my chest. "And that's Vuyo, you probably *recognize* him, he's TikTok famous, the video of him flying down the stairs in a shopping cart and then wiping out got one million views, so cool . . . and that's Nina-M I was telling you about, she thinks she's this big beauty blogger because Kylie Jenner liked one of her posts or something, but really, she's not." I looked over at Nina-M; she was lying on the grass pouting at a selfie stick. I was getting a real education from Teagan all right. But it had nothing to do with the geography of the school and everything to do with getting a better glimpse into the characters that I was now forced to cohabit with.

And it was for all these above reasons that I now found myself sitting on our cool kitchen floor after school, listening to my favorite artist, Grimes, while eating ice cream straight out of the tub with the biggest spoon I could find.

"Hey, Captain Zac Sparrow." My brother, Zac, walked into the kitchen, and I smiled up at him. I still called him Captain Sparrow sometimes, a throwback to his pirate obsession phase. Kids on the spectrum tend to develop obsessions with things. But as quickly as they develop, they suddenly change. One day it's pirates, and the next . . . *who knows.*

"Want some?" I passed him the spoon and patted the floor next to me. Zac is probably the only person in the world who isn't going to judge me for eating ice cream on the floor, unlike my mother, who scrutinizes every morsel I put into my mouth. She rarely says anything, though, which makes it worse in a way.

Zac took the spoon from me and immediately scooped up some vanilla ice cream. We only have vanilla in the house because Zac only eats white foods: plain yogurt, pasta, potatoes—not the healthiest diet. We make sure to give him a vanilla "milkshake" everyday, which is really a vitamin-enriched drink, because he refuses to eat anything with colors. He says he can feel the colors fighting each other in his stomach. This idea that colors could possibly be alive and interacting with each other has always intrigued me. In art there's a concept called simultaneous contrast; it refers to the way that two different colors affect each other when placed side by side. It's an illusion where one color can change how we perceive the other one. But I've often wondered if it isn't an illusion for Zac, whether he is somehow capable of experiencing things in life that no one else can.

"How was your day?" I asked.

"I built a mousetrap that I think can actually catch mice when I put cheese in it to lure them in but I don't know what kind of cheese they like yet and I only like the white cheese but maybe they like the yellow cheese or the one with holes but I don't know where to get that cheese from so I'm going to experiment with the white cheese first."

"That sounds cool. What are you going to do with the mice you catch?"

"I was thinking I could train them like they train those dogs at the airport that sniff the luggage for drugs and stuff on the conveyer belt but I wouldn't train them to sniff I would train them to be undercover spies like they have in the CIA."

"Spies. Wow." I smiled. I loved the way my brother's brain worked. While other kids were playing with toys or kicking balls around, he was engineering intricate traps, building solar-powered devices, and making electrical currents from potatoes and lemons. He's a total genius in so many ways, but ask him to do something simple like brush his teeth and it falls apart; the toothpaste tastes too strong, the water is too wet, the bristles are too hard.

"Maybe I could take the mice to my new school, and they could spy on the people there?" I offered thoughtfully and then watched him for a while, trying to gauge what kind of a mood he was in. It was always hard to interpret his moods. While the angry moods were easy to read, the subtler emotions in between were trickier. But his shoulders were relaxed, he wasn't flapping or clicking his fingers, he was eating, so I broached the subject tentatively. "How was school today? Did you try to escape again?"

"It was better," he mumbled. "Escaping was not necessary." He shoved another spoonful into his mouth and I smiled to myself with relief.

"Maybe I could make microscopic cameras that we could strap onto the mice's heads that no one can see and they can film everything that happens at your school and then we could download it onto my computer and watch it like a movie and make popcorn," he said through a mouthful of ice cream.

I laughed. I wanted to pull him into a hug, or kiss him on the cheek, but didn't. He's not great with touching; you can only touch him if he initiates it. Sometimes I crave any kind of physical contact with him.

"Ice cream in the afternoon!" We both looked up as my mother swanned in. "Not very nutritious," she added. "Besides, milk is not actually good for us. It's basically antibiotic-laden pus. You should google it."

"Really?" I tried to hide the sarcasm in my voice, but wasn't sure it was working. By her own admission, she'd gleaned this little nugget of info from Google. She'd probably also dipped her toe into the pool of fake Facebook junk that swirled around us on a daily basis. The kind that had people believing that the earth was flat, and that humans were being secretly microchipped by aliens. My mother buys into all of it. She never used to, but in the evenings when she's all alone, you can find her frantically googling and watching YouTube videos about how the world government is made up of reptilians. I'm always amazed by her propensity to believe in the utterly unbelievable. Dr. Finkelstein said she's probably unable to sit alone at night with her feelings, so grabs hold of any distraction she can find. Well, I could think of at least ten other, healthier distractions she could choose.

"It's not like there's much in the fridge," I offered up flatly.

"It's not like I've had any time to go shopping!" She sounded snappy now, and I decided to back off. No use in pointing out that the fridge was mostly empty and the house was still largely unfurnished since the second furniture delivery truck hadn't arrived yet. It felt like we were living in a vast, hollow cavern; squatting in emptiness, waiting for our lives to begin. Our lives, which only a few days ago had been packed up into boxes, labeled, and loaded.

She sighed loudly. She did this a lot and it always made a flicker of guilt break through the general anger I felt toward her. "I'll try to go to the shops tomorrow. I wanted to get Zac settled first, and I have all these new business meetings."

"Sure," I muttered quietly, almost to myself. I didn't really believe her. I'd probably be the one buying the groceries, phoning the logistics company to track down our furniture, and filling out all of Zac's forms for his new OT and speech therapists.

"What are you doing now?" she asked.

"Mmmm, I'll have to look at my busy diary and get back to you." I shoved an extra-large spoon into my mouth, pus or no pus.

"Lori Palmer. No need for that tone!" She put her hand on her hip and raised her eyebrows at me. They barely peeped over the rims of her big, designer sunglasses.

"Lori Palmer," Zac repeated. He usually repeats words when he gets overwhelmed, when things around him aren't completely calm, and suddenly, I felt bad for being sarcastic. Not because it was directed at my mom, but because it had unsettled Zac.

"Why? Would you like me to do something?" I asked as sweetly as possible.

"I've got that shoot here today. We're shooting an ad for my business. It will only take about an hour." She pulled her glasses off and looked at me.

"Mom! What's . . . why . . . what have you done?"

"Just had a little thread lift around my eyes." She reached up and touched them gently. They were a completely different shape than what they'd been this morning. "But don't worry, the doctor assured me the redness would be gone in an hour. Besides, it's nothing my bangs can't cover." She fluffed her bangs and put her sunglasses back on, and her newly taut eyes disappeared.

I tried not to shake my head disapprovingly. But honestly, I still wasn't used to this new version of my mother. The woman who came home with a new face every so often. About a year ago she'd come home with lips that were twice their normal size, and then a little while after that, a forehead that no longer moved. It reminded me of a sculpture—flat, smooth, unmovable marble. I'd overheard her on the phone telling one of her friends that she wanted the forehead of a twenty-seven-year-old. Funny, that was the exact same age as my father's girlfriend, Maddy.

"Maybe you and Zac could go out and have a *real* snack somewhere?" She passed me her credit card; it was a dismissive gesture. The kind that told me she didn't want us here lest we interfere with the stupendously important ad for her real estate company, Palm Luxury Realty.

She'd gotten half of my father's money in their long, messy divorce, and ever since then, she'd rebranded herself as the queen of luxury real estate and cosmetic enhancement.

"Thanks, Lori. I owe you one."

One? In my opinion, she owed me more than one. She owed me a couple of thousand, one for every single day since *that day.* The day the doves cried.

I stood up and gestured for Zac to follow, just as my phone beeped.

DAD: How was your first day?

I put it back into my pocket without answering. I was angry with him too.

5

By the time I got to school for day two at BWH, I was late. Not because I'd overslept or forgotten to set my alarm, but because it had taken an eternity to get Zac to agree to go to school. I ended up stepping in after watching my mother negotiate unsuccessfully with him for half an hour, getting more and more worked up as she went. In the end, I promised that if he went to school, when we got home we could go to the beach and build a giant sandcastle with five turrets, secret passages for all the mouse spies, as well as a deep moat to keep enemies out. I also promised I would take him to school, despite the fact I was due in class in ten minutes.

At least my mother had done one thing right when she'd rented the monstrosity we now called home: the house was exactly four blocks from my new school and five from my brother's.

But that was its only redeeming feature. Not to sound like an art snob here, but this house was an affront to just about every single one of my aesthetic sensibilities, with its shiny, silver colonnade entrance, blue mirrored glass frontage, and the large lion sculptures with wings that flanked the biggest front door known to humankind. I couldn't help but wonder how we'd gone from cool, downtown industrial to . . . *this*? Whatever *this* was trying so hard to be. I guess it made sense that my mother would have chosen a house like this. Over the top, shiny facade. Screaming to be seen by everyone who drove past.

It was hot again today. The weather in Cape Town was different from Joburg. The air here was thick and sticky, like stepping into a steam room, whereas home was dry. You could move through the heat freely at home, but here it felt like it clung to you, weighing you down as the day went by.

I'd anticipated the heat today, though, and was wearing much cooler clothes and extra deodorant. I'd put on my favorite T-shirt, the one with the Andy Warhol pop art soup can print. This was my go-to shirt, and slipping it on felt like chatting to an old friend. You know why I love this shirt so much? Because it takes something so ordinary—a can of Campbell's soup—and elevates it to art. I've often wondered if Warhol was able to see things in everyday objects that no one else could see. Could he look below the surface of something and find the thing inside it that made it beautiful and special?

I finally skidded into a parking place at school thirty minutes late for class. And when I made my way up the long stairs and into the building, and managed to find the right classroom, I was utterly traumatized to discover that I was sitting next to Amber, in the front row.

I hate the front row. I feel like I'm being watched when I sit there, which of course, I am. The anxiety of all those eyes boring holes into your back felt overwhelming, and with Amber next to me, these feelings were only intensified. So much so that when I pulled my water bottle out to quench my dry, nervous mouth, my hands were shaking so much that I spilled water on her book, ruining the work she'd done, while also wetting her skirt. By some cruel twist of fate, it seemed I was destined to go through life at BWH continuously pissing off the likes of Amber—the one girl at school you didn't want to piss off.

And like my first day at BWH, this day also just deteriorated. Because I soon discovered that wearing a soup can on my clothing had *not* been a good idea. This became evident when the Three Ts cornered me in the bathroom.

"Do you, like, really, really like, like, *soup*, like, a lot?" Teagan asked.

I wanted to open my mouth and shout, *Do you, like, really, really like, like, saying like, like, a lot? Like?* But didn't.

"Isn't it, like, too hot, like, for soup, like?" Teagan asked. (Okay, so I'm lying about all the *likes*. They weren't really saying them, but I was imagining them in my head.)

"Yeah, I'd understand it if it was a smoothie or something," the one called Tasandra added thoughtfully.

"*Oh em gee*, that's such a good idea!" Teagan clasped her hands enthusiastically. "We should get shirts made with our favorite smoothies on them, and then we wouldn't need to open our mouths to order them, we could just point at our shirts."

What. The. Hell! Had I heard that correctly? I stared in shock, watching Tasandra and Teagan as they looked like they were really considering this as a legitimate new way of ordering their favorite blended drinks. And then something strange happened. Thembi, the tall, golden-brown goddess, tilted her head to the side and looked at my shirt again.

"Isn't that by a famous artist?" she asked.

"Andy Warhol," I replied quietly.

"He did those pictures of Marilyn Monroe and the cows. I saw them when I was in New York."

"You saw original Andy Warhols?"

"Yeah, they're cool," she said and then turned around. This seemed to be the cue for the other Ts to follow. I stared after them as they walked toward the door.

That hadn't really happened, had it? Because surely someone like her hadn't just called my shirt cool? The other two Ts had no idea who Andy Warhol was, and to be honest, a little flicker of artistic superiority had rushed through me, but Thembi . . . she seemed different somehow. There was something about her I couldn't put my finger on. I caught one last glimpse of her arm as she closed the door behind her. The warm light from the passage beyond the bathroom seemed to accentuate the gold of her skin for a second. I mentally made a note to try to re-create that color; *how much gold would I need to add to brown to get that?*

"Teagan has a point, you know?" I heard a flush and looked up as Amber walked out of one of the stalls. Her long blond hair had been fastened on top of her head in a messy bun. The kind that you knew she'd spent hours perfecting in front of the mirror. Just the right amount of mess for Insta-worthy, curated casualness. I'd spent such a long time wishing that girls like Amber would like me. That they would open their arms and invite me into their inner girly sanctums. We would all do our hair and makeup together. Gossip about the guys and get ready to go out to parties.

That had never happened, and even though I had my own little, happy clique now, there was still this tiny part of me that craved some kind of affirmation from an Amber. *I hate that part of me.*

"No one likes soup that much that they put it on a shirt."

"It's not about liking soup." I swallowed.

Her face scrunched up like she was sucking on a lemon. "Then what's it about?"

"It's art."

"Art!" She rolled her eyes. A sense of inferiority swelled inside me. *Why did girls like her make me feel this way?* And she knew it, because she asserted her dominance even more when she slowly, pointedly dabbed a tissue over the wet mark on her skirt. When she'd sufficiently rubbed my face in it, she crunched the tissue up, and then with a casualness that bordered on utter disdain, threw it at the trash can and then shrugged when it missed and fell to the floor.

"By the way, *Lauri*," she said, deliberately mispronouncing my name. "I think you forgot something yesterday. I saved it for you." She smiled. It was glacial. The kind of smile that would make hell freeze over.

I reached out to take whatever she was giving me, and when I saw what it was, embarrassment plugged my throat closed.

My button.

She gave me a smug smile and then exited the bathroom with a low, evil-sounding chuckle. The kind a witch might make while dropping the severed heads of small, innocent, woodland creatures into a fiery cauldron. I picked up her tissue and threw it into the bin. How had this become my life? Living the ultimate teen cliché where a girl like *her* was picking on a girl like *me*?

6

I dragged myself and my humiliated soup can shirt out of the bathroom, and as much as I like to give off the vibe—*whenever possible*—that I'm cool and unaffected by such puerile, immature behavior, it's all a lie.

Because I am. I *am* affected by it. It *does* get to me, and it cuts me right to the quick, and now I wished that I had my regular afternoon appointment with Dr. Finkelstein. I pulled up the message she'd sent me with the number for a therapist in Cape Town. While my phone was out, I decided to send the guys a quick WhatsApp. I needed something familiar in my life right now. Something I could anchor myself with.

WhatsApp Group: How You Doin'???

I smiled to myself whenever I read the group name. Two years ago we'd binged all of *Friends*, and this had become our official greeting for a while. That was a happy time.

LORI: This place is crazy! You wouldn't believe it

GUY: Do tell

ANDILE: Are the guys there hot tho?

LORI: You're such a gay cliché

ANDILE: 🙄 But you love me anyway

LORI: 😸 Who wouldn't!

ANDILE: And what are the girls like? Are they a bunch of hot Mean Girls?

LORI: Some of them seem okay, I guess. But then there's Amber . . .

GUY: AAAHH! There's always an "Amber" isn't there?

LORI: And she already hates me . . . I guess I did break her nails and spill water on her

ANDILE: Bad girl

LORI: It was an accident, but now she has it out for me

GUY: Just put that gorgeous head of yours up in the air and be yourself

ANDILE: Totally. Everyone will love you

ANDILE: Well, maybe Amber won't. But that's okay. Who wants to be friends with her anyway 😰

LORI: I gotta run, don't want to be late for class

GUY: We miss you xxx

LORI: Me too

GUY: Big time!

ANDILE: I miss you more than Guy

GUY: That's just because Musi broke up with you

LORI: Noooo. Why?

ANDILE: He decided he wasn't gay . . . again!

GUY: Confused "straight" guys are the worst! They should just come out as bi. Like me. Best of both worlds

ANDILE: 😳

LORI: Okay! Love you all. Have to go

ANDILE: 😺

GUY: Bye. Slay the day!

Slay the day. I smiled. It was so cheesy, but we loved saying it to each other. The conversation with the guys had made me feel a little less lost and I started typing another message.

LORI: Hi, my name is Lori. I got your number from Dr. Finkelstein. I've just moved to Cape Town and she recommended you as a therapist. Wondering where you are and if you have any time to see me?

I started to slip my phone back into my bag, not anticipating an immediate response. But it beeped.

DR. STRIDE: Lori! Of course. I've heard great things about you from Pamela. I'd love to see you. How's tomorrow afternoon at 3:00?

LORI: I'm not sure I can make this week, I have to look after my brother in the afternoons at the moment. What about next week?

DR. STRIDE: You're welcome to bring him.

LORI: I'm not sure

DR. STRIDE: There's plenty to do here. I have a huge garden he can explore

I looked at her message and paused. I always dreaded this moment, when I had to explain it. *Explain him.* And it always felt wrong, as if I was betraying Zac, disrespecting his right to privacy. *But that's the thing with autism, sometimes it's impossible to hide.*

LORI: My brother doesn't like stranger's homes. He's not very comfortable in them. He's on the autism spectrum.

DR. STRIDE: No problem. Whatever suits you 😊

Smiley face? This woman didn't sound like a normal therapist at all.

LORI: I'll ask my mom whether she can look after Zac tomorrow and get back to you later

DR. STRIDE: Perfect. I look forward to working together

What were the chances that my mom wasn't busy tomorrow afternoon with some important meeting/advert/eyebrow lift? Since coming here, looking after Zac seemed to have become my responsibility. Back home we'd had an au pair three times a week, but now it was just me, and my mom was hardly home anymore either. I loved spending time with Zac, but school was going to get busy and I wasn't going to be able to do that every day.

The day sort of tumbled on from there. I went from one class to another in a silent daze. Moving through the crowds of people, down the passages, and up the flights of stairs . . . alone. This was nothing like art school. Firstly, there was no art here, other than some after-school club, and secondly, everything was so formal, despite the lack of school uniforms. Desks and chairs and lines and neat rows. Also, the kids here were completely different from the ones I was used to. Everyone here seemed so made up—perfect, polished, pretty. I felt so uncomfortable here; every step I took felt like I was wading through a swamp of quicksand that was trying to suck me under. And then it was lunchtime.

I hate eating in front of people. I'm scared that like my mom, they might also be taking an inventory of everything I put into my mouth. Watching the fat girl eat with curiosity, like an animal in the zoo. So I walked straight out of the cafeteria and strolled around school, and without Teagan by my side, I noticed things I hadn't seen the day before, like all the #motivational posters on the walls.

I find this kind of thing so distasteful. Like those motivational speakers who ooze fake humility in that totally pseudo, sincere manner. Big smiles, power suits, gelled hair, telling you how they used to get bullied when they were young and understand what you're going through—*And for only R999.99 you can be like them if you buy their Ten Steps to Success program, guaranteed to give you brighter, whiter, bigger smiles, thicker wallets, and thinner thighs, but wait, there's more.* I stopped and read a poster.

"'Good, better, best. Never let it rest.'" Ugh.

"'Today's struggle is tomorrow's strength.'" Double *ugh*. But the next one made me stop dead in my tracks.

"'When you start seeing your worth, you'll find it harder to stay around people who don't.'"

My worth. The word punched me in the gut. Most of my worth had been tied up in the fact I was an artist. People knew that, they respected that, I was even semicool because of it. But any semblance of cool I'd once possessed, had been left behind in Joburg, with my old life. I walked all the way down to the field at the far end of the school. There was a really nice tree there that provided just the right amount of dappled shade. In the distance, some guys—the jocky ones—were tossing a rugby ball around. And because I didn't want them to think that I was there to watch—that would be mortifying—I turned my back to the field and sat down.

I could eat my sandwich in peace here and draw something in the sketchbook I carried around with me. I flipped the book open and took out my 2B pencil. It was the perfect pencil for sketching: soft, yet still hard enough, giving just the right combination of perfect lines and shading. I decided to sketch my sandwich wrapper, so I crumpled it and dropped it to the ground. But just as I was about to take a bite and lower my pencil to the paper, something whacked me on the back. My entire body fell forward and my face hit the ground.

"What . . . ah . . . what?" I scrambled to my feet in a state of shock. What was that? A bomb? A meteorite? A . . . a . . . a . . .

Bloody rugby ball. Loud laughter erupted behind me and I froze. *Had that been on purpose?* I certainly wasn't going to wait around to find out. I grabbed my things and was just about to rush off when I heard a voice.

"You okay?" I turned, only to find *him* standing there.

Jake Jock Jones Double Barrel.

"Sorry about that. Vuyo got a bit carried away," he said. Vuyo, I knew that name . . . oh, TikTok-famous guy who deliberately fell down flights of stairs. God, I hoped he hadn't filmed that: I don't want to be trending tomorrow.

"Sure. No worries. Sorry," I replied, shrugging. This was my default response to things like this. I brushed them off with carefully rehearsed nonchalance. I'd learned that when you reacted, it spurred them on. *Dulling your emotions and reactions was the only way for girls like me to handle situations like this.*

"Why're you saying sorry?" he asked.

"Uh . . . what?"

"*I'm* sorry," he said. "You were just sitting here, having lunch."

"Oh. Okay. Thanks . . . I think." I blinked a few times, utterly confused.

He smiled at me. *He really was gorgeous.* Still, not my type.

But there was no denying his obvious hotness. Michelangelo believed that beauty could be boiled down to a simple equation. The golden ratio that dictated how features should fit together in perfect, mathematical symmetry. But Jake's hotness seemed to defy this. His lopsided smile, the scar through his left eyebrow, the random and imperfect waves in his hair, the way it was mostly brown except for those gold strands that made it look like the sun was directly above him, casting a constant glow over him. Nothing about his face was in proportion, and yet it fit together perfectly. Michelangelo was definitely wrong.

"I'm Jake, by the way." And then he did something strange. He extended his hand for me to shake.

"I—I know," I stammered, taking it sheepishly. "Lori."

"I know," he said.

And then, as quickly as he'd appeared, he was gone. He jogged back to his friends, who were all still laughing.

"Shut up," Jake shouted, throwing the ball at Vuyo.

"Don't be a dickhead," Vuyo said when the ball collided with him. I think a look must have passed between them, because suddenly Vuyo looked over at me and waved.

"*Sorry!*" he yelled.

The day grew progressively worse after the ball incident. Just when I was starting to think the people at BWH weren't as bad as I'd initially thought, Amber proved me wrong. She'd teased me as I'd walked past her and a group of her friends, *Well, I guess she needed bread to go with that soup.*

They'd all laughed and I hadn't understood why until I'd gone to the bathroom and realized my sandwich had smudged across my shirt. Clearly, I'd fallen on top of it when the ball had hit me.

So when the last bell finally rang, I couldn't get out of there fast enough. When I was safely in my car again, I looked back at the school. Strange really, that this brightly colored building with its sunshine-yellow walls and sky-blue roof could be such a dark place. In the 1500s an artist called Hieronymus Bosch painted these disturbingly dark images of hell, and I couldn't help but wonder if he shouldn't have included Amber and BWH in his famous oil paintings.

The drive to my brother's school was a quick one, and very unlike my walk back from school in Joburg. Everything here was so clean. Pristine. Even the streets looked shiny and manicured, like all the people and cars that inhabited them. There was a neatness and orderliness to this place that Joburg didn't have, and it felt suffocating. But it also felt made up in some way, like a stage set that had been meticulously designed and then professionally lit, just waiting for gorgeous actors to start whatever scene was next. Everything about this place felt like a performance, nothing was out of place, *except me.*

I pulled up to a traffic light and then choked on an intake of breath when I came face-to-face with my mother staring down at me from a streetlight. Her arms were folded, her hair was shiny and overstyled, and her smile was so big it reminded me of the Cheshire Cat. Another performance.

Palm Luxury Realty. Your luxury specialist.

I pulled off as soon as the light turned green, but it wasn't long before I saw her again. This time she was standing in front of a massive house. Arms open wide, porcelain-veneered Cheshire smile.

Welcome to your new luxury home.

I shook my head in disapproval; I could do that now. What the hell had happened to my mother to turn her into this strange face on a poster? Well, I suppose catching your husband in a hot tub with a much younger woman will do that to you. Not that I was meant to know any of this, of course. But I'd overheard them arguing late one night when they thought I was asleep. And believe me, I wish I had been asleep, because I know more than any child should know about their parents' relationship. Like the fact they "hadn't made love in over a year," according to my dad. I throw up in my mouth a little every time I think of that. My mother replied that she'd sacrificed everything for this family. She'd once been his business partner, but had given that up to stay home and look after *his* kids so *he* could go out and follow *his* dreams. *What about my dreams?* she'd said. To which my father had replied that she wasn't the woman he'd married anymore. She was no longer fun and had lost herself somewhere between school runs, the PTA, bake sales, and worrying about which nonstick pan or washing detergent was best.

I guess that was the thing that caused my mother's one-eighty. This complete and sudden transformation that now found her staring down at me from posters with that smile plastered across her face, looking like she fit in so well around here. I didn't get her at all. She painted herself as this perfect mother, and by all outward appearances she probably looked like one, but she wasn't. And I didn't even want perfection from her, I just wanted something that wasn't *this*. Whatever *this* was.

I've thought back on that time a lot, to when my parents were still together. And I can't figure out how I hadn't seen it coming. Surely, I should have known that my father was planning on leaving us? Because he hadn't left just my mom for *her*, he'd left me and Zac, too, and if I thought about it like that, it made me want to cry, even after all these years.

I finally arrived at the Lighthouse. That was the name of my brother's new school. And allow me to make a quick observation related to the naming of these kinds of schools. There always seems to be a trend toward overloading the light thematics: the Lantern Learning Center, Stars Academy, Sunshine Kids. As if they're trying to disguise the undeniable truth of it all, which is often far from bright and shiny.

But as I climbed out of the car, panic knocked me in the ribs. I hoped Zac hadn't lost it today, tipped over a table, or run from class. I hoped they weren't going to say he could no longer be a pupil here. *Then this move would have been for nothing.* I took a deep breath and walked in.

The inside of the school was awesome, and today I was really able to look around. It was unlike any of the other schools he'd been to, and looked more like a house than an actual school. I walked through the central courtyard, filled with bright, colored plants and a small veggie garden, and headed in the direction of his classroom. A kid with thick glasses ran past me on his tiptoes. I smiled; Zac used to run on his tiptoes. It took craploads of physical therapy just to get him to walk flat on his feet. I remember the day he was able to do that; we'd celebrated as if he'd won the Nobel Prize.

"Hello?" I stuck my head into his classroom.

His teacher, Mrs. Edwards, looked up from her desk. "Hi."

"I'm here to fetch Zac." I glanced into the classroom, but it was empty. "How was he today?" I asked apprehensively.

"It took him a while to settle, but when he did, he was great."

"Really? He was?"

She graced me with a warm, reassuring smile. "Don't worry, he's going to fit in well here." She said it with such confidence that I *almost* believed her. But we'd thought that about the last four schools.

"They're all down on the sports field. Can I show you where it is?" she offered.

"It's okay. I know where it is. Thanks."

When I reached the field, I scanned the sides for Zac. There's no way they would get him to play a sport. He detests any kind of activity with rules that aren't his own, and he also hates the noise and excitement of sports. But when I didn't see him sitting there, another stab of panic hit me. I scanned the field, looking frantically from child to child to child and then . . . I was gobsmacked.

There he was. He was holding a tennis racket and someone was helping him hit a big, blue ball with it. I didn't want to disturb them, so I found a spot on a small wall and sat down to watch. It looked like they were playing a mash-up of tennis meets soccer meets volleyball meets cricket. And clearly there were no rules, either, which quickly become evident when Zac hit the ball and then hopped on one leg to a Hula-Hoop, which he then picked up and wiggled around his hips.

The guy who helped him hit the ball ran up to him with his hand in the air. "That's it, buddy! High five!" And then I was downright floored to see Zac give this stranger a high five.

But I was even more floored—literally, I almost fell off the wall and landed on the floor—when the stranger turned around and I saw who it was.

7

Jake Jock Kick Me in the Back Handshake-Hot Jones Double Barrel!

He looked so out of place here, and I blinked rapidly to make sure I wasn't hallucinating. *I wasn't.* There he was, high-fiving my brother, and it was so strange and utterly surreal that I felt like I'd been suddenly sucked into the canvas of a Salvador Dalí painting, jumping over melted clocks as a giant eyeball stared on.

I didn't want to see him. Not since the embarrassing ball incident, followed by the even more embarrassing sandwich incident. *Crap! What to do?*

Hide behind a bush? Wait for him to leave then nab my brother and make a stealthy run for it? But just as I was playing these rather ridiculous scenarios out in my head, it happened . . .

"*Lori!*" Zac screamed so loudly that I was sure everyone as far away as BWH looked up. He waved, and as he did, Jake's head began to turn.

It was as if everything started playing out in dramatic slow motion—perhaps even to some dark, ominous soundtrack. Jake's head turned slowly, so slooooowly and then . . . *bam!* Eye contact. Followed by a look of recognition and then . . .

Small smile. *Why was he smiling at me?*

Small wave. *Why was he waving at me?*

And then he started walking toward me. *Oh crap!*

I tried to keep cool. I tried to look so indifferent and unfazed and above it all, but knew I was failing dismally. I concentrated hard on trying to get my facial features to behave normally, even though I could feel them wanting to do a bunch of things that would probably just make me look like a weirdo.

Hand on hip? Would that help my cause?

Arms folded? Would that make me look cooler? Or would that just make me look like I had one giant boob?

Run hand through hair nonchalantly? No, it would probably just get stuck in the curly knots.

I was overthinking this to the extreme, and it made me so acutely aware of all my body parts and where they were, and what they were and weren't doing.

Jake and my brother were coming closer as I shuffled nervously from foot to foot, and then someone joined them. A girl about my brother's age ran up to Jake and put an arm around his waist.

"Hey, Lori," Jake said when he finally reached me.

"What the *hell* are you doing here?" The words flew out of my mouth before I knew what I was saying.

"What the *hell*? *Hell*?" my brother repeated.

Jake laughed and I started to apologize. "Sorry, I didn't mean to . . ."

He laughed even more when the girl holding on to him started giggling.

"No need to say sorry," he said for the second time that day.

I stopped talking and pursed my lips tightly for fear that something else might fly out. An awkward lull forced itself into the conversation, and seemed to linger there until I couldn't take it a second longer and had to break it.

"Zac is my brother," I gushed. "He's my brother." I'm not sure why I repeated it, but I did.

"That's cool." Jake smiled down at Zac. "He's awesome."

My jaw loosened. People seldom called my brother awesome, and if they did, it certainly didn't sound as sincere as when Jake said it.

"This is my sister, Lisa." He looked down at the girl who had attached herself to him tightly. She had the same blue eyes as his and her hair was up in cute ponytails, flecks of golden curls in the sea of brown, just like his.

"What do you say?" Jake asked.

"Nice to meet you," she said overly loudly with a smile so big her eyes disappeared into her cheeks.

"Nice to meet you too," I replied, and then without warning, she hugged me.

I glanced at Zac. I knew what he was thinking. He didn't like it when other people showed me affection; he got strangely jealous, even though he didn't show much affection himself. When she finally let go of me, I walked over to Zac and held my hand out. He hesitated for a few moments and then took it and moved to my side possessively, giving Lisa a scowl as he went. Sometimes he can come across as rude, but he's not, I swear, he just struggles to express certain emotions. This is one of the hardest parts of having a brother like Zac—few get to see the boy that I do. They only see the "bad" and make their assumptions based on that. I'm always trying to convince them of his other side, the side that isn't too abrupt and doesn't scream in public if he's having a sensory meltdown. The world is cheated out of this other version of my brother, and maybe that's one of the saddest things about it all.

"Zac played an amazing game of hoop ball today," Jake said, breaking my train of thought.

"Hoop ball?" I asked.

"It's a combination of Hula-Hooping, tennis, soccer, baseball, and volleyball. We all made the rules up together."

"We?"

"I volunteer here once a week, doing sports with the kids," he qualified.

"And he's the best," his sister quickly added. "The *best*."

"Best. Best," Zac echoed and then fluttered his fingers together. I looked up at Jake; it was usually around this stage, when Zac started doing something weird, that people backed off. But Jake didn't flinch.

"We better get going." I inched away from Jake and Lisa.

"We're going to the beach now to build a giant sandcastle with five turrets and a moat and underground tunnels for my mouse spies and a fridge in it too in case we get thirsty while we build it because we wouldn't want to get dehydrated and then have to go to the doctor and be put on a drip. You can come with us?" The words flew out of Zac's mouth like bullets from a machine gun.

"Uh . . . um . . . Zac." I turned to him. "I'm sure that Jake and Lisa have a lot of things to do this afternoon. Maybe we can just build it ourselves?"

I didn't want Zac to be heartbroken when yet another person turned down one of the impromptu social invitations that he always seemed to deliver at the wrong time, and usually in the most inappropriate way possible.

"Just how big is this castle going to be?" Jake asked.

"Big. Like huge. In fact, it's going to be the biggest sandcastle ever built and then I'm going to call the *Guinness Book of Records* and they will come out and take photos of it."

"*Whoa!*" Lisa lifted off the ground, that was how excited she looked.

"Sounds like you're going to need some extra hands?" Jake raised his brows at me.

"Sorry . . . you . . . uh, you want to . . . ?"

"Yeah. Totally." Jake looked at me and our eyes met and—*Be still my beating heart.* No seriously, be still!

"Which beach?" he asked, running a hand through his hair and letting it flop back down into his face. I tried not to stare at that one strand that seemed to have wrapped around itself, creating that perfect, circular curl.

"I don't know their names. I just know it's the one below our house. We live in Clifton."

"What does your house look like? I surf a lot, so know most of the beach houses."

Of course he surfed.

"It's the white one. With the blinding silver pillars and the reflective, blue glass front. It kind of looks like it's meant to be in Greece but somehow found its way to Africa instead."

Jake laughed. "I know that house. Wasn't it owned by Will Smith?"

"Julio Iglesias," I clarified. "Not exactly like Will Smith, but I guess they do both make music . . . *sort of.*"

At that, he laughed—*again.* "My mom loves Julio Iglesias! I can't wait to tell her that."

"All moms love Julio," I said. "He's so cheesy. And he has a lot of chest hair. He's like the Spanish Hasselhoff."

Jake laughed even harder, and I couldn't remember the last time someone had found me this funny, well, other than the art-school guys. "I can't believe you live in Julio's house," Jake mused.

"What's funny? Why are you laughing? It's too loud." Zac let go of my hand and put his hands over his ears.

"Sorry, we'll whisper." Jake lowered his voice, and then looked at me and winked.

Wait . . . *did he just wink at me?* And again, I was transported straight back into the dreamlike canvas of a surrealist. This had never happened to me before! Guys did not wink at me, and certainly not guys like Jake Jones-Bloody-Evans!

"Should we meet on the beach in front of your house at five, when it's not so hot?" he asked, but despite the fact he was looking at me, it took me a moment to register what he was saying.

"You were being serious?" I asked.

"Unless five is too late? Or we could do it another day?"

"Today!" Zac raised his voice.

"Five it is then," Jake said, and pulled his phone out. "Swap numbers in case something changes?"

My already loosened jaw now tumbled to the ground, and I hoped he couldn't see my shocked, dangling tonsils. I pulled my phone out, almost dropping it because my fingers were shaking.

We exchanged numbers and then he walked away, tossing a casual, "See you soon," over his shoulder.

But there was nothing casual about this at all. Casual was watching Netflix in your pajamas with the guys. Casual was your cousins coming around on a Sunday afternoon. Casual was *not* hot Jake coming 'round to your house to build sandcastles!

8

I stood on our lawn and looked at the beach. There was no sign of Jake or Lisa, and I wasn't totally convinced they were coming either. *Why would he want to come here and build a sandcastle with us?* To be honest, a part of me hoped he wouldn't come. I didn't exactly have much experience when it came to hanging out with (straight) guys, let alone popular ones who probably talked about things I knew nothing about; our rugby world cup win, whey protein, and whatever else was on jockish conversational offer.

No. That was a lie. When I said I didn't have much experience with (straight) guys, what I really meant to say was that I have *zero* experience. I am a total cliché: *the fat girl who's never been kissed.* I can't even pretend that it's intentional, that I'm saving myself for the "right guy." *Because I'm not.* I would literally kiss anyone at this stage, just to say I'd done it. Andile once offered up his lips as practice, and I was so desperate that I'd almost considered them, *almost.*

And the more I *don't* do it, the more awkward it becomes and the less I think that it will ever happen. And the less it happens, the more afraid I become that when it finally does, I'll be terrible at it. It's a vicious cycle. And don't even get me started on sex—I've totally written that activity off. I can't stand naked in front of the mirror myself, how on earth am I meant to get naked in front of someone else? No, I was probably going to die a virgin, or worse, I would have to find someone on those creepy websites for men who fantasize about feeding cake to fat women while the women slap them with their stomach folds. It's strange how fat is either reviled or fetishized. There's no middle ground for it in our society, is there? A place where fat can just exist as it is. Where it isn't one thing or the other.

"Let's go, let's go. *Go!*" Zac pushed me toward the steep, rocky path at the bottom of the garden that led to the beach.

"Okay. Let's go." I held my hand out for him and this time he took it. I was just about to prep him gently for the fact that Jake and Lisa might not be coming when two figures appeared on the beach. He'd said he was coming, but honestly, I hadn't quite believed him. Luckily for me, the small part that *had* believed him had convinced the part that *hadn't* to change into something a little nicer, splash on some mascara, and smudge on some bronzer so I didn't look so pale. I'm not a big fan of makeup—you would think I'd be good at it because I'm an artist, but I'm not. I tried to contour once with a NikkieTutorial. Let's just say it didn't end well.

"Look!" Zac jumped and almost threw himself down the steep path.

"*Wait!*" I grabbed him by his shirt before he plunged to the ground. Sometimes he's got zero impulse control.

We walked down the path together, Zac pulling against me like a horse on a bit, as Lisa and Jake made their way along the beach. And then, as if both parties had timed it perfectly, we all arrived at the same spot at the exact same time.

"Um, h-hi," I murmured awkwardly, although that hadn't been the intention at all. I'd actually been hoping for a cool, dis-interested kind of "hi." The kind of "hi" that would give Jake the impression I was a girl about town, who'd seen and done things, was totally cool, comfortable with hanging out with the guys, and down for whatevs! Instead, my "hi" kind of screamed *insecure, virgin girl*.

"Hey," Jake said. Now that "hey" was cool. That "hey" was a hey about town, and that "hey" was defs down for whatevs! I was so jealous of his "hey."

"I can't wait to build a sandcastle!" Lisa jumped up and down as if she wasn't bound by gravity. She never stopped moving, it seemed. Her movements and voice also had a certain punctuated urgency to them.

"*With five turrets and a moat!*" Zac raised his voice and flapped his fingers a little.

"Of course, those are the most important parts!" Jake said with a reassuring smile, which seemed to relax Zac somewhat.

Jake looked at me and gave me a tiny nod; I wasn't used to nods, either, and my eyes widened in shock. When Zac raised his voice in public people usually shook their heads in blatant disap-proval. On one occasion, a woman had actually walked up to us and reprimanded my mother for allowing her child to behave like that in public. My mother had been so apologetic, but I refuse to apologize for Zac's behavior. My mother always does, though. As if his "mess" isn't compatible with her projected perfection. I like my brother's mess.

But Jake seemed completely nonjudgmental. And I couldn't help it, I smiled at him. For a second, our eyes locked and wow, he did have rather nice eyes. Especially in this late-afternoon glow. *What color were they? Cobalt, azure, no . . . cerulean blue!* That's it. A little bit dusty with the slightest hint of green. I looked away quickly when a fluttering feeling started deep in my belly.

"I brought a cooler with some drinks, a bucket with some spades, and a few towels to sit on," Jake explained.

"You come prepared," I said, not daring to make cerulean contact amid all the fluttering. I mentally scolded myself for allowing the flutter in the first place. Girls like me shouldn't flutter for guys like Jake. But I was fluttering. And now I couldn't stop saying fluttering in my head. I cleared my throat and shuffled my foot in the sand awkwardly. I looked down, utterly horrified to see sand particles sticking to the hairs on my toes. I quickly curled them under. I wasn't used to this open-toed way of life. I needed to shave there!

The sandcastle building was going well. Jake took the lead, and Lisa and Zac did whatever he said. I couldn't quite believe how diplomatic and calm Zac was being; it made me somewhat uneasy, though. The calm before a potential storm, perhaps? Sometimes it felt like I was balancing on a knife-edge with Zac, always holding my breath, never able to fully relax. Always waiting and watching for it to come crashing down around me. But as time went on, I began to exhale slightly. They melded into a perfect little team—shaping and digging and smoothing until, from those millions of tiny grains of sand, something castle-like started to emerge. Watching them, I felt like I was watching a pointillist paint. Small points of paint on a canvas coming together to form the bigger picture. There was something almost hypnotic about watching them work, and eventually I allowed myself to relax.

But trying to get comfortable on the sand was another story altogether. I'd already tried several sitting variations, but nothing was working.

1. Crouched on my haunches. At first, this seemed okay. That was until I looked down and realized how my upper thighs looked squished together. Everything sort of bulged out at the knee. This might have been vaguely all right if it hadn't been for the fact that in this position, under the pressure, it really brought out the shape of my cellulite. And with the sun setting behind us, shadows were being cast from all the indentations.

2. Propped up on my knees. This also worked for a while, until the wind picked up and pulled at my skirt. I tried to push it between my thighs to hold it down, but this just made me look like I was wearing very tight cycling shorts.

3. Legs crossed. No! Not enough skirt to cover every upper-thigh area, not to mention another sort of area.

4. Sitting with legs to the side. Also not great, since the entire side of my white thigh was now fully on display. But at least in this position the cellulite was more minimal and the skirt didn't flap, so I went with it. I pulled a towel onto my lap to help hide everything a little better. (Sometimes I carry an extra hoodie around with me, even on warm days, to drape over my lap if the need arises.)

I hated feeling like this, though—uncomfortable in my own skin. Constantly fiddling with my clothing, whether it was pants that needed pulling up at the waist because they'd rolled down due to the force of a rogue stomach bulge, or having to pull my boobs back into my bra after leaning over to pick something up off the floor.

But the more I watched Zac building the castle, the more I began to forget my physical discomfort. I hardly ever saw him play like this. He was so relaxed—not obsessive at all. In fact, after several unsuccessful attempts at a turret, he let the idea go. *Do you know how huge that is?* One of the characteristics of his autism is mentally getting stuck on something. He once talked about our new microwave for three full days. Every conversation was about the microwave: *how it looked, how it sounded, where we should put it, what we should put in it.* He had so many questions about it and the way it worked, I'd had to turn to Google for the answers to satisfy his insatiable curiosity. I like to think of it like this: his brain's like a washing machine, and sometimes a thought gets stuck in the spin cycle. That's the only way to describe it. Currently, he's obsessed with snakes and the universe. Which means that he knows more about black holes and neurotoxic venom than most of the experts, which is kind of brilliant and amazing if you think about it.

After another half hour or so, Jake finally broke away from the two of them and crawled over to me. My body immediately stiffened, and once again, I was acutely aware of myself and all that work to get comfortable was gone in a puff of sand.

"Hey." He sat next to me.

"Hey," I replied, copying his tone because it just seemed so cool and smooth.

"They're playing well together."

"I know. I'm surprised. Playdates often end badly, especially if Zac becomes obsessed with doing something one way and the other person doesn't want to."

"Kids on the spectrum have a hard time reading other people's emotions. It makes it hard to play with others."

"How do you know he's on the autism spectrum?" I knew I hadn't told him this.

"It's pretty obvious. To me, anyway." He smiled.

"Of course. Yes! You coach them, the hula ball . . ." For some reason, I'd almost forgotten this part.

"Hoop ball," he corrected with another small smile. "We're trying to get it recognized as an official Olympic sport."

"You are?"

Jake eyed me for a moment or two and then burst out laughing. "Joking." He nudged me playfully on my arm and—

Wait. Hang on a moment here. Let's pause. Have I, Lori Palmer, just been nudged playfully on the arm *by a straight guy*? This had never happened to me before. I'd never been nudged. Not even close. Not even a half nudge. And never by someone this hot, even though he wasn't my type. *Oh, who the hell was I kidding,* Jake was everyone's type, and now my arm felt like it was on fire, and then, because I was a totally inexperienced dork, I froze. Instead of nudging him back or coming up with a clever, funny comeback, I simply turned to a block of ice. An awkward silence engulfed us and my mind raced, thinking of something to say that would break it.

"So Lisa, is she . . . ?" I let the question hang in the air.

"ADHD," he replied.

"Zac's also dyslexic. He's struggling with reading and writing."

"Lisa's also struggling academically. She has some unspecified learning difficulties too."

"Don't you hate that word *unspecified*." I threw some air quotes around. "I mean, if the experts don't know what it is, then what are we supposed to do about it? It's such a cop-out . . . *unspecified*!"

"Totally," Jake agreed. "Or what about when they first think it's auditory processing issues, and then it's ADHD, inattentive type, but then, no, it's actually ADHD, hyperactive, impulsive type."

"I know! Zac went to a million doctors. He even went for an EEG and an MRI before someone finally diagnosed him correctly." I paused, a stab in my side. Familiar stab. "I—I was relieved when he was diagnosed. Before that I just thought he was . . . irritating."

"Yeah, I know what you mean." Jake turned to me, his voice getting softer. "I thought Lisa was just badly behaved. I was a bit of a dick to her sometimes."

We fell into a silence for a while, letting the gravity of our words wash over us.

"How are your mom and dad with it?" he asked.

I shrugged. "They're divorced. Not because of that. My mom works a lot." It was all I could manage to say about the matter, and I could see Jake was waiting for more, but honestly, I didn't really know what else to say.

Jake nodded, though, as if he'd understood what I'd meant with that vague statement, even if I hadn't understood it myself.

"My mom got really depressed when Lisa was diagnosed. She had to go to therapy and take antidepressants for a while. She blamed herself." He looked down at the sand when he said it.

"That must have been hard." My voice softened to match the sudden mood shift.

"She's fine now, though." He looked up at me briefly, and in that moment, I felt inexplicably close to him.

"My mom throws money at Zac's autism. Best schools, best occupational therapists, equine therapy, speech therapy, cognitive behavioral therapy. But I think she does it not just because it's good for him—*which it is*—but because she doesn't know how to deal with it. Sometimes I think I know more about it, and how to deal with it, than her."

A smile broke out across his face. "It's so good to talk to someone my age who gets this stuff," he said on a long, loud exhale. As if he'd been holding his breath this entire conversation, waiting to let it out, and now he had.

"Yeah!" I reiterated, and also breathed out. I hadn't realized I was also holding my breath. "I've never spoken to anyone like this before. Well, not to anyone who wasn't secretly judging."

"Me neither. It's really, really good." Jake paused, and I could sense there was something heavy weighing his pause down. "Sometimes I feel lonely," he said. I sat up straight; this was the last thing I'd expected a guy like him to say. "There're support groups and therapists for parents, but what about us? Who do we talk to about this stuff?"

My chest contracted. "I know what you mean. I have these amazing friends, Guy and Andile, and they're so understanding and supportive, but they just don't understand it. *Really understand.* Sometimes I want to tell them things, but don't."

He looked me straight in the eyes, as if he'd deliberately sought them out. I tried to hold on to his gaze, but let it go when the flutter reared its head again.

"Tell you what," he said. "Let's start a kind of support group."

"With who?"

"Just us." He smiled.

"I don't think you can call two people a group."

"A support coupling then?" His perfectly imperfect lopsided smile grew even more.

"What will we do? Meet in some recreational hall and drink bad coffee while we share our feelings?"

"I think you're confused, that's an AA meeting. My dad goes to them, they also serve stale doughnuts."

"Oh. Sorry, I didn't mean to make fun of, uh, sorry . . ."

"It's cool. He's been sober for twenty-five years. I've never even seen him drink."

"That's amazing."

"Yeah, I'm proud of the dude," he said playfully.

I waited for him to speak again. But he didn't, so I changed the subject, still worried that I might have offended him. "So, back to our support coupling. How would it work?"

"Well, we have each other's numbers, so we can message each other when we feel we *need* to talk to someone."

"That might be often. I always feel like I *need* to talk to someone," I chirped.

"We can also just message each other when we feel like it too." A softer, huskier version of his voice made my cheeks warm up, and I quickly looked out to sea. I didn't want him to see my face in case he got the wrong idea, like I was swooning over him. *Which I was!*

Thankfully, Lisa came over and broke the awkward moment. "I need to pee!" She was crossing her legs tightly. "*Now!*"

Jake jumped up. "Okay, we'll leave."

"Can't hold it. I'm going to explooooooode." She bent over at the waist, contorting her face into a painful-looking grimace.

"You can come to our house."

Jake looked relieved. "Thanks!"

"Are we going now?" Zac asked and my heart dropped. Getting Zac to leave a place if he was enjoying himself was usually difficult.

"We can come back later," I offered quickly, but couldn't believe my eyes when he shrugged and started walking toward the house.

"I'm going to be honest," Jake said as we all hurried up the steps, "I've always wanted to see this place. Hope you're up for a guided tour."

"Sure." I pulled the massive sliding door open and stepped inside. I was struggling to take this all in, though. Hot, popular guy, who had nudged my shoulder and told me we were starting a support coupling, was in my house with his sister.

Could this day get any more bizarre?

9

I stood in the open-plan kitchen, holding on to the big marble island in the middle of it. From here, I had a view into the lounge where Zac was sitting on the sofa watching TV, as well as a view to the door of the guest bathroom, where Jake was. He was standing outside, leaning against the wall in this way that made him look like a male model.

"Remember to wash your hands," I heard him say.

A voice came back immediately. "Yeeees!"

"Just reminding you," he replied, and then walked toward the kitchen as if he was on a damn catwalk.

My body stiffened in response to his approaching presence. And the closer he got, the more it felt like my muscles were now made of cement. Everything froze, except for my heart, which was racing. And the closer he got, the more worried I became that he would actually hear my beating heart.

"So?" He reached the marble countertop and placed his hands on it.

It felt like a desert wind had blown in from nowhere and filled my mouth with dry crunchy sand. I tried to talk . . .

"Soooooo," I returned in a voice that sounded strange and high-pitched. Why was the presence of a hot man making me talk like this?

He grinned. Small, cute, lopsided. And then there was silence. He seemed to be waiting for something, and that was when I remembered.

"Oh! The house. See it, you want?" I cringed at my Yoda-like delivery. I've always envied those people who are naturally cool. Coolness seems to ooze out of their pores and float around them like a giant, shiny aura. Everything seems to come easily to them; they joke and laugh and exist in the world with a kind of comfortable ease that I've never had. For the most part my life feels like I'm lugging around a giant cactus. It prickles, it hurts, and very often, it itches. And right now, I was desperately trying *not* to scratch my head, where a nervous, psychosomatic itch had formed.

"I mean unless you don't want to show me aro—"

"No!" I cut him off, way too enthusiastically. I quickly tried to adjust, stating less eagerly this time, "Noooo, it's cool. I mean, sure, whatever."

We heard the toilet flush, and both turned as Lisa walked out, wiping her wet hands on her shirt as she went. I glanced at Jake as he gave a small, pride-filled smile. I got that. Pride for the small things that others take for granted because for them, it's a given.

Nothing is ever a given with kids like Zac and Lisa. In fact, you could say that the only given is that nothing ever is.

Jake and I watched as Lisa sat down next to Zac on the sofa. He was busy lining all the TV remotes up next to him in a perfect, straight line. Small to big. "You think they'll be okay there for a while?" I asked.

"It's not like we're going far." He raised a brow to me in query, and I nodded.

"Hey, guys, why don't you watch *Teen Titans*?" I called out to Lisa and Zac, who were sitting side by side on the couch now.

"I LOOVVE *Teen Titans*!" Lisa jumped up enthusiastically and knocked one of the remotes off the couch. Zac glared at her.

"They are supposed to be in a line!" he scolded. I lurched forward, ready to step in and diffuse the situation, when Lisa picked the remote up and carefully put it back. I exhaled relief when Zac looked at it and nodded, as if acknowledging that all was now right in his world again.

"Right, let the tour begin, I guess." I walked up the stairs that led to the second level. Why anyone needed a house built on three levels was really beyond me. Why anyone needed three lounges, two dining rooms, and six bedrooms was also beyond my grasp.

"Most of our furniture hasn't arrived from Joburg yet, so you could say we're embracing minimalism," I said, staring into the hollow space in front of us.

"Wow! This is insane." Jake walked up to the floor-to-ceiling glass window and looked out over the ocean. The sun was finally starting to sink lower in the sky, and it was casting an orangey, pink light over everything. "Going to be honest. I didn't really want to see the house. I just wanted to see this view. It's awesome."

"It's okay, I guess."

"Okay? You guess?" He turned. "What could be better than this?"

"Truthfully, I'm more of a city kinda girl."

He looked at me curiously for a while. "Give yourself a few months. The sea has a way of getting into you."

I seriously doubted that. My dislike of water was deeply ingrained in me, had been for years, and if I closed my eyes and thought about it, I was instantly transported back to that moment that I was forced to hate it.

We started walking again, up the other staircase that led to the bedrooms. We did a brief walk-through of the rooms; I left mine out since it still looked like a bomb had gone off in a clothing store. We'd gotten into this slow, step-by-step rhythm of walking together through the house until . . .

"*What the hell!*" Jake's shrill shout made me jump, and I swung around as he scurried onto a chair.

"What?" His panic had set mine off.

"There!" He pointed at the floor, ashen faced.

I looked down and . . . "Oh, that."

"Yes, *that*?" His eyes were glued to the spot by my feet where a snake was slithering past.

I bent down and picked it up; it coiled around my fingers like it always did.

"Oh my God. What are you doing, Lori? Put it down!"

"Don't worry, it's Zac's pet. She's a brown house snake, she must have escaped again." I pulled the snake up to my face and stared at it. "Isn't that right, Miss Hiss." It stuck its tongue out at me belligerently.

I looked up at Jake; he was still perched on the chair with eyes that looked like they were about to launch out of his head, and I couldn't help it . . . I burst out laughing. His white cheeks flushed red as he jumped off the chair, struck a pose, and then ran his hand through his hair.

"Yeah, I meant to do that." His attempt at a cool recovery made me laugh even more.

"Wanna hold her?" I held my hand out, and he fumbled backward again.

"No. Not really."

"Don't like snakes?"

"Uh . . . no!"

I shook my head at him. "You know, you scream like a girl when you're scared."

"Don't tell anyone. My reputation would be ruined," he joked.

"Who would I tell?" I walked into Zac's room and put Miss Hiss back into her terrarium.

"This is seriously a pet?" Jake leaned in and peered into her tank.

"It's better than the tarantula," I confessed.

He scrunched his face up, but I could see he was smiling. "You live in a weird house."

"I wonder what Julio would say?" I said, and he chuckled. These perfect, somewhat mesmerizing strands of hair tumbled into his face, and he looked hotter right now than he'd ever looked before, especially with that warm orange light streaming through the big window, casting all kinds of golden highlights across his face. He looked like a work of art created by one of the old masters. He should be framed and hung on some great museum wall for all to see, and to be honest, it perturbed me that I was thinking about him like this.

"I—I'm going to check on Zac and Lisa, I'll be quick. If you go up the other staircase, it leads to a roof terrace," I shouted over my shoulder as I rushed down the stairs. I glanced over the railing to the TV room below, where Lisa and Zac were sitting happily. I watched them for a while, a tiny lump forming in my throat. It was rare to see Zac so chilled, and it made my heart feel like it was going to burst.

When I was satisfied that all was well, I started back up the stairs, and that's when it hit me. It hit me all at once and my intestines twisted themselves up like a lasso.

"Crap!" I started running. There was something up there that I didn't want him to see. Didn't want anyone to see.

I raced up the stairs and burst onto the roof terrace, immediately scanning it for Jake. But he wasn't there. "No, no, no!" He could only be in one place now—the *one* place I didn't want him to be. I raced across the rooftop and threw the door to the hot tub room open. Only, it was too late.

My heart sank. It fell into my feet, crawled out of my toes, and pooled on the floor below me and then, I wanted to die of embarrassment.

I wished I could rewind. Go back in time and stop him from coming up here.

10

There he was, standing, staring at it. The last portfolio piece if I wanted to get into the Blackwell Art Institute—the most prestigious art college in South Africa—was a self-portrait. It was supposed to represent me as an artist and in some moment of insanity, I'd taken a photo of myself in front of the mirror, without a top on. I'd turned sideways to the mirror, taking the photo over my shoulder; the side of my face and back took up most of the shot, there was no boob, thankfully. But what you did see were all the various folds and flaps and other things that began with an *F*. Back fat, jean bulging fat, side boob fat. And the worst thing about all of this was that *he* was looking at the photo that I'd blown up, printed out, and stuck up on the wall. I'd only managed to paint my face so far, meticulously converting the photographic details into brushstrokes. The rest of me, my body, was unfinished. Because it was just too confronting to paint.

"It's . . . it's . . ." I stuttered, unable to finish the sentence because I had no idea what the sentence was. What did I say to this? To him looking at a half-naked picture of me.

Silence. A silence so strangely loud, almost as if something buzzed inside it. The molecules in the air seemed to vibrate, and they filled the room with this kind of expanding energy. As if there was a giant balloon in the room that was being blown up. Bigger, bigger, bigger . . . it felt like the balloon was about to pop. The sound would be deafening. And then he turned and looked at me, something strange etched into his face. I paused, waiting for the hammer of judgment to fall. Only it didn't.

"You are so good." He dragged the words out, placing emphasis on each one individually. He pointed at the canvas, and I glanced at it. Wet, red curls, falling over my shoulders, freckles like millions of stars splattered across my cheeks and nose and shoulders, and that small white scar on my forehead from the time I'd fallen off my bike as a child, all laid out for him to see in crisp high definition.

"You're an artist." He was looking straight at me now, and I took a step forward. All I wanted to do was reach out and rip that photo down. I'd never been that naked in front of anyone before. Even myself. The day I'd taken that photo was one of the only days that I'd looked at myself like that, and I'd only been able to do it for a moment.

"It looks exactly like you." And then much to my horror, he walked right up to the canvas and leaned in. "How do you do that? Make it look *exactly* like the photo?"

"I practice."

Jake shot me a look over his shoulder. "I could practice every day for years and wouldn't be able to do this. You've got a gift."

I looked back at my canvas. It was painted in my usual, hyper-realistic style. A true-life depiction right down to the minutest detail. I've always been good at seeing the details in things. Always been good at spotting the smallest things that others don't seem to see. The way light falls on objects, the way shadows darken and obscure them.

"It's insanely good."

"It's okay, I guess," I whispered under my breath. Compliments always made me feel uneasy and off center.

"What's it for?"

"It's a final portfolio piece, I'm trying to get into this art school. They only accept twenty people each year."

"You'll definitely get in." He said it with such confidence. As if it was a fact. Irrefutable, like the earth going around the sun or the grass being green or his eyes having turned a deep, cobalt blue in this darker light.

I looked up at the ceiling and then quickly back down at my feet. Looking everywhere in the room except at him.

"When will you finish it?" he asked. My throat tightened.

"Don't know. Don't know if I want to." Which was the truth. Despite thinking that I could, I just didn't know if I could go through with it, whether I could actually face the truth of myself long enough, and in so much crystal-clear detail, to be able to paint it.

"You should *definitely* finish it."

"We should get back down to Zac and Lisa, and also, it's a bit late, my brother needs to eat at a certain time and—"

"Sure, of course. Routine is important." He moved toward the door, away from the photo, and relief washed over me in waves that almost made me cry.

We walked out the door and this time, I quickly turned the key in the lock. Locking the door behind me, locking away a secret I didn't want anyone to see. But I knew that he'd seen it, and I didn't know how I was ever going to look him in the eye again.

11

I wanted to get through the next day at school without seeing Jake. We might have hung out yesterday, but let's be honest, it was more of a playdate for our siblings. Besides, I knew enough about the way the world worked to know that when at school, in front of his friends, he wouldn't be talking to me. Guys like that didn't talk to girls like me in front of their friends. Those were just the unspoken high school rules.

Besides, I was too embarrassed to talk to him anyway. He'd seen me seminaked. *What did he think of me?* He was probably used to seeing girls from the Hot List like Nina-M and Amber naked; all long and svelte and impossibly pretzel-thin.

But Jake proved hard to avoid at school, because he was absolutely everywhere. I spent the day ducking behind pillars and walking in the opposite direction, and at second break, I confined myself to an empty class at the end of the hall where I spent time doodling in my drawing book. But when the bell rang and I looked down at my book, I realized that I'd drawn what looked like the waves in Jake's hair.

I had my first session with Dr. Stride that afternoon. My mother had sighed loudly and told me that although she had numerous wildly important things to do, she would look after Zac. She said this as if it was the biggest imposition in the world. As if she was doing me the greatest favor known to humanity. When I was growing up, my mom was the kind of mother who would rush to school and drop off a book, or my lunch, if I'd forgotten it. She was the kind of mom who drove me across town for extra art lessons. Everyone used to tell me what a great mom I had. How she was always there for me—for everyone.

That Barb is a saint, they declared when she swooped in and saved the school bake sale after one of the tables collapsed and all the cupcakes slid off and fell into a sticky pile on the floor.

How does she do it all? they asked when she took me to school, rushed off to do soup kitchen for the needy, defrosted the freezer, cooked supper, and still managed to help me with my biology project and organize my dad's end-of-year office party.

But that was then, and this was now. And the mother of now was not a person I understood at all. On one hand, she acted like Zac was an imposition, but on the other, she'd uprooted our lives to put him in the best school money could buy. My mother was this basket of contradictions that didn't seem to fit together quite right, much like the features of her face. Over the last few days I'd started to wonder if moving here had more to do with fulfilling her dream of becoming a luxury real estate mogul in Africa's most expensive city than finding the right school for Zac. Could she be that selfish?

I drove down the main street of Clifton. It was glistening—pristine in the afternoon sun. It sparkled with cleanliness in a way that was almost unnatural, as if someone had run a disinfectant wipe across its surface. No germs. No dust. No dirt. Nothing to tarnish its appearance of perfection.

I hate perfection. Well, that's not entirely true. I have a complicated love-hate relationship with it. I seek it out, yet I'll never admit that out loud. I want it, I don't want it; I try to loathe it, I pretend it offends me, but I always strive for it. But for someone like me, it's an elusive dream. Because I'm nothing like those perfect girls at school, and if you ask outside Lori whether she wants to be like them, she'll say no and roll her eyes, but if you ask the other Lori—inside Lori—what she wants, *you'll get a totally different answer.*

Perhaps that's why I love art. It's the one place in the world I get to be honest, because inside-Lori makes the art and her art is perfect. Every line. Every smudge. Every soft contour and darkened purposeful shadow. Whether ink, paint, or charcoal, every time I bring my weapon of choice down to the paper, I strive for perfection. Maybe it's how I make sense of my messy outward world. I take all the disorder—the colors and splashes and strokes and stripes—and order them all. Just like Zac does with his remote controls. He makes his little part of the world less overwhelming when he puts them all into neat lines.

I stopped at the traffic light and looked to my left, and that's when it caught my eye. It hung in the middle of the shop window as if framed. As if it was special. Dangling from an invisible pair of hands that were presenting it to the world. The dress was long and glittery gold. It hung in a way that made it look alive and moving, like a waterfall. But not a violent crashing one; rather an elegant trickle of water slipping down a rock face. Gliding down, long and smooth, and pooling at the bottom in a frothy, thick impasto of lace and beads. A girl like me would never admit it out loud—I could hardly even admit it to myself—but I envied girls who could wear dresses like that. And in some fantasy in my mind, some made-up version of myself and my life, I *am* the girl in that dress. I am the girl at the dance with *that* boy on my arm and everyone is looking at us. Barbie and Ken. The belle of the ball. All eyes on me, and I'm smiling my huge, white, perfect smile—because in my fantasy I also go to the same dentist everyone at BWH goes to. I have defined cheekbones and no double chin. I have collarbones so deep that when I climb out of the shower, small pools of water gather in them.

I sighed. Because all of that couldn't be further from reality.

But still, the dress was gorgeous, and it reminded me of Joburg . . . *golden, shimmery, Egoli.* It looked like the dress that the singer Miriam Makeba wore on the front cover of *Drum* magazine in 1955. And what could be more Jozi than that? Her pictures hung on the walls of Maggie's, and suddenly I missed home so much I wanted to cry, and this dress seemed like the only thing in this entire place that reminded me of it.

A loud honk made me jump, and I realized that I'd been looking for so long that the traffic light had turned green. I pulled away and told myself not to think of that golden dress in the window again. Thinking about things like that only caused pain.

12

I rang the bell on the wall and waited.

"Hello?" An upbeat voice crackled through the speaker.

"Hi, it's Lori for Dr. Stride."

"Lori! Come in." A loud buzz, followed by a click as the gate unlocked. I pushed it open and was immediately greeted by an arrow and a sign that read To HEAD SHRINKER. Weird therapist humor, I guess. I followed the path past the main house until I reached a cottage around the back. The door was open and I stuck my head inside.

"Hellooo," I called out to no reply.

I crept in and glanced around. *Wow!* It looked like a unicorn had thrown up in here. I had never seen so many bright, mismatching colors in my life. Neon-yellow cushions on a bright, purple couch. A floral wingback chair, and a gold-sequined otto-man. Orchids of varying sizes and colors, a round, red coffee table, butterfly wallpaper, and so many snow globes.

"Hello," I called again and waited.

"Lori!" I swung around when I heard the voice, and then I stopped and stared. Because standing in the doorway was, undoubtedly, the person who'd decorated this room.

"Lori. I've heard so much about you. Come outside, you're just in time." She waved her arm at me, and I was immediately drawn to her nails. Long and purple and bedazzled.

She was like no mental health professional I'd ever met before. Mental health professionals, in my experience, always wore muted, subtle colors, not bright purple from head to toe. I'd always assumed their desaturated palettes were because they didn't want to project their personalities too much. They were the ultimate neutral canvas, and if they did wear any adornments, it was usually a beaded earring or some kind of rustic scarf, the sort of scarf that screamed "I'm an academic." The kind of scarf you could imagine engaged in deep discussions about Freud in an ivy-walled building. I flicked my eyes up at her wall and scanned it, running them over the degrees that lined it, just to confirm she was who she claimed to be. And then my eyes stopped. It took my brain a few moments to figure out what I was looking at, but when I did, I tried to stifle my gasp.

Sure, it was abstract, sure it was blue and purple and glittery, sure there were butterflies flapping about on it. But when I real-ized what the subject matter was, *really* was, well . . .

What would I call it exactly, *vagina art*? I looked at the certifi-cate that hung next to the painting. Certified Sex Therapist.

I took a step backward. "I'm not sure . . . I mean, am I at

the right place?" I asked the woman wearing the bright, purple kimono dress with pink and yellow tassels that flapped in the breeze. "Are you a . . ."—I could barely get the words out—"sex therapist?"

"Sure." She nodded. "But that's just one of my specializations."

"Okay," I muttered reticently.

"Are you here for that?" she asked, her tone dead serious.

"*What!?*" I spluttered, almost choking on a fleck of saliva I'd inhaled in my shocked state. "No, oh, no, that's not . . . I mean, I'm not . . . that's a—"

"A hard no?" she asked with a smile.

I nodded quickly, dying of embarrassment inside.

"Well, no worries," she said casually, as if this conversation didn't embarrass her in the slightest. "Come outside." She waved her arm at me. "Like I said, it's perfect timing, *mos.*"

Mos? She was mixing some Afrikaans slang into her speech, something that many Capetonians of mixed racial descent did. I'd just never heard a psychologist be so informal before, and it threw me a little—although I did like the way it sounded. It made the language transform into something more vibrant and alive-sounding, like mixing paint colors together to create a totally unique color.

I walked onto a patio that faced a large garden. It was beautiful here, I had to admit that. Table Mountain rose in the distance, and her garden was one of those overgrown types where things had been left to go wild and tangle, like something out of a fairy tale.

"What am I just in time for?" I inspected the garden in front of me, an inkling of suspicion forming in my belly.

"Getting our hands dirty." She moved toward a table and picked up a small spade.

JO WATSON

"Are we . . . burying something?"

"Yes, my last client," she said and then burst out laughing so loudly that a small bird in a nearby tree got a fright and flew away quickly.

I looked at her. The suspicion was no longer just an inkling, and my heart thumped against my chest.

"Just joking!" She stopped laughing and passed me the spade. "You're okay with getting your hands dirty, right?"

"It depends."

"But you're an artist, aren't you? Pamela says you're an incredible one, so I would imagine you're often covered in paint," she offered with a big smile.

"Yes," I half mumbled under my breath. I had no idea where this conversation was going.

"Soil is just another medium of expression. Come, the plants are calling." She pranced off, and I followed her up the path tentatively. When she reached a large flower bed, she lowered herself onto her knees, then patted the ground next to her.

"Come. Sit. I hate being indoors. Especially on days like this." She inhaled long and loud. "Great day, isn't it?"

"I guess," I said very noncommittally. I suppose I could have said what I really thought—that the day wasn't nice at all, it was muggy, the sun was trying way too hard, making the air feel thick, making me sweat and freckle—but I didn't.

I lowered myself to my knees; it wasn't comfortable. Fat girls on their knees, not the most comfortable thing. Our weight pressing down onto our legs, pins and needles in feet as blood circulation is cut off. God, I hoped my toes weren't going to fall off or something. Imagine that. I arrive at my new therapist with ten toes and leave with none. I wonder if that would be considered malpractice? And then I looked over at Dr. Stride again, and something hit me. Something obvious and glaring, and I wondered if this was the reason Dr. Finkelstein had sent me here—the thought made me so embarrassed that my cheeks went red. Because Dr. Stride was large. Okay, now I'm using a euphemism. She was fat, and I couldn't believe that I was only noticing it now. I guess when I'd first seen her I'd been distracted by all the color. She was also tall, with big feet, hands, and ears. Nothing about her was delicate or subtle; everything about her demanded that you notice her, and I got the distinct impression she didn't care either.

"What are we doing?" I asked, withdrawing my eyes and inspecting the flower bed in front of us. It was crammed with succulents of all shapes and colors and sizes. They were woven together like stitches on a tapestry. Swooping patterns and swirls, like a living work of art.

"I need to reorganize this bed. It's time for a change." And then, without warning, she grabbed the plants and started yanking them out of the soil.

"Uh . . . wait!" I said automatically. "Aren't you going to kill them?" I was shocked, as she looked at me, clutching handfuls of succulents, their roots dangling like little nooses. Some of their leaves had fallen off and were now lying on the dirt.

"Nope. It's the great thing about succulents. You can be rough with them. They're basically indestructible."

"Really?" I inspected the plants. It was hard to imagine that these were indestructible. That any plants were indestructible and that we could be this rough with them.

"Looks can be deceiving." She raised her thick, high-arched brows at me. "They're stronger than they look." She pulled another one out of the ground. "Go for it. Take some out. Just pull. Or use your spade, whatever." She pointed at the gray, rose-shaped plants in front of us. I reached out slowly and was just about to pull one when I stopped.

"Sorry, why are we doing this?"

"Would you rather be sitting inside on the couch?"

I glanced back over my shoulder at the cottage behind me, and then turned back to the flower bed, the powder-blue sky, Table Mountain, and the huge clouds that rolled over it, draping the mountain in a white tablecloth. "No. It's nice here." I reached for the spade but stopped myself again.

"Are you sure you're a real therapist?" I looked her up and down. She certainly didn't look like one, with her fire engine red hair glinting in the sun.

"What do you think?" she asked.

"That was a very therapist answer."

"And how does that make you feel, Lori?" she asked playfully, and then chuckled.

"Fine!" We laughed together. I reached into the flower bed and sank my spade into the soil. I began to raise the soil when something caught my eye.

"Oh no! I think I cut it in half." I watched as a poor earthworm writhed frantically in the soil.

Dr. Stride leaned in. "*Ag*, don't worry. They're just as resilient as these plants. It should regenerate its tail."

"Really?" I picked the worm up gently with my spade and put it to one side.

"Nature really is quite the metaphor for life, isn't it?" She leaned back on her knees and looked straight at me now. Something in her gaze made me sit up stiffly. She was looking at me as if she could see straight inside me. As if she understood every single part of me, even though we'd just met.

"Take these leaves for example"—she ripped some succulent leaves off and tossed them haphazardly into the flower bed—"even these will grow again. Pull the leaves off, and baby plants grow out of them. First the bright-pink roots stretch out and then perfect, miniature plants. It's called propagation."

I looked over at the discarded leaves. I couldn't imagine them surviving like that. Surely, they'd just wither up and die.

"These things are amazing, they're designed to survive and regrow, no matter how they've been broken. Even this stem . . ." She snapped the stem off the plant, leaving the head in one hand and the stem in the other. She moved some soil away, made two small indents, and placed the pieces into the ground.

"The stem will grow other plants on it, and the head will grow roots that burrow into the soil again, and both will be just as strong—*maybe even more so*—than they were before. And so the cycle continues."

I looked up at her; she was staring at me again, meaningfully. "Humans break too. Bad experiences, past events, trauma . . ." Her meaningful look increased, her penetrating gaze holding mine. "But with time, with therapy, with love, we grow again. Brand new and perfect, like these will."

"That was also a very therapist thing to say."

"Told you I was a real therapist."

We sat in silence for a while as I looked out over the flower bed in front of me, imagining not plants this time, but people. Broken bits and pieces of human remains, all of them in various stages of regrowth and change.

"So, what say we finish this bed and get to know each other

before we jump into our work. I think twice a week will be good to see each other."

My head jerked up. "Twice?"

"I don't believe in doing therapy forever," she said. "Lying about on the couch all Freudian and talking for hours and hours about how your mom messed you up, and how that time you didn't get the right birthday present from your dad made you feel unloved."

"Huh?" I couldn't hide my shock. "That's kind of what I thought therapy was."

"Not my therapy." She shook her head. "I like to set meaningful goals with my clients and then work with them to achieve them."

"O-okay."

"Good!" She clapped her soil-covered hands together. "So, tell me your story, Lori."

"What would you like to know?"

"Everything."

"Well . . ." I started and then stopped. Everything was very broad and nebulous. Like casting a tiny net into a massive ocean, hoping to catch something. "I don't know what to say."

"Let's start smaller. What do you like about yourself?" She ripped some more plants out of the soil and placed them on the grass.

"What do I what?"

"Like about yourself," she repeated.

"I—I . . ." I stopped dead. *What did I like about myself?* For some reason this question absolutely floored me. No one had ever asked me this before, and I'd never stopped to think about it either. The question repeated in my brain, confusing me more by the second. "I don't know," I finally managed. I could instantly see this was the wrong answer. I could see that in the way Dr. Stride was tutting out loud and shaking her own head, just in case I still needed it confirmed.

"Well, that's not good enough," she said.

"Excuse me?"

"Right, homework for next session—" she started.

"Homework?"

"Write a list of things you like about yourself."

My insides wrapped themselves into a tight ball. I was starting to feel very uncomfortable with this conversation.

"Or draw them, if that makes you feel more comfortable," she added quickly.

"Okay," I said slowly and thoughtfully. "I'll try."

And then she gave me the most dazzling smile I'd ever seen. "Right, these echeverias have remained comfortable for too long, let's pull them out."

"Echa what?" I asked.

"They're called echeverias. Don't you just love that word. E-che-ve-riaaaa. Rolls off your tongue, *ne*?"

Despite what I was feeling, I couldn't help but laugh at this. Dr. Stride was unlike any therapist I'd ever been to before, and I didn't know if that was a good or bad thing. But I knew it was something.

13

Things I Like about Myself by Lori Palmer

I stared down at the writing in my notebook and tapped the page with my pen. *Things I liked about myself.* Why was this so hard? Why did it feel like I couldn't think of one bloody thing to say? I closed my book and looked out over the ocean.

Ever since Jake had pointed out its beauty, I was appreciating it for the first time. Some artists, like Turner, had spent their entire lives painting the sea. Fascinated by it, studying it, capturing its every mood. I watched it closely, paying special attention to the way the light danced on its rippled surface. The way the light became a silvery liquid, riding the surf until it disappeared into the white froth on the shore. And the blue, it was far more complex than I'd previously thought. I could see that it was made up of hundreds of different hues. It was patchy, like an artist's palette, all the colors blending together perfectly to form this massive thing that seemed alive, living and breathing all on its own.

I also thought about the succulents. For some reason, I hadn't been able to get them out of my head. How you could pull them apart, break them up, and they would spring back to life. And then I thought about the time I'd been pulled apart, and I wondered if I'd sprung back to life yet since the incident.

Truthfully, it was more a series of incidents carried out over the course of several years. The relentless, schoolyard bullying that had culminated in that moment in the water six years ago. Even now, if I close my eyes, *I still feel like I'm underwater again.* That moment is never far away and I return to it in my mind more often than I should.

It started out as a normal day, like any other day would. I've often wondered why I didn't get some kind of a feeling about it. Surely, when a day like that comes around that changes your entire life, changes you, there should be some kind of warning. An inkling in your bones that when the sun sets that day, nothing will ever be the same again. But there was nothing. Nothing, that is, until I'd hit the water.

The hard push of a hand on my back that sent me flying through the air. The feeling of panic as I fell into the pool unexpectedly, smashing into the surface, which felt as if it was made of concrete. Pain. The cold rush of water shooting up my nose and into my mouth. Instant headache. My arms desperately trying to grab something, anything . . . but nothing. And then sinking. Going deeper. The world above me blurring and distorting behind a wall of rippling water.

The silence was the most frightening part. The absence of

sound, like I was no longer a part of the world above me. Like I was somewhere else entirely. A new world, where there was no air, no gravity, no noise, and no hope of ever breathing again.

My lungs were on fire and I'd tried to come up for air, I really had . . . *at first*. But every time I did, a strong hand forced me back down. First hand, Bradley. Second hand, Mandla. Third, Johan. Forth, Bradley again. Pushing my head back underwater, again and again and again until I stopped fighting, gave up, and let myself sink deeper.

And in that moment of giving up, an unexpected feeling of calm washed over me, and I remember thinking that I could just close my eyes now and let go. *It would be so easy.* It would be a matter of moments until the blackness came and swallowed me up, and then I would never have to hear the teasing again. See their taunting faces. Listen to their jeers and manic cackles, the venomous words they spat at me on a daily basis. Words that cut through me like blades, leaving me red and raw and bloody.

I've never told anyone that before. That I let go like that and no longer fought. That I was quite happy to watch those laughing faces above me vanish entirely. Not even Dr. Finkelstein, who would probably read something into it that wasn't there. *Or was it there?* Sometimes I think about that moment and wonder why I was so okay with it all ending like that. I could have tried harder to swim away, I could have fought harder with my nails and teeth. But I didn't. I went under and stayed under.

A teacher finally jumped in and pulled me out, and when I opened my eyes again, I was back in the world I thought I was going to leave behind. That was when all my panic started and my parents sent me to therapy. The kids got suspended only for three days over that, but my suspension has lasted years. Because even though that moment physically ended, it has never really left me. It's always inside, lurking just below the surface. Waiting to pull me back under again. The only thing that got me through those years was art—sorting through all the pain and anger and fear, and rearranging it all into beautiful brushstrokes. Tears mixing into the paint from all the crying, blood mixing in from me pulling at my cuticles in utter panic.

That was a very dark time in my life, and it was then, after that incident, I went to art school. A fresh start. A place where I was good at something, and accepted because of it. And bonus, no swimming pool in sight! But now I'd moved to Cape Town, and this whole place was a damn giant swimming pool. I got up off my bed and pulled my curtains shut; maybe the sea wasn't as beautiful as I thought after all. I sat back down on my bed and opened my laptop. I went to YouTube and typed the words *succulent propagation* into the search bar. The screen filled with videos and I watched them, getting caught up in the strange and magical world where broken bits and pieces grew new arms and legs. Their shapes and colors intrigued me too—there was something about them that made them different; they were the antiplants. Unlike pretty, sweet-smelling roses or lilies or all those other plants you see in floral arrangements, these guys were badass somehow. From blacks and grays to almost neon greens. Spikes and thorns and pointy bits, or soft, plump cushions. A collage of textures and colors that seemed so out of this world that they were almost alien. I was so drawn in that I almost choked on my Coke Zero when the ad came on. Because there she was. My mom. Emerging from behind a massive palm tree on our patio, wearing a leopard print jumpsuit.

"Hi, I'm Barbara Palmer, of Palm Luxury Realty, and I'm here to tell you that finding your dream house is easier than you think."

She raised a pair of binoculars to her eyes and then looked around. Her acting was so bad that I wanted to melt into my bed. I couldn't believe what I was seeing. She lowered the binoculars with an unnatural jolt and then stepped through the palm leaves, dramatically swooshing her hands around, as if she was walking through a dense jungle.

"Oh no." I raised my hands to my face; they hovered just below my eyes, as if they wanted to stop me from seeing this train wreck. But I couldn't look away.

"At Palm Luxury Realty, we pride ourselves on matching people with their perfect homes."

She turned dramatically and put her hands on her hips; her huge hair bounced and pooled around her shoulders, as if it was alive.

"Whether it's a trendy penthouse in the heart of the city, a mansion on the plush lawns of Bishopscourt, or a seaside villa in Clifton . . . like this!*"*

I jerked back as she shouted that part and swung her arms in the air. The camera raced up into the sky until it was looking down on our house.

"No, no, no." I shook my head. My mother was making the biggest fool of herself in this badly made infomercial. She might as well be selling an As Seen On TV product that just didn't work, or that we never knew we needed—like a handheld device that sliced your cucumbers into perfect heart shapes, because until now we never knew how much we needed heart-shaped cucumbers. I watched in horror as my mother continued.

The camera swooped back down, and now she was sitting at a table with a stack of papers in front of her and a big bottle of champagne in an ice bucket.

"And we will take care of everything, all the tedious paperwork, all the admin—all you have to do is sit back and wait, until we . . ."

She stood up with a huge bunch of keys in her hand.

" . . . put your dream home in the palm *of your hand."*

She smiled as a man's arm entered the shot. She threw her head back and laughed (I'm not sure why) as she placed the bunch of keys into the hand and then looked straight into the camera again.

"So, call me, Barbara Palmer, and let me make your luxury real estate dreams come true."

And then, to end this horror show on a high note, she shook the champagne, popped the cork, and laughed as the golden bubbles flew into the air. I slammed my laptop closed. I felt like I was in the *Twilight Zone*—some surreal, strange space where I was no longer in actual reality, but in some strange upside-down version of life.

I jumped off my bed and paced my room a few times. With

each passing day, this person who was meant to be my mother was becoming more of a stranger to me. Who was this woman who made bad internet ads, wore leopard print, got her lips and eyes done, and spoke in a corny language? I didn't know anymore who this new person was that was inhabiting my mother's body like an alien growing inside her. And I guess I hadn't really known since that day. The day the doves cried.

14

It was four years ago, on the twenty-first of April 2017, when everything went down. I remember waking up that morning and lying in bed before school, randomly scrolling through social media. A song started playing that I'd never heard before, "When Doves Cry." There was something so haunting and strange about it. A tortured melody of discordant, aching sounds, a voice that sounded deep at times and then impossibly high. Tense. Jarring and yet beautiful too. I clicked on a link and watched, fascinated by the strange, sexual video. This glam-looking, androgynous man crawling across a purple-lit floor. His eyes looked like they held a secret, and when he looked straight into the camera, you got the feeling he would never tell anyone what that secret was . . . but he knew what yours were too.

I watched to the end of the video, and then read the words that floated onto the screen. He had died one year ago, Prince. A rock legend. I googled his name and news articles came up reporting on his tragic, untimely demise, and the one-year anniversary of his death. And then on the way home from school I walked past a record store and saw one of his albums in the window. *And that's when I got the hysterical call from my mother.*

"Your brother has had an accident at school. . . . Needs emergency surgery . . . can't get a hold of your dad. . . . Is he home? . . . Know where he is?"

No. I didn't know where he was. He'd been working a lot recently, and was hardly home. A big development that his real estate company was working on, he'd said. I put the phone down in a state of shock. I'd called my grandmother and asked her to take me to the hospital. I'll never forget walking into the hospital room; the atmosphere was like that song.

My brother was lying in the bed, his arm wrapped in a cast, fast asleep. A woman and a man in white coats were talking to my mother in hushed tones—my mother looked wide-eyed and afraid. There was a sense of urgency in the air like something was coming. A policeman and the school principal were standing outside the room.

"Why is there a policeman here?" I heard myself ask. My mom and the two doctors turned around. I read the titles on their white coats: surgeon, psychiatrist.

"Is he going to die?" I was suddenly hysterical. I didn't know what to make of the strange tension in the room, the way the principal kept glancing at us through the glass as she talked to the police officer outside, and the way my mother was wringing her hands together tightly.

The surgeon stepped forward. "Your brother is going to be fine. It was a severe fracture but we've put it back together."

"Why is the principal here? Why is she talking to a policeman? Why is a psychiatrist here?"

Finally, the whole story was relayed to me.

My brother had had a total meltdown at school. They hadn't been able to stop him. He'd run outside, climbed up the tallest tree in the middle of the playground, and no one had been able to get him down—they were afraid he would jump if they tried. They'd called the fire department but when they'd put the ladder up, he'd jumped. Police had to be called in when accidents "like this" happened at school. The way they'd said *like this* left me feeling cold. The principal seemed upset with my mother too; she kept saying that she'd warned my parents something like this could happen. She'd told them that Zac needed to be evaluated, but they weren't listening.

It was the first time I'd ever heard the word that I know so well now: autism. It was the principal who'd suggested it to my parents months ago, and now it was the psychiatrist who was giving my mother the name of a neurodevelopmental pediatrician, and speaking of evaluations and possible occupational therapy and all those things that have become so normal to me over the years, but that seemed so strange to me then.

I remember standing there and knowing that this all made sense. I'd watched Zac since he was a baby, and something about him had always seemed different. The way he played on his own in the corner and didn't really engage with others. How he refused to eat to the point of becoming thin, and then how he would only eat certain foods, and they all had to be on separate plates and at certain temperatures. The words he used, so brilliant and advanced for his age I wasn't even sure where he'd heard them. The way he jumped and freaked out at the smallest sounds, the way he became obsessed with things to the point that you wanted to go crazy . . . and then, like a tidal wave, there was truth in what the principal was telling my mother, even if I didn't understand it then like I did now.

My mother was devastated, though. So confused, and she kept trying to call my dad. Finally, his receptionist suggested that he might be at his new development, and that was when my mother went looking for him. I'd stayed with Zac, who was sleeping peacefully, like a cherub. A perfect angel.

Over the years, I'd been so impatient with him and grown so irritated that I'd locked him out of my room. I'd shouted at him when he'd repeated my words back to me or gone on about something nonstop for hours, and I remember feeling so guilty and promising him that from that day forward, I would be the best sister I could be to him. I laid my hand on his cheek; it was soft and his eyelashes were so long. He made this little noise when he breathed out, and his lips kind of squished together like they had when he was a baby, and when he opened his eyes slowly and smiled at me, it felt like someone punched me in the stomach. He hardly ever smiled.

"I jumped out of the tree," he whispered.

"I know."

"I didn't fly though," he said and then he did something so strange and bizarre that I can only think it was because of the cocktail of drugs he was on. He reached up and put his little chubby hand on my cheek. I laid my hand over his and held on tightly, never wanting this moment of contact to end.

"Please don't try to fly again," I urged him.

He closed his eyes and shook his head a little. "I won't. Night, night, Lori."

I think I finally knew what it was to *really* love a sibling that night. I'd dozed off for a moment, with my head on the bed, holding on to his hand, when my parents came back. The air suddenly became thick with tension, so much tension you could almost taste it, bitter on your tongue. I'd kept my eyes closed and listened to the conversation that played out while they thought I was sleeping.

My father was having an affair with a realtor in her twenties named Maddy. My mother had found them celebrating in the hot tub with champagne after selling the last of their development in record time. He was apparently "in love" and moving out of our home to be with her. My mom begged him to stay. They could go to therapy, they could work it out, lots of couples managed to get through this, but he wasn't interested. And the more he said no, the more my mother groveled and the more I wanted to scream and cry. I had to bite down so hard on my lip that night to stop myself from making a sound that it was bruised for a week afterward. And that was the day that everything changed. *The day the doves cried.*

The next morning, I woke up to find my mom sitting at the hospital window, looking out over Joburg, drinking coffee. She had this strange, distant look in her eyes, and she's had it ever since. As if something inside her died that day. Zac began all the millions of evaluations that week and was finally diagnosed. Life around me began to revolve around everyone else, and suddenly I was lost in it all. My mom worried about my brother, and how to screw my father over in the divorce and get his money. My father worried about Zac, and his new girlfriend, and how to keep his money in the divorce. And somewhere along the way, it felt like no one was worrying about me anymore.

But at least one good thing came out of it: my bond with Zac. I probably wouldn't exchange anything for that. Even if everything had to fall apart in order for me to get it.

Things I Like about Myself by Lori Palmer
I'm a good sister.

15

The days at BWH came and went, came and went. The weekend passed. And then more days at school passed. I'd *almost* successfully managed to evade Jake, until isiZulu class, where I found myself sitting in front of him again. I didn't greet him or meet his eyes. I couldn't. The image of him looking at my photo was so fresh in my mind that clammy embarrassment still wiggled its way over my skin like an itchy rash. But he didn't greet me either. He also didn't make eye contact. Like I said, I knew how things worked around here—but even though I did, it still hurt me more than it should have. *So much for our support coupling.*

And then it was Friday. I'd been at BWH for a whole week and a half, and it was the day of the compulsory water polo match. I'd been caught between this strange feeling of dreading it but also being intrigued to see Jake in his so-called natural habitat. The swimming complex at the school was enormous. The Olympic-sized pool was lined on all sides by stadium benches that reached up high. I wasn't scared of heights, but I was scared of water, so I headed for the top of the stands.

The whole of BWH was there, taking up one entire side of the stadium, while the other team's school, all dressed in red, was taking up the opposite side. Amber and the Ts, and some other girls whose names I didn't know, were standing in the front, pom-poms in hand, clearly ready to start the cheering. I scanned them, and Thembi immediately caught my eye.

She looked so beautiful in her pale-blue cheerleading outfit—tall, and the contrast of the pale blue against her dark skin looked amazing. She reminded me of Miss South Africa, Shudufhadzo Musida, with her shaved head, her high-arched brows, and skin that seemed golden in the light. She was one of those girls you hear stories about—some talent scout sees them buying bread in their pajamas at a shop, and then they have an international modeling contract because they're *that* stunning. I looked over at Amber, she was very much the Queen Bee. The one who seemed to control everyone around her. Even the Ts were listening to her. She was talking and smiling and gesticulating happily, but I wasn't buying any of her supposed sweetness. I could see that Amber was hiding something dangerous under that baby-blue cheerleader's outfit. Behind those big, bright smiles was a sinister side. Like the color cadmium red. Beautiful, vibrant, beloved by artists like Matisse, Cézanne, and Bacon. But utterly toxic. Something so beautiful, so seemingly full of life . . . so *deadly*. I couldn't help but wonder if anyone else saw it, or if it was just me? I turned away from Amber and looked around.

Nina-M was filming something, probably for her beauty blog—she was putting an SPF cream on her face and talking about it. I overheard her say something about the importance of wearing sunscreen. TikTok-famous Vuyo was making someone film him while he stuck straws up his nose and then tried to shoot them out at targets.

My phone buzzed in my pocket and I pulled it out. Another message from my dad.

DAD: Just checking in. Hope school is going well. Call me when you can, I have something I need to talk to you about. Love you

I bit my lip. Tears prickled in my eyes and I quickly wiped them away. I didn't know if I was more angry or sad when it came to him. I turned Notifications off and put my phone away just as a massive cheer rose up and everyone turned to the left. I did the same, and then there he was. Walking toward the pool followed by his team. I sat up straight, my breath hitching in my throat and something familiar flapping in my stomach. I held my breath, watching him, and then I think I forgot how to breathe altogether. It happened in slow motion—well, that's how it seemed, anyway. He reached up and started pulling his T-shirt off and then in one swift movement, he tossed it onto a chair and turned.

My bottom jaw felt like it snapped off. I imagined it tumbling down the grandstand and landing at his feet. It might even land in the water with a splash and sink to the bottom of the pool. Because in all my years, I'd never seen anything like it. Abs so defined and perfect they looked like a six-pack of pudding cups you wanted to reach out and rip open. And then, in one swift, graceful move, the pudding cups disappeared as he dived into the pool. His dive was so flawless that it barely made a splash, and when he bobbed back up to the surface, he was smiling. The pool was clearly his happy place.

The game started, and despite myself, despite all the things I liked to tell myself about how I hated watching sports and that they held no interest for me . . . *my interest was held*. It was held as the ball flew through the air from one side of the pool to the other. As water crashed and bodies smashed, and how Jake would rise up out of the water, as if standing on something. It seemed impossible that someone could get so high out of the water. He threw the ball into the net so hard that water covered the people seated poolside. I was transfixed as he did this over and over again. He kept scoring and the school kept cheering, and Amber and the Ts kept jumping, and without warning, I found myself on my feet. I found myself clapping and jumping and getting swept up in the game until the final goal, the moment of silent awe afterward, and then the explosion of joy that swept over the stadium like a giant wave. And by the end of the match my hands were red from clapping, my throat was sore from shouting, and my legs had never had so much exercise in my life. And strangely—bizarrely—I felt a part of something that I'd never imagined I would ever feel a part of.

Jake and the team climbed out of the pool and fell into a group hug, and I couldn't help but smile. I was just about to sit down again when Jake hit the ball into the air and everyone looked up. The ball traveled higher and higher and then unexpectedly, as if it had bumped into an invisible wall, it stopped. It hovered for a second or two and then . . . *chaos*.

The ball was falling. I looked around. Amber was scrambling up the grandstand with the determination of someone trying to catch the bouquet at a wedding. She was getting closer, coming toward me with such speed. I looked up.

"Oh my goodn—" The ball was headed straight for my face, and everyone in the stadium had turned to watch. I closed my eyes and held out my hands, blocking my face and winced as the ball hit my fingers. And then it stopped. *Wait . . . had I just caught it?* There was deathly silence. If a pin were to drop from the sky right now, I'm sure the sound would have echoed through the stadium like a clap of thunder. I finally opened my eyes and looked around. Everyone was staring at me, including Amber. But hers was not a stare. Hers was a vile, hateful glare. I glanced at the pool. Jake was looking at me too. And then he smiled, and the whole stadium burst into eardrum-shattering cheers.

16

After the excitement of the game, followed by the awkward, yet in some strange way, exhilarating feeling of being the center of an entire stadium's attention, I decided to get out of there. Besides, I had therapy. I was making my way across the parking lot when I heard him calling.

"Hey!"

I turned to find Jake standing there, in his full BWH water polo tracksuit. This was the first time we'd spoken in almost a week. Wet tendrils of hair peeped out from under his cap, his smile was huge, and his eyes seemed so very cerulean right now. He walked toward me, and I felt that familiar, visceral reaction to his presence once more.

"Congratulations," I gushed without restraint.

"Thanks."

"Good game. Well, I mean, I've never watched a water polo match before, so I guess I can't say whether it was a good game per se, but it seemed like a good game."

His smile grew. "It was a good game."

"You scored a lot of goals . . . uh, is that what you call them? Or hoops, or tries, or whatever."

He laughed. "Goals. I did!" He said it with such a matter-of-fact tone that it made him even hotter.

"Are you coming to the party tonight?" he asked, and I shrugged in question. "There's a party to celebrate our win tonight at Vuyo's house, you must come."

"No. It's okay. Besides, I don't really know anyone, and I haven't been invited or anything, or—"

"I'm inviting you."

"You are?" I asked, squinting and shielding my face from the bright sun.

He chuckled. "Unless me saying 'you must come' is not an invitation." And then, without any kind of warning, he pulled his cap off and pushed it down over my head.

"Uh . . . thanks." I reached up and touched the cap, surprised by this gesture.

"The party starts at seven. He's just down the road from you. 101 Bay Drive. Everyone is going to be there." He looked excited, but I wasn't.

I broke eye contact with him. I was awkward at parties. In truth, I felt more alone in social gatherings than I did when I was actually alone. Besides, I'd never gone to a party without my two wingmen.

"Think about it. No pressure." His voice had taken on a different tone now. One that seemed to convey meaning, as if he knew what I was thinking.

"Party! Party! Party!" I whipped my head around when I heard the chant. Two other water polo guys were running up to me. *Why were they coming toward me?*

"Dude, nice catch! See you at the party!" the one guy almost shouted in my face and then they both rushed over, tackled Jake, and hoisted him onto their shoulders.

Jake turned to me as he was being carried away and shot me a smile followed by a small shrug. I didn't quite know how to interpret that.

"I got invited to a party tonight," I said, sinking my spade into the soil. We'd uprooted all the succulents and were now putting them back into the soil in a swirling pattern. Dr. Stride, who insisted I call her Vicki now, looked up at me, soil smeared across her rounded face. "Are you going?"

"Nah, don't think so." I tried to make it sound like I was somewhat irritated that I'd been invited to the party. Somewhat put out. I was too cool for stupid water polo parties. My artistic sensibilities were beyond all that.

Vicki stopped what she was doing and looked straight at me. She didn't believe me. I could see it in her intense gaze. I'd done enough therapy in my life to understand *that look*. The look they give when they know there's more to a story than meets the eye. I put my hand on my hip defiantly, ready to challenge her. But when she looked down at my hand, I released it, giving up my show of bravado.

"Okay, okay. I know what you're thinking," I blurted.

"What am I thinking?"

"You're thinking that despite my nonchalant act here, that actually, when it comes down to it, I *do* want to go to the party in some way. Deep down inside."

"Do you?" she asked.

"Parties intimidate me. I feel panicky and nervous at them, but at the same time, I want to go to them, even though I say I don't. I don't know, it's like I want the things I tell myself I don't want because I'm afraid of getting them, *or not getting them*, or something."

"That was profound." She smiled.

I shrugged.

"The best therapist in the world is the one right inside you." She pointed at me.

"You know that sounded totally cheesy, right?"

"Sometimes we therapists can be cheesy."

"Yeah, with your succulent analogies and strange labia art hanging on the wall."

"Labia art?"

"Yes." I turned and pointed at the office. "That purple piece with all the butterflies flying out of it."

She seemed confused for a second or two and then a look of recognition washed over her face, followed by amusement. "Those are butterflies flying out of a dark cave. It's meant to symbolize your mind and the freeing of emotions from it. I painted it myself."

"Oh." And now I was mortified.

She paused and seemed to consider me for a moment.

"Don't!" I pointed an accusatory finger at her.

"Don't what?"

"Don't say something like, 'Well, it's interesting that you saw a labia, Lori. That must be indicative of something else.'"

"Is it?"

"*Psssh!* No!"

"Well, Freud would say that what you saw was a representation of your innermost secret desires."

"Thought you didn't do Freud."

Then she laughed. "Ag, nah. I don't. Honestly, when I finished the painting I also thought it looked less like a cave and more like something else! I should probably not quit my day job, ne?"

Vicki threw her head back and laughed so heartily that it was hard not to join in. She was a strange one, all right. Today she was wearing bright orange, from head to toe. A bright-orange kaftan accessorized with bright-orange rubber boots. Even her nails were orange. She had presence. And it wasn't her size that gave her that; it was something else. Her energy. Her openness. And obviously the fact she looked like a massive traffic beacon helped too. I bent back down to continue with the garden.

"Who invited you to the party?" she asked after a brief moment of silence.

"Just this guy, Jake." I tried to brush it off and make it sound like it held no weight and quickly added, "And some other guys I don't even know."

"Jake?" she asked, honing in on that name, my attempt at subterfuge clearly not working.

"Our siblings go to the same school." I sat up straight. "The Lighthouse. He volunteers there. We got talking."

There was a long pause and I got the sense she was gathering her thoughts, or mentally jotting something down. "Must be challenging, having a brother with special needs."

"Sometimes," I confessed, and guilt instantly whacked me in the rib cage. "I love him. A lot, though," I quickly qualified.

She smiled. "I know you do. But sometimes I think we often ignore or overlook how challenging it can be for a sibling."

"Why?" I asked.

"Well, parents often go to therapy and there're classes and coaches for parents, but not many resources for the siblings."

"That's exactly what Jake and I were saying."

"And of course, most of the parents' energy tends to go toward the sibling with special needs, and often the neurotypical sibling's needs don't get met."

"That's not his fault, though," I said quickly, feeling like I needed to defend him.

"Of course it's not. It's no one's fault. It is the way it is. But that doesn't mean it's not hard sometimes."

I looked away quickly. I didn't want to acknowledge what she was saying at all.

"How's your relationship with your parents?" She picked up a bright, pink succulent and shoved it in the soil.

"I'd say that my relationship with my dad is pretty nonexistent at the moment. He decided to cheat on my mom with a twenty-something-year-old and walked out on us."

She stood up. "The clichéd male midlife crisis?"

"I'd say. And so would that bright-red sports car he's now driving."

I didn't want to add that I was particularly hurt and angry with him at the moment. I'd asked if I could stay in Joburg with him, only for a few months, just until I'd finished school. *Sorry, honey. It's just bad timing, because Maddy and I are in the middle of moving into a new place.*

"It happens more often than you think," Vicki said, pulling me from my painful thoughts. "Half my clients who come for couple's therapy have gone through it. But it can be worked through."

"He didn't want to go to therapy. He's in love," I said bitterly, hating that I sounded exactly like my mother. But honestly, I was bitter. More than bitter. It made me feel sick to my stomach to think of my dad as a guy who had sex in a hot tub. He was my dad. He wasn't meant to be having sex and falling in love, he was too old. It was gross, not to mention truly and utterly selfish.

"How's your mom?" she asked.

"She should be in therapy if you ask me." I paused and looked at her for a while. "Ever heard of Barbara Palmer of Palm Luxury Realty?"

"Noooo! Of the YouTube videos? Seriously?"

"That would be she." I picked up one of the succulents and placed it in the center of the area I'd just cleared, perhaps with a little more hostility than I should have.

"So in the last few years, your brother was diagnosed with autism, your parents went through what I'm guessing was a very acrimonious divorce, you've had your childhood perceptions of your parents shattered—your dad as the protector of the family and your mom as a nurturer and carer—and you've moved schools and cities. That's a lot for anyone. I'm sure you've been deeply affected by all of it."

"I guess." I tried to sound dismissive again, but I knew it wasn't working. She looked at me for the longest time, and I got the feeling she could see that this was the last thing in the world I wanted to talk about, which in therapist terms meant that this was now the *only* thing she wanted to talk about.

"How are the panic attacks?" she asked. When I didn't answer right away, she continued: "You gave Dr. Finkelstein permission to share your details with me. I hope you still feel comfortable with that?"

"Yes. Sure." I stopped talking. The bubble of panic rose up inside me when I talked about the panic. Just thinking about it seemed to bring it to life. "I almost had one the other day, at school." I looked away and focused my attention on the flower bed again.

"That's not surprising. You're under a lot of stress at the moment. What stopped it?"

"A fake fire alarm."

"Are you taking your medication?" she asked.

I rolled my eyes and looked down at the ground, fiddling with my hands.

"There's nothing wrong with taking medication." She leaned closer to me and her voice took on a firm tone. "If you were a diabetic would you deny yourself insulin?"

"No," I whispered. I'd heard this before from Dr. Finkelstein so many times. *Anxiety is just as real as any other chronic condition.* But still . . . sometimes it just felt like a sign of weakness, like I was incapable of "just getting over it."

As if reading my mind, she said, "Anxiety and depression aren't things you just get over. And they don't make you weak, or less than. Some of the most interesting and brilliant people I know have a mental illness. Just look at the greatest artists of our time. Edvard Munch said he suffered from depression and agora- phobia, and look what art came out of that."

"*The Scream*. I love that painting."

"Beethoven is speculated to have had bipolar disorder and then there's van Gogh."

"He cut off his ear," I said flatly.

"And isn't it great we have medication these days to help prevent things like ear cutting?"

"Point taken."

"Of course you took my point. My point is good, ne," she said, dazzling me with one of those big smiles of hers. "Tell me more about this Jake?"

"Not much to tell, really." *Well, that was just not true.* "Our siblings had a playdate on the beach the other day and built a sandcastle."

"It's good that you're making friends here."

"I wouldn't exactly say we're friends. If our siblings weren't at the same school, we would never have spoken."

"So, you think the only way it's possible for him to be friends with you is if your siblings are friends?"

"Well, obviously!" I stated emphatically.

"Explain." Her tone was demanding.

"What do you mean?"

"It's not obvious to me." She said it so matter of factly that it caught me off guard.

I lowered my head; shame and embarrassment bubbled up inside me. "He's the most popular guy at school and I'm . . ." I paused and waved my arm around myself a few times. "You know, I'm . . ." I waved my arm even more. "You know!"

"Trying to swat a fly?" she asked.

I looked at her pointedly. "You know what I'm trying to say."

"Say it." Her eyes dug into me.

"You of all people must know what I mean," I heard myself hiss at her.

"No, I don't, not if you don't tell me."

I looked straight back at her. Her eyes were challenging me. I stood up, looked around, and dropped the spade on the ground angrily.

"You know what, this is stupid." I threw my arms in the air. "I mean, what are we even doing? This isn't therapy. I'm digging around in a garden for heaven's sake."

Vicki stood up, too, rising to the challenge.

"What do you want me to say?" I asked sarcastically.

She shrugged, and it pissed me off.

"Right! Okay. How 'bout this? Fat, ugly!" I shot those words out at her, and then gasped. I took a step back.

"Is that the first time you've said those words out loud?"

I nodded.

"And how did they sound?"

I bit down on my lip as my throat constricted. "Terrible," I confessed.

"Would you ever call someone that out loud?" she asked. "Me, for instance. Would you ever call me that to my face?"

"No. Never."

"And yet, that's what you're calling yourself in your head every single day." Her voice took on a soft, compassionate tone. "Probably more often than you think."

The first small tear escaped my eye and slid down my cheek. "Yes," I whispered, so choked up that the word barely came out of my mouth.

"Who called you those words?"

Tears stung my eyes and I blinked. "The kids at school. Not at art school, the one before."

"And did you like it, when they called you that?" she asked.

"Of course not. What do you think? I mean, they even tried to drown me once."

"And yet . . ." She left the sentence open ended and looked at me, as if pushing me to fill in the blanks. But I couldn't.

"And yet, *what*?"

"And yet you continue calling yourself those things. So the bullying hasn't really stopped, has it? Except you're the one bullying yourself this time."

Her words hit me like a lightning bolt. "I guess when you put it like that."

"How do you think your best friends would describe you if I phoned them and asked?"

"Andile and Guy?" I forced a smile. "Not like that."

"Then what?"

"Creative. Fun. Caring. Loyal." I paused, almost not daring to say the next work. "Pretty, especially when I wear red lipstick."

"And do you believe them when they say you look pretty?" she asked.

"I don't know. I mean, I think they think I do."

"Where's that sketchbook you carry around with you?" She clicked her fingers.

"In my bag."

"I want you to take it out and write something down for me."

I reached into my bag unenthusiastically and pulled out my book. I walked over to the garden table and sat down. "What?"

"My goals," she said, and I scribbled the words down. "Number one, to be your best friend."

I wrote and then stopped. "I don't know what you mean?"

"If I was your best friend and someone had just called me fat and ugly"—I cringed as she said those words—"what would you do?"

"Tell them to back off. Tell them to shut the hell up."

"Exactly." She nodded at me. "Now you need to do that for yourself."

I finally understood what she was saying; I needed to shut those intrusive voices in my head down.

She walked over to the table and sat down. "So, this party tonight?"

"I don't know." I shook my head.

"I think you should go. In fact, I insist you go. In fact . . ." She pulled my sketch pad away from me and scribbled across the page in bold lettering and then pushed it back.

"'Go to the party. Wear red lipstick! Doctor's orders!!!!!'" I read out loud and chuckled. "Seriously?"

"Seriously."

I looked down at my watch. It was almost time for the end of the session. "Okay. I'll go," I conceded.

"Good. Then I'll see you on Tuesday again."

"Tuesday." I began walking away but she quickly ran up to me again.

"Here. Take these." I held my hands open as she dropped something into my palms: succulent leaves.

"Lay them on some soil. Give them a little bit of water in a spray bottle, not that much, and watch them grow." She closed my hand around the leaves. "We start small. A fine mist of water, a few good words to ourself, and we keep it up every day. And one day, we won't believe what we've grown into."

"What if I kill them?"

"You won't. They're very resilient. More resilient than they know!"

I chuckled. "You love your plant analogies, don't you?"

Her face lit up. "Party! Wear lipstick! Look fabulous. You're okay. You're doing well. More than well."

"I'm okay. I'm doing well." I repeated the words, and for some reason, almost believed it when she said it. No one had said that to me in a while, forever maybe.

17

I found myself standing in front of the mirror once more, trying to decide what to wear. I grabbed one of my only dresses and put it on. It was a plain black T-shirt dress that hung loose, to just above my knee. I turned sideways and sighed. My boobs were so big that the dress sort of hung off them like a massive tent. It made the dress shorter in the front than in the back.

"Wait!" I said as I realized my inner bully had kicked in without me even noticing. Vicki was right—I probably wasn't aware of how many times a day I said that to myself.

"Lipstick!" I turned away from the mirror and reached into the makeup bag I seldom used. I rolled up the lipstick and spread it across my lips, careful not to go outside the lines, and then I dived back into my cupboard and grabbed a pair of red sneakers.

I was a sneaker girl through and through; the idea of heels simply struck terror into my heart. Maybe for a thinner, more agile girl the idea of walking on spikes was okay, but to a girl like me, it wasn't. I laced up my sneakers and then took one last look at myself.

Fine. I looked fine. "Fine," I said out loud and then shot myself some half-assed thumbs-up. This was good . . . a little mist of water, or whatever.

When I reached the bottom of the stairs, I found my mother sitting on one of our couches, which had finally arrived from Joburg today. The room was so huge that the furniture drowned in it.

"Where are you going?" she asked. She looked like a small grain of sand in the vast room. Our house was cold and lifeless. White walls and hollow, empty rooms that echoed when we talked. I felt like I was looking into the eyes of a cold, dead fish. The kind you see lying on a bed of ice at the grocery store. White isn't really a color, you know. It's more a trick of light, or a trick our eyes play when it mixes all the wavelengths to see it. White is the absence of any specific color. It's a nothing. An empty. Just like this house, and just like the woman sitting on that couch with the faraway eyes.

"Out," I said dismissively.

"You've put on lipstick." For some reason her comment made me feel self-conscious. I lifted my hand to my mouth and wondered if I should take the makeup off.

"What time will you be back?" She stood up and her heels clicked on the floor, echoing through the room.

"This house is too big. It echoes."

She stopped walking and looked at me strangely for a moment. "One should really focus on the positives, not the negatives, Lori."

"Huh?"

"I've been reading this book—"

OMG. I think I blacked out at this stage, or my ears just automatically closed. Whenever my mom started a sentence with "I've been reading a book," or "I googled it," I just knew some diatribe of strange information was about to come out, whether it was about thoughts manifesting physical things, or how waking up and meditating before the start of each day would make you a millionaire before the end of the year. I zoned out as her lips began moving at speed.

". . . proven . . . scientific fact . . . negativity and negative words . . . water molecules . . . manifesting . . . actual electromagnetic energy . . . laws of attraction . . ."

Her lips flapped, her mouth opened and closed and she was talking at me as if she was a preprogrammed robot. I couldn't remember the last time my mother and I'd had a real conversation. Her version of conversation was reciting to me whatever theory she was currently obsessed with. Last month it was some crystal that could remove negativity from the air and attract "wealth abundance," whatever that meant.

"Okay, okay, I have to go." I started to turn away from her, cutting the lecture short.

"*I have to have a house like this!*" she suddenly yelled. It was so abrupt and jarring that I swung around in shock. Her voice echoed around the room, and the walls repeated her words back to me twice before it was silent again.

"If I am Barbara Palmer of Palm *Luxury* Realty, I need to project the image of luxury at all times. I have a reputation to uphold. I have to remain true to my personal brand. Have you seen my new ad?" On closer inspection, her eyes looked red around the rims, as if she'd been crying.

"Yes," I said flatly.

"And what is more luxurious, what says and lives and breathes luxury more than this house?" Then she turned around and walked in a small circle. She seemed very agitated tonight. More so than usual.

"Besides, have you seen what your father just bought?" She said this part almost under her breath, as if I was *almost* not meant to hear it. But I had. My mother swears blind that she doesn't badmouth my dad, but she does. Not that I blame her, I guess. "That penthouse at *their* new development." She lowered herself onto the couch again. "I wonder if they'll be getting married there too. Might as well, since it started there."

"What?" I moved closer to her.

"What?" she replied glibly.

"You just said that they might as well get married there?"

"Oh, didn't he tell you?"

"Tell me what?"

"That he and *that woman* are getting married." In all the time my father had been with Maddy, my mom had never called her by her name. My brother and I used to go there every second weekend and Maddy tried so hard with us, but it always felt awkward. But Zac adored my dad; I had too. More than adored him. I'd idolized him and put him on such a pedestal that when he'd fallen off it, the ground beneath my feet had shaken. In many ways, it was still shaking, and my feet had never really found solid ground since.

"Not that I care, of course," she said. "Why the hell would I care? You know I have a fifty-million-rand listing in Bishopscourt. That YouTube ad is paying off. It's been viewed over a hundred thousand times, I'm basically viral. I'm a . . . what do you call it?" She looked at me and clicked her fingers. "You know what I mean, a social . . . what do they call it . . . influencer. I'm a social influencer."

"Wait . . . " I shook my head, trying to process this information. I was still stuck on the news that my father was engaged and hadn't told me. "They're getting married. When did this happen? When did he tell you?"

"Do you know what the commission on fifty million is?" She completely ignored my question.

My stomach constricted. I wanted to yell at her. I wanted to yell that she needed to snap back to reality. She'd been so far gone for so long, she needed to come back down to earth and reenter the atmosphere. I wondered if the woman that I used to know as my mother was even in there anymore. In that body that was starting to look so strange. Those lips and tight forehead and wide eyes that were starting to remind me more of a Picasso than an actual person.

I took a deep breath. "I'm going out," I said slowly and calmly.

"Does Zac know?"

"He's listening to music. I didn't tell him."

"You know how he can get when you don't tell him things like that."

I put my hand on my hip. "Why don't you tell him this time," I spat sarcastically.

"Lori Pa—"

"Yeah, yeah, that's my name." I cut her off abruptly; I hoped my angry tone hid what I was really feeling inside right now. *Pain.* We stared at each other for a minute, eyes locked, and I wished so much that she would open her mouth and actually talk to me for once. Like a real person. Like a mom. That she would say something of actual value. Something that mattered and meant something. But she didn't.

"You have to melt Zac tonight, remember," I said, breaking the tense silence. She looked at me blankly and I sighed. "On the Pilates ball. You have to roll him around, like the occupational therapist explained. It calms him before bed."

Why did I remember these things and my mother didn't?

"Sure, sure." She flapped her hand in the air flippantly. "I know that."

"He only likes to be melted on the blue ball, not the gray one."

"I thought the blue one popped?" she asked.

"I ordered another one from Takealot."

"Oh right! That's right. I know that," she said, sounding very far away again, and I wondered where she'd just gone. Maybe she went back to the same place inside herself over and over again. Maybe it was Dad and Maddy in the hot tub, like it was with me in the pool. Maybe that was the place she returned to? I looked at her, *really* looked at her. She seemed shorter tonight somehow, even though she was wearing heels, and I couldn't help but feel just a little bit sorry for her.

"What? Do I have something on my face?" She reached up and touched her cheeks.

"No, Mom, you don't."

"Good. Good. I have a Zoom call with a potential client now. Investment banker. Totally loaded. Looking for a holiday home." She fluffed her hair up and smiled at me. That Cheshire smile was back and so was Barbara Palmer and with it, my sympathy was gone again.

I shook my head. I didn't know what to say to her. So I didn't say anything. I walked out the door and closed it behind me.

As soon as I was alone in the car, I pulled my phone out and went to WhatsApp. I clicked on my dad's profile and read the messages he'd sent me.

DAD: Please call me

DAD: Hey, I would really like to talk to you. I have something important to tell you

My heart sank. I went to Maddy's Instagram profile and I couldn't hold back the tears when I read her latest status update, complete with the photo of the glittery ring on her finger. I dropped my phone onto the passenger seat and drove without looking back at it.

18

I parked my car in the long row of vehicles that snaked down Vuyo's street. I could hear the music from here. A deep bass shook the ground and I recognized it as a Black Coffee tune. I could feel the song "Drive" underneath my feet as it moved through the concrete like an unstoppable wave, and I wondered if it was telling me something—Get in your car and drive away, Lori! But I didn't. I took a deep breath and tried to pull my dress down; it felt like it had gotten caught between my butt cheeks and was rising up in the back. Another fat girl problem, usually a result of wearing a skirt, sitting down, and then standing up again. I felt so out of place here. Everything inside me told me I didn't want to be here, but I certainly didn't want to go home either.

When I got closer to the house, I stopped. Everyone was

inside. I could see them all dancing through the massive glass front. Throngs of happy people jumping up and down together, their body parts and clothes and colors melting together like an impressionist painting and then . . . *there he was.* Someone had lifted him onto their shoulders, and he was laughing as if he was having the time of his life.

I took a step back. *What the hell was I doing here?* I didn't belong here. I couldn't do this. I didn't care that I'd promised the doc, and that I'd smeared my lips red. All I cared about was the sweaty ache in my belly and the thump in my heart, and that building anxiety that made my feet feel like they were swelling. I was just about to obey the song and head right back to my car when I felt two massive arms around my shoulders. I jumped in fright.

"You caught the baaaaaalllllll!" someone yelled in my ear.

"*Yeeaah!*" another voice shouted, and suddenly I had two people screaming in my face at once. I was totally disoriented for a second until I recognized them as the two water polo players who had called me *dude* earlier. They smelled of vodka, overly sweet cotton candy vape, and cologne so strong it caught in the back of my nose.

The one put his hand up in front of my face and I wasn't sure what to do with it. So I did the only thing I could think of: I gave it a tentative high five. This seemed to be the right move because he wrapped his fingers through mine and forced my arm into the air for a mutual fist pump.

"Caught the fucking ball!" the other one screamed, and then I was being dragged toward the house. Caught up in a flurry of drunken, BWH cheer. I tried to pull away.

"I—I was . . . just . . . going." I tried to stop this forward momentum I'd been caught up in, like a riptide carrying me away.

"Party!" the one shouted enthusiastically, still pulling me. Pulling me all the way down the driveway and into the house. But as soon as I was there, the arms disappeared and so did the guys, and I was left standing all alone in a sea of mostly strangers.

I scanned the room for a friendly face. But they were few and far between. Very few and so far between. I felt far between. Between worlds and places and standing somewhere so unfamiliar and feeling like I didn't belong here, only apparently, I did? It seemed that everyone knew who I was, not by name, but that I was the girl who caught the *fucking* ball, and apparently that made me a someone. So much so that Vuyo was showing me the video of my catch on TikTok.

"It's already got ten thousand likes," he said, and this made me so uncomfortable I wanted to turn and run.

And then Thembi and the Ts started walking toward me. They should be a girl band. I looked to my left. Amber was approaching too. Looked to my right, the Ts. Left, Amber. Right, Ts, left Amber until . . . perfect timing. Like two swells crashing against each other, they were all upon me at once.

"Hiya," I said lamely.

"Hey," Thembi spoke. She seemed to be the leader of the Ts. I wasn't sure where Amber fit into the mix. She seemed to be a part of two different groups. The Ts and what I'd come to refer to in my head as the Goldilocks gang. What was weird about BWH was that it had cliques all right, but they all seemed to be of a similar ilk. Slight variations here and there, but all cut from the same cloth—probably Egyptian cotton, thread count off the charts. But there didn't seem to be the usual school extremes here. These groups were only slight variations of the same theme.

"Is that a Huda matte lipstick?" Thembi asked, looking at my matte red lips.

I raised my hand to my mouth and covered it slightly. Damn, I shouldn't have worn the lipstick. What was she going to say now? It didn't suit me. What was a girl like me doing wearing lipstick like this? "I think so," I muttered.

"Cool," she said casually. "That stuff was so sold out. You couldn't get it for months. No one makes matte lipstick like she does, though." I looked over at the other Ts, who both seemed to be inspecting my lips too. The only reason I owned this lipstick was because Maddy had gotten it for me, she was cool that way. She knew what everyone was wearing and wasn't wearing, and she was always trying to bond with me over this—I guess she really didn't know me. And then, out of the blue, I was being ambushed again.

"You have to drink with Jake," a guy said and started pulling me again.

"Wait . . . no." I pulled back.

"Dude, that's the rule. Whoever catches the ball, drinks!"

"But . . ."

Another arm wrapped around my shoulders. This time it was Amber's. I didn't much like the way she was looking at me.

"You have to," she crooned in my ear. "It's tradition." She pulled me into the crowd and a chant started.

"Shooters! Shooters! Shooters!" People flocked around me, and I began to feel very claustrophobic. Drowning in a sea of people. And then, through the crowd a familiar face appeared and my heart did a very involuntary series of backflips.

"Hey," Jake said, looking at me.

"Hey," I mumbled back.

"Shooters! Shooters! Shooters! Shooters! Shooters! Shooters!" The chant got louder, and a bright blue and white shooter was thrust into my hand. The colors of BWH.

The crowd leaned in and I looked over at Jake, who was raising the glass to his lips. I raised mine slowly and then brought my nose over it to sniff.

"Oh God!" I half choked as the blue liquid suddenly flew into my face as someone knocked the bottom of my glass. It dripped down my chin, and the rest splashed across my dress and forehead. Out of the corner of my eye I saw Amber laughing. Her head was back, her mouth was open, and because of the way the light was positioned straight above her, it was dark and shadowy inside. Like a bloody black mamba. *Did you know that just two drops of black mamba venom can kill a person in twenty minutes?*

But no one else was laughing. Everyone else was cheering me on, as if this was all part of the game. I looked up at Jake, and while everyone was distracted, he spilled his drink into a nearby potted plant. No one seemed to have noticed. Except me. And then everyone lost interest in Jake and me as more blue and white shooters got poured and passed around.

I walked away, trying to wipe the sticky liquid off me.

"Where you going?" I heard Amber shout from behind me, a taunting tone in her voice. But I didn't look back. *Why was she such a bitch?* I walked into the kitchen and washed my hands in the sink. I felt dizzy. Not from the drink; I'd barely swallowed any of it. I felt dizzy because I really didn't want to be here any longer. This crowd. This noise. This house. *This everything.* My phone rang and I scrambled to pull it out of my bag. It was my mother, and when I answered it, she sounded hysterical.

"Your brother is having a total meltdown because you're not

here." I could hear Zac screaming in the background. "You need to come home."

I hung up and actually breathed a sigh of relief; at least I had a reason to go.

19

The beep of the phone sent me scrambling across the room. I grabbed it and held it tightly to my chest, hoping the sound wouldn't wake Zac. It had taken me two hours to get him to sleep. I crept from his bedroom and closed the door behind me.

JAKE: Hey r u awake?

LORI: Hey. I'm awake

JAKE: You left the party suddenly. Everything okay?

I scrunched my face up when I read his message, twice. I couldn't believe he'd even noticed.

LORI: Zac had a meltdown when he realized I wasn't home. My mom was struggling to calm him

JAKE: Is he okay now?

LORI: He's asleep, so yeah

JAKE: When Lisa can't sleep I sometimes download ASMR videos. She really likes them

LORI: 😂 Like those Russian women who whisper strangely at you?

JAKE: 😂 She really likes the one where they rub slime over the microphone for an hour

LORI: Ha-hah! How is that supposed to be relaxing?

JAKE: IDK, I once watched a guy pop Bubble Wrap for an hour

LORI: 😂

LORI: How's the party?

JAKE: I left. It was getting a bit hectic

LORI: Won't they notice if the guest of honor isn't there?

JAKE: Nah, they're too drunk

LORI: They were drunk when I arrived, can't imagine what they're like now

JAKE: They'd started doing body shots

LORI: Not your thing?

JAKE: Not really

LORI: Cos you don't drink?

JAKE: Oh . . .

JAKE: You noticed that?

LORI: I don't think anyone else did, tho

There was a pause in the conversation and I walked down to the kitchen as I waited for his response.

JAKE: You know how I told you my dad is a recovering alcoholic?

LORI: Yeah?

JAKE: Well, they say that stuff can be genetic, so I don't really do it

LORI: Smart!

JAKE: My dad took me to a meeting once, and when I heard some of the stories, I thought it was better not to

LORI: Like what?

JAKE: This one guy went to the bottle store and left his kids in the car for hours because he got drunk and forgot where he parked. The baby almost died

LORI: That's crazy!

JAKE: Yup!

JAKE: You're the first person who noticed I don't drink

LORI: Seriously, no one else knows?

JAKE: I guess they're all too self-involved to notice

JAKE: Or maybe they're not watching me closely enough

I coughed a little as the carbonated bubbles of the Coke Zero I'd just opened got stuck in my throat. I hoped he didn't think I was watching him closely now.

JAKE: Wanna do a playdate this weekend? Lisa has been begging me all week to play with Zac. He's her new favorite person. I think she has her first crush! 😼

I almost dropped my Coke on the floor as a voice in my head screamed at me. *Perhaps Lisa isn't the only one who has a crush. Shut up*, I imaginary screamed back at the voice.

LORI: Sure. What do you have in mind?

JAKE: I assume that malls and theme parks are out?

LORI: Totally! Zac can't handle places like that. Too much stimuli. He'll have a meltdown and then you'll have to drag him out which makes you feel guilty and look like a child abuser

JAKE: Been there, done that . . .

I smiled at this. It was so nice to talk to someone who got this stuff.

LORI: 😊 So if not theme parks and malls, then where?

JAKE: Let me think about it. But what about tomorrow at 2?

LORI: That's cool

JAKE: Okay. I'll message you in the morning with an idea

LORI: Cool

JAKE: Cool

JAKE: P.S. . . . sorry about the snake

LORI: ?

JAKE: Well, I've been thinking . . .

JAKE: It wasn't very chivalrous of me. Jumping up on a chair like that while it was at your feet

LORI: LOL

LORI: Plus, you screamed like a girl

JAKE: SMH

JAKE: Next time we're in a potentially deadly situation, I promise I'll protect you!

The flutter. It was back. It was huge now! And it filled my stomach.

LORI: What kind of deadly situation would we find ourselves in?

JAKE: IDK, a few months ago a gorilla escaped from the zoo here

LORI: You'd protect me from an escaped gorilla?

JAKE: Sure! Why not

LORI: Ok. Question. Would you rather be bitten by a snake, or a gorilla?

JAKE: 😆

LORI: This is a serious question, Jake

JAKE: Ok. Snake. There is antivenom

JAKE: Besides, a gorilla would probably take my whole arm off

LORI: So true

JAKE: This is officially the weirdest conversation I think I've ever had

LORI: LOL

LORI: Me too

There was another pause and my heart raced and pounded and bashed about in my chest as if it could not be controlled.

JAKE: Night Lori!

LORI: Night, Jake

I walked back up the stairs with the biggest smile on my face and was about to go to my bedroom when I heard a small, muffled sound coming from my mom's room. I peered through the open crack in her door and saw her lying in the middle of the bed with her back to the door. Her shoulders were shaking as if she was crying. Crumped tissues lay strewn on the bed and in the middle of it all was a big book titled *Step into Your Personal Power*. My smile faded instantly, and I quietly pulled her door shut.

20

Zac and I were in my car, driving to the Kirstenbosch gardens for the first time. Google Maps took us all the way around Table Mountain National Park, so no matter what direction you drove in, the mountain was a constant in your window. What I liked most about Table Mountain was not the mountain itself, but the trees that dotted it. Tall and crooked and bent over by the wind. They were all leaning as if they might fall over at any moment, as if one more gust of wind could uproot them and toss them through the air. I connected my phone to the car and pressed Play on one of our favorite songs of the moment. One of the things I loved about our relationship was how important music was to both of us. We could listen to music together for hours without saying a word, and yet feel like we'd communicated everything. The song

"Nebula" by XOV came on, and we both turned and shared a small smile before the beat kicked in and we found ourselves bobbing our heads back and forth. I think Zac likes this song so much because it speaks to one of his obsessions.

"Did you know," Zac said over the music, "that there are over three thousand nebulae in the Milky Way?"

"Wow," I replied. "Did you know that Tutankhamun was an ancient Egyptian pharaoh who lived thousands of years ago, and when he became king, he was the same age as you?" I offered up another fact about some of the other lyrics in the song. Zac loved facts; he got so excited about learning new information that no one else knew and I often found myself googling interesting facts just to tell him.

"He was eight years and five months?" he asked, being his usual literal self.

I nodded. "Somewhere around there."

"Around where?" he asked, and I tried to stop my smile.

"Around here!" I pointed out the windshield, distracting him. "Look how cool and big this mountain is."

Zac leaned forward and stared up and the mountain, and I made a mental note to google some facts about Table Mountain later.

The song continued and I could see Zac was thinking. I sometimes wish I could be inside his brain for a day, to see how it all works in there. To see the connections it makes and . . . and . . . *sometimes I wish I knew how he felt about me.* He's never told me that he loves me spontaneously. It's usually in response to me saying it, and I've often wondered if he just says it back because he thinks it's what he's supposed to say. He struggles to show affection, even though I know he feels it. I just wish he was able to express it more often to me. It's weird, Zac is the one person in my life that I invest more in than anyone else, and I'm not even sure how he *really* feels about me.

We arrived at the Kirstenbosch gardens five minutes before two, and I was barely able to contain Zac, he was so excited. He jumped out of the car and I had to grab him by the shirt before he raced into traffic.

"Cars!" I said quickly as I yanked him to a stop.

"Cars," he repeated.

"You wouldn't want to be squashed like a pancake."

He turned and looked at me. "People can't be pancakes."

I widened my eyes at him playfully. "You never know."

He folded his arms. "Impossible. Pancakes are made of eggs and flour and we are made of blood and flesh and bones."

"Mmmm . . . good point. I guess bloody, bony pancakes would taste gross."

"What would taste gross?" a familiar voice asked.

I turned. It was Jake. Messy hair blowing in the breeze. Casual T-shirt with a small hole at the collar, which for some reason, made him seem even hotter to me. Imperfect. He was holding Lisa's hand. She beamed at Zac, and he looked away quickly, his cheeks going bright, tomato red.

"We were discussing how gross it would be if pancakes were made from people," I said.

Jake laughed and then gave me a smile. *Killer smile.*

"I can't escape weird conversations with you." He sounded amused. We had an in-joke already. An actual in-joke.

"Eeeew. Why, *why* would you want to make a pancake from people?" Lisa shouted the one *why*. She had this unique way of talking in which some words reached out from the sentences and punched the air.

"It's impossible to make pancakes from people," Zac quickly jumped in, moving over to Lisa and talking at her intensely. I watched with a smile as Lisa offered up some ways in which that might be possible, Zac rebutting each one with huge hand movements as he talked loudly and quickly. Jake moved over and stood next to me.

"Never a boring moment," he said playfully.

"Never." I watched Zac and Lisa as they discussed how the most you could do was put human hair or cut fingernails into a pancake. The idea made my stomach churn.

Out of the corner of my eye I saw that Jake had turned his head and looked at me. Dear Lord! Should I turn and look at him too. *Should I . . . ?*

Yes! my brain screamed at me again, much like it had last night. Okay . . . I'd officially lost my mind.

But the voice ignored the concerns over my sanity and whispered to me again, *But do it casually . . . calm . . . casual . . . act cooooool . . .*

But I didn't.

After paying, we all walked into the gardens and I was immediately struck by how sprawling they were. The mountain itself seemed to rise up out of the garden, emerald rolling hills, carpets of flowers so luminous and pink, large aloes—geometric and spikey, and almost alien-looking. Trees that looked like they had been growing here for hundreds of years, their branches huge and tangled—prehistoric-looking, like gnarled dinosaur claws. As we walked in silence across the lawns, Lisa ran ahead of us at top speed, bouncing across the lawn as if her feet barely touched it. Zac looked at me and rolled his eyes.

"I hate running," he huffed.

"I know. You don't have to."

"I won't." He released my hand and folded his arms tightly across his chest. He really does hate running, it makes his heart beat too fast, which makes him feel anxious. And also, he constantly worries about things like dehydration. We once watched a documentary about being stranded on an island, and the narrator had said that your first priority should be finding water, or else dehydration would set in. Ever since then, Zac has been preoccupied with getting enough fluids. He gets anxious if we don't have his special blue water bottle on hand at all times.

Jake and I hadn't spoken since entering the park. Instead we walked together at the same speed, our strides matching, in a silence that wasn't uncomfortable at all. We were like this for about five minutes before Jake announced that we'd arrived at our destination, a wooden walkway with steel railings that wound into the thick undergrowth and disappeared behind a tree.

"This is called the Boomslang," Jake said.

"Boomslang," Zac quickly repeated. "Tree snake. Highly venomous snake with back fangs that mainly lives in the trees. Hemotoxic venom. You'll bleed to death if it bites you."

"I'm impressed," Jake said.

"I know everything there is to know about snakes. Snakes and dinosaurs and the universe and remote controls and batteries and now I am going to know everything about Tutankhamun who was the king of Egypt when he was eight years and five months old."

I laughed at this, and all I wanted to do was pull him into a hug to express how much I loved him and thought he had the coolest brain in the entire universe.

Jake held his arm out for Zac and Lisa, indicating the way. "Shall we?"

JO WATSON

"What?" Zac asked.

"Shall we go?" Jake qualified.

"*Wait!*" Lisa yelled, holding her hands up in the air dramatically. "Are there snakes there? Because I *haaattte* snakes."

"Don't worry, I know what to do if we see a snake," Zac said quickly, and walked straight onto the bridge. "I can recognize all snakes, so I'll keep you safe."

"Okay," Lisa replied and followed him.

We stood there and watched as the kids walked off a little way ahead of us.

"Irony is," I said, "he probably does know what to do if we see a snake." I walked onto the bridge.

"Seems like you do too." Jake shot me a playful look. Teasing and oh-so-cute, and I felt all crumbly and warm. Like a freshly baked apple pie. I looked away quickly so it didn't look like I was considering putting a scoop of ice cream on his head and eating him with a spoon.

The bridge we were on curved up from the ground, and soon it felt like we were walking among the treetops. As the sky above us disappeared behind a green ceiling, I felt encased in a magical world of tangled branches and leaves. The breeze was soft and gentle, the leaves swayed, and every now and then a bright-blue patch of sky could be seen through the greenery. And then something caught my eye. A particularly interesting leaf hung from one of the trees. It was long and wrinkled, and yet in the middle of it, a round hole. As if someone had pushed a pencil through the leaf. I peered through the hole at a bright-red ladybug below. I pulled my phone out and zoomed in. The light was perfect, rushing through the dappled leaves, creating an intricate web of light and shadows. As it cast a glow across the foliage, the light seemed to reveal a magical world that only it could show me.

I checked the picture on my phone, and when it was perfect, when one of the shadows was casting its magic over the leaf and the ladybug, I took it. Jake walked over to me and looked down at the phone.

"You take amazing photos."

"Thanks." I went to Instagram and chose my filter; always black and white. And then I loaded the picture. Jake pulled his phone out.

"What's your Insta?" he asked.

"JustLori."

"Cool." I watched as Jake searched Instagram.

"Wow, you have a lot of followers."

"I guess." I tried to play it down a little. I didn't want him thinking I was posing as an influencer, like Nina-M or my mother.

"Why no pictures of yourself?" he asked.

"I don't know." I shrugged glibly, acting like I didn't know the answer to that question, even though I did. I only took photos of things I deemed beautiful and interesting, and that had never been me. It was the ladybug, or the autumn leaf. The broken bottle on the pavement, the soap bubble floating in the air, the cobweb wet from morning dew, or the broken tree branch after the storm.

"You're seriously good at art and photography." Jake slipped his phone back into his pocket and then, just before we started walking again, he gave my shoulder a tiny nudge. Or had that been a mistake?

"What school were you at in Joburg?" he asked.

"The art school."

"That's a bit different to Bay Water High."

"That would be an understatement. You know, we don't even have sports at art school."

"And then you come here and discover that everything basically revolves around sports." He turned to me and then started walking backward down the bridge, facing me. I could feel my cheeks flush, and it wasn't from the sun that was now shining on me as we exited the canopy.

"So, what did you do for fun in Joburg?" he asked. "I assume it wasn't going to parties to celebrate me single-handedly winning the water polo championship." He smiled jokingly.

I smiled back. "No."

"So, what?"

"Hang with my friends. Go to art galleries and concerts. There was this cool jazz club we used to hang out in, Maggie's. Go to the ballet sometimes. Vintage clothing shopping, or shopping for vinyls at this really gross charity store that always had rats, but you could buy the coolest stuff there. Listening to music."

"Basically, nothing like your life here."

"Nope."

"What music do you listen to—wait, no, let me guess—it's probably some weird, cool band that someone like me has never heard about?"

I laughed at this. "Someone like you?"

"Yeah. You and your arty Joburg scene is just waaaay too cool for us simple jocks down at BWH, right?" He was definitely teasing me now. It was strange and exhilarating, all at the same time. And I didn't know what to make of it.

"Probably," I teased back.

"So, what do you listen to?"

"Have you heard of Grimes?"

"Who what what?" he asked with an amused smile.

I laughed.

"Tell me about her or him, or they." He seemed genuinely interested in what I was saying. Which was strange.

"Well, *she* kind of looks like this strange alien, pixie creature, but in a really cool way. She's like a living piece of art, and she makes music that's not really *just* music, it's a patchwork of sounds and vocals that you can't really hear, but you somehow understand . . . I guess that doesn't make much sense. It's hard to describe her music. It kind of paints a picture of something and you're not really sure what it is at first, you have to listen to it over and over again until you can see it. And she does everything herself. She even shoots her own videos—" I paused. "I don't know, it speaks to me even though I don't actually know what it's saying half the time. I also like XOV and The Knife and Fever Ray, they're all Swedish and make dark, electronic pop music, or . . . I don't know what you would call it."

He stopped walking and looked at me strangely. And then a slow smile spread across his face. The smile seemed to migrate from the corners of his mouth and travel up into his eyes, which now seemed brighter and bluer than they had ever been before. "Anything but JustLori. I don't think I've met anyone who listens to dark Swedish music."

"Thanks, I think? Or not? Is that a good thing, or a bad thing?" I asked, stumbling over my words.

He laughed. "See." He spun around and turned his back to me and then shot me a look over his shoulder that literally stopped my heart, dead. *D.E.A.D!* For a split second my heart ceased to beat and my blood ceased to flow and everything felt hot and cold and blurry and crystal clear all at the same time. *Wait . . .* what was going on here?

21

WhatsApp Group: How You Doin'???

LORI: How do you know if someone likes you? Quick! I need urgent assistance here

ANDILE: Wait . . . who's liking who?

GUY: What kind of like?

LORI: Like, like like

GUY: Smooching, touching, heart like?

ANDILE: Ha-hah! Smooching???

LORI: Shut up, you can tease me later. I'm in a public bathroom, and I need to get out, so . . . how do you know if someone likes you?

ANDILE: They ask you a lot of questions about yourself

GUY: And they listen. Genuinely interested

Okay, check!

ANDILE: They find an excuse to touch you . . . even if it's brief

Twice and counting.

GUY: Tease and joke with you, in a cute playful way

Check!

ANDILE: Want to spend time with you

He asked us out today.

ANDILE: Smile at you a lot

Yes, yes, yes . . .

GUY: Flirt with you

LORI: How do you know if they're flirting?

ANDILE: Trust me, you'll know

LORI: How?

ANDILE: You'll get that feeling

LORI: What feeling?

ANDILE: It's hard to explain, but it makes you feel drunk and giddy and stoned all at the same time

Oh my God. That's how I felt right now!

ANDILE: Why? Do you think someone likes you?

LORI: IDK

LORI: I mean . . .

But how could he like me? Me. Of all people. Of all the girls who inhabited the bright-yellow corridors of BWH. Why me? I sighed. I was clearly reading into this, letting my imagination gallop away from me. He was just a friendly guy. Our siblings were friends, so we were hanging out, by proxy.

LORI: No

LORI: Don't worry about it

LORI: Gotta go

I walked out of the bathroom and up to the patch of grass everyone was seated on.

"Why did you take so long?" Zac asked firmly. "Were you having a poop?"

"Oh my God." My face flamed hot as Lisa and Jake burst out laughing.

"No! No! I was messaging someone." I waved my phone in the air. The very last thing I wanted was Jake imagining me doing . . . *that*! Sometimes I wish Zac had a social filter, but he doesn't. He will ask the most inappropriate questions, at the worst times, at the top of his voice usually. He's the master of creating awkward moments. Like that time he loudly asked while I was buying tampons what they were used for. The other shoppers had all turned and looked, me with a bright-pink box of tampons in my hand. Why don't they make tampon boxes in more discreet colors? Even pastel pink would have done—not the luminous, cerise thing I was clutching in my hand.

I lowered myself onto the grass carefully while everyone watched me like I was a neon-colored tampon box.

"Can I have some water?" Zac piped up.

"Sure." I reached into my bag, and took his special bottle out. It's the only water bottle he'll drink out of, because it's blue and has a pop-up straw. For the most part, Zac wears only the color blue, and wherever possible, prefers only blue belongings. He's also fascinated by the way the straw pops up, and always opens and closes it three times before drinking.

"I don't want to get dehydrated," he said, opening and closing the lid three times before finally taking a sip. It was long and slow, and when he was done, I took the bottle away and popped it back into my bag.

"Can I have my snack?" Zac asked.

I pulled the bag of crisps out of my bag and passed it to him. He paused and looked at them.

"Sorry," I said. "They didn't have your usual ones, but I did check, they are white."

He looked at the bag and shook his head. "I'm not hungry anymore."

"Why don't you go play with Lisa?" Jake asked.

Zac turned and looked at him blankly. "I don't like the game she's playing."

"Well, why don't you ask her to play another game?" Jake suggested.

"Like what?"

"What games do you like to play?" Jake asked. Zac looked confused. I knew why. The truth is that Zac doesn't actually play games, not in the sense that other kids do. He's never played games imaginatively; instead, he prefers practical activities like building machines or taking them apart, creating experiments, or constructing forts and obstacle courses for the snake.

"Here." I swung around and pulled his binoculars out of my bag. "Why don't you and Lisa go and see what you can find lurking in the bushes."

At that, he perked up, grabbed the binoculars from my hands, and walked off happily. When it looked like they'd found something to do together, I felt Jake turn to me.

"What did you mean when you said, 'they are white'?" Jake asked.

"Oh, Zac only eats white food. We are still working on that in therapy," I said. "You know, sooo autistic."

Jake smiled back at me. "Sooo autistic," he echoed with a tone in his voice that told me he wasn't mocking Zac at all. In fact, it sounded affectionate, just like mine had. This made me smile, probably more than I should have.

"Can I ask you another question?" he asked.

"Sure."

"Have you been avoiding me at school?"

"What? I mean . . . no. It's just been busy and confusing what with the new schedule and . . . I don't think so . . ." My words fell out of my mouth like randomly dropped marbles, and in that moment, I wished I was one of these people who was more confident and chilled, and less me. "You've been avoiding me too!" I said quickly.

"So you *have* been avoiding me, then?"

"So have you."

"When did I avoid you?" Jake asked.

"In isiZulu." I shrugged to make it look like although I'd said this, it really didn't bother me. So what! I didn't care . . . *but I did care.*

"*You* were avoiding *me* in Zulu," Jake said.

"No. I wasn't."

"Um . . ." Jake leaned forward. "I tried to catch your eye to say hello but you looked away and then didn't look at me again."

"No. You looked away and didn't look at me again."

Jake chuckled, low and soft under his breath.

"What?" I asked.

"Clearly, we got our wires crossed. I thought you were avoiding me because you didn't want anyone asking how we knew each other, because you didn't want anyone to know about Zac and—"

"No!" I cut him off quickly. "It's not that. I don't care who knows about Zac. I'm not ashamed of him, at all. It's not that. Trust me!"

"Cool," he said, and then went quiet for a while. "No one knows about Lisa, or that I volunteer at Lighthouse."

"Why?" I asked.

"I guess I don't want people to judge."

There was a heavy full stop to that sentence that lingered in the air around him. And I didn't know if he meant he didn't want people to judge Lisa or didn't want people to judge him.

"People can be judgy," I replied quietly.

"Like my gran. She doesn't believe in ADHD. She thinks Lisa is just badly behaved and my parents need to be stricter with her."

"That's such crap!" I sat up on my knees. "You know this friend of my mom's told us that you can cure autism by cutting out all gluten when she saw Zac eating a sandwich for lunch."

"That's insane! You can't cure it."

"I know! I bloody told her where the hell to get off! Much to my mother's horror, of course."

Jake smiled. "We needed you last year, then."

"For what?"

"There were protestors outside the school holding up signs protesting psychiatric diagnoses of children so young."

"Screw them! They just don't know what it's like. Getting the diagnosis is the good part; you have something to work with after that. Before the diagnosis, you have no idea what's going on; afterward you at least have a way of moving forward with therapies and things. If I'd been here, I would have ripped their stupid signs up, bloody hell!"

Jake smiled at me, slowly again.

"What?" I asked.

"You speak your mind. I like that."

"I do?"

"Yeah. And you're not afraid to stand up for Zac and advocate for him."

"Well, yes! If I don't, who will?"

Jake's smile wavered. "I don't think I do that for Lisa as much as you do for Zac. If I did, all my friends at school would know about her and Lighthouse." He looked down at the grass and pulled some blades out.

"You volunteer at her school! You're here with her now!" I said emphatically, and this seemed to make his face soften again.

"So, I have a bit of a confession to make," Jake said.

"What?"

"You know that fire alarm in assembly?"

"Yeah?"

"Well, that was me," he said.

"What? Why?"

"It looked like you needed saving from Amber, especially after the crappy Monday morning you had last week."

"What do you mean?" I asked.

"I saw you at the Lighthouse on Zac's first day when he tried to climb over the fence . . ." He tapered off.

"You saw that?"

"Sorry. It looked hectic."

And then a thought hit me and I quickly looked down. "So you saw me . . . I mean . . . ?"

"Yes." His voice was filled with compassion.

"Oh." I pulled at a thread in the picnic blanket feeling vulnerable, exposed, and embarrassed.

"Don't worry, we all need a good cry sometimes." His voice was almost a whisper.

I raised my eyes slowly and looked up at him. He gave me a small grin. "Besides, it was nice to piss Amber off."

"I thought you and Amber were together?"

"*Together* might be too much of a strong word for it."

"Well, according to Teagan you were making your way down the Hot List, starting with Amber behind the bleachers." I regretted it the second those words were out of my mouth. They made me sound like I cared who he made out with, which I didn't!

Now you're just lying to yourself, babe, Imaginary Voice mocked.

He laughed. "You shouldn't believe everything you hear. BWH thrives on gossip. It's like the invisible currency everyone uses there."

"She's really pretty, though," I heard myself say, and again, regretted it.

"I guess." He went quiet for a while and looked thoughtful. "But she can also be pretty mean and very clingy. I kissed her once and I think she was already planning our wedding."

"It would probably be a beautiful wedding," I offered. "Although, I'm not sure I would be invited. I think she hates me."

"She hates anyone who isn't like her," Jake added.

"I would have thought that a guy like you would be with someone like Amber."

At that, he leaned back on his elbows and eyed me. "Why, cos I'm the jock and she's the hot, mean girl? You watch too many clichéd American teen movies, Anything but JustLori."

"I don't." I laughed.

"Oh, I forgot! You probably watch arty black and white French films with subtitles and angsty, moody lighting."

"I am so *not* that kind of person."

"And I am so *not* that kind of person either," he said firmly.

"Maybe there was a time when I used to be, but that was before Lisa and the Lighthouse and things like that. That stuff changes you."

"So, I won't find you on TikTok throwing yourself down a flight of stairs with straws up your nose?" I asked playfully.

He laughed. "You know how many millions of followers he has?"

"I can't believe I'm at the same school as a guy who's a celebrity for sticking straws up his nose."

But this time, Jake didn't laugh. He glanced at Lisa and Zac, and I followed his gaze. I knew what he was thinking without having to ask. When you have siblings like we do, it really puts things into perspective. The things that your peers are doing can look like such a waste of time and energy.

Having siblings like we do means having to grow up quicker. It means that life isn't always just a party. There's a serious side to it, filled with heartbreak and pain, and sometimes the greatest joy too. When he caught my eye again, it was as if he knew that I was thinking the exact same thing. It was strange and exhilarating and warm. Nice. *More than nice . . .*

"This was cool," I said, standing by my car. Jake was holding Lisa's hand; it was cute to see how close they were, and of course this just made him even more attractive, which at this stage was almost impossible to believe.

"We should do this again. It's nice to find a friend for Lisa," he replied, and I instantly deflated. *Had he only enjoyed this because his sister now had a playmate?* His phone beeped and he turned his attention to it.

"Amber. It's the summer dance in a few weeks. She wants to go with me." He shook his head. "Are you going?"

"To the dance? Uh . . . no." I tried to hide the shock in my voice, but I think I failed.

"You should come."

"Nah." I shrugged, trying to brush it all off. "I don't really do dances, and certainly not royal-themed ones." I rolled my eyes, trying to give off that cool, disinterested vibe. I was above this; above puerile dances and who cared about the royals anyway, Kate *who*?

"It's not that bad," he said.

"It's not really my scene." I started opening my car door in an attempt to put an end to this awkward conversation.

He looked at me as if he was trying to decide whether he believed me. Was I that transparent? Could he hear that mad voice in my brain shouting, *If you ask me, I'll go!* I couldn't risk him seeing that, so I quickly turned.

"Well, thanks again. Zac had a really nice time." I started climbing into the car.

"Okay!" He and Lisa waved at us. "But think about the dance, everyone will be there. I'll be there. It will be fun. Or maybe it won't be fun and we can laugh at everyone together," he said as I closed the door and pulled away.

22

When we got home, Zac was exhausted and immediately deposited himself in front of the TV. I opened the fridge and sighed loudly. My mother still hadn't gone grocery shopping, like she'd promised.

"Mom?" I called out, but got no reply.

I walked up the stairs and called again. But when I still hadn't gotten a reply, I headed to her bedroom. The door was closed and I knocked. "Mom?" I turned the handle and walked into an empty bedroom. I walked across her room to her bathroom and that was when I saw it . . .

"Mom! Oh my crap." I turned and covered my eyes as quickly as I could and stumbled backward. "What the hell are you doing?"

"Lori, language! And why didn't you knock?"

"I did knock! You didn't answer . . . why, *why* didn't you answer?"

"I was busy."

I held my head and shook it. "I can see that."

"What do you want?" she asked.

"I want to go grocery shopping. Can I take your card?"

"It's in my bag on the bed."

"Right! Okay, I'm going. Bye." I rushed over to her bag, grabbed the card, and was just about to leave the room when she stopped me.

"Everyone is doing it!" she called out loudly.

"Can we not talk about this, please," I mumbled under my breath.

"Swiping right and left and online dating and Tinder and Cupid's Match and Grindr—"

"Grindr is for gay guys, Mom!" I cut her off.

"You know what I mean. How else am I meant to find someone at my age, Lori?" Her voice had taken on a high-pitched quality that reeked of a kind of desperation that left me feeling sick. "The dating scene has changed so much since I was dating. You know, we used to go to the drive-in and have milkshakes and hold hands if we were lucky—"

"You didn't grow up in the 1950s."

"I might as well have. That's how different it is. Now it's all online and profile pics and winky faces and emojis and likes and, and, and . . . *your dad is engaged*!" Her voice quivered as she yelled this part, and I genuinely felt sorry for her. As much as she was trying, she couldn't hide the pain in her voice.

"I suppose you would have me never date again? I bet your father would like that." I heard her walk out of the bathroom and I hoped she'd put clothes on over that lacy underwear she was wearing. "You don't understand what it's like at my age to be divorced, a single working mom looking after two kids and trying to build a career and personal brand."

At that I turned, anger pushing away any sympathy I'd felt a second ago. "Looking after two kids? Is that what you think you do?" I asked. She had wrapped herself in a dressing gown now. "As far as I can see, you're too busy sexting to go grocery shopping."

"Sext—*What?*" She gasped.

"Oh, don't pretend to be shocked . . . sending half-naked pics to God knows who on the internet. You know what psychopaths are out there? Have you never watched *Dr. Phil*? *I can't believe this.* You're a mom! I mean, if anyone should be sending half-naked pics, it's me! The teenager. Not my middle-aged mother."

"I wasn't sending half-naked pics."

"Well, it looked like that to me."

"I was only taking a portrait shot of myself for my profile pic."

"In your bra?"

"I wasn't going to show my bra. I put a lot of work into my décolletage," she said back.

What the hell was a décolletage? I held my hands up in the air. "Whatever. I'm going." I turned and started walking out the door.

"I wasn't going to show my bra," she shouted after me, but I ignored her. "Do you want me to die alone and lonely? Is that what you want?" she called after me as I exited and closed the door. "I'm crossing the threshold of negativity and stepping into my positive purpose!" I heard her shout as I rushed down the stairs and hightailed it out of there.

23

I'd finished buying the groceries and was driving home while angrily shoving chocolate into my mouth, which I knew I shouldn't be doing. The fact that I had a slightly underactive thyroid meant that I was susceptible to weight gain, and the fact that I was a stress eater meant that I really knew how to pile it on. If gaining weight was an Olympic sport, I'd probably take home the gold medal. I just hoped the medal was one of those chocolate ones wrapped in gold tinfoil.

With each mouthful, I tried to push away the image of my mother pouting into the bathroom mirror in her underwear. But I feared that image had been forever burned into my brain. I would be on my deathbed, almost blind, and I would still be able to see my half-naked mother acting sexy in front of the mirror, and what was worse about the whole thing? My forty-five-year-old mother had a better bloody body than me! It was gross and disgusting enough imagining my dad having sex in a hot tub but now I had to imagine my mom on some dating site sending sexy pics to men who would probably send her *you know what rhymes with stick* pics back!

They were my parents, not some horny teens, and yet they were acting like it, and I really didn't know what to do with the strange emotions that I felt when I thought about that. You're not meant to think about your parents like that. I felt traumatized, hurt, and angry, and totally repulsed. There should be a new word for this emotion. I didn't know what it was, but I knew I needed to try to push it away, hence the chocolate.

I had my mother's credit card on me and, if I was a bad teen, I would probably go and buy something really expensive that I didn't even need just to get back at her for mentally and emotionally scarring me for the rest of my life.

I stopped at a traffic light and looked to my left, and there it was again. Calling out to me. Telling me that I should come and take a closer look.

You should come to the dance. . . . His words echoed in my head.

I parked my car and walked inside the shop. There was no one in sight. A staircase at the back of the shop caught my attention and I could vaguely hear someone upstairs. I moved straight over to the dress, the gold one, and when I was close enough, I ran my hand over it. The fabric was soft and luxurious. Cool to the touch. I reached for the hanger and pulled it off, and then, without thinking, walked over to the full-length mirror and held it in front of me. It was so beautiful, the way the light caught the material as it fell to the ground like melted, liquid gold being poured. It was so delicate-looking, like something special and fragile and rare. I wanted to buy it and hang it in my cupboard so I had something gold and shimmery to look at in the morning. This dress reminded me of Joburg at sunset, Maggie's jazz café, and my favorite contemporary artist, Lina Iris Viktor, who used 24-karat gold leaf in her paintings. I tried to imagine what I would look like wearing it. I imagined myself inside one of Lina's paintings—a goddess draped in real gold, staring back from the canvas with confidence and intensity, like she does. I looked over my shoulder at the staircase; the voice had stopped. I looked around the shop, still empty. On the street, no one was walking past. I bit my lip and looked over at the changing room behind me.

It probably wouldn't fit me, though. I pulled at the material; it was stretchy. I glanced over my shoulder at the staircase one last time and then quickly made a beeline for the change room. I closed the curtain, pulled my clothes off as quickly as possible, lest I change my mind, and slipped the dress on. And then I turned and gasped.

I stared at myself and my heart started to break, piece by piece by piece. *I looked terrible.* I looked nothing like the imagined work of art I thought I would be. On me, the dress looked totally transformed. How had I taken something so beautiful and turned it into something so hideous? My throat tightened and I could feel the salty sting of tears creeping up into the back of it. My body had ruined this dress. *I had ruined it.*

"It's not the right cut for your body type," a voice said, and I swung around. There was a large crack in the curtain of the changing room and *she* was standing right there.

"Thembi!" I looked around to see if the other Ts were there, or worse, Amber.

"You left the curtain slightly open," she replied in her signature deadpan way. She grabbed the curtain, and to my horror, pulled it aside, revealing more and more of me as I stood there feeling so uncomfortable in my skin. And even though I was wearing a dress, I felt more naked now than I had when Jake had seen my photo.

Thembi seemed totally unfazed, though. She looked me up and down and I wanted to melt into the ground. Vanish. I struggled to fight back the tears as she walked around me, scrutinizing every angle. "Is it for the dance?" she asked.

"*No!*" I said as quickly as I could. I didn't want her thinking I was expecting to go to the dance and then wondering who was going to ask me.

"My father's wedding!" It was the only thing I could think of.

"You're too short to wear a long dress like this, you definitely need something that hangs just under your knee, it will be more flattering." Her tone was still deadpan, and it gave nothing away of what she was thinking and feeling.

"What . . . what are you doing here?" I finally managed to ask.

"I work here, on the weekend. I'm going to be a designer," she stated matter of factly.

"Cool," I said. Even though this wasn't cool. There was nothing cool about the most gorgeous girl at school seeing me like this.

"I'm trying to get into the Paris School of Fashion Design," she continued. "They only accept a few people each year. You have to be outstanding, so . . ." She shrugged, and suddenly looked slightly vulnerable. Her voice had taken on a tone I hadn't heard before. "I want it so badly, you know?"

I nodded at her, but didn't speak. I couldn't. My mouth felt like it would no longer work, what with my tongue feeling ten times bigger than it usually was. I feared that if I opened my mouth and tried to form words that they would just come out slurred.

"The color doesn't suit your complexion either," she stated, her flat tone back. "You need a much more vibrant color. I would even go as far as saying you should wear red. Bright red, like your lips last night. Or maybe emerald green, complements your red hair."

"Uh . . ." I took a step backward. I wanted to get out of here so badly. I wanted to run.

"A 1950s cut, maybe. Capped sleeves, cinched waist, very @fullerfigurefullerbust, that kind of thing. You've got a similar vibe to her," she said, putting her hand on her hip.

Who the hell was @fullerfigurefullerbust?

I felt myself flush, and the prickle of self-consciousness made me sweat. I had to get out of this dress.

"Well, cool, I have to . . . uh . . ." I took another step backward, just as a phone delivered a loud ring. Thembi looked at the phone in her hand and then quickly looked back at me.

"I have to take this." I nodded as she raised the phone to her ear and started talking.

"Yes, hi." She spoke into the phone and I watched her intently. "Her dress is almost ready. I was just finishing some of the beading upstairs . . ." A pause as she listened. "I'll go check quickly." She rushed up the staircase and disappeared again, and the relief that washed over me was palpable. As fast as I could, I pulled the dress off, put my own clothes back on, and ran, tossing the dress on an ottoman as I went. As soon as I was out of the shop, the second my feet touched the ground, the tears came.

24

I turned my back on the shop and walked away as fast as I could. My heart thumped and my chest was tight and sore and . . . *I was in the pool again*. The wetness on my face confirmed it. The world was starting to disappear behind a veil of blurry water.

Not now. Not now . . .

I continued walking. Nothing around me looked familiar anymore and I couldn't remember where I'd left my car. But that didn't seem important right now. I was so embarrassed. The embarrassment clawed its way across my cheeks, making them red and hot. As I walked, the ground beneath me felt like it was curving under me, making it hard to keep my balance. The pavement seemed to twist around a singular point, bending and lifting to meet me, like I was inside a work of anamorphic art. But as I continued, I finally saw what the singular point was, and it stopped me dead in my tracks.

Red and white danger tape was wrapped around four bright-orange cones standing upright on the pavement. As I was trying to figure out what this dramatic show was for, two women walked past me.

"You think they would have fixed this by now," one woman—the one with the high clickety-click heels—said as she stomped past and stepped over one of the bright-orange cones. "It's so ugly, plus it's dangerous."

"And it's been like this for months," the other one in sporty trainers and tight activewear pants said. "Letting our roads go to ruin like this. And everyone has complained, but you think they've fixed it!"

"I know. Such a bloody eyesore!" clicky heel added. I looked up and watched these two women walk away, the one casting an almost disgusted glance over her shoulder at whatever this thing was. This thing that was so damn offensive to their sensibilities. I looked down expecting to see . . . well, I wasn't sure exactly. But when I saw it, I was shocked.

Was that all? This disgusting thing that seemed so offensive to the women, and to the city, which had cordoned it off like something that didn't belong here. There, on the pavement, was a small pothole and running out from it, a crack in the concrete. I took a step closer. Was I missing something?

Okay, sure, the crack was fairly large and the pothole was big enough that someone's Chihuahua might be tripped up, but still.

I stared. Something inside me started to stir. It was small at first. A feeling I couldn't name, a feeling that seemed too far away to recognize. Floating just outside my consciousness, flapping just beyond my grasp. I closed my eyes and in my head I reached out and grabbed it, the feeling that was floating past me and when I did . . . *anger.*

Red-hot anger rushed through me like a dart down my spine. My eyes flicked open and I looked around, taking in every detail of my surroundings. I stared at the rows of perfect glass-fronted shops, the coffee shops and restaurants, their expensive chairs and tables dotting the pavement, a red carpet leading into gold doors, the champagne bar, polished crystal flutes hanging upside down just waiting for fashionable people to slip their extra-plump lips over them. The potted plants, meticu-lously manicured lollipop trees in perfect rows along the street. The upmarket optometrist, rows of YSL, Dolce & Gabbana, and Bulgari blinging and shining in the sun. Aesthetic dentist Dr. Smile, for your perfect, bright-white smile. Vegan smoothie bar, goji berries, and chia seeds and all those things that prom-ised to clean you out, make your insides as perfect as your outsides. The cars, rows of them parallel-parked to perfection: Range Rovers, G wagons, and Porsche Cayennes. My head spun as I looked around. Not a leaf out of place, not a hair, not a non-white tooth in sight, not a lump or bump or drop of cholesterol. It was all so perfect here. This suburb, this little bubble, this little part of the world, was the representation of all that was flawless and faultless. And then among it all, like it was trying to squeeze itself into a dress it had no right wearing, a crack. A hole. A small blemish on the smooth surface of perfection. I looked down again. This was the only imperfect thing about this place, *apart from me.* And like me, it was alone in this champagne-colored world of bubbles and downward facing dog. Cordoned off like it had a disease. Sullied. Dirty. Imperfect.

And then it hit me. I looked around once more and then pulled my car keys out of my bag. I knew what needed to be done. I just needed to find my car first.

25

I parked my car in the side street. It was two in the morning and everything was dark. I grabbed Jake's BWH cap off the backseat and put it on my head in an attempt to mask my face. I rushed over to the crack; my heart was beating in my chest, but not in a bad way. Not in a way that made me feel panicky, but in a way that made me feel alive and exhilarated. I'd never done anything like this before in my entire life, and a part of me couldn't believe I was even doing it, *but I was.*

I pushed the tape aside and put my bag down. Gave one last look around before I opened it and spilled the brushes and cans of paint onto the road. They tumbled out and sounded so loud, like rocks falling over the edge of a cliff. Maybe it was loud because there were no other sounds around; maybe it was loud because all my senses felt heightened. I felt like I was on fire. I could see better, think better, and smell better. There was a buzz and a hiss that felt like it was radiating throughout my entire body, zapping all my cells to life.

I took a deep breath and looked at the hole and crack one last time. It was broken now, but it would grow again. I grabbed the first can of spray paint and shook it. I'd never worked with spray paint before, never even thought to work with it. I'd seen artists use it, so I knew it was difficult, and that there was a technique to it, but for some reason when I'd seen it in the shop and held it in my hand, it had felt as if it was meant to be there. As if I would know what to do with it. And I did.

I squeezed the nozzle and the paint sprayed out, a jet of color into the night. I lowered it to the ground and began. It felt instinctive. Like I'd done this a million times before. The painting flowed through me like the tide, as if I had no control over any of it. It was coming from somewhere else and I was just a conductor tapping into some far-off collective artistic consciousness. The shapes and pictures flowed down my arm, into my hand, and out of the can. I felt this strange combination of being far away from my body but more connected to the world around me at the same time. Connected to all the tiny minutiae: the ant running across the pavement, the small breeze making the leaf move across the street. I was seeing everything all at once, the tiny dots and pieces that make everything up, as well as the bigger picture. Zoomed in and out at the same time as the painting rushed out of me, as I used a combination of spray cans and big brushes with wild abandoned strokes. This was nothing like the art I usually did, but despite that it just tumbled out of me and fell onto the ground. Out of the hole, into the crack, all the way across the road, up the garbage can on the other side. And I felt, I felt . . .

Alive.

In that moment, dirty and paint-stained, on my hands and knees on the side of the road in the middle of the night, I felt more connected to something greater than myself than I'd ever felt before. I felt imbued with a kind of purpose that I didn't even know I had. Even if I didn't quite understand what that purpose was exactly, I could feel that what I was doing was important and that it meant something.

26

I tried to cover my yawn in class, but I was exhausted. After painting, I'd gotten home when the sun was almost up, and then collapsed into bed. I'd thought I could sleep late Sunday morning, but an alarm had gone off, reminding me that I needed to finish my self-portrait for Blackwell. I'd flown out of bed and spent all day painting. I'd stared at my half-completed self-portrait for hours first, not knowing what to do with it, or how to complete it. I didn't have time to paint the rest of my body, nor did I want to. My perfectly painted face hovered in the middle of the white canvas like it was attached to an invisible body. It looked incomplete, but I was running out of time, so I'd done a quick patch job to make it look like the body was obscured by shadows. I'd stayed awake all night finishing it and had woken up early to post it.

The bell for recess finally rang after four periods of exhausted hell, and I dragged my feet to the cafeteria. Today I was too damn tired to care if anyone saw me eating—I needed sustenance right now. I needed a high-caffeine, high-sugar rush that would wake me up enough for the rest of the day. Heading to the cafeteria, I caught sight of Thembi out of the corner of my eye and ducked behind a pillar. I didn't want to see her. I could imagine what she was saying to the others today.

You won't believe it, but Lori came to the shop and tried on a dress that made her look like a fat whore.

Fat whore. Why do those words even go together? Someone had scribbled that on my locker once and I couldn't understand it. Just because I'm fat, I'm automatically a whore?? How does me being fat make me a whore? How did fat become such an offensive thing to others when I'm the one carrying it, not you?

I kept my head low as I joined the cafeteria line. Thembi and the Ts were sitting all the way at the other end of the room, and at the table next to them, Jake and the water polo gang. Some of them still looked like they were nursing a hangover. But as I stood in the line I overheard a snippet of conversation that made my ears prick up.

". . . right across the road from the Champagne Bar . . ."

". . . saw it on Twitter . . ."

". . . I don't know, some flowers or something . . ."

I broke away from the line, pulled my phone out, and started searching. It didn't take long to find it . . . *my art*. I found it on the class WhatsApp group—someone had posted it while driving past. Then I found it on a local Facebook group I'd joined when I'd arrived, Clifton Residents. Someone had posted it there and then others had shared it. I followed some of the shares and landed on

Twitter, where it was being discussed. Some local, online news sites and a few blogs had even picked up on it. I turned around and power marched to the bathroom, where I closed myself in a cubicle so I could look through it all in peace. I clicked on the news article and started reading.

> *This morning residents of Clifton were greeted with an artwork that seems to have appeared overnight. The mystery artist took it upon themselves to use a pot-hole and crack in the pavement—which the residents have been complaining about for months—to paint an elaborate floral scene with the words "I am beautiful" written across the road, breathing life into the once considered unsightly blemish.*

It hadn't crossed my mind—not for a second—that my work would cause such a scene. I went to Twitter, and then to Instagram, to the hashtag #Iambeautiful and read through some of the comments.

It makes you see things from a different perspective, one person Tweeted.

I've been stepping over that hole for months, wishing it was fixed, but now I hope they never do, someone else posted.

Excitement filled me. My hair stood on end and something prickled at the base of my neck. But the excitement was short-lived, because when I stepped out of the toilet, Thembi was waiting for me.

"Thembi . . . uh . . . hi!" I stammered stupidly. She looked gorgeous, as usual. She was wearing a pristine white jumpsuit and white sneakers. The white looked even brighter against her dark skin. It seemed like an outfit that was so impossibly unattainable for a girl like me—I'm not sure jumpsuits were intended for people who weren't svelte and slinky, and also, how do you keep something like that so clean? And yet, here it was, gleaming. As if it had been bleached. Her clothes were different from everyone else's at school; they seemed high fashion, as if she was about to hit the catwalk.

"Hey, Lori!" she said quickly. It was the first time I'd heard her say my name; it was weird.

"What are you doing here?" I moved to the sink and washed my hands, even though I hadn't gone to the toilet. But I wouldn't want her thinking I was some kind of dirty nonwasher.

"I was waiting for you," she declared matter of factly. She had a peculiar way about her. Her voice was somewhat monotone, and everything that came out of her mouth seemed to hold the same relevance, whether she was saying your name or telling you she'd seen Andy Warhols.

I turned the tap off and hung my head. "If this is about the dress, I'm sorry I didn't hang it up, I was in a rush."

"I gathered that," she said. I forced myself to look at her in the mirror, desperately trying not to show any emotion, or, well, anything that would give away what I was feeling inside.

"Did you see that art on the street yesterday morning?" she asked. "It's actually just across the road from the shop." She walked over to the mirror and pulled a lipstick from her bag. She dragged the color across her mouth—a dark, matte mauve. She was so pretty.

"No," I shook my head, lying.

"It's cool."

"Cool!" I repeated. There was an awkward lull in the conversation as she stared at my reflection in the mirror.

"I could make it, if you want?" she blurted out, turning to face me. "A dress. For your dad's wedding."

"Sorry?"

"I know what you're thinking. Why would you let *me* make you a dress when you can clearly afford to shop at Simone Couture? But what you don't know about me, is that I'm going to be a famous designer one day, so in a few years' time you can say that before she was even famous, you owned an original Thembikile design." She reached into her bag and pulled out a bottle of perfume.

"Sorry, what?"

"Look, honestly, you'd actually be doing me a favor." She spritzed herself with the most divine-smelling scent. "I need something else for my portfolio. The Paris school, remember?"

"Why don't you make a dress for Amber, or Tasandra, or one of your other friends?"

"I've already done that. And now I want to work on something for the fuller figure." The words came out of her mouth unemotionally and I cringed.

"Plus-sized fashion is one of the fastest growing trends. I'd be stupid to ignore it like some of those other narrow-minded designers do." She rattled the words off, and I listened for the judgment in her tone, but . . . *there was none*? I'd never had someone talk to me in such a direct manner about my size, without a hint of judgment or sarcasm in their voice. Or maybe that was just her strange, flat way of speaking?

"So, what do you say?" she asked again.

"Uh . . ." I looked up blankly and blinked. This was still not completely registering. Thembi leaned in expectantly, as if waiting for my answer. I formed my lips into what was meant to be an

N shape. *N* for no, but instead, something totally different came out and I didn't know why.

"Okay? I guess . . ."

"Excellent," she replied and then flashed me a small smile.

Crap! What had I just done? Had I just agreed to let the most gorgeous girl at school take measurements of my body? I bet my upper arm measured the same as her waist.

"I'm going to make you look incredible. When I'm done, no one will be looking at the bride, trust me." She spritzed the perfume into the air and then traipsed through the mist like she was in a perfume commercial shoot in Monte Carlo or something equally glamorous like that.

"Here's my number." She pulled a business card out of her bag and handed it to me. I looked down at the white card with glossy, embossed white writing on it, very chic.

Thembikile Designs

"Okay, I'll call you," I said as she walked out of the room, leaving a lingering floral scent behind her.

27

"How was the party?" Vicki was knee-deep in the flower bed. This time I wasn't helping her—I was sitting at the table in the garden sketching the various succulents. I wanted to study them; they'd become somewhat of an obsession to me lately. My muse, if you like.

"It was okay."

"Did you wear red lipstick?"

I looked up at her and smiled. "Yup."

"And have you been silencing your inner bully?"

I stopped drawing and closed my book. "Something really strange happened today."

She sat back on her haunches and looked at me through her red heart-shaped sunglasses.

"This girl at school, this really pretty, popular girl, offered to make me a dress."

"Oh?" she leaned in, looking interested.

"She works in this shop that I went into and she saw me and . . . *crap*. It's stupid, isn't it? And I completely regret agreeing to it now. I don't actually know why I agreed to it. It feels weird."

"How so?"

"I don't know. She says she needs a design for her portfolio and wanted to do a fuller-figured dress, or . . ." I tapered off when I saw how Vicki was looking at me. She had that therapist look on her face. The one that bores into your soul and attempts to drag your innermost thoughts out. "I know what you're going to say," I said.

"What am I going to say?"

"That I should do it. That it will push me out of my comfort zone, that it might even be good for my self-image to have a dress made for me, or something like that."

"Is that what you think I'll say?"

"Maybe it will even be a slap in the face for my inner bully."

She turned away from me and sank her hands back into the soil. "I wasn't actually going to say that, so I'm glad you didn't listen to me."

"What were you going to say?"

"I was going to say not to do anything that makes you uncomfortable. Baby steps, you know. But I can see that I was wrong." She peered over the rim of her glasses and raised her eyebrows up and down. "It's good. You're challenging yourself. And who knows, maybe this will be your Oprah a-ha moment."

"You like Oprah?" I asked.

"Not as much as I like *Desperate Housewives of Beverly Hills*."

I laughed. "You mixed the shows up. It's *Desperate Housewives* and then *The Real Housewives of Beverly Hills*."

She shook her head. "I didn't mix it. It was totally intentional."

"You know, my mom's kind of starting to look a bit like Lisa Rinna, the one with the huge lips."

Vicki paused and looked at me for a while. "So, I take it you disapprove of cosmetic enhancement?" She pointed to her forehead. "I've been known to use a little from time to time. Smooth these damn wrinkles out, ne." She ran a hand over her forehead.

"I mean, I guess . . . I don't know." I looked at her forehead and now I just felt bad. "I don't recognize my mom anymore. That's my point. She looks totally different. She *is* totally different. I caught her sexting someone the other day. She's online dating now."

"What did she used to be like?" she asked.

"Not like this. Not someone with such big hair who reads these trite, motivational books that tell you you can be a millionaire overnight if you step into your personal purpose, and who believes in conspiracy theories about world governments trying to control us with radio waves and stuff like that," I rattled off. "She's ridiculous. She's like this caricature of herself."

Vicki rose to her feet and adjusted her big yellow sun hat.

"She sounds very lost. She's looking for something," she said quietly.

"Lost?" I closed my book angrily. I didn't agree with this statement. My mother wasn't lost, she was very much found and in your face.

"Sounds like she's lonely and desperately searching for meaning. Sounds like she's lost trust in people and the world around her." Vicki took a step closer to me.

"And how do you come to that conclusion?" A flicker of

inexplicable anger flared inside me. I'd wanted Vicki to agree with me, tell me how ridiculous my mom was, not paint her as some sort of poor victim.

"People who bury themselves in self-help and motivational books are often searching for meaning in their lives. People who readily jump to believe in every conspiracy theory out there are distrustful of the people and world around them. They see the world as a dangerous place that is out to get them."

I stared at Vicki and then blinked at her rapidly, feelings of irritation and anger swirling inside me.

"Have I told you about cactuses yet?"

I rolled my eyes at her. "No."

She smiled. "Brace yourself."

I folded my arms and sat back in the chair, waiting for this new plant analogy to drop.

"There's this thing you can do with them, called grafting. You cut a piece of one species off and then stick it onto a wounded part of another cactus species and it starts growing again."

"Sorry, what?"

She walked over to a small wall, picked up a pot and then placed it on the table in front of me. I stared at the strange thing. A long, straight, green cactus looked completely disproportionate with a bulbous purple ball growing from the top of it, and off that, things that looked like feelers reached up. It looked like a Frankenstein creature that had been pieced together crudely.

"All these different pieces are from different plants, that have just been put together?" I pointed at it.

"Yes. You tape them to the wounded host, and they will attach themselves and grow, and then become something completely new. You can keep going, putting as many different parts as you want, until the plant no longer resembles its original form."

"What's this got to do with my mom?"

"Your mom seems to be sticking all sorts of things over her wounds. Bits and pieces that don't fit with the person she once was, that's why she's unrecognizable to you. Like this. It looks nothing like it used to look, trust me."

"Are you saying that's bad?" I asked.

She shrugged. "What do you think?"

I shrugged back. I didn't actually know. "The divorce really messed her up. I guess finding your husband in a hot tub with someone else will do that."

"So maybe she's trying to repair herself with all these things? The giant billboards? The house? The lips? The books? The sexy pictures? The money? She's trying to find something to fill the gap. The gap left by your father and the divorce."

I sat up straight. "Are you saying I should feel sorry for her?"

"Do you?"

"Do I . . . ?" I thought about this for a moment and then that anger surged again. "No! I don't. Her little cactus extravaganza is completely selfish and ridiculous and—" My alarm beeped and cut me off. I looked down at the time and jumped out of my seat. "I've got to go early today. The cactus is rushing out to a meeting and I have to get home to look after Zac." I grabbed my drawing book.

"You're a really good sister," she called as I went. I stopped walking and stood there, feet frozen to the ground.

"Has anyone ever told you that?"

I shook my head. "Not really."

"Well, you are."

"I try. But sometimes I wish my mother did more. Instead of sexting strange guys on the internet who, for all she knows, are serial killers and stalkers, and making terrible bloody YouTube videos and trying to sell half of Cape Town because she is Barbara Palmer of Palm Luxury Realty. And it feels like we haven't had a real conversation in years. Nothing that comes out of her mouth is real. But I guess she's not real anymore, so how could anything she says be real, and sometimes I just think I hate her." I said that last part and then gasped, shocked that those words had come out of my mouth. I'd thought them, but never said them. Vicki shook her head at me.

"I don't think you hate her, Lori. But I don't think you get what you need from her—*what you deserve from her*—and I think it hurts. Same goes for your dad. Their divorce didn't just mess your mom up." She said that last part pointedly, and I knew what she meant. I don't like to admit how hurt I was by the divorce and my father's infidelity. It's not like he cheated on me, but sometimes it feels that way.

"Have you ever really spoken to your dad about the divorce, and how it made you feel?" she asked.

"He's engaged now." The words flew out of my mouth. "She's only twenty-seven."

"I'm sure that must be confusing."

I looked down at my feet, but didn't answer.

"And your mom? Have you spoken to her about the divorce? How it made you feel?"

I shook my head again.

"So you've lost your voice. You've bottled everything up inside. And the thing about bottling is that inevitably it must come out again. And if the bottle is shaken just a little, it might explode."

"Mmmm," I mumbled. I knew what she meant. Because sometimes it did feel like I was on the verge of some kind of explosion.

"You have such a powerful voice, Lori," she said, but I shook my head. This couldn't be further from reality. "You do, you just haven't realized it yet." And then she smiled. Strange and conspiratorial. "By the way, did you see that artwork that everyone is talking about? The succulents?"

"Oh. You know?" I said.

Her smile broadened. "Ag, I suspected. But now I know."

I felt my cheeks blush again and then smiled a little to myself.

"You're a real artist, Lori. You see beauty in things that other people don't." She walked up to me and then placed her big hands on my shoulders. I was taken aback by the move; none of my other therapists had ever touched me. But it felt comforting and reassuring. "And now, we just need you to see that same beauty in yourself." She squeezed my shoulders. "Homework for next session, bring me that list of the things you like about yourself! I need to see it."

I nodded at her. "I will."

"And use your voice!" she shouted after me as I left.

28

Things I Like about Myself by Lori Palmer
I'm a good sister.
I'm a real artist.

The next day in the middle of class, my name wafted through the loudspeaker. I was to report to the school counselor's office. My first thought was that they'd found out I was the graffiti artist and now I might be in trouble. A follow-up article had been done in which they'd mentioned just how illegal it was to paint over a national road. And then another thought hit me, worse than the first—that something bad had happened to Zac. I stood up and rushed out, twenty pairs of eyes staring at me. I walked up to the counselor's door and knocked nervously.

"Come in," a male voice returned.

I pushed the door open and stared at the man behind the desk. I hoped my face didn't betray what I was thinking—*I was thinking a lot.* He was standing behind the desk, bleached-blond hair, bright-orange tan, and teeth a new shade of white: uber-hyper-white. He was also wearing an offensively bright Hawaiian T-shirt and was lifting weights.

"Twelve, thirteen," he counted as the weights moved up and down. "Take a seat. Pull up a chair. Just finishing my reps . . . fourteen, fifteen . . ."

I sat down and watched him as he pumped the weights, hard.

"*Twenty!*" he declared finally. He walked over to the water dispenser in the corner and turned to me. "H_2O?"

"Huh?" It took me a second. "Oh. Water. Right. No. Thanks."

"Cool beans." He poured himself a cup and then strode back to the desk. *Who said cool beans?*

He sat loudly, collapsing into his chair. He downed the water, scrunched up the plastic cup and then, as if rehearsed, as if he was trying to show off, he tossed it over his shoulder where it fell into the trash can. He looked so pleased with himself I almost expected him to jump up and say "Booya!" But he didn't. Thank goodness for small mercies.

He crossed his leg and a big, orange calf muscle bulged. I guess in some circles, some women might find this kind of thing attractive. I tried not to stare, but his shorts were so short that I was sure I could see up them. They were the kind that a ball—or two—might pop out of. And suddenly, I found myself wondering if his balls were as orange as his legs.

"So, Lori Palmer." He placed his hand on the desk in front of us. "I'm Xander Brown."

Xander Orange was more like it. "Nice to meet you," I said and looked down at his fingers, which he was now tapping against the desk. I blinked a few times when I noticed the unusual negative space on the table.

"Shark attack," he said, holding up his hand, displaying his obviously missing middle finger. And then he stood up and hoisted up part of his shirt to reveal a massive jagged scar that ran the length of his waist. "Got me right down to the liver. A few more millimeters and he would have ripped it right out of me."

"Oh. Okay . . . that's, um . . . wow!" I offered up, unsure of how to reply to this.

"I tried to poke him in the eye." He held his hand up again. "And that's when he took my finger."

He sat back down in the chair. "I was surfing and was just about to come out of my roundhouse cutback when it came at me. And you know what?" He leaned over the table and locked eyes with me.

"What?"

"There was a moment where we looked at each other. Eyeball to eyeball. And I swear I heard him say—with his mind"—he cleared his throat dramatically—"'This is my territory, buddy.'" He said it in a strange, gruff voice, which I assumed was meant to be the shark's voice. But why would a shark say "buddy" if he was planning on biting you?

And then he smacked his hands together loudly and I flinched. "And *bam*! He was on me. Sank his teeth straight in and tossed me around like a rag doll. Like I weighed nothing! And I'll tell you what, Lori. I didn't feel a thing, not a thing, that's how much adrenaline was pumping through my veins."

"Oh, I'm sorry to hear that," I said lamely.

"*No!* Not sorry, Lori. Not sorry at all. Because if he hadn't gotten me, I wouldn't be the man I am today, and I certainly wouldn't have written . . ." He swiveled his chair around, pulled something off the shelf and then passed it to me. ". . . *this!*"

I looked down at the book in my hands. *Staring Death in the (Shark) Eye.* A giant, creepy shark's eye stared back at me from the cover.

"Open it up, read the dedication." He pointed at the book and clicked his fingers together.

I opened it and read loudly, "'Dedicated to the shark who bit me.'"

"Bingo! Binnnng-gooo! But why did I dedicate this book to the shark, you're probably thinking?" he asked, but I got the feeling it was a rhetorical question, so I didn't answer. "Because my whole life changed after that. I got out of a very toxic relationship, moved from Durban to Cape Town, and that's when I made the decision to write about my experiences, become a motivational speaker and school counselor."

I put the book back on the table and nodded. "Sounds, uh, good."

"It is all good. All great. The universe is good. You just have to listen to it. And do you think I gave up surfing after that?" he asked.

"Yes."

"*No!* No, Lori, I didn't."

"You didn't?"

"No. Fall off the old bike, dust yourself off, and get back up. Or in my case, go to the hospital, have five blood transfusions, three hundred and fifty-six stitches, and a kidney removed. Booya!" This time he did say that.

"Oh." I was floored. This guy was a total nutcase.

"So!" He banged his hand on the desk again. "Lori. You're probably wondering why you're here?"

"I am."

"Well, as school counselor, I always like to check in with our lucky new pupils who've joined the BWH family. Just to make sure they're happy. BWH is a special place and I want everyone to have the best experience possible. So are you?"

"Am I what?"

"Having the best experience possible?"

"Sure. I guess."

"Good! And is there anything troubling you?"

"No."

"Excellent. Anything confusing about your schedule, or classes?"

I shook my head.

"Great!"

"Making friends?" he asked.

"Uh . . ." I hesitated. I thought about Jake and me. Were we friends? I guess we were. I tried to stop myself from smiling and nodded. "Yes, making friends."

"Fan-*tas*-tic! Have you thought about joining any after-school clubs? Netball maybe?" he asked.

"Netball?" I scoffed.

"You have a great pair of hands on you. I saw you catch the ball at the water polo game."

I couldn't help it, but I chuckled. "*That* was a total accident, I assure you."

He sat back in his chair and folded his arms. "There are no accidents, Lori. Only meant-to-be's."

"Meant-to-be's," I repeated. "Right."

And then he stood up and clapped his hands together enthusiastically. "Looks like you are fitting in perfectly, Lori! Really embracing the BWH spirit."

I gave a halfhearted nod. I wanted to say "I wouldn't go that far," but didn't.

"Great to meet you, Lori, and if you ever need anything . . . please, you know where I am."

Was this it? My big counseling session? It must have been, because suddenly he was holding his office door open for me.

"Sure. I know where you are."

"And here . . ." He ran back to his desk and picked up the book. "I'll even autograph it for you," he said, signing it with a flurry. "But don't tell anyone else, or they'll all be wanting autographs." He laughed at that and then gave it to me. "Read it. Learn from it. Take it all in. And remember, everything you ever wanted is on the other side of fear." He dazzled me with a blinding smile. So big and bright, just like everyone else around here. Just like my mother's Cheshire poster smile. Everyone here seemed to radiate positivity like sunbeams—throw them lemons, and you'd be sure to get lemonade. Maybe even pink lemonade. But I knew that my mother's poster smile was fake, and I wondered if his was too? I walked out of his office and closed the door behind me. I stood there in a contemplative, confused silence for a while, trying to absorb all this BWH strangeness.

"Lori." Jake walked toward me, catching me off guard. "I see you met Xander." He pointed at the book.

"I did indeed."

"Did he autograph it?"

I flipped it open and showed him.

"He spelled your name wrong." I looked down at my name spelled L-o-r-r-y, and for some reason felt flattered that Jake had noticed this.

"I suppose he told you about the shark?"

"Yup," I said as we both started walking down the corridor together. "And how he almost lost his liver. *Wait,* is that why he's so orange? Isn't that a liver thing?"

"It's just bad self-tan. You should see his Tinder profile pic, Vuyo showed it to me."

"Oh?"

"Let's just say, if you think he looks orange in real life . . ."

I laughed at this. It was hard to imagine anything being more orange. A tangerine maybe.

"So, what are you doing tomorrow evening? Around five?" he asked.

"Nothing."

"Cool, because it's Lisa's birthday tomorrow. We don't make a big deal of it. She gets really stressed about it."

"Zac too." I thought back to his disastrous birthday party of a few years ago.

"We don't have parties for her. She gets too—"

"Overwhelmed." I cut him off. "I know. We don't do parties for Zac either."

We both stopped walking and looked at each other. I could see he was feeling the same thing I was, so I voiced it. "It sucks for them that they can't enjoy those kinds of things."

"It does."

We looked at each other for a moment. And then we both smiled. I don't know why he was smiling, exactly. But I knew why I was.

Because you luurve him. You wanna have babies with him, the voice in my head sang at me mockingly. God, I was getting sick of her. I quickly broke eye contact and carried on walking.

"We usually do a quiet family thing at home. But I know she would love it if Zac came," he said, catching up to me. "She told me today that Zac is her BFF."

I stopped walking. "Zac's not great at other people's houses. I wouldn't want him to freak out and ruin her party."

Suddenly, that hand, *that hand* that belonged to Jake Jones-Evans, was on my shoulder, and my whole body, every single microscopic cell in it, reacted. It burst into flames and burned with the intensity of a million exploding stars.

"Don't worry. He can freak out. No one will judge."

"If you're sure?"

"I'm inviting you, aren't I? And it would mean the world to Lisa."

"BFFs? They're so cute," I said.

"They are."

"Okay, cool," I conceded.

"I'll text you the details." He looked back down at the book in my hands. "Chapter seven's a real eye-opener."

"I'll be sure to read it, then," I replied.

And then he turned and walked away from me. I stared after him. I hadn't intended to, but I felt his sudden absence so acutely that all I could do was watch him walk away. My stare was interrupted when I heard a giggle. I looked to my left and there she was. Amber. Staring at me with a smile plastered across her face, the kind of smile a shark might have before it calls you buddy and then rips an organ out and spits it onto the cold, hard floor.

29

I was nervous about meeting Jake's parents, but I didn't want to show it, for Zac's sake, because he'd been tapping his fingers against the dashboard nervously the whole way there.

"Will she like her present?" he asked, sounding almost panicked.

"I'm sure," I replied calmly.

"How do you know?"

"Well, I asked Jake what she liked and he said making jewelry, so I think she'll love it."

"Do you think she will like the beads I chose? They are blue. Blue is the best color. Even though it's normally not for girls. They like pink, but I don't like pink."

"I'm sure she will love the blue." We'd been to a craft store earlier that day to buy Lisa a present, and then I'd painted her a card and Zac had written in it.

"Did you bring my water bottle?" He fiddled with his seat belt now.

"Yes."

"Did you bring my binoculars?" he asked.

"I did."

"Did you know Dad is getting married?" he asked. I whipped around in my seat and stared at him.

"How do you know?"

"I heard Mom saying it on the phone, 'Can you believe it, Sue. He's actually marrying that woman. He's actually marrying that homewrecking bitch.'"

"Whoa!" I held my hand up.

"That's what Mom said!"

"I know. I know. But remember, that's a bad word and you can't say it in front of people."

"Like I'm not allowed to say *crap*?"

"Exactly like that."

"Why can't I say *bitch*?" he asked again.

"Because it's considered offensive."

"A bitch is a female dog."

"I know. But it can also mean something else. And the other thing is a bad word."

He was quiet and thoughtful for a while before speaking again. "I don't think they should allow words to mean two things, it's too confusing."

I smiled at him. "You're right. There should be a rule about that."

"There should."

I looked at him for a while as he shuffled in his seat. "So, how do you feel about Dad marrying Maddy?" I asked.

He shrugged. I think this complicated emotional concept was probably beyond his grasp, but I felt like I needed to ask it anyway.

"He doesn't love Mom anymore," he stated matter of factly.

"Well, not in that way."

"What way?"

"He doesn't love her in a romantic way anymore," I explained.

"How many ways can you love someone?" he asked.

"A lot. Romantically, or in a friendship way, a brother-sister way, like I love you, or the way you love Miss Hiss," I explained. There was a pause and he looked out the window thoughtfully.

And then he spoke and my heart felt like it wanted to explode. "I love Lisa. She's my best friend."

I reached out and was just about to put my hand on his shoulder but pulled away. "It's good to have a best friend," I said as we pulled up to Jake's house.

"Do you love Jake?"

"Wh-what? No . . . what? No." I spluttered. Hearing those words out loud made me feel all strange and tingly. "*Pfft!* Nooooo!"

"So, he's not your friend, then?" he asked.

"Uh . . ." I was stumped by my blunt brother. "It's complicated."

"How?" he pressed.

"It just is."

"How?" He kept going.

"It's more complicated when you're older."

"How does being older make it more complicated?" He just wasn't letting this go, and I knew I needed to end it now, or else these questions would follow us into Jake's house.

"Hey, did you see there's a new documentary about the universe on Netflix? We should watch it tonight!" I jumped out of the car, hoping to change the subject.

"Really? What about the universe? Because if it's about nebulae, I don't need to watch it. I already know everything about nebulae."

"I'm not sure. We'll have to find out. Come, let's go!"

"But if it's about black holes, that would be cool. Did you know that gravity in a black hole is so strong that it sucks everything in?"

I tried to hide my smile. My distraction had worked.

Jake's house was farther up the hill, not close to the sea like ours, and unlike my house and Vuyo's house, it wasn't modern at all. Instead, it had a quaint beach cottage vibe to it, and I liked it instantly. I preferred houses like this that had character, or had something about them that made them unique and interesting, but not in the way that ours was "interesting."

I straightened my black dress, looked down at my gold Adidas sneakers, and then rang the doorbell. My heart beat a little faster in anticipation of seeing him. But it wasn't him who answered the door.

"Hi, you must be Lori, and this must be the Zac. We've heard so much about you," said a gorgeous woman with blue eyes like Jake's. "I'm Judy."

"Hi, Judy. Lori," I said anxiously.

"Come in." She held the door open for us.

"Come in, come in," Zac repeated.

"He's a little nervous," I whispered to her.

She smiled and whispered back. "It's okay."

"*Zaaaac!*" Lisa skidded up, shouting.

Zac put his hands over his ears and Lisa came to an abrupt halt.

"Sorry," she whispered with her finger over her lips. "Let's whisper. *Shhhhh!* Let's whisper."

Zac took his hands off his ears; he seemed satisfied with this solution.

"I'm going to watch a documentary about the universe tonight with my sister," he whispered back to her. "I hope it's about black holes and not nebulae."

"I want to show you my room!" Lisa said excitedly.

"Here!" Zac pulled her present out and thrust it toward her with little finesse.

"That's so sweet, you shouldn't have," Judy said to me.

"I want to show you my bedroom," Lisa stated again, and this time Zac looked up at me for reassurance.

"It's okay. I'll be right here."

"Can I have my water bottle?" He held his hand up and I passed it to him. And with that, he and Lisa were off down the passage. I stared after them.

"Don't worry, they'll be fine." I felt a sudden reassuring hand on my shoulder.

I smiled. "Oh, here's her card, I almost forgot." I handed Lisa's birthday card over and Judy studied it carefully.

"This is beautiful. Where did you buy it?"

"I painted it. They're succulents." I blushed slightly.

"You painted this? It's incredible."

"Lori is an amazing artist." I heard a familiar voice and turned to see Jake as he walked around the corner. I tried not to beam at him stupidly.

You do luuurve him. Great, the voice in my head was back.

"I'm kind of good, I guess," I stumbled.

"Kind of good?" Jake said. "That's an understatement."

"Well . . . thanks." I felt coy. I felt flutterings. I felt all sorts of things that I hoped Judy and Jake didn't see.

"Hi, there, I'm Mike." Jake's dad appeared and held his hand out for me to shake.

"Hi. Lori." This was all so peculiar and I felt completely out of my depth here. I'd never met a guy's parents before, and I felt strange and nervous and . . .

"Sorry, do you mind if I use the bathroom?" I suddenly blurted without even realizing I was going to say that.

"Let me show you where it is." Judy walked me to the guest bathroom and I quickly went in and pulled my phone out.

WhatsApp Group: How You Doin'???

LORI: Guess where I am?

ANDILE: Where?

LORI: In Jake's house. In his guest bathroom to be more specific

ANDILE: Are you hiding?

LORI: Yes, sort of

LORI: I'm meeting his parents and I feel like a total blithering dorky dork

GUY: Oooh, meeting the parents. This must be serious

Of course I'd filled the guys in on everything that had happened between Jake and me so far. Broke down every moment as if doing a postmortem. I typed quickly.

LORI: It's not like that. He invited Zac around because it's his sister's birthday

GUY: Are you sure that's the only reason?

LORI: YES! Stop making more of this. We're just friends because our siblings hang out

ANDILE: Friends . . . and you're hiding in his toilet messaging us? Because that's what you do when you're JUST friends with someone

LORI: I don't know how to act in front of his parents. I feel like I'm being a weirdo

ANDILE: Just be yourself!

GUY: Totally

GUY: Besides, you are a little weird anyway

LORI: I don't want to be weird. I want to be normal

ANDILE: BOOORING

LORI: Crap! This is so 😱

LORI: I gotta go

GUY: And you gotta stop messaging us from inside bathrooms!

ANDILE: Don't hide for too long, you wouldn't want them to think you are taking a giant dump! 😂😂😂💩

LORI: OMG, not again

GUY: Wait, what do you mean not again?

LORI: Never mind. Long story

GUY: We've got time

LORI: I don't. Gotta run

LORI: Bye

I exited the bathroom and followed the sounds of chatter. Mike, Judy, and Jake were standing in the living room, which had been decorated with pink balloons and streamers. On the table stood a large chocolate cake with a mermaid on top of it, as well as a bowl of chips and some candy. Judy smiled at me again; she had a smile like Jake's—big and open, and with the ability to set you at ease. "Thanks so much for coming this evening."

"It's a pleasure."

"Lisa hasn't stopped talking about Zac since he arrived at school, and Jake's told us all about you too," she said.

At that, I stiffened, trying to ignore the last part of her statement in case I went a bright, fire engine red. "It's really nice that Zac's found someone to play with," I said.

"And it's nice that Jake's found someone his age to talk to too," she added quickly.

"It's nice," I said softly. The word *nice* suddenly sounded wrong. Like when you say any word too many times in a row, it stops sounding like English.

"Should we call them in to cut the cake?" she asked.

I nodded and almost said "nice" again, but stopped myself. "Mmm-hmm," I mumbled instead, which was probably just as bad as saying "nice."

I glanced at the cake reticently. Zac hated brown food the most. Said it reminded him of poop.

"Oh, wait." Jake raced off to the kitchen and came back moments later holding a vanilla cupcake in his hands. "We got this for Zac."

"Oh my gosh . . . that's so kind of you guys. Really, that's so..." I couldn't say any more, I felt so emotional. This small, yet incredibly kind gesture made me want to cry. It wasn't often that gestures like this were made on Zac's behalf. The world can be a cruel place for people like him—if you don't fit into the box, well, there's no place for you. But this cupcake was a place. A safe place. And those were rare.

After we'd whisper-sung "Happy Birthday," opened some

presents, and eaten some cake, I found myself standing outside on the balcony looking down at the sea in the distance. It looked calm now, like a still pond.

"Okay, seriously, how can you still prefer the city, over . . . *this*?" Jake walked all the way up to me. "Look!" He waved his arm across the vista in front of us. The sun was starting to dip lower in the sky, casting a bright, white light across the surface of the calm water, making it look like liquid mercury.

I shrugged. "I suppose it's pretty cool."

"Pretty cool?" he repeated. "You can't beat this."

I laughed. "But have you seen downtown Joburg at sunset?"

"Don't have to. This is better."

I turned and faced him. "Just before the sun goes down completely, there's this moment when the whole city changes. The Nelson Mandela Bridge flickers to life, red and green and purple, and sometimes, if you're lucky, a train comes in at just the right time and all its windows are illuminated and it's like a serpent of light coiling under the bridge. And then in the distance, the Hillbrow Tower turns on, bright pink and blue. And then Ponte lights up, and the sun turns the sky a bright orange, and it looks like all the gray concrete has turned to gold."

I finished talking, and Jake stepped closer. He was looking at me in a way that stole the breath right out of my lungs.

"I get it now. You're like a magpie." He smiled.

"Sorry?"

"You like shiny things." He looked down at my shoes and I wiggled my toes in them.

"I've never thought of myself like that before, but I guess I do."

"Fine, fine!" He leaned over the railing. "If shiny things are your thing, I'm going to have to show you something."

"What?" I also leaned over the railing; our shoulders almost touched.

"I'll have to take you there later."

"When?"

"Tonight? After you take Zac home, you think you can come out for a couple of hours?"

"Sure. If my mom is there to look after Zac."

"Great." And then he turned his head to me and nudged me with his shoulder. Again. This was the third nudge, *and yes,* I was counting. "You're going to take one look at this and totally forget Joburg."

"I doubt that."

He looked back at the sea and nodded. "Trust me on this. I'm going to turn the city girl into a sea lover."

"Okay, I'm off now." Jake's dad came up behind us and we both spun around. "I'll see you tomorrow evening."

"Is something wrong?" Jake asked.

"Just some issues at the farm," his dad replied. "Terrible timing. Of course, it would happen today. But what can you do."

Jake nodded as if this was a common occurrence.

"Really nice meeting you, Lori." He smiled at me. "And thanks so much for coming, it made Lisa's birthday so much more special."

"It's a pleasure. Glad we were here," I said, looking at this clean-cut, suited man. It was hard to imagine him ever being an alcoholic. But maybe that was judgmental of me; what did I think alcoholics looked like, anyway?

I watched him closely as he kissed Judy good-bye on the forehead. I felt a little twinge in my chest when I remembered my dad doing that with my mom. He always kissed her good-bye, even in the months leading up to the divorce. That thought made me feel even worse. When he was gone, I turned to Jake.

"I didn't know your dad was a farmer," I said.

Jake laughed and shook his head. "He's an engineer, he works in renewable energy. The company he works for has a wind farm just out of Cape Town. He goes there pretty often, especially if there are technical issues."

"Zac would love it there. He's really into anything that involves electricity, batteries, and solar-powered devices. Things I know nothing about—he's way smarter than me."

"I think he's smarter than all of us," Jake said. "So, what about it?"

"What about what?" I asked.

"Still up for that adventure tonight?"

"Sure." I looked over at Judy, who was starting to clean up inside.

"Wait, let me help you," I said as I rushed back inside to help pick up the bits of torn birthday wrapping paper that had been strewn across the floor.

"That's so kind of you, Lori." She shot me another one of her supersmiles. Her smile was real, though. You could see it. "Totally unnecessary, since you're *our* guest. But lovely. Thank you."

"It's a pleasure." I felt myself smiling back at her, a genuine smile, and from it I had to conclude that . . .

> *Things I Like about Myself by Lori Palmer*
> *I'm a good sister.*
> *I'm a real artist.*
> *I, Lori Palmer, am officially good with parents!*

30

"So, where're we going?" We'd been driving in Jake's car for thirty minutes already.

"Can't tell you. It'll ruin the surprise." He flashed me a grin. "Want to listen to music?"

"Sure. What do you have?"

"Here." He passed me his phone, a self-satisfied look glinting in his eye.

I eyed him suspiciously and then opened his music. "You downloaded her!"

He nodded. "Yup!"

I chuckled as I scrolled through all the recently downloaded songs by Grimes.

"Which one is your favorite?" he asked.

"Depends what I'm doing?"

"Which one is your favorite for driving?"

"Good question." I continued scrolling until I saw it. "How about this." I pressed Play and the song "Violence," with its strange, whispery, inaudible vocals, burst through the speakers. I waited for the beat to kick in; that dreamlike, eerie combination of synth sounds that was so addictive. We listened in silence for a while and then he turned his head to me.

"It's cool. I don't understand a word she's saying, but it's cool."

"I think that's the point." I smiled at him and the flutter in my stomach was back. "So, you went and downloaded Grimes after I told you about her?" I asked, feeling a strange combination of being flattered and flustered at the same time.

"I also got some XOV, but couldn't find those knives," he said, and I laughed.

"The Knife. Singular."

Jake smiled. *That smile.* That smile that felt like it held all the power of a million exploding nuclear weapons. I quickly looked out the window. It was no longer safe to look directly at him, or else I might be incinerated.

We drove for a few more songs and then he slowed down. We made a turn onto a small street that wound down toward the sea, and soon, we'd parked by the beach. He looked out over the sea and then shook his head. "Crap. Don't tell me it's not here tonight."

"What is?"

We climbed out of the car. "Do you mind walking?" He bent down and started unlacing his sneakers.

I regarded the beach. I wasn't a massive fan of walking on it.

When you're fat, walking on soft sand usually just feels like walking on a hamster wheel—you don't go very far. And also, you have to think about things like chafing, a pain no thin girl would ever know. But I agreed and took my shoes off. We ambled onto the beach— the sand was soft and cool, and the feel of it slipping between my toes was nicer than I'd expected. We walked in silence for a while; the only sounds were the waves crashing against the shore and then racing up onto the sand only to disappear into it. The beach was so much nicer at night, and I wondered why going to the beach at night wasn't a thing. If it was, I might even go. There was something peaceful and beautiful, almost mystical about the sea and the beach at night. The water was a deep, rich gray color and in patches it was turned brilliant silver from the moonlight reflecting off it. And the sky was so black. Sure, there were stars, but between those stars was a blackness so intense that it felt like the sky had been painted Vantablack, the darkest color known to man.

"What are we looking for?" I asked, finally breaking the silence between us.

"Let's walk around that corner." He pointed at a large group of rocks. "And if it's not there, then you win and city trumps sea."

We walked up to the rocks and I noticed that if I was to go around them, I would have to wade through ankle-deep water. I looked down at the cold, dark water and took a deep breath. *Did you know you can drown in an inch of water?* I closed my eyes and took my first step. The cold water hit me like sharp blades around my ankle and I inhaled sharply and flicked my eyes open. Panicky terror welled up inside me, but I tried to push it down. This was the most water I'd been in since the incident; I only showered now. I made it around the corner and when I saw what was there, my mouth fell open and a loud gasp escaped it.

31

Blue. Turquoise, electric blue. Brilliant and luminous and glowing and flickering as if it were alive inside the waves. The sand looked like it was dotted with millions of bright blue stars that had somehow fallen from the Milky Way.

"Wha . . . what is that?" I asked, staring at the shore in front of us.

"It's called bioluminescence. It's created by algae lighting up the water."

"It's amazing." I walked toward one of the rocks on the beach and sat down. Jake sat next to me, but I didn't look at him; I was too wrapped up in this moment. This bright-blue, luminous, lit-up moment. I'd never seen anything like it and it was, it was . . .

"So, better than Joburg at sunset?" he asked.

I nodded, searching for the words to describe this display. Mother Nature had a flare for the dramatic, that's for sure. "It's certainly up there," I finally said.

"Up there?" Out of the corner of my eye, I saw him turn and look at me.

"Okay, fine. You win." I didn't bother to conceal the smile that was pulling at the corners of my mouth.

He jumped up. "I win?"

"You win."

"Hell, yeah," he said, and then tried to do a cartwheel on the beach. I burst out laughing as he tumbled down with a thud. He immediately put his hands behind his head and crossed his legs. "I meant to do that?" he said, looking up at the sky.

"Sure," I teased back. "Like you meant to jump up on a chair."

I laughed and when it tapered off, Jake rolled to face me, his whole body propped up on the sand.

"You know you're going to be completely covered in sand?" I said.

"I like the sand."

"Personally, I'm not a fan. It gets into too many unwanted places."

He smiled at this, and then for some reason, there was a tense lull in the conversation that made me feel somewhat nervous, even though I didn't know why.

"You're not a fan of the water either." It was a statement, not a question.

I shook my head and looked out over the sea. "Bad experience once."

"What happened?"

My stomach tightened. "I almost drowned."

"In the sea?"

"No. School pool."

"How?" he pressed gently.

I sighed. *How much should I tell him?* How much should I let him in? I bit my lip when I felt a squeezing in my throat. "Kids can be mean bastards," I whispered, and this time looked directly at him.

He sat up farther on the sand and leaned in, as if totally engrossed in what I was saying. "What did they do?"

"They pushed me in. I tried to come up for air, but . . . they kept pushing my head down. Over and over again."

"Assholes." He said it as if he really meant it. As if he was angry on my behalf. "Why you?"

I was taken aback by the question. Couldn't he put two and two together? Me in a swimsuit. At a pool. In front of my classmates. It didn't take a genius to figure it out.

"I guess . . ." I started slowly. Feeling nervous. Feeling ashamed. Feeling . . . *everything.* "They teased me a lot. Because I was . . ." I paused. *Use a euphemism, Lori. Don't actually say it out loud.* "Different," I offered.

He studied me for what seemed like the longest time. If he hadn't worked out what I meant, then I certainly wasn't going to explain it further. And then finally, after what felt like a forever under his probing gaze, he spoke.

"Lisa and Zac are different. Different is cool. Different isn't boring like everyone else at BWH."

"Wait . . . .you think everyone at BWH is boring?"

"Don't you?"

"I mean . . . for the most part. But I didn't think you would."

He sat up fully on the sand. "Are you saying *I'm* boring?"

I smiled. "No."

"You think I'm boring. Don't you? Cos I don't listen to weird Swedish music."

"No." I smiled.

"Then why're you smiling like that?"

I covered my mouth with my hand and shook my head. "Not smiling."

"Yes. You are."

I giggled this time, my hand still pressed to my mouth.

He eyed me for a while. "I'll just have to prove to you that I'm not."

"And how are you gonna do that?" I asked.

"I'll think of something. Besides, how do you know I don't listen to superunderground ukulele music?"

"Do you?"

"I don't," he said flatly, which made me laugh even more. "Do you?"

I shook my head. "But I know this one guy back at art school who plays in a ukulele band."

"Of course you do." *That smile again.* Atomic bomb smile. Exploding star smile. Big bloody bang smile. It made me feel stupid, and giddy, as if the rock below me was spinning, and then he broke eye contact and flopped back down on the sand.

"So why do you think everyone at BWH is boring?" I asked, once the rock had stopped spinning.

His shoulders slumped. "Maybe boring is the wrong word. Maybe it's more that they all seem to have these perfect, oblivious lives. They don't have siblings like we do, or a dad who goes to AA meetings, or a mom who was really depressed for a while." He shrugged. "Not that I'm complaining, or trying to imply those things are bad, it's just . . . I don't know if I'm making sense?"

"You are. I know what you mean." Because I did. My parents were divorced, my mother was a sexter, and my dad was engaged to a woman who was young enough to be my older sister. And then there was Zac. It made me feel different from everyone else, and now I realized that despite all outward appearances to the contrary, Jake felt different too.

"That's why I love swimming," he said.

"Why?"

"It's so silent and still under the water. Everything else disappears down there."

I swallowed nervously and looked at my feet as the feeling of being underwater came back to me. Jake must have sensed this and changed the subject.

"So, did you finish your portrait?" he asked.

"Kind of. Although, I'm not sure it's very good."

"Trust me, it is!" he said, sinking his feet into the sand now.

"What are you doing next year? I mean, obviously, you're going somewhere fancy, cos you've been given a big fat water polo scholarship," I teased.

He nodded. "I have."

"Naturally."

"I'm going to study sports psychology." He rolled over onto his back again, sand spilling off his feet as he did. "I want to build on what I'm doing with the kids at the Lighthouse. Every week I see how good sport is for them, not just physically, you know? They make friends, they learn to share, learn teamwork, learn to resolve conflicts. I think I'd like to work with special needs kids in the future."

Oh dear. . . be still my beating heart. I always knew he was a good guy, but really, this had taken him to a whole new level.

What was he going to say next, that he'd saved a blind, starving kitten with three legs from a well and then nursed it back to health with his bare hands and a teeny-tiny syringe?

And then Jake pointed at the sky. "Shooting star. Make a wish!"

"What?" I looked up just in time to see the last flash of light disappear into the Vantablackness.

He turned and looked up at me. "Did you make a wish?" he asked.

My cheeks went red and hot. "I did." I reached down and picked up a handful of sand and watched the grains run through my fingers and fall back onto the beach. *I did make a wish.* One that I dare not ever wish for. Girls like me don't make wishes like that. Girls like me know better than to wish for things they will never get.

But in that perfect moment, with Jake on the beach, and the blue glow and the stars and the cool sea breeze and the fluttering in my stomach and the slight, giddy dizziness I felt when he looked at me . . . *I'd wished.* Even though I knew it wouldn't come true.

32

I'd woken up in a good mood; the night with Jake had been nice. But my mood quickly deteriorated when I was caught off guard by a call. I didn't check the caller ID and when I answered, it was my dad.

"Lori, I've been trying to get hold of you." He sounded nervous.

"Dad. Hi. I can't speak now, I'm going to be late for school."

"Five minutes, please. I wanted to tell you something."

"I know," I said, not able to hide the anger in my voice.

"How do you—"

"When your fiancé posts photos of her ring on Facebook, Instagram, and Twitter, it's kind of a dead giveaway."

There was a moment of silence before his audible sigh made the phone crackle and hiss. "I didn't want you to find out like that. I've been trying to call and message you."

I kept quiet. I didn't know what to say to him. I felt voiceless, like Vicki had said. What I really wanted to say was how much he'd hurt me when he said I couldn't stay with him. I wanted to tell him how hurt and abandoned—and now, replaced—I felt. But I didn't.

"I've got to go. School," I said quickly.

"Okay. I love you, Lori." It sounded like a plea, not a statement.

"Sure, me too." I hung up, slipped the phone into my bag, and raced to school. But when I got there, Amber walked straight up to me.

"Hey, L," she said in this soft, singsong voice.

I blinked a few times. No one had ever called me L; my name was short enough already. Besides, that L had a distinctly passive-aggressive tone to it. Or maybe it was just aggressive—there didn't seem to be anything passive about the way she was staring at me now.

"What?" I asked, suspiciously.

"So, how's life at BWH?" Her pseudosweet tone laced with invisible daggers told me I should probably run away rather than stay here and listen to what she was about to say.

"It's okay."

"Making friends? Meeting new people?"

"I guess."

She sighed and then stopped walking. "So just a word of advice, as a friend—"

"I didn't know we were friends?"

"Well, you know what I mean."

I felt like shouting in her face that I had no idea what she meant, but didn't.

"Mmm-hmmm?" I mumbled.

JO WATSON

"Thing is with Jake—" she started.

"Jake! Why are we talking about him? What does he have to do with—" I wanted to slap myself for saying that. It had come out strange and emotional and sideways, and her smiling at me now was confirmation that she'd gotten the exact reaction out of me that she'd wanted to get.

"It's just, I can see how you feel about him." Her eyes zoned in on mine, and I swear, she was trying to see right into my brain.

I looked away quickly, in case she did possess some supernatural witchy powers.

"We're just friends. No, our siblings are friends!"

"Oh, L." She put her hand on my shoulder. "I saw how you looked at him outside Xander's office. I mean, I don't blame you, he's, well, *he's Jake*." She tilted her head to the side, condescension practically oozing from her eyeballs. "But he *is* Jake. You know what I mean. *Jake!*" She was saying his name *a lot*. "I just don't want to see you get hurt. You know what I mean?"

"Not really."

"He's not really the kind of guy to do relationships. He gets around. If you know what I mean?"

Stop saying, If you know what I mean? I screamed in my head.

"And . . ." she continued, "if he does do relationship, well, I'm not sure you're his . . . *type*. If you get my vibe?"

"What?" I stared at her in utter shock, her words like a knife slipping between my ribs.

"I think you know *exactly* what I mean." There was such venom in her voice, and suddenly I wanted to cry. I felt like Lori Fatty Palmer all over again. But I wasn't going to give Amber the satisfaction of seeing me hurt.

Why was she such a cow? Why had she taken such an instant

dislike to me? Because I'd ruined her moment in assembly, snapped her nail, spilled some water on her, caught the ball, had the drink with Jake? Or did she just hate me because I was fat? Was there this unspoken rule somewhere that said girls like her should hate girls like me? And did they know what they did to us? Did they know that this moment would stay with us, *me*, for the rest of my life? Three words from them in a fleeting second would be words I would hear echoed in my head a million times over.

She flipped her hair, almost hitting me in the face, and then sauntered away. "See you around, L."

33

I sat at the kitchen counter, eating chocolate pudding. It had been a few days since my phone call with my dad and a few days since Amber had said those things to me. But the anxious hole that she'd cut out of my chest with her vicious words was still there and still needed filling. It was so big and gaping that I knew nothing would fill it, though, certainly not chocolate. Things like chocolate only ended up making the hole deeper. After what she'd said to me, and the way she'd been watching me ever since, I'd avoided looking at Jake at school. I didn't want to give her any more fuel to pour over my head, but it was hard to ignore him because we'd fallen into this habit of texting each other constantly. And pretending he didn't exist at school would just be weird. But every time I looked at him, or spoke to him, a bolt of anxiety gripped me and I found myself looking around for Amber.

I looked up from the pudding cup. Zac was curled up on the couch, half-eaten dinner in front of him, watching TV, and my mother had headphones on while power walking on her treadmill. Every now and then I would hear a . . .

"*I am bold. I am bright. I am beautiful.*"

I watched her for a while, thinking about what Vicki had said. Was she just sad and lonely? Didn't she trust the world around her? I thought about her lying in bed the other night, surrounded by tear-soaked tissues, but stopped when my phone suddenly rang. I jumped when I saw the caller ID. My heart thumped in my chest. *This was it!*

"Crap!" I knocked the chocolate pudding over my phone while trying to answer. "Craaap!" I grabbed a cloth and wiped my phone frantically.

"Crap, crap, crap!" Zac was on his feet, looking at me with concern.

"*Shhh.*" I raised my finger to my lips.

"*Shhhhhh,*" he shushed back at me, clearly unnerved by my outburst.

"I can't, Zac. I can't now. I need . . . *Mom!*" I yelled.

She didn't reply. She'd turned up the speed on her treadmill. "*Bold. Bright. Beautiful. Bold. Bright. Beautiful.*" She swung her arms so hard that they looked like they would snap off at the elbows.

"*Mom!*" I yelled again.

"*Mom! Mom! Mom!*" Zac shouted. But still, she didn't look up.

I grabbed my chocolate-smeared phone and raced for the guest toilet. I slammed the door behind me and sat on the floor with my back against the door.

JO WATSON

"Lori!" Zac called as he banged on the door.

"Not now. Please," I begged.

I took a deep breath and answered the phone. This must be good news. They said they would email us, but they were phoning me!

"Hi. Lori speaking." I tried to sound like I hadn't just locked myself in a toilet.

"Lori. Hi." I recognized the voice immediately. The dean of Blackwell. I remembered her voice so clearly from my initial interview. She had this deep, husky voice, I was sure it was from smoking far too many cigarettes in dark, dusty, Parisian art studios. She'd studied art at the University of Paris in the '60s—only the best art school in the world. Some years back I'd dreamt of studying there, too, but I'd given up on that—I couldn't be that far away from Zac, especially with my mom the way she was.

"Hi. Imogen . . . um, Mrs. Blackwell, uh . . ." I stuttered.

"Imogen is fine," she replied.

"Cool."

"I wanted to call you and tell you that we've made our final selection for next year."

"You have?" I tried to sound calm, despite the pounding in my chest.

"Yes. And I'm afraid, Lori, that we didn't choose you."

"Y-y-you didn't?"

"*Lori!*" Zac screamed and banged on the door again.

I covered the receiver with my hand and banged back. "Stop it, Zac," I hissed through the door.

"Everything okay?" Imogen asked.

"Yes. Sorry, baby brother, uh, I thought you were going to email us?"

"Well, we did email everyone else, but I wanted to talk to you personally."

"Why?"

"The thing is, Lori, you're an incredibly talented artist. And when this process began, none of us thought we wouldn't be choosing you for next year."

"So . . . why didn't you?"

"You're technically brilliant. Probably the most technically talented artist I've seen in years, but we all just felt that with your last painting, none of us knew who you were as an artist."

"What do you mean?"

"Well, the painting didn't really have a voice."

"A voice?" *Why did I keep hearing this word?*

"Yes. What are you the artist saying about the subject? What emotion are you trying to convey? We felt it was more like a photograph. We know that's your particular style, but we just wanted to see something *more* from you. Something a little different."

"Something with a voice," I echoed.

"Exactly. We wanted to see work that had an opinion. That said something. Technique can be taught, but art is not about technique and perfection. It's about what the artist is trying to convey with their work. Your portrait lacked that, making it feel unfinished."

"Unfinished?" I repeated and wanted to cry. That's because it was unfinished. Technically, I hadn't painted what I'd set out to paint. My hand went moist and sweaty against the phone.

"*Lori!*" Zac banged on the door again.

"Do you have to go?" Imogen asked.

"Uh, no. I mean, yes . . . I don't know. I . . ."

"We're very sorry. We had really high hopes for you," she said.

JO WATSON

"We still do. And we want you to reapply again next year. Perhaps take this year to think about what I said, and try and find your unique perspective and voice."

"I don't understand what you mean? I thought I had a voice, I thought I had a . . ." I tapered off. "What is a voice? Can you at least tell me what I have to do to get it?" I could hear the desperation in my voice now, and I hated it.

"A voice isn't something you can explain, and I can't tell you how to get one either. But it's the thing that distinguishes a good painter from an artist."

"And my worked lacked that?"

She sighed. "Yes."

"*Lori! Lori! Lori!*" The banging on the door got louder.

"I've got to go," I said quickly.

"I understand." Imogen sounded sympathetic now. "I'm sure we'll speak again."

"Yes. No . . . sure . . . I . . . good-bye." I put the phone down and felt my body move as Zac pushed at the door so hard that I jerked forward.

I stood up and swung the door open. "*What?! What?! What?!*" I screamed at him. "Can't you see I'm busy? Can't you see I needed a moment! Can't you!!" I lost it. I could feel it all slipping away and as much as I wanted to reel it in, I couldn't. The bottle was going to burst open and everything was going to explode out.

"*Lori!*" my mother yelled and rushed toward me.

"Lori, Lori," Zac repeated urgently as he flapped his hands in the air.

"See what you've done!" My mother moved to Zac, but he swatted at her.

"Sorry . . . I . . ."

"You should be sorry. You should." My mother tried to pull Zac into a bear hug, but he pushed her away. "Look what you've done, Lori!" She shook her head disapprovingly, as if I was the bad guy, and this made me furious. All the rage and sadness and frustration I'd been lugging around for so long, built inside me, like a growing tornado. Swirling, spinning, kicking up dust until . . . *touch down*. It collided with the ground, the bungee cord snapped, and the bloody bottle burst open.

"*You know what . . .*" I shouted back. "All I needed was two minutes to myself. *Two!* And I can't ever get that. Is that too much to ask from you?" I pushed past my mother and rushed for the front door. Zac ran after me, and my mother pulled him back by his shirt.

"I was doing my exercises," she called after me, trying to control the now-hysterical Zac.

"You're always doing something, Mom," I spat.

"Well, I'm very busy. I am running a company, and I'm trying to break into the market here, and I am trying to build my personal br—"

"Stop! Just stop." I looked at her, tears in my eyes.

"Stop! Stop! Stop!" Zac broke free of my mom and rushed to the corner of the room, where he flung himself down.

My mother looked at Zac and then shook her head. Her eyes moved back to me, but she wasn't really looking at me. Not really. She seemed to look through me. As if I was invisible. As if the things I said and did meant nothing. It broke my heart.

"Oh, and by the way. In case you care at all, that was Blackwell. I didn't get in! Apparently, I don't have a voice. But I'm pretty sure that suits you, since now I won't be going off and I can stay here and help you around the house, grocery shop, look after Zac while you sell your fifty-million-rand home in bloody Constantia."

"Bishopscourt," my mother corrected.

"Sorry, what?"

"The house is in Bishopscourt."

At that, I turned and left.

Things I Like about Myself by Lori Palmer
I'm a good sister.
I'm a real artist.
I, Lori Palmer, am officially good with parents!

34

I found myself driving around, again. I didn't know what to do with myself. The feelings of total rejection, inadequacy, and anger mixed together to form some kind of uberemotion. One that was hard to describe, but inexplicably big. So big that it felt like it wrapped about my entire body like a heavy duvet on a cold night. Only it wasn't cold. It was hot, and the feeling was starting to make me sweat.

I had no idea where I was going. I didn't know this place, and everything here looked the same. Mountains. Sea. Big houses. Mountains. Sea. Big houses. The indistinguishable mountain looked the same from all sides, a generic blob of rocks, and suddenly, I hated it.

The road I was on snaked around the mountain, the sea to

my right. I was sandwiched between two great big things and suddenly, I felt like I couldn't breathe under the weight of them dwarfing me. Pressing down on me. Pushing. Squeezing and then . . . *I'm underwater again.*

An anchor tied to my foot. Swells pulling me under. Water in my mouth and nose, and I'm coughing and spluttering. I tried to take a deep breath, but it felt like my bra was strangling my rib cage like a python come alive. I reached out and blasted the air conditioning, pointing it into my face. I opened my mouth and let the cold air rush in. I tried to suck it into my lungs, I tried and tried and . . .

My name is Lori Palmer. I am seventeen years old. I live at the . . . the . . . "Shit!" *I live at . . . I live in Clifton. My name is Lori Palmer. I am seventeen years old. I live in Clifton, Cape Town. My name is Lori . . .*

But much like it hadn't worked in the school hall, it wasn't working now. I pulled onto the side of the road. My heart was jackhammering inside me. I had this heavy pain in the middle of my chest, as if I was lying down and someone had placed a brick on me. My breathing felt labored and I fought for air.

I was drowning. Dry drowning. Like those kids you hear of who get water in their lungs while swimming and then go to sleep later that night and drown.

Was I going to drown somehow?

I scrambled for my phone and opened Google Maps. I typed in the word *hospital* and it brought up the nearest one. It was only five kilometers away. A seven-minute drive. I breathed a small sigh of relief. Sometimes, when I'm like this—*when I know on some level this is just a panic attack, but on another level, a more powerful one, I'm convinced I'm having a heart attack*—I like to check where the nearest hospital is. It calms me a little. And when it's this bad, I like to drive in the direction of the hospital, just in case.

I started driving again, toward the hospital. I drove for about six minutes, and as soon as the hospital came into view, I felt a lot better. Even still, I decided I would circle around it a few times, just until the rest of the panic subsided. But as I turned the corner, something caught my attention.

A small cross on the side of the road. It had been there a long time. The rain had rotted the wood, wind had blown it askew, and weeds were growing around the base of it. It looked alone, forgotten, *invisible*. I parked my car and looked around. It was dark. No one was here, and for some reason I couldn't explain, I felt drawn to look at it. It was as if it was calling in a voice I couldn't quite hear but at the same time, knew I had to listen to. I walked over to the cross and bent down to read the name on it.

Rose Maponyane 1997-2015

I read her name in my head and there was something so familiar about how it sounded. Not familiar like I'd known her, but another kind of familiar that I didn't understand at all. I quickly did the mental math and realized that Rose had been just a little bit older than me when she'd died. Right here on the corner of this road, against the streetlight that still bore the scars of it. The old, now-rusted dent in the pole told her final story.

It was so hard to wrap my head around the fact that someone had taken their last breath here. Right by my feet. Someone had ceased to exist on the spot I was now standing on. I was alive— my heart was beating and my lungs were drawing in air—but she was gone, and yet we were both here. The thought was so overwhelming that it felt like my brain was stretching in order to contemplate it.

I bet she was loved. I bet if her family drove past and saw this cross, they would hate to think of her all alone and forgotten on this dark street corner, nothing but the bent-over pole to show that she'd once been alive.

My bag of paints was still in the trunk of my car, and suddenly I knew what I needed to do. I needed to show the world that this broken-down cross was so much more than that. That it had been a person. A *Rose.* A girl with dreams and ambitions, who'd once been alive and breathing. I needed to bring Rose back to life, I needed to give her a voice, *I needed to.* A loud, screaming voice so she wouldn't be overlooked and forgotten on this lonely street corner anymore. So *she* wouldn't be invisible. With one last glance over my shoulder to make sure I was all alone, I grabbed my paints.

And again, just like the first time, like something strange and surreal that defied all the known physical laws of right here and right now, *it happened.* It flowed through me. I felt plugged into and caught up in a moment that seemed so much bigger than myself. It was infinite. To the stars and back. Shooting past Earth and the moon, racing toward Mercury, past Jupiter, slingshotting around Pluto and then rushing back to me, through me, into my fingers, and out of the can of paint.

When I was finished, I looked back at my art and realized that something was missing. The last piece I'd done had been completely anonymous, but this time, I was going to make sure that the world knew that I was here too, with Rose. So, I moved to the edge of the artwork and tagged it.

35

"Oh my . . ." I sat up in bed, shocked when I saw my Instagram feed. My fingers hovered over the video for a moment and then I clicked and watched.

"*Cape Town residents were once again greeted by another work of street art this morning,*" the news reporter said while standing by my artwork. "*This one was done here, where six years ago college student Rose Maponyane was killed by her boyfriend in a car accident. After an explosive argument that led to domestic violence, she escaped their home by car, only to be pursued by him. The incident of gender-based violence ended in a fatal accident for Rose that night, and the story made national headlines when her boyfriend did not get the maximum jail sentence for his crime. We spoke to her parents.*"

I gasped. I hadn't meant to paint around such a famous cross.

"*We love it*," her emotional father said. "*Someone has brought our daughter back to life and now she'll never be forgotten.*" The man looked straight into the camera now. "*Whoever did it, if you are watching, thank you.*"

A tear escaped my eye and snaked down my cheek. The news reporter spoke again.

"*But while her parents might be pleased, police spokesperson Relibogile Mashingo warned that under the antigraffiti bylaws, artists must apply for permits before painting in a public space. If they do so without one, it's considered destruction of public property and comes with a fifteen-thousand-rand fine or three months in jail.*"

"Crap!" I inhaled sharply.

"*Local residents are also praising the anonymous artist who is taking the neglected and forgotten of Cape Town and breathing new life into it. So, Cape Town, the question is, could we have our very own Banksy?*"

I lowered my phone and blinked a few times in utter shock.

"Banksy," I repeated out loud. I put my hands over my mouth. "Bansky." I climbed out of my bed and stood in the middle of the floor, looking out over the sea. It looked different this morning. Not as foreboding in some way. Not as big. It was strange to no longer feel dwarfed by the thing that had made me feel so small only last night. I walked back to my computer and opened it again, typing Rose's name into the search bar. Story after story quickly filled the page. Stories about the surge in gender-based violence in South Africa. Stories about Rose herself—she'd been studying to become a social worker—and stories calling for harsher sentences for perpetrators of gender-based violence. My art had started this important conversation that had now taken flight across the media, and I couldn't quite believe it. I grabbed my pencil and amended my list once again.

> *Things I Like about Myself by Lori Palmer*
> ~~*I'm a good sister.*~~
> *I'm a real artist (despite what Blackwell says!).*
> ~~*I, Lori Palmer, am officially good with parents!*~~

I tapped my pencil against the list and knew what I needed to do. I got dressed and knocked on Zac's door.

"Hello," I called quietly, and then pushed it open. Zac was sitting on the floor, surrounded by dozens of batteries that he was busy attaching together with wires.

"What you doing?" I asked.

"I am going to create the world's biggest battery, and then I'm going to be in the *Guinness Book of Records*."

"I bet you are." I sat down on the floor next to him. "Can I help?"

He nodded, and then showed me what to do. We sat in silence, working for a while before I spoke.

"I'm really sorry about last night. I lost my temper and it wasn't cool. I shouldn't have shouted at you like that."

He stopped what he was doing and looked at me. "Who was on the phone?"

I sighed. "Just this lady." I brushed it off.

"From where?"

"From this place that I wanted to study art." My stomach knotted.

"Why do you need to study art, you are so good at it already. You should also be in the *Guinness Book of Records*."

I gave him a smile. "Thanks. But I reckon you'll make it into the *Guinness Book of Records* before I do."

He observed me for a while. "Probably." And then he looked back down and continued making his battery.

"So, are we cool?" I asked softly.

There was a long pause between us, and I waited for him to speak again. Waited for him to forgive me. "Can you google Tutankhamun and tell me about him?" he finally said, breaking the prolonged silence.

"Sure." I pulled my phone out, went to Wikipedia and scrolled. "Look at this." I turned my phone around and showed Zac. "This is made of pure gold."

Zac leaned in. "Is that his face?"

"I think so."

Zac studied the face for a while. "You know gold is the best conductor of electricity."

"I didn't know that." I put my phone away and carried on attaching the batteries to the wires. "Maybe," I leaned over to him and whispered, "we should borrow some of mom's bangles and attach them to this giant battery and see what happens?"

At that, his face lit up. I smiled. I loved it when his face lit up like this. When his mind grabbed onto something that interested him. When something deep inside that diverse web of firing, flickering neurons sprang to life in a way that I would probably never understand. But then his face fell.

"What?" I asked.

"Promise you won't be mean to me like that again?"

My heart thumped in my throat. "I promise."

"Promise?" he repeated.

"Cross my heart," I said.

He looked confused and I quickly realized my mistake.

"What does cross your heart mean? How do you cross your heart? With what?"

I shook my head and smiled. "Never mind, it's a stupid saying."

"It is, because you can't cross your heart. Your heart is inside your body, how do you cross it?"

"You're right." I put my head down and attached another two batteries until my mother stuck her head around the door.

"Lori, you're up?" she said in a strange tone.

"Mom." Zac jumped up. "I need one of your bangles."

She looked at him curiously but slipped one off and handed it to him. "Don't lose it."

He shook his head and stared at the bangle with such intensity that I knew he was about to go into one of his happy creation bubbles.

"Can I talk to you downstairs?" my mom asked, forcing a big, white, veneered smile.

"Sure." We walked downstairs and as soon as we had, she jumped straight into it.

"About last night," she started. "I'm sorry you didn't get into Blackwell, I know how much it meant to you. But there's an excellent art degree at the University of Cape Town, and then you would be able to see Zac more."

I nodded, even though I didn't want to go there. I wanted to go to Blackwell.

"Anyway, I know I've been very busy lately with the move and my business, and now also trying to build my online personal brand."

If I had to hear the words *personal brand* again, as if my mom was Kim Kardashian, I thought I might get sick.

"So why don't you go out today, go out for the whole day and tonight, do whatever you like. Go to a party, stay out late. Whatever. I'll look after Zac. And also, I wanted to tell you that I think we should start looking for a nanny to help on some afternoons, because all the responsibility is falling to you at the moment, which isn't fair. I'm sure you have lots of other things you need to do."

"Okay." I nodded. "That's a good idea. We'll have to interview them very carefully, though."

"Of course."

"They need to have experience with kids like Zac."

"Of course," she repeated. "I've already contacted a very reputable agency that deals specifically with that."

I looked at my mom, and she smiled at me. I was a bit taken aback by this sudden change of heart she seemed to be having. But I also felt grateful for it too. I was excited about the idea of having some time on my own. But when she and Zac went out, I felt strangely alone in this massive house and had no idea what to do with myself. I flopped down on the couch and pulled my phone out. If I was in Joburg, the guys would come over. We might watch some Netflix, we might go out for coffee, or go to Maggie's and sip whiskey and pretend it tasted good because we looked so cool doing it. We might go scrounging through some secondhand shops, seeing what treasures we could find there. And then I thought of something. I reached into my bag and pulled out Thembi's business card. I stared at it for ages before typing her a message.

LORI: What you doing today?
THEMBI: Nothing. You want to go fabric shopping?
LORI: Sure

THEMBI: What's your address, I'll come fetch you

I sent her my address and was about to put my phone away when I remembered something she'd said. I went to Google and typed in @fullerfigurefullerbust. I followed the link to her Instagram page, and when I saw the pictures, I sat up straight on the couch. I stared at them, thumbing over the screen as the pictures flew by.

She was absolutely gorgeous. This voluptuous redhead with perfect, flicked eyeliner and red lips. Posing in sexy lingerie, not caring that her stomach had rolls or her legs had cellulite. She looked so confident and sexy and . . .

I burst out laughing. *Looked nothing like me.*

36

Thembi and I spent the day buying fabrics for my dress. It had started out weirdly; I didn't know how to act around her, with her strange monotone replies. But after a while I kind of realized that she was just like that, always giving short, sharp answers to people and not putting much effort into her tone. In fact, she reminded me of Zac a little.

And by the time we'd finished shopping, we were chatting away like friends who'd known each other for years. I was surprised by how easily conversation flowed. I'm not sure why I'm always so surprised when I get on well with someone. Dr. Finkelstein said that I put up a protective wall around myself. That I go through life expecting people to be horrible to me, and when they're not, it surprises me. Like with Jake. While I was thrilled, okay, more than thrilled, we were hanging out, it still surprised me.

When Thembi and I had finished shopping, we headed back to her house.

"Oh." Thembi stopped us before slipping her keys into the front door. "Don't say anything to my parents about fashion design, they don't know that I'm doing it next year."

"What?" I asked.

"They think I'm going to study medicine to follow in their footsteps. They don't know that I've applied to the Paris School of Fashion Design."

"Crap!"

"Yeah, crap," Thembi echoed.

"Are you going to tell them?"

She forced a grimace. "I'm going to have to at some stage. Especially when they realize I didn't even apply for medicine."

I stared at her, and she shrugged playfully. But I could see there was nothing playful about the shrug. Painful maybe.

"I'm destined to be a designer, Lori. Besides, I hate blood." She turned the key and the massive door swung open.

"Hey." She walked inside and called out, her tone flatter than usual.

"Hey, love." Her mom came around the corner and I tried not to do a double take when I saw her. And when her dad appeared, I had to try even harder.

"Mom, Dad, this is Lori Palmer, she's new. She just moved here from Joburg."

"Lori, hello. Nice to meet you." Her mom extended her hand for me to shake, and so did her dad. They both looked so different than Thembi, and it wasn't their skin color—that wasn't the reason I'd had to remind my jaw not to fall open.

Thembi's mom wore a pair of old beige corduroy pants and an ill-fitting paisley blouse in orange and brown. Her hair was long, almost down to her lower back, and looked like it had never been dyed. The rough, gray strands breaking up the dark brown made her look older than she probably was. She wore no makeup and the only adornments on her body were two strange wooden earrings hanging from her lobes. I turned my attention to her dad; he was also gray-haired, and looked even older because he was wearing one of those tweed jackets with the brown leather patches over the elbows. This was not what I was expecting. I was expecting glamour and glitz, a mother in Gucci and a dad like Kanye and . . .

"We're going to study upstairs," Thembi quickly said. "We have a biology test."

I nodded quickly, feeling uncomfortable about this lie I was caught in the middle of.

"I suppose we don't have to remind you how important biology is?" Her mother had a strange, probing tone in her voice.

"I know." Thembi nodded.

Her father looked at her strangely now. "You're withholding. Is there something you want to tell us?"

"Dad, can we not do this now, please."

"Do what?" her father asked.

"Can you not analyze me for one day?"

"I'm just saying, your body language and tone seem to be concealing something." Her dad leaned in.

"Are you slipping behind at school?" her mother asked. "Is that why Lori is here to help you study?"

"No, Mom." Thembi started walking off, and I gave her parents a quick smile before following her.

"Can I bring you girls some juice or something?" her mom shouted after us as we walked up the staircase.

"No, thanks," Thembi replied without looking back. We walked into her room, and again, it was not what I'd been expecting . . . *at all*. It was neat. Precise. And so bloody brown and cream and beige.

"I know," she said with a long sigh. "It's disgusting."

I spun around. "Well, I wouldn't say that, but . . . it's not what I expected."

"Yeah, I know." She kicked her shoes off and then moved over to a small bar fridge by her desk. She took out two bottles of sparkling water and handed me one. I didn't know what I was more impressed by, the bar fridge or the fact the bottles had her name on them.

"It's a water delivery service. They deliver bottles with our names on them and then pick them up at the end of the week and return them filled the next day. My parents say that water is the single most important thing for optimal brain function."

"I see." I took the lid off and sipped. I should remember that for Zac.

"I forgot to tell you, I'm adopted," she said glibly.

"Yeah, I kind of guessed that." I walked in a small circle and then sat down on the leather couch against the wall. "Your parents seem, very . . ." I was searching for the words.

"Different?" She sat down next to me. "My dad is a child and adolescent psychiatrist and my mother is a neuroanthropologist."

"A what?" I asked.

"She studies the ways that culture influences the structure of the brain and vice versa. She's a professor at UCT and my dad has published a million books called *A Thriving Adolescent*,

Understand Your Teen, and my personal favorite, *Learn to Speak Teen*."

I chuckled at this.

"You have to watch your tone around him. Trust me, he will scrutinize everything you do and say. It's like living with a surveillance camera pointed at you."

I looked at Thembi and wondered if that was the reason for her short, sharp, often flat way of speaking. She'd trained herself to have a neutral tone at all times.

"Sometimes, it's so exhausting." She sighed loudly.

"And they think you're going to study medicine?"

"Apparently, I'm destined to be the next great neuropsychiatrist, or surgeon. Their greatest fear is that I would settle for something as pedestrian as a general practitioner."

"They have no idea you want to do fashion?"

She shook her head. "I must have gotten my creative genes from my biological parents. Reality is, I don't care about the brain. All I care about is how to make the body beautiful."

"Do you know who they are, your biological parents?" I asked.

"Nope."

I looked down at the bottle in my hand, and watched the condensation slip down the side and trickle onto my hand.

"Sometimes I think I'm adopted, but no one bothered telling me," I said.

"Why?" she asked.

I paused. I would normally never get this personal with someone so quickly, but Thembi had let me into her world. "You know Barbara Palmer of Palm Luxury Realty."

She sat up straight and her eyes widened. "You're shitting me? That's your mom? The one from all the YouTube videos?" The flatness in her tone was gone now, and I got a feeling I was starting to glimpse the real Thembi.

"The very same."

"And I thought my mom was weird. You know, she brings Neanderthal skulls to our house. And I once found human brain dissections in our freezer, and my dad once psychoanalyzed me because I told him I had a dream about being a peanut butter sandwich."

I burst out laughing. "That's equally weird!"

"And your dad?" she asked.

"My parents are divorced. My dad screwed some twenty-something-year-old in a hot tub."

"More and more interesting by the minute." She paused. "I wish my parents would get divorced." There was now a hint of sadness in her voice.

"You don't. Trust me."

"No, I do. They can't stand each other sometimes."

"They don't look like it."

"Looks can be deceiving. My dad thinks his research and career are more important than my mother's, and she thinks hers are . . . their jobs are the most important things to them."

"My brother is autistic," I blurted out for some strange reason, and immediately regretted it.

"My mother always says that neurodiversity is the next step in the evolution of the human brain. That neurodiverse brains actually have a competitive edge. Some companies are even seeking to employ neurodiverse people."

"Really?" I went quiet and thoughtful for a moment, while I considered this. Perhaps it was true. The idea that Zac's autism was some kind of a mistake had never sat right with me. I'd never viewed his brain as defective in any way. If anything, I'd always seen it as superior in the way it functioned, and saw things and drew connections that others couldn't. There was genius inside Zac, and perhaps the world around us was just defective because it couldn't understand his rare and special gifts.

"I wish I had a sibling." Thembi broke my train of thought. "But they only wanted one so they could focus all their energy on creating the perfect child." She stood up and walked into the middle of the room. "Oh well, they're going to be so disappointed when they realize that I'm far from perfect."

Thembi pulled a small stepladder out from under her bed and climbed onto it.

"What are you doing?" I asked as she reached up and pulled on the string hanging from the ceiling. As she did, the ceiling opened and a staircase folded out from the attic.

"We're going up to my real bedroom," she said with a mischievous smile, and started climbing. I followed her, and when I got up there, I looked around the room in shock.

"What the . . . ?" Now this, *this* was what I'd expected. The walls were covered in cutouts from magazines—models wearing amazing clothes, walking down catwalks. In the middle of the room stood one of those dressmaking busts, bright fabrics draped over its shoulders. A table was covered in patterns and fabrics, piles of tape measures, and more scissors than she probably needed.

"How do your parents not know you have this room?" I asked.

"They do. They just don't know what's in it. They believe in giving teens privacy and their own space, to allow us to express in a healthy manner." She said that last part with a put-on voice; I guess it was meant to sound like her father.

She put the bag down and pulled out the fabrics we'd chosen—

well, that she'd guided me to choose. I still wasn't sure about them. I rarely deviated from black, and here were these bright emerald greens. But in a way, I didn't really care, since I was never going to wear this dress anyway. I wouldn't dream of wearing anything like this, and I probably—definitely—wasn't going to my dad's wedding, or the dance.

"Okay." Thembi turned to me. "I need to measure you."

My stomach dropped. She might as well get the scale out and weigh me too. It's amazing how much power a number on a scale can hold. How much your self-worth can be wrapped up in those few little digits. I once read that your weight isn't a constant, it actually depends on where you weigh yourself, because weight is the measure of how much gravity pulls on your body. So, if I was on the moon, I would weigh less. How I wished we lived on the moon right now.

"Uh . . . okay," I said tentatively, trying to shut up my inner bully, who was being very vocal right now. My heart pounded in my chest as Thembi flipped a small book open, put a pencil behind her ear, and draped a tape measure around her neck.

What's she going to think of you when she realizes how fat you are? the bully whispered in my ear. I took a deep breath and mentally told her to back the hell off. (I was trying a more aggressive approach with her now!)

"Stand here." Thembi pointed and I moved. She seemed a little far away now; she had that same look I got when I was about to start a painting. When I stare at a blank canvas and see a million possibilities of what it could be. Michelangelo once said that the sculpture was already inside the marble, his job was just to chisel it out. I wondered if that was the same for fabrics? The design was already there, just waiting to be cut out and sewn together.

I waited for her to descend with her tape measure. I hoped she wasn't going to turn around and say we hadn't bought enough material, because she'd underestimated my size. But she didn't say a word as she zoned out and wrapped and unwrapped the tape, instructing me to lift arms and put them down until . . .

"You have such huge boobs," she declared.

"Oh, I . . ." I quickly folded my arms, feeling self-conscious.

She leaned over to the table and scribbled my bust measurement down. "I would give anything to have even ten percent of those. I'm as flat as a board."

"What?" I said, taken aback.

"I was so self-conscious when everyone was getting bras." She shook her head. "That was a crap time for me." She said it casually, but it was anything but casual to me. I stared at her. I couldn't believe that this person in front of me, this gorgeous, perfect-looking person, had something she was insecure about. It had never occurred to me that people who looked like her would have anything to feel insecure about. I wanted absolutely everything she had, and she was saying she wanted something of mine. She looked up at me again.

"I asked my parents for a boob job for my sixteenth birthday." She smiled. "You can imagine how that idea went down. My father thought I was having some teen identity crisis."

"I go to a therapist," I said, without thinking.

"I went to a therapist, too, for a while," she said, and I blinked. Why would someone like her need to go to a therapist?

"Wh-what did you go for?" I asked, even though I probably knew I shouldn't.

"A while back, I sort of had some issues about being adopted. It's weird not knowing where you come from sometimes; I guess that also makes it hard to know where you fit."

"Oh," I said, thrown by how candid she was being with me.

"Why do you go to a therapist?"

"Uh . . . anxiety," I whispered, almost under my breath. I half expected her to look up at me with shock. But she didn't even flinch.

"We're done here." She put down the measuring tape.

"Okay." I breathed a small sigh of relief and then moved away and started looking at the walls.

"Did you do these?" I asked, pointing to one of the many sketches on the wall.

"Yes." She came and stood next to me.

"They're really good."

"I know. Watch out, Paris Fashion Week!" I laughed and Thembi joined in. What she lacked in boobs, she made up for in confidence, and I admired that. Her phone beeped and she glanced at the screen, immediately rolling her eyes.

"What?" I asked.

"My boyfriend is acting shady. We were supposed to go out tonight, and he's canceling on me. Something's up."

"What do you think it is?"

She dropped her phone on the chair and then shrugged. "Don't know. Are you dating anyone?" she asked, and I burst out laughing. She looked at me blankly, as if she didn't know why I was laughing.

"No," I said quickly.

"Leave your boyfriend or girlfriend in Joburg?"

"Well, kind of. I sort of left two back there . . . well, they're my best friends, but they call me their girlfriend. Guy always jokes that we're the only nonsexual threesome in the world." I turned when I heard arguing coming from downstairs. Thembi threw her hands in the air in frustration.

"They couldn't just wait a couple of hours before they started this! At least until you've left."

I stood there awkwardly and tried not to listen as Thembi flopped into a chair, her usual bravado and confidence slipping off her. I felt sorry for her.

"I'm sure it will be over soon," she said apologetically. "They're 'expressing' themselves." She gestured air quotes. "Apparently, it's all part of having a healthy relationship. If you ask me, I don't really know how healthy their relationship actually is."

"My parents never used to fight. And they got divorced. Maybe you're meant to fight sometimes," I offered.

"Or maybe humans aren't meant to be with one person for the rest of their lives. Maybe we were meant to be with a person for a period of time, get what we need from them in that moment, and then move on?" she said thoughtfully, and I immediately thought of Jake.

"Or maybe, some relationships are just toxic. Look what happened to Rose Maponyane. Did you see that art?"

My throat immediately tightened at the mention of it, and all I could manage was a small nod.

"Imagine getting into a relationship with someone who actually ends up harming you, or worse, killing you?" she said and looked straight at me. "It's scary. But that's a reality for many women in this country. And I tell you, whoever painted that stuff should be given a medal."

I looked down at my hands when she said this, and that's when I noticed the small dot of red paint on one of my nails. I rubbed it off quickly. I didn't know if I deserved a medal; in fact, a part of me felt that I didn't deserve this kind of praise at all. I had stumbled upon Rose by accident in a way; I hadn't even known who she was. Banksy knew what he was saying with his art. Did I?

There are no such things as accidents. Only meant-to-be's. I heard Xander's words in my head, but was suddenly distracted when my phone beeped. I scrambled to get it out of my pocket. I looked at the screen and felt my cheeks go warm. I hoped Thembi hadn't noticed that.

"Who is it?" she asked.

I shrugged. "No one." Only it was someone. *It was Jake.*

37

I waited until I got home to read Jake's message.

JAKE: Super late notice . . . totally random question. I have tickets for a show at the planetarium tonight. One of the parents at school gave them to me, he works there, do you guys want to come?

A hollow pit formed in the bottom of my stomach.

LORI: Sorry, I only saw your message now

LORI: Sounds cool, but Zac is out with my mom tonight

JAKE: I was starting to wonder if you were ignoring me

LORI: No. Sorry

JAKE: We don't have to take the kids

LORI: What do you mean?

JAKE: Just us

LORI: To the planetarium?

LORI: With you?

JAKE: 😄 yes

JAKE: I know it's random, but it could be fun

JAKE: When did you last go to the planetarium?

LORI: I don't think I've ever been

JAKE: First time for everything then

My heart started beating faster. Like a date. *Was this a date?*

LORI: Sure. Okay. I mean . . .

JAKE: OMG, you don't sound keen. Is it the idea of a planetarium or the idea of going with me?

LORI: No, it's nothing like that. I'm just surprised, I guess

JAKE: Why?

LORI: I just imagined us hanging out with our siblings in tow. You know

JAKE: So you don't want to be friends with JUST me?

LORI: That's not what I'm saying

JAKE: We hung out on the beach the other night, I couldn't have been such crappy company?

LORI: OMG, no. I didn't mean that

JAKE: I'm starting to get really offended here . . .

LORI: Please don't. That's not my intention

JAKE: 😔 How boring do you think I am?

LORI: I WANT TO GO OUT WITH YOU!!!

There was a pause and my embarrassment made me want to melt into the floor as I waited for his response.

JAKE: Wow! Caps. Multiple exclamation marks

LORI: I mean, it would be cool to go to the planetarium

JAKE: With me?

LORI: Sure. Why not

JAKE: Okay, so planetarium starts at seven

LORI: Shall we meet there?

JAKE: Sure 😊 I usually offer to pick the girl up, but you're not like any other girl I've ever met. Anything but JustLori . . .

I stared at the message. What did that dot, dot, dot mean? And how did I respond to it? I typed:

LORI: See you soon . . .

Adding some dots too. Just in case the moment called for more. Another message popped up on the screen.

JAKE: . . .

Oh my, now what? Four dots? Too many? My finger hovered over the dots, trying to figure out how many dots were appropriate. If dots were even appropriate anymore? He sent me another message.

JAKE: 😊

I breathed a sigh of relief, at least we'd left the dots behind. I'd never been a fan of pointillism. So I sent him a smiley face back, too, whatever that actually meant. I really sucked at this, didn't I?

—⁓—

We walked into the planetarium and stopped when we saw the poster for the show. A bright, cartoony-colored poster hung on the wall. I read it out loud:

"Bob and Sipho Fly to the Moon."

I turned and looked at Jake. He half grimaced, half smiled.

"Yeeeeah, I guess he was expecting me to come with Lisa."

I laughed.

"Let's go anyway," he said, handing the tickets in.

The show kicked off, and it was definitely aimed at kids,

but somehow that didn't matter. By the end of it, we were both laughing our heads off and screaming out with the audience, "*Five, four, three, two, one . . . blast off!*" We stumbled out of there forty-five minutes later, the biggest smiles plastered across our faces, and I realized that I hadn't laughed like that since being with the guys in Joburg.

"Thanks for that," I said to him, still smiling. "I needed it."

"What?"

"A good laugh. I don't think I've had one like this since leaving Joburg."

We ambled into the parking lot, and I was just about to walk to my car when he stopped me.

"Hey, let's walk. There's a cool park around the corner. Besides . . ." He paused and looked at me and I felt that bloody flutter again. "I don't really feel like going home."

"Cool," I said, trying to act casual, even though on the inside I was exploding with excitement. We walked into the park. The sun was still up, and the light was soft and diffuse. Beautiful. Once again, the mountain took up prominence in the background. It was always there, no matter where you went in Cape Town, like a beacon that guided you to the same spot every single time.

"You know, there was this painter called Pierneef, he painted Table Mountain once. But not from the angle that everyone else paints it from. He chose this lesser-known angle and for years there was this fierce debate about whether it was even Table Mountain? But it was. He just chose to look at it differently, not like everyone else did, as if he saw something in it that no one else saw. You should see the way he paints trees and clouds and landscapes . . ." I stopped walking and looked up at the mountain. I could feel Jake next to me, but I was so wrapped up in my thoughts now. "I would love to spend a day looking through his eyes—he sees the world in such a unique way. Imagine being able to see things like that? To be able to look at things in a way no one else can. I think Zac looks at things like that too. From an angle that no one else in the world would ever think to look at it," I finished, and slowly turned. Jake was standing next to me, but unlike me, he wasn't looking up at the mountain . . . his gaze felt hot and sticky on my skin.

"What?" I could barely get that word out, my mouth was so dry.

He looked away, as if he was feeling what I was. *Was he?* "You do look at the world like that."

"I do?" I asked.

He looked at me again. His eyes were no longer that light, bright-cerulean blue. They had darkened into navy. "No one else I know sees a city at sunset like you do." And then he turned and started walking away from me. I followed, and we walked in silence for a while, him with his stormy, navy eyes and me with my now growing-redder-by-the-second candy apple–red cheeks. We must have walked in silence for five minutes before he spoke again.

"What's the one thing you miss most about Joburg? Other than friends and sunsets?" he asked.

"That's easy, summer afternoon thunderstorms."

"Really?"

"I used to go up onto the roof of our building to watch them."

"Aren't you supposed to *not* be on a roof in a storm?" he asked sarcastically.

I smiled at him. "But if you're not, you miss out."

"Miss out on what?"

"Everything."

"Like what?"

I stopped walking and turned to face him. "The world feels alive right before a storm. The air has this crackle to it, and it just makes you feel . . . feel . . . *I don't know*, a little bit crazy. Like you can do anything because there aren't any rules anymore. Something so much bigger than you looms, and it makes you feel humbled and a little terrified all at the same time," I said, thinking back to one storm specifically. The one where the winds came hot and full and beat against my face and clothes and pulled at my hair until it was wild and matted. When the clouds had gathered purple and black, suffocating the blue sky. "And then there's this moment, just before the lightning comes, when everything feels frightened. Even the atoms in the air. They buzz with this antici-pation, and an unseen energy builds up and you can almost feel it rushing through you. And the lightning is so loud that you have to cover your ears. And then when the clouds finally burst open, it's just the best feeling." I smiled and then shrugged. "You proba-bly think I'm weird now, right?"

"Yeah, I do. Totally weird . . . *but also kind of cool*." That last part was a soft whisper. A small sound on the breeze, but I caught it, and before I knew what I was doing . . . before I'd even thought the words and given my lips permission to speak them, I heard them:

"I think you're cool too." *Dot, dot, dot.* Yes! This was a dot, dot, dot moment if ever there was one.

He smiled. "So not an uncultured, boring jock who knows nothing about art and cool Swedish music."

I laughed. "I never said you were boring."

He gave me another smile; this time it was slightly naughty.

The smiled moved into his eyes. Azure blue this time. They glinted with the same magic that you feel just before the storm. "I still have to prove to you that I'm not boring."

Our eyes locked and the lightning struck, deep inside my belly. But then he broke the moment.

"Hey, want something to eat?" He pointed at a food truck parked on one of the paths.

I shook my head. No way was I eating in front of him. "I've already eaten." I lied. I was starving.

We walked away from the food truck, him with a giant hot dog in his hands, me with a Coke Zero. They had given me one of those biodegradable straws, the type made of cardboard. Look, I was all for saving the planet, really, but these straws got soggy between your lips and turned to mush. I watched out of the corner of my eye as Jake opened his mouth widely, tilted his head to the side for easy access and then shoved half the hot dog in. My stomach rumbled, quietly, thank goodness.

"You know, I once got into such shit in this park."

"You did?"

"Last year, we knew this barman at the hotel across the road and he used to get us a bottle of whiskey sometimes. He skimmed a little off the shots he poured. So we used to come here and drink it, and then we got caught."

"What happened?"

"I drank too much one night, and passed out on a bench, and a security guard found me and called my dad."

"Crap!"

"That's when my dad took me to that AA meeting."

"And you haven't drank since then?" I asked.

"Nope. It's not like he told me to stop drinking, but he did want to show me what the potential consequences were, since addiction can be genetic."

"Why do you hide the fact you don't drink?"

He shrugged. It wasn't his usual cool and casual shrug. "Probably the same reason I don't tell people about Lisa."

"Scared of being judged?"

"Does that make me a coward?" he turned and asked.

I glanced at him to gauge his body language. His shoulders were a little more slumped than usual, as if he were carrying just a little bit of extra weight. "I don't know. I'm the last person in the world you should ask. I'm always scared I'm being secretly judged. I'm scared of everything."

"You? Never!" he said.

"What do you mean?"

"You don't give a crap—in a good way! You have opinions about things. You voice them. You tell strangers off in supermarkets. You'd rip up protestor's signs. I did nothing but stand there and watch them. You're brave . . . I'm the coward."

"What?" I swung around and looked at him. "Brave? I don't . . . no. I'm . . . not. Trust me."

We'd been talking so much that I hadn't noticed we'd walked all the way through the park. I was about to suggest we turn back when something caught my attention. I turned to look at it, *needed to look at it,* and just like I'd felt when I'd seen Rose's cross, I was pulled toward it. Jake came up next to me and we stood in utter silence as we took it in. No one dared to speak.

"How are you supposed to find her like that?" I finally broke the silence, and reached out to touch the tattered piece of paper with the old, weather-beaten photocopy on it.

"'Natasha Lewis was last seen wearing a pink Dora the Explorer

T-shirt and blue shorts playing outside her parents' house in Table View on February 21, 2021. She is eight years old, weighs approximately twenty-five kilos and her height is one hundred and twenty-five centimeters.'"

The words seemed to reach out from the paper and kick me in the gut.

"She's the same age as Lisa," Jake said.

"Yeah."

"I can't imagine what I would do if Lisa went missing." His voice was somber as he stepped forward and stood right next to me. Shoulder to shoulder we looked at the small poster together. A sense of gravity filled the air around us, so heavy and oppressive that it pushed against me, forcing my feet into the ground. I felt stuck. Unable to move and look away.

"Her family must be going crazy," I offered up. "I would be going crazy."

"Maybe she's been found . . ." Jake took his phone out and started googling. It was darker now, and the light from his phone cast a glow across his face.

"And . . . ?" I asked.

"Why is it so hard to get information on missing kids?" He held his phone up. "I can't find any updates on her, just a tiny article about her going missing. That's all."

"How have we not heard about this girl on the news?" I asked.

"Did you know," he exclaimed, "that a child goes missing every five hours in South Africa?" He held his phone up and a screen of little smiling faces stared back at me from it. All of them lost now. No longer smiling.

"No wonder we haven't heard of *this* girl." I looked back at her poster thoughtfully, this small, pixelated black and white photocopy of a once-happy child, clinging to the wall, held in place by one dirty piece of tape. The other side had come loose and when the breeze blew, the paper flapped in the wind like a butterfly trapped in a jar.

"It pisses me off." Jake's tone changed and I turned around and looked at him. "If Lisa went missing, I would want the whole country to know about it. I wouldn't want her to just be a piece of paper on a wall somewhere." He started walking again and I followed him.

"Me too. Especially here, in a country that has such a problem with violence toward women and girls." I looked back at the small letter-sized poster on the massive wall. The wall dwarfed it, spread out around it until the paper was a mere speck on the face of this massive thing. Like a barnacle on the side of a blue whale, it was almost invisible. This girl should not be invisible. Like Rose, she deserved to be seen. She deserved to scream loudly from this wall to be found.

"I wish there was something I could do," he said quietly, almost to himself this time.

"Me too." But there was something I could do. My paints were at home, though, and it was too early to start. *But I was going to do something.*

We walked a little more; the mood had changed between us.

"You want to have some coffee, or something?" Jake pointed to a coffee shop across the street.

"Sure, if you're cool with that?" I tried to sound unfazed.

"Yeah, it would be nice," he replied. We walked across the road, sat down at a table on the pavement, and ordered coffee. There was a warm breeze and I could hear music playing somewhere in the distance.

"Did you see what that graffiti artist did to that cross on the side of the road?" he asked suddenly, and I stiffened. Did he know it was me?

"Yes? What about it?" I couldn't hide the anxiety in my voice.

"I thought you'd like it, since you're an artist."

Not according to Imogen, a small voice in my head said.

"So you think it's cool what she's doing? The art. Not bad, like the police say?"

"How do you know it's a she?"

"Just a guess." I looked away quickly, trying to hide everything that was going on inside me.

He was thoughtful for a moment and looked at me. I sat up straight in my chair now, waiting for him to speak again and deliver his verdict.

"I think it's cool," he finally said. "That guy who killed Rose should have gotten a longer sentence, everyone is saying that. And I read that it's putting pressure on the justice system and the government to take a closer look at gender-based violence. Whoever they are, they're really doing something important."

"What are they doing?" The words were right on the tip of my tongue, and I pursed my lips together to stop them from tumbling out. But they were building up inside me at such a speed that I didn't know if I would be able to hold them back much longer.

"Well, they clearly have a purpose. They're trying to make a statement with their work. Get people thinking and talking, and maybe even change the way things are done."

I nodded. "I guess."

"Definitely!" he quickly added. "I wonder who it is?" He looked thoughtful. The words were now dancing on my tongue. Fast. Frantic. As if they were desperate to come out. Banging on the inside of my lips, trying to force them open.

"I wish we could contact them," he said.

"Why?"

"They should come here and paint something on the wall for Natasha. So she's not forgotten. Like Rose."

"It's *me*!" I blurted out, and then slapped my hands over my mouth and looked around.

"What's you?" he asked, leaning across the table.

"It's me. The person. The art. I did it." I whispered this time.

"Seriously?"

"Yes!"

He stared at me for a while, and then a small smile twitched in the corners of his eyes. "Of course it's you. The card you painted for Lisa, same flowers, I should have seen it!"

"It's a flowering echeveria. Most people don't know that succulents bloom, but they do."

And then a huge smile swept across his face. *That smile.* That one that seemed to hold all kinds of mysterious magical powers that reduced me to dust. "That's the coolest thing I've ever heard."

"Really?"

"It's amazing. You're famous. Everyone in Cape Town is talking about it, you were in the news. I should, like, get your autograph."

"No one can know. I could get into serious trouble."

And then he reached over and grabbed my hands. The move caught me so off guard and I flinched so hard that the coffee on the table spilled a little.

"You have to do something for Natasha. People need to know that she's still missing."

I smiled at him. "I'm going to," I whispered.

"You are?"

"Yes. Later tonight. But you can't say anything, promise me?"

"Never!" He squeezed my hands, and I stared down at them. I felt such a rush of something surging through me.

"I'll help you," he said. "I'll keep watch and hand you your paints."

"You don't have to." I shook my head.

"I want to. I . . . *need to*. I can't explain it, but I know I need to help you." I looked up at him. Looked straight into those massive blue eyes of his and felt myself melt.

"Your art has the power to change things, Lori," he said. "I told you you were brave."

I kept looking into his eyes. I couldn't look away, and they seemed to pull a smile out of me that was mirrored on Jake's face. I nodded at him. "Okay, you can help."

Things I Like about Myself by Lori Palmer
I'm a good sister.
I'm a real artist (despite what Blackwell says!).
I, Lori Palmer, am officially good with parents!
I have a voice. There is power in my art.
I am brave!

38

We met up again at eleven that night, when the streets were quiet and all the coffee shops had closed. When I got back to the park from driving home and fetching my paints, Jake was already waiting for me.

"You ready to do this?" he asked.

I nodded.

I put my earbuds in and pressed Play. A Grimes song sprang to life in my ears: "My Name Is Dark." Grungy, electric, industrial sounds burst into my ears and I thought this was the perfect song for this moment.

And very soon, without even thinking about it, almost forgetting that Jake was there, I was swept up in the sounds and the painting. I began painting Natasha's face: big and colorful and huge across the whole wall. With each sweep of my can and paint-brush, I bought her face to life. The strokes flowed out of me, like they had before. This was so different than my usual, precise style of painting. There was nothing perfect and controlled about what I was doing now. It was messy and spontaneous and . . . *could this be my voice?* The one Imogen had spoken about?

I looked over at Jake a few times while I was painting. He sat on the bench, legs crossed, eyes fixed on me the entire time. And when I was finally done, when Natasha's face was as large as I could make it, I wrote the words *Find Me* across the painting and tagged it. But as soon as I'd finished, I felt a tug on my arm. I took my earbuds out and swung around.

"Someone's coming," Jake hissed loudly. He gathered all the paints into my bag and then pulled me with him as he started running through the park. My heart was beating in my chest as we ducked behind a tree together. We peered around the trunk and my heart missed a beat when I saw who it was. A security guard, patrolling the perimeter. We slapped our hands over our mouths and stared in shock as he approached the freshly painted wall. He was going to see it at any second, only he didn't. His walkie-talkie made a sound, and he walked off in the other direction.

Jake and I looked at each other, wide-eyed, still holding our breath. But when the guard was out of sight, we both burst out laughing. We tried to stifle the nervous laughter, which only made it worse, until we were both gasping for air. We stumbled to our feet and held on to each other's shoulders for support. *Oh God, it hurt! My ribs hurt.* Finally, the laughter tapered off and we found ourselves standing opposite each other. We stayed like that for a while, until Jake broke the moment.

"What's the time?" he asked.

I looked at my phone. "Eleven fifty-five."

His smile grew. "That's perfect. But we have to run."

"Where?"

"Come!" And then he was running again.

I tried to keep up. I wasn't built for running. My boobs were *definitely* not built for running, and I tried to cross my arms over them as I went, without being obvious. "Where are we going?" I asked, in-between big, unfit breaths that I couldn't hide.

"Somewhere *not* boring!" he shouted over his shoulder.

I continued to follow him but soon it felt like my legs would give out; thankfully we finally stopped. I looked around. We were standing in the middle of a large lawn. "What are we doing here?"

"Remember I told you I fell asleep here once?"

"Yes."

"Well, it was on that bench." He pointed. "And something woke me up."

"What?"

"Wait for it . . ." He looked down at his watch. "Wait for it . . ."

"Wait for what?"

"Quick! Give me your phone," Jake said, holding out his hand, his phone in the other one.

"Why?" I asked.

"Trust me," he said. I gave him my phone and he tossed them both to the side; they landed on the soft, manicured grass with zero thud.

"Okay, what are we waiting fo—" I put my hands in the air as the wetness rushed at me. The sprinklers were huge, the kind that rose up out of the lawn, and then covered everything like rain.

"Aaaaahhh! This is amazing," I squealed.

"It might not be a Joburg thunderstorm, but"—Jake came closer to me—"it's the best I can do."

"I love it," I said, looking up into the night sky. The stars twinkled above me, like they had in the planetarium. The water rushed down my face, washing over me. I put my hands in the air and twirled around in a circle. Smiling and laughing, because in that moment—that wet, starry, after-painting moment—I felt an emotion I didn't feel that often, of being completely, utterly, happily free.

"I'm going to do it this time," Jake said, and I looked over at him as he attempted another cartwheel flip thing. He slipped on the wet ground this time and fell onto his back.

I laughed. "You need to stop doing that. You clearly suck at it." I rushed over to him and he held his hand out for me. I grabbed it, pulled as hard as I could, and he sprang back up.

"This is incredible, thank you," I blurted; he was standing right in front of me now.

"You're incredible," he said.

Whoooosh! The sound of my heart launching out of my chest. Flying out of me and into the sky.

"I am?" My voice shook.

"What you did on the wall . . . imagine if they find that girl because of you. And what you did for Rose . . . you're the most interesting person I've ever met, by far. Anything but JustLori."

"I—I . . . don't know what to say," I whispered, the water still rushing over me.

"You can answer a question for me." He moved closer. His eyes had changed once again. This time they were a turquoise color that was so bright it outshone everything here.

"What question?"

"So, Amber kind of told me something."

"Wh-wh . . . what did she say?" A bang in my chest pushed all the good feelings out of me. Anything Amber had to say wouldn't be good.

"She told me that you're into me."

"What?!" I shook my head, almost hysterically as the first wave of embarrassment threatened to knock me to the ground. "No. I'm not . . . I swear. I . . . no!" I protested loud and long, and a part of me didn't know why. *Just say it, Lori,* one part of me screamed. But the other part was saying something completely different: *Guys like him don't like girls like Lori Fatty Palmer.*

A strange expression contorted the features of his face and I wondered if he could hear the voices in my head too. I tried to recover from this as best as I could, the only way I knew how.

"Wait, did you think I was?" I forced amusement into my voice as if this was the craziest, funniest thing I'd ever heard in my life. Except it wasn't, it was so mortifying, and despite the cool water rushing over me, my skin was boiling.

"Well, I kind of . . ." His face dropped.

"Kind of what?" I asked as he stepped again, almost closing the gap between us entirely.

"Never mind," he said softly, looking down. The water splashed over his face, and he'd never looked hotter than he looked right now. He looked down at me again and then everything went silent. I can't explain the feeling, and I don't really know *how* it happened. It was something that couldn't be controlled. Like the formation of the great galaxies, the colliding of black holes with their infinite gravitational force. We were like that. Pulling, falling, closer, until . . . *I was kissing him.*

Time stood still and sped up at the same time. Everything

around me buzzed and hummed and although my eyes were closed, I could see colors. Indescribable colors blending together to form hues and shades that I'd never seen before. Every smell, every feeling, every sound was crisp and clean and sharp, like living in superhigh definition. And yet, it was also soft, diffuse. Slightly fuzzy around the edges. The moment was a stack of contradictions. Mixed emotions. A million thoughts. I opened my eyes again.

I concentrated on all the tiny details—the infinitesimal things of the moment—so I could remember them all. His smell. The way his lips felt rough and smooth all at the same time. The way a water droplet clung to his eyelash, pulling it down. The way the water felt slipping down the nape of my neck and trickling into my clothes. Slipping down my spine. The way his breath was hot but the water cold. The way his tongue felt, gliding across mine, the way it caused these other feelings, explosions starting in my face, racing down my body—arms, fingers, legs, and toes. This was a good kiss. A great kiss. He was an amazing kisser, and for all my previous fears and worries, my mouth and lips and tongue seemed to know exactly what to do. This was confirmed when Jake let out the softest moan against my lips, by far the hottest moment of my entire existence. And I knew right there and then that . . .

Things I Like about Myself by Lori Palmer
I'm a good sister.
I'm a real artist (despite what Blackwell says!).
I, Lori Palmer, am officially good with parents!
I have a voice. There is power in my art.
I am brave!
I am a great kisser!

But then one of the voices in my head interrupted the moment. I tried to push it away but I couldn't. It started repeating Amber's words.

She's right you know, do you really think a guy like Jake could like a girl like you? My inner bully started laughing, and I tried to ignore her. But then, when his hands left my face, trailed down my shoulders and arms, and slipped around my waist . . . *I pulled away.*

"No. I . . . I . . ." I put my hand over my mouth and walked backward, away from him. He looked shocked. "I'm sorry, I didn't mean to," I said, shaking my head.

He seemed even more shocked now, as I bent down and picked up my bag of paints.

He ran his hands through his wet hair. "Shit. Did I just read that totally wrong?"

I started nodding my head, and then shaking it. "It's late. I have to go." I quickly turned and ran away.

"Lori! Lori!" I heard him call after me, but I didn't turn back.

Things I Like about Myself by Lori Palmer
I'm a good sister.
I'm a real artist (despite what Blackwell says!).
~~I, Lori Palmer, am officially good with parents!~~
I have a voice. There is power in my art.
~~I am brave!~~
I am a great kisser!

39

I pulled into the garage at top speed, almost bumping into a car I didn't recognize parked by our curb. My mind was racing after that kiss. I'd imagined this moment in my head, fantasized about my first kiss, but then when it had happened, I'd completely freaked out. Especially because it had been with Jake and his hands had been touching my body like *that*. I jumped out of the car just as my phone beeped.

JAKE: Are you okay?

My fingers shook as I typed back.

LORI: Fine. Sorry. Had to go

JAKE: Are you sure?

LORI: Yup. Sure.

JAKE: I'm sorry about what happened. I hope I didn't offend you or . . .

JAKE: Actually, what did just happen?

Oh crap. I didn't know what to say to him. I'd wanted Jake to kiss me, and then it had happened and it had felt so damn good, until those voices started gnawing away at me, poking the fires of self-doubt until they raged so big and bright inside me. He must think I was absolutely mad. I was just about to start typing when a message from him came in.

JAKE: I'm sorry

JAKE: I shouldn't have done that

JAKE: You made it VERY clear you weren't interested in me in that way, and I shouldn't have done that

JAKE: Sorry

JAKE: Will you forgive me?

I gaped at his message. I could feel and see the very thing I'd wanted so badly being yanked away from me, and I had no one else to blame but myself.

LORI: All forgiven

I typed quickly then slipped my phone into my pocket. I grabbed my bag of spray paints and rushed into the house, still soaking wet, and ran straight for the hot tub room on the roof to stash them. I didn't want anyone to find them in my bedroom. I pushed the door open and when I did . . .

"*Whaaaat?* What? What? What?" was all I could manage as I stared at my mother in the hot tub. She wasn't alone.

"Lori! I thought you were out for the night."

I dropped my bag of paints to the floor. They landed with a thud, adding an auditory exclamation mark to this moment.

"I came back, Mom. I mean . . . what the hell are you—"

And then I saw him, and just when I thought my shock levels couldn't skyrocket any more, I pointed a shaking finger at him.

"You! How did you? Why are you? What the hell are you doing in the hot tub with my mother?"

"You know him?" my mother asked, she looked so shocked that I swear, I think I saw her eyebrows actually move. She was so shocked she broke her Botox.

"Xander is my school counselor," I said flatly.

My mom turned to the man in the hot tub. "I thought you said you were a motivational speaker?"

"Really, Mom? Really? Is that what you got out of that statement?"

"Your Tinder profile says motivational speaker," she continued.

"He is," I barked. "He got bitten by a shark or some crap and wrote a book. I have a copy if you want to borrow it. . . . It's auto-graphed," I said sarcastically.

My mom buried her head in her hands, and I wondered if this is what my dad had done all those years ago when my mom had caught him in the hot tub. God, my family was dysfunctional. We hadn't always been this way. I'm sure we were happy and normal once, but that seemed so long ago that maybe I'd just imagined it.

"Lori, I didn't know that he worked at your school, if I had I would never have—"

"That is such crap, Mom! Of course you would have. Because you don't care about anyone else but yourself. If Xander over there"—I pointed—"had been carrying blue and white BWH pom-poms and wearing a shirt that read 'Bay Water High' I doubt you would have been put off. Seriously." I turned around and held my head. "And here I thought you were trying to be a real mom again . . ." I stopped talking as something painful dawned on me.

"Oh, wait. This is why you told me to go out. It had nothing to do with me, but everything to do with you and what you wanted."

There was a pause. A strange beat and then Xander started climbing out of the water.

"Oh no." I averted my eyes, I didn't want to see him in his swimsuit.

"Lori, I understand you must be feeling very confused, and even angry right now. Those are very, very real emotions and I'm sure—"

"Don't." I pointed a finger at him. "Don't do that. I have my own psychologist."

"You know, when that shark bit me at first I felt totally traumatized."

I threw my arms in the air. "Will you shut up about the bloody shark!"

"Everyone has a shark in their life, Lori, and we all have to overcome its bite."

"*What the hell?*" I screamed out at the universe. "Has the world gone mad?"

My mother stood up now. "I'm allowed to date, Lori. I am a sensual woman in my prime and I—"

"*No!*" I held my hand up to stop her talking. "Don't go there. Please!"

"There is nothing to be ashamed about, having a healthy sexu—"

"*La-la-la!*" I put my hands over my ears. I didn't want to know about my mother's sex life. Ever. I would rather hell froze over.

"*Lori!*" she shouted. "I'm trying to talk to you." She paused and eyed me up and down. "Besides, look at you, you're sopping wet. Maybe I should ask what *you've* been up to?"

I burst out laughing. "Now you're trying to talk to me like a mother. What happened to go out and do whatever?" I continued to laugh; it was a hysterical, panicked laugh that soon turned into a tearless sob. I looked from my mother to Xander, and then I just grabbed my paints and ran back to my car.

I was driving, again. I'd never just driven like this in Joburg. I guess I'd never felt such a need to get away from it all. But the driving did little to distance me from all the feelings; in fact, I was just lugging them along with me. I went up Chapman's Peak, the long road that took you around the mountain was supposed to be the most beautiful part of Cape Town. But I was struggling to see any beauty in this place anymore. After driving aimlessly for an hour, I decided to head back. I couldn't run from this forever, but as I headed back, I saw it . . . *my mother.*

She was smiling down at me from a giant billboard, and it pissed me off. Her face blocked the view behind her, to the sea and the mountain, and I'd never wanted to unsee anything more in my entire life. It pissed me off so much that when the traffic light turned green on this dark, empty street, I didn't pull away. Instead, I parked my car and stared at her, our eyes locked in an intense death stare. And then I nodded at her, because I knew what needed to happen. I grabbed my bag of paints and Jake's BWH cap, and climbed out of the car.

40

I woke up the next morning at around noon. I don't think I'd ever slept this late, but I'd been out all night. I walked downstairs to find my mother sitting in the lounge. I didn't bother to say hello until I heard her talking to someone. And then I saw who she was talking to.

"Where's Zac. Is he all right?" I asked. The last time I'd seen police was the day the doves cried.

My mother turned slowly, avoiding eye contact. "Zac's fine. He's in his room. These gentlemen are here about the vandalism."

"What vandalism?" I asked quietly.

"My billboard. Some criminal painted over the entire thing. Painted me into the background, as if I was invisible. Can you believe it?" She turned back to the police. "And as I was saying, that advertising space cost me fifty thousand rand! And now someone in Cape Town is running around destroying public property. It's disgraceful."

One of the policemen nodded. "We'll definitely look into it, but these things rarely get solved. Unless someone actually saw who did it."

"Well, someone must have seen something!" Her voice went up ten octaves. "Billboards don't just get painted over by ghosts." She swooshed her arms in the air and her golden bangles clanked together loudly. The sharp sound made me feel sick. "If I were you, I would start looking into rival real estate companies."

Oh crap! "Mom, I doubt it's that," I said, coming forward.

"Of course it is. It's corporate sabotage!" She raised her voice even more. "It has to be a rival estate agent. They're probably jealous that I've just arrived and already have the top listings, or . . ." She looked very thoughtful for a while. "I'd look into my ex-husband, too, and his fiancé. Definitely his fiancé, she cannot be trusted, that one. I took half his money in the divorce and I know they're not happy about it."

"Mom. I'm sure it's not Dad." I looked at the policeman and shook my head, panic rising inside me. "It can't be my dad. He lives in Joburg. It's not him," I assured them.

Okay, in retrospect, this had been a *very* bad idea. But I hadn't been thinking straight. Last night I'd just lost control; the bottle lid had popped open and everything had burst out.

"It's probably the Cape Town Bansky," one of the policemen offered.

"Why do you say that?" my mom asked.

"They struck again last night at a museum. They like to make political and social statements, perhaps they're protesting the billboard. I know some of the residents didn't like it when it went up, said it detracted from the natural beauty of the environment. There was even a petition signed to get it taken down. So maybe it's that."

"Well, whoever it is, I won't stop until I bring them down," my mom said. Her voice had taken on a low, ominous tone now.

I rushed upstairs and went to the online *Cape Times*. And there it was. Everywhere. Natasha's face was smeared across every social media page there was.

"*Did Cape Town's Banksy strike twice last night?*" I read one of the headlines out loud and adrenaline poured into my veins, making my heart beat faster. I took a deep breath and continued, skimming over a few sentences until I came to the important bits.

> *Cape Town's very own Banksy chose to bring atten-*
> *tion to a missing girl last night. Natasha Lewis was*
> *taken from outside her home six months ago and is*
> *still missing. Her family became frustrated by the lack*
> *of progress on the case and took it upon themselves to*
> *put up missing posters, but didn't get any new leads.*
> *They said that since this morning, the help line has*
> *been ringing nonstop with people offering to assist in*
> *the search, and a few people have even provided new*
> *leads for the police to follow. Her parents are grateful to*
> *the artist who chose to highlight their daughter's plight,*
> *but this time the city of Cape Town is hitting back. A*
> *police spokesperson said that they would make it their*
> *priority to find whoever did this, because this time the*
> *artwork was done on a national heritage site, the Iziko*

South African Museum. They have also said they will
be painting over the mural even though various activist
groups, including Women's Voices, a group dedicated to
bringing attention to gender-based violence, have said
that they will do whatever it takes to stop them. Their
leader, Lodi Mbeki, said that they applaud whoever
the artist was. And a few kilometers away in Clifton,
a huge billboard for Palm Luxury Realty was also
painted over. The billboard caused some controversy
when it was put up on the picturesque street, blocking
the view. Residents even signed a petition to have it
removed. Could Cape Town's Banksy be concurring?
The cost to advertise on the billboard is fifty thousand
rand, and the latest advertiser, Barbara Palmer, can't
be happy . . .

There was more, but I stopped. I was officially in serious trouble. I carried on flicking through social media—Natasha's and Rose's faces dominated, along with small pictures of my mother's billboard here and there.

My phone beeped and I looked down at it.

VICKI: Seems like Cape Town's Banksy struck twice last night. Are you okay?

LORI: Shit. I don't know. My mom has called the cops. They're here at the house and apparently I painted a heritage site!!!!

VICKI: I think you should probably hang up your spray paints for a little while until this blows over

LORI: I will! I will!

VICKI: I had a cancellation tomorrow at two, do you want to take it?

LORI: Okay. See you then

VICKI: Take care of yourself. And for what it's worth . . . I think it's bloody cool what you're doing

I sat in my room for a while, and stared out my window at the sea. I felt very out of my depths here; I'd never done anything like this before. I'd always been a good girl. Never a rebel. And now look at me, literally wanted by the police.

41

"So you kissed him and then ran away?" Vicki asked, crossing her legs in the chair. She was wearing a giant purple sun hat today, and we were sitting by her pool.

"Yeah," I replied.

"And do you know why you ran?" she asked.

"I think it was because of what Amber said to me." I ran my fingers around the hem of my dress nervously.

"The reason you ran had nothing to do with what Amber said to you and everything to do with what you say to yourself."

I leaned back in my chair. "Are we back to my inner bitchy bully?"

"Until you learn to silence her, you're going to run away from all the good things you deserve."

"What do you mean?"

"Lori, your fears and insecurities and what you think about yourself, those things are all sabotaging you, and if you don't learn to silence those voices, you're never going to have the things in life that you deserve."

"Okay, be direct, won't you."

"It's true. You never finished that painting for Blackwell properly because you were too afraid to paint your body as you saw it."

"Wait, are you saying that I sabotaged my chance of getting in?" I sat up in my chair and glared at her.

"I'm just saying that your fears are stopping you from having the things in life that you want and deserve."

"So you're saying I deserve Jake? That someone like me deserves *him*?"

"Why not?"

I shook my head. "You don't get it. You're not my age. You don't understand how the world works these days. It's easy for you to say that, when you're sitting over there."

She pulled her hat off and put it on the table in front of her. "Tell me how your world works."

I sighed. "The girl like me, the fat girl, is only good for a few things. She's either the best friend who's really easy to talk to, the funny girl who makes everyone laugh, the sassy fat girl, or the weird fat girl . . . she is those things—and those are supporting roles, by the way. They're not leading roles. They're not the leading roles in the big Hollywood rom-coms. *No!* We don't get to be stars in our own rom-coms, we don't get *that guy*. We don't get Jake Jones-Evans—star water-polo player, hottest guy at school— unless we're in the pages of some unrealistic YA book that totally throws social conventions out the window and sets itself in this totally made-up world where fat girls win and the guy looks past all her cellulite and sees the girl inside. We don't get that."

"And yet last night you were kissing *that guy* under a sprinkler," she said, eyeballing me. "Maybe this world you're referring to is not as unrealistic as you think. Maybe your view on the world is actually the outdated one, fueled by your own faulty beliefs about yourself. You're still living in a world where plus-sized models have never looked hot on Instagram and Lizzo never took to the stage."

"The kissing was an accident!" I said.

"There're no such things as accidents," she replied.

"Now you sound like Xander Orange," I said.

"Maybe he's right about that one."

"Fine, then it was this weird thing that happened because we were caught up in a moment and there was fake rain and running and painting and we thought we were going to get caught, but we didn't so there was relief and excitement and, and, and . . . *and*!" I huffed loudly and folded my arms. "Just and."

"And?" she probed.

"Yes, and!"

"And what?"

"And have I told you how much I hate the body positivity movement on Instagram." I sat straight up now.

"Why?" she asked.

"Well, it's just one more way to make the rest of us feel crappy about ourselves. Because if you're not totally happy with your curves and embracing them and posting pictures of yourself in bikinis, then there's something wrong with you. It's like, if you're fat these days, you have to be positive and happy about it. You have to be okay to show it off to the world. There's no middle ground. What if I don't want to be fat? Am I then betraying my kind, who are all waving the flag against fat shaming and being happy with who they are? Maybe I'm not happy with who I am."

"And maybe that has nothing to do with being fat?" she said.

"Huh?" I looked at her and blinked.

"Do you think if you were thin you would be happy with yourself?"

"Uh . . . *yes*!" I said.

She shook her head. "I don't think you would. I think you would still find something to criticize, and still find a way of putting yourself down."

I shook my head and then tears welled up. "No, I don't think so. I think I would be happy if I was skinny because then all the bad things wouldn't have happened to me."

"Tell me about the bad things." Vicki leaned in closer and locked eyes with me.

"His name was Bradley Marcello." I spat the words out quickly. "We were twelve and I had such a huge crush on him. I'd had a crush for two years. And then one night, at Libby and Rachel's party—the most popular girls at school—they told me that Bradley wanted to play seven minutes in heaven. You know the game where you go into a closet with someone you like and do whatever?" I looked at her and she nodded. "I was naïve and stupid and an idiot to go, because of course they locked me in the closet. There was no Bradley. Just me, alone and scared in the dark cupboard for what felt like hours."

She waited for a while and let me cry. They were familiar tears, I'd cried them many times before. And when the last of them was out, she passed me a handful of tissues. I dabbed my face. "Was that when the panic attacks started?" she asked.

I nodded. "I think it started building then, but they really started after the pool." I took a deep breath. It was jagged and jerky and hurt my ribs. "When they pushed me in and then held my head underwater. Why are people so disgusted by fat? Why do they literally want to drown you because you weigh more? Is it so gross and distasteful, like that crack in the pavement?"

"And look what you did to that crack. You made it beautiful."

I turned and looked up at the mountain—this defining feature that seemed to be intrinsic to Cape Town in every way.

"He touched my waist," I suddenly said.

"Who?"

"Jake. He touched my waist, and no one has ever touched me there, *like that*. I—I . . . didn't want him to feel it. Because it's . . ." I looked away from the mountain—looking at it was irritating for some reason. It seemed to be looking down at me expectantly now. "What if he'll want to do more than touch my waist?" I looked over at her now.

"I'm sure he will," she said. "He's an eighteen-year-old guy. I'm sure he wants to do a lot more than touch your waist." She shot me a very penetrating stare. "And I'm sure you do too."

"I've never thought of myself in that way," I whispered.

"As desirable?"

"Mmm-hmmm," I mumbled.

There was a silence again; the breeze blew and made the surface of the pool ripple.

"This is a complicated and exciting time for you, Lori," she finally said.

I sat up and turned to her. "Is that seriously what you're going to say to me now? Complicated and exciting?"

"Well, it is. You're coming into your own. You're finding your voice in this art that is so powerful, it's got the whole city's attention. You're discovering new things about yourself, making new friends, and entering into a romantic relationship for the first time. You were thrown out of your comfort zone when you came here and guess what, this was probably the best thing that could have ever happened to you."

"Things with my mom and dad have never been worse, though," I quickly said. "So how can this move be the best thing?"

"Sometimes things have to hit rock bottom before they get better."

"I think finding your mom in a hot tub with your school counselor is pretty much rock bloody bottom, not to mention finding out your dad is marrying a woman who could be your sister."

"Homework." She stood up and clapped her hands together.

"What about it?" I asked.

"How's your list?"

"It's okay, I guess."

She eyed me suspiciously. I didn't think my list had been going that well, to be honest. I'd crossed and uncrossed so many things that I no longer knew what was even written there anymore.

"Well, now you have new homework," she said. "I want you to stand in front of your mirror naked and look at yourself."

"*What?*" I almost choked on a fleck of spit as it shot down the back of my throat. "Can't I just do the list?"

She shook her head. "Start small, in your underwear maybe. And look at yourself. Really look. Look at everything. Get to know it. Maybe you'll surprise yourself and find something you like?"

"And if I don't?"

"Then you're going to learn to like the parts you dislike.

Because if you don't learn to like them and become comfortable with them, no one will be able to put their hands on your waist without you running away."

I folded my arms and looked at her. "Are you sex therapizing me now?"

She raised her eyebrows at me. "Nothing gets past you, ne."

I sighed. "I haven't seen myself naked in . . . a while."

"Well, I think it's time to meet that part of yourself again."

"You know this is completely weird and lame and is probably something that I would find recommended in some hashtag self-help book."

"Maybe it's in the self-help books for a reason."

I rolled my eyes; no way I was doing this week's homework. I turned when I heard a noise behind us, and that was when I noticed the man in the navy suit. He stood there looking very 007-ish, if I do say so myself. He was hot. Older, but totally hot.

"Sorry, I didn't mean to disturb." He looked at me apologetically for a moment and then looked over at Vicki. "Sorry, I thought your session today was canceled, or I would never have disturbed you."

I shook my head. "It's okay." *Who was he?*

"It was canceled, and then filled again. Sorry, I forgot to tell you," Vicki said, looking over her shoulder at this man.

He gave me a killer smile and then mouthed another sorry my way. He walked up to Vicki and then to my surprise, leaned down and planted a kiss on her forehead.

"I'm leaving now. I'll probably be back at ten," he said so sweetly and lovingly.

She smiled up at him. "Hurry home," she said.

He gave me a small wave before he walked away. I stared after him in shock. I looked back at Vicki only when she cleared her throat and put her big hat back on.

"Mmm-hmm," she said. "See, we fat girls do get the hot guy too. Sometimes we do actually get to be the stars in our own Hollywood rom-coms." And with that, she put her glasses back on her face and lay back in her lounger, smiling. I watched her for a bit.

"You see, Lori, what you have to realize is that these hetero-normative beauty standards that we all hold ourselves up to are total crap! They've been forced on us by magazines and catwalks and the beauty industry. And women everywhere are finally fighting back, taking to the stage and Instagram and showing the world that we can be hot too. Besides, beauty often has very little to do with outward appearances. Take an artist like Picasso—he certainly wasn't painting what would be called beautiful. Francis Bacon, Frida Kahlo, the list goes on. But how do you look at those paintings? As great works of art. As things that contain beauty. The concept of beauty, and what others find beautiful, is complicated and layered. It's not as simple as a flat stomach and a perfect face. Some find great beauty in a person's laugh, in their mind . . . bloody hell, some people like feet. And the sooner you realize that, the better. I had to learn to measure my self-worth and beauty by a different yardstick—I know I'm no great beauty, but I also know that the other qualities I possess make me hot as hell! And someone, one day, maybe sooner than you think, is going to look at you and think you are the most beautiful woman in the world, just like someone looks at me like that." She turned to me and pulled her glasses down her nose and looked at me over them. "See, I really do know how the world works."

42

The next week went by in this strange, awkward daze. I felt like I was trying to walk on eggshells, which if you think about it, is pretty ridiculous for someone my size. Because those things would just turn to dust under my feet. My mom and I hadn't spoken, Jake and I hadn't really spoken, and I felt like I was going batty. Vicki's words had been tormenting me too. During another session she'd pointed out how my self-worth had become so entwined in the numbers on the scale. And for as long as I did that, I would be letting the bullies win, because I was still bullying myself. Until I learned to measure my self-worth by other means, I would be stuck in this cycle of self-sabotage, pushing away the things I really wanted and deserved—like Jake, and like wearing a beautiful dress.

We also talked about my panic attacks and I was given more homework: tackling those irrational fears around my anxiety. Like when I'm sure I'm going to die and have a stroke because my heart is beating so fast, or when I'm sure I'll drown in the air. She taught me some breathing techniques for when the panic attacks hit, and we practiced good self-talk and focused on the things I liked about myself. We talked a lot about the dress that Thembi was making me, and how I needed to see myself in a different light, and that maybe this was an opportunity to do so. We spoke a lot about Jake, not necessarily just him, but guys like him, and how it was ridiculous for me to think that I would never have sex and be loved at my size. That was impossible, she said. She made me read articles, and research and arm myself with knowledge that I'd never had before. Now I'm not saying I was all cured and #bodypostivity vibes were flowing out of my pores, and I'm not saying I thought I deserved to be kissed by someone like Jake yet; I was far from that. Very far. And I still hadn't managed to stand in front of the mirror yet either.

And then on Thursday, Xander called me into his office again. I went more reluctantly this time.

"Come in," he called as I knocked on the door.

He wasn't pumping weights and drinking H_2O this time. He also wasn't smiling as much and didn't look as orange, but maybe that was my imagination.

"Please, sit, Lori." His voice was more somber and therapisty this time. Like he was trying to overcompensate for something. Not hard to guess what. It might have had something to do with me catching him in the hot tub with my mom. I wonder if I'd caught them precoital or post? I wasn't actually sure what was worse.

"I wanted to circle round and touch base with you regarding the other night," he said.

I instantly cringed at the "touch base" thing, and I could see he knew he'd chosen the wrong words.

He cleared his throat. "Debrief. I want to debrief."

I rolled my eyes at these buzzwords he was using. "Okay."

He looked away, as if he couldn't hold my gaze. "What happened with your mother the other night . . ." He tapered off and I waited for him to speak.

"Yeees." I leaned in.

"I would never have considered allowing anything to happen if I'd known that you were her daughter. My priorities are always, *always*, to my students and their well-being." He looked up at me and forced a smile. "Nothing is more important than the happiness of my students. And I would never want to do anything to jeopardize that. I always strive to put their needs first, and do whatever I can to help them, and I feel like I failed you, and . . ." He paused, ran his hand through his hair, looking genuinely tormented, and I was thrown. "I'm sorry."

I stared at him as he fiddled with his fingers, looking so upset by this ordeal that I actually believed what he was saying to me. In his strange way—his strange, sharky, cool beans kind of way—he really cared for the students here at BWH. With his short-handed, clichéd, two cents–worth therapy and big white teeth.

"And I want you to know that it's over between your mother and me. . . . She's a remarkable woman, though, your mother," he said softly. "Very inspiring." He gave me a small smile and I forced one back at him. "So . . ." He clapped his hands together and I flinched. "Is it forgiven?" he asked.

I nodded. Just because I wanted to get this over and done with. "Sure."

"Good. Chapter nine in my book is all about forgiveness. Forgiving your enemies, forgiving yourself."

"I'll make sure I read it then." I didn't mean that, though. I walked out of his office and breathed a sigh of relief, but it was short-lived when I found Jake standing there, waiting for me.

"I heard them call your name over the intercom," he said. "We haven't really had a chance to talk since, so . . . can we?"

"Won't you be missing class?"

"I have a free period now, so it seems we're both free."

"Okay." We walked down the passage, much like we had at the park the other night, which seemed so long ago now. No one said a word, although there were so many words to say. It was as if the whole passage we were walking down was filled with these massive, invisible words that were just waiting to be spoken. And finally Jake did.

"Did I . . . did I screw it all up?" he asked.

I turned and looked at him. "No."

"It feels like I did. The kiss messed it all up." He was looking at me in a way that made me want to kiss him all over again. I wanted to tell him that I had actually messed it up—well, all those bullies in my head had.

"No, you didn't mess it up," I said again.

"You sure?"

I forced a smile at him. It was so damn hard. "No. You didn't."

He exhaled an audible breath, as if he'd been holding it. "Great! So we can move past this and be friends again? I really, really like our friendship. I've never met anyone like you, and anyone I can talk to like I talk to you, and I would hate to lose that. Seriously."

"It's already been moved past. It's forgotten." *Crap.* That wasn't really what I wanted to say. What I really wanted to say was, Let's *not* move on. Let's never move on from that moment, ever. Let's kiss again. And let's not stop once we start.

"Great! Friends!" His face lit up and it was like a hot dagger in my gut.

I didn't want to be friends. And how could we? How could we go back to the way things were, now that we'd kissed? We carried on walking together, and even though he looked a lot happier and lighter, I was not.

"Are you going to the vigil tonight?" he asked.

"What vigil?"

"Haven't you heard about it? For Natasha. Tonight at seven they're holding a candlelight vigil for her, and also to stop the repainting of the wall."

"Really?"

"Yes."

I turned and started walking again. "I don't know," I said quickly. "I might have to look after Zac."

"Me neither, I have this water polo dinner thing." We walked in silence to the end of the corridor and then Jake looked at his phone.

"Free period almost over."

"Sure. Cool."

"Friends still?" he asked. "I'm just checking again."

"Friends." I agreed, even though, right now, *friends* felt like the ultimate *F* word.

"Great, because you're a good friend, Lori."

Things I Like about Myself by Lori Palmer
I'm a good sister.
I'm a real artist (despite what Blackwell says!).
~~I, Lori Palmer, am officially good with parents!~~
I have a voice. There is power in my art.
~~I am brave!~~
I am a great kisser!
I'm a good friend (even if I don't really want to be just a friend).

43

It looked like half of Cape Town had turned up. Press and media trucks lined the small street and people holding posters walked in unison up the road chanting, "Find Me. Find Me."

I stared at the scene playing out in front of me. I had done this. It had started with the crack, and then Rose, and now this. And perhaps it hadn't started quite as consciously as it now was. But it had started, and now it couldn't be stopped. This was the most significant thing I'd ever done in my seventeen years on the planet. And prior to today, I'd had no idea that I was even capable of doing something like this.

Candles had been lit and placed on the ground around Natasha's painting. People bowed their heads in silent prayer, and some were walking up to the wall and laying flowers below it. To my left, a City of Cape Town truck was parked, and three men with paintbrushes stood with unopened cans of white paint at their feet. A ring of people holding hands had formed around them, stopping them from approaching the wall. The feeling in the air was palpable. It tingled and pulsed with a sense of greatness and importance . . . and uncertainty. This moment was balancing on a precipice, and anything could tip it over, one way or the other.

And then someone broke through the crowd and walked up to a box that had been placed in front of the wall. She was young, Black, cool-looking, and was wearing a Dora the Explorer T-shirt with Natasha's face on it. The face *I* had painted. She climbed onto the box and everyone applauded. She introduced herself and talked about the epidemic of gender-based violence ripping the country apart. I pushed my way through the tightly packed crowd, bustling past shoulders and arms and signs held in the air.

Finally, I got to the front. I wanted to see the woman who was talking more clearly. I stopped listening to her words at some stage, though—I didn't need to. I could see what she was saying, her hands raised in the air, fists clenching, the vein bulging in her forehead as she spat her words out at volume. She was angry. And so was everyone else. I felt caught up in this massive thing—I could feel it expanding around me, like the universe must have done at the moment of the big bang. Starting at a singularity, an infinite tiny point, and then suddenly space and time were rushing out of that point, building atoms and grains of dust and soon moons and planets and solar systems and entire galaxies, a universe. That's how big this felt.

And then the woman on the stage was crying as two people were called up. They were Natasha's parents, and soon there wasn't a dry eye around. Not even mine. I was also crying. Softly at first, but then harder and harder until I was falling into the arms of total strangers as we hugged and linked hands, bound together by this one common thing. As I stood there, my arm around the woman next to me, my hand slipped into the person's to my right, and I felt a part of something and I couldn't help but think, I had helped do this.

Me!

Things I Like about Myself by Lori Palmer
I'm a good sister.
I'm a real artist (despite what Blackwell says!).
I, Lori Palmer, am officially good with parents!
I have a voice. There is power in my art.
I am brave!
I am a great kisser!
I'm a good friend (even if I don't really want to be just a friend).
My voice can start a movement!

44

Thembi called the next day to say my dress was ready.

I arrived at her house and she greeted me excitedly. "My parents are out, so we have the whole house to ourselves." There was such a sense of relief in her voice, I could relate.

"Have they found the person who trashed your mom's billboard yet?" she asked as we walked up the stairs.

"No. Shame," I said, trying to make that sound genuine.

"I wish I knew who did it though, I'd be rich."

"Why?"

"Haven't you seen the reward she put out?"

"No?"

"It's on her YouTube channel, and she posted it on Facebook."

My stomach lurched. I pulled my phone out and went to her

business page and there it was, my mother talking to the camera offering up a R10, 000 reward for information leading to the capture of the scandalous vandal.

"Crap," I whispered under my breath as we reached Thembi's room. I'd hoped it would have blown over. But I should have known better. My mom was like a pit bull when she got an idea into her head.

Thembi looked at me excitedly. "Are you ready?"

I looked at the dress stand in front of me. It was draped in white cloth and I couldn't see a thing.

"I guess," I said softly, not so sure I was.

"You're going to look amazing in it," she announced, and then in one swift movement she pulled the sheet off and revealed the dress.

"So I know I said something shorter would be better, but I decided to make it long, but look here." She pulled the bottom of the dress. "I've put a really high slit in it, so when you walk it will open up and give this sense of movement, so it's like this long/short hybrid."

"The neckline is so . . . low?" I looked at the plunging V-neck; it seemed to plunge down forever.

"You have such great boobs, though, it's going to make them look amazing."

"And it looks really tight in the middle."

"Yes. Cinched and ruched waist, it's going to give you an hourglass figure. And of course, to accentuate that even more, I did this beadwork under the bust, to draw your eye in, not that it needs much drawing. Capped lace sleeves, I know you said you didn't like your shoulders, so I thought this would be flattering but not make the dress feel too old and claustrophobic."

I stared at it. It was utterly beautiful, the way the light glinted off the swirl of green beads that curled around themselves and disappeared into the green fabric as if they were part of it. It reminded me of van Gogh's *Green Wheat Field*; the energetic, green brushstrokes combining together to create a sense of movement, as if the painting was alive, but . . . I could *never* wear something like this.

"You don't like it?" Thembi asked, sounding deflated.

"*No*. It's not that, I . . ." Tears worked their way up my throat. "I've never worn anything like it before. I've never thought I could wear anything like this, I—I'm not sure it will look good on me." I couldn't fight the avalanche of emotions rushing over and out of me right now.

"Babe." I felt a hand on my arm. "Do not insult me. Trust me, I know what looks good on people and what doesn't. You think I would put you in something that didn't look good?"

"No." I turned and looked at her.

"You're going to look amazing in this, especially after I've done your makeup for the photo shoot. And don't worry, I did a makeup and hair course too. I thought I would probably need to know those things while I was starting out as a junior designer, but when I get more established, I'm sure I'll have hair and makeup people flocking to work with me."

"Sorry, photo shoot?"

"For my portfolio. I have to send them the sketches of the dress, a mood board, and then also shoot the dress."

"Me? You want me to be in a photo shoot?"

She looked at me for a moment or two, then her face dropped. "No one will ever see the pics, I promise. Just me and the lecturer."

I looked over at the dress and shook my head a little. "I don't think I can. I don't think I—I . . . it's . . . I can't." I looked over at Thembi and then shook my head so hard that my neck felt like it was going to break. "I'm so sorry, I know you've worked so hard on it but I just . . . I can't." And then I turned and ran from her house.

Things I Like about Myself by Lori Palmer
I'm a good sister.
I'm a real artist (despite what Blackwell says!).
~~I, Lori Palmer, am officially good with parents!~~
I have a voice. There is power in my art.
~~I am brave!~~
I am a great kisser!
I'm a good friend (even if I don't really want to be just a friend).
My voice can start a movement!

45

I'd turned my phone off and had collapsed on my bed. I didn't want Thembi to call me. I felt like I'd let her down. . . . *Or maybe you let yourself down?* a soft voice whispered in my ear.

"Crap!" I buried my face in my pillow. Now Vicki's voice had also joined the peanut gallery in my head. As if the cacophony couldn't get any bigger. I kicked my legs a few times and then screamed into my pillow, because I wasn't sure I knew what I was feeling. The sound of my door opening made me turn. It was Zac.

"What's wrong?" he asked, looking perturbed.

"Nothing." I wiped my face and tried to flatten my hair.

"You look funny," he stated.

"Really?" I must be a sight if Zac had noticed.

"Your face looks red and ugly. You don't look pretty anymore."

"What?" I asked, standing up off my bed.

"You always look pretty. Now you look ugly. I don't like it." He folded his arms across his chest.

"You think I'm pretty?" I was totally taken aback by this.

"I think you are the third prettiest girl in the world," he stated matter of factly.

"Oh. Who are number one and two?"

"Well, Mom and Lisa of course," he said.

"Did I used to be number two before Lisa came along?" I asked, taking a step closer to him.

"Yes."

"You think I'm pretty," I repeated.

"But not when your eyes are red like that."

And this time I didn't hold back, I walked straight up to him and pulled him into a hug. "Come here." I squeezed him hard and he tried to pull away from me. "I'm not letting you go this time," I said, squishing a massive kiss on his cheek. He wiggled even more and I knew he was reaching absolute capacity now, so I let him go and he ran from my room. I smiled, pleased that I'd managed to steal a kiss and a hug.

"I'm the third prettiest girl in the world," I whispered, and then closed and locked my bedroom door. I walked over to the mirror and looked at my reflection. It stared back at me with that same cold, relentless look it had a few weeks ago. But this time, I wasn't going to take crap from it.

But . . . what if I was going to hate the person I was about to meet? What if all I could see were the flaws? I closed my eyes and took a deep breath. And when I finally opened them again, I locked eyes with the person staring back at me. We gave each other a firm and determined nod. We were in this together, me and my reflection. We could do this!

I pulled my T-shirt off and dropped it to the floor, and then looked at the torso in front of me. The first thing I noticed was the color. I was pale, and my broad shoulders and chest were covered in freckles that I'd never really liked before. I focused all my attention on the freckles before looking anywhere else. I stared so long and so hard at them that they seemed to transform in front of my eyes and suddenly, they didn't look like freckles anymore.

I moved closer to the mirror and lifted my finger to one of the freckles and joined the dots, like joining the stars in the constellations. And when I was finished, I shook my head in utter disbelief.

I walked over to my makeup bag and pulled out a red lip liner, and then carefully lowered it to the first freckle and traced the dots again. This time I left a trail of red behind, and when I was done, there it was. As clear and perfect as one of my paintings: *a heart.*

The freckles on my chest made a perfect heart shape, just above my left breast. I looked at it and smiled. I had no idea that under all those things I usually hated, something like this would have appeared.

I turned sideways and looked at my arm and my eye immediately sought out another image. I lifted the red lip liner again and followed the dots. This time a star appeared, a little wonky, some arms longer than the others, but it was a star. I turned the other way, looked at my other arm and shoulders, and immediately saw more images. I traced them excitedly; I'd uncovered a hidden world that I never knew existed until now. I pulled my pants off and looked at my legs. On my upper thigh, a sickle moon. On my other thigh, a flower.

JO WATSON

I stopped tracing the images and met the mirror's gaze once more. This time, it wasn't looking back at me like it usually was. A strange feeling washed over me as I dragged my eye from one red drawing to the next. I didn't see the flab and stretch marks and cellulite this time. I saw something else entirely. I saw a work of art reflected back at me. Sure, not a perfect work of art, but a work of art nonetheless. A work in progress maybe? I looked at the fingerprint patchwork of drawings on my skin—*they were all mine.* No one in the world had this pattern of lines and dots and curves.

The white stretch marks on my hips looked like a tiger's stripes in the moonlight, and I swear, the cellulite on my upper thighs reminded me of waves crashing against the shore. I was seeing myself through the eyes of an artist now. Like Pierneef and the mountain, like Turner and the sea, like Warhol and the soup can, and all the other great artists who chose to look at life through a different set of lenses. Who sought out and found beauty in things that no one else did. And right now, I was seeing that beauty in myself. Reflected back at me, but this time, *not* seeing its faults. I swept my eyes over my body and then turned slowly, looking at every last part of me. This was *my* body. It was unique, and if bodies like mine didn't exist, everyone would look the same. Every artwork in the world would look identical; nothing would stand out anymore. Nothing would be different. And the world would be as boring as hell.

> *Things I Like about Myself by Lori Palmer*
> *I'm a good sister.*
> *I'm a real artist (despite what Blackwell says!).*
> ~~*I, Lori Palmer, am officially good with parents!*~~

I have a voice. There is power in my art.

~~I am brave!~~

I am a great kisser!

I'm a good friend (even if I don't really want to be just a friend).

My voice can start a movement!

My body is a work of art!

46

I rang the doorbell frantically until Thembi opened the door.

"I'm ready! I can do this!" I pushed past her and rushed straight up to her room, where I took up a position in the middle of the floor. I filled the entire space with my newfound confidence, until it grew so big that it pressed into the walls around me.

I was careful not to let go of it, though—I knew it might waver. This feeling might be short-lived and soon slip through my fingers like grains of sand. But while I had a firm grasp on it, I was going to use it. Wield it like the powerful weapon it was.

Thembi put her hands on her hips and smiled at me. "I never doubted it for a second." And then, we started.

An hour later I stood face-to-face once more with another

mirror, although this time, it was draped in a white sheet. My hair and makeup had been done, and I was in the dress.

"Wait, here. I bought you something I thought would go with the dress." She rushed off and returned with a box. "Your size, right?"

I stared down at the box she'd just placed in my hands. "Did you buy these for me?"

"It's my way of saying thanks for letting me do this, I really needed it."

"These are . . . they're, *wow*, gorgeous. But I've never worn high heels."

"You've *what*?" The shock on her face was comical.

I laughed. "You sound just like my friends."

"Well, they're right! How the hell have you never worn high heels?"

I shrugged. "You know . . ."

"Cos big gals can't wear high heels. Because Ashley Graham is walking around in flats all day. And what about Tess Holliday? Shuffling about in slippers?"

"Well, they're, like, you know. Fashionable, stylish, gorgeous," I said.

"Excuse me . . ." she whipped the cloth off the mirror, "and you're not?"

"Oh my God!" I did a double take. I only thought those happened in cartoons, but they didn't. My head snapped back and forth as I stared at a version of myself that I'd never seen before. This was a Cinderella moment right here, and I knew how clichéd it was on some level, but I didn't care. Right now, I was going to revel in it. Soak it all in like a sponge. "I can't believe it's me."

"Don't cry! You'll ruin your makeup." Thembi fanned my eyes as they started tearing up.

"Thank you," I said.

"For what?"

"For making me look like this."

"I didn't make you anything. It was always there, the genius designer in me just knew how to bring it out."

I turned and smiled at her. She smiled back at me, and suddenly I felt like I could tell her.

"I was actually trying on that dress in the shop for the dance," I confessed.

"Why did you say it was your dad's wedding?"

"I don't know. I guess I felt like you would think who the hell is going to ask her to the summer dance? I thought you'd laugh or something. Tell the others at school."

"I'd never do that. Besides, I know what it's like," she said.

"What what's like?"

"Being bullied."

"How?"

"When I was younger, people used to tease me because I was adopted. This one kid at school told me my parents didn't really love me."

"What a prick!"

She shrugged. "I kicked his sandcastle down in the sandpit. I got even. So are you . . . ?"

"Am I what?"

"Going to the dance?"

I shook my head. "No. I'm not."

"Why don't you come with me?" she asked in her usual matter-of-fact tone.

"Aren't you going with your boyfriend?"

"Nah. I dumped him. He's been cheating."

"Seriously? What a dick."

"I know! Total asshole, but I made myself a killer dress and I look amazing in it, so I have to go." She smiled at me.

"I don't know," I replied.

"Stop saying you don't know. We'll go together and *everyone* will stare at us as we walk in. There will be whispers and gossip because everyone will wonder if we're an item, and everyone will be talking about it until the end of the year. At least we'll give them something interesting to talk about, instead of all their usual crap! And we'll look so gorgeous that everyone will be jealous and then everyone will want original Thembikiles and I'll say, 'Wait in line.'"

I looked at myself in the mirror, and nodded. "Okay."

"Great, let's do this photo shoot!" Thembi turned and headed for the door.

"Give me a moment. There's something I need to do."

She gave me a little look, as if she understood what I meant and exited the room. I bent down, kicked my shoes off, and then slowly, carefully, resting one hand on the edge of her desk, climbed into the high heels. I wobbled a few times, flapped my arms to stop myself from falling, but when I finally felt steadier, I turned back to the mirror.

I looked at the shoes on my feet first, followed their curves all the way to my ankles, traced the lines of my legs, up to the slit in the dress—I'd never worn anything that showed this much leg—I dragged my eyes higher, over the plush fabric, observing how it clung to my body like a second skin, how it clung to my hips and then tapered into my waist. The beads glinted at me, accentuating my breasts, which looked—*wow!* I had the best breasts I'd ever seen!

My eyes trailed from my breasts to my neck and then my face. I inhaled sharply. I had cheekbones and long lashes and powder that made me shimmer. Red lips, big and voluptuous and so kissable, if I did say so myself. My hair was up. Messy, red, curly tendrils falling down casually. As if I had put no effort into this look. As if I looked this good when I woke up.

This was really me.

Me.

I pulled my phone out and slowly, nervously took a picture of myself.

With shaking hands, I went to Instagram and chose a filter. This time I wouldn't use black and white. This time it would be in full color. Because I was color. I was every single shade of an artist's palette. And for the first time in my life, I wanted the world to see me like this. I took a deep breath and was just about to post the picture when I stopped. I lowered my fingers to the keyboard and typed #bodypositive.

Things I Like about Myself by Lori Palmer
I'm a good sister.
I'm a real artist (despite what Blackwell says!).
~~I, Lori Palmer, am officially good with parents!~~
I have a voice. There is power in my art.
I am brave!
I am a great kisser!
I'm a good friend (even if I don't really want to be just a friend).
My voice can start a movement!
My body is a work of art!
I have great boobs. I mean . . . AHMAZING!
I am hot!

47

WhatsApp Group: How You Doin'???

ANDILE: OMG, how gorgeous is that photo of you?

LORI: Thanks

GUY: Serious, how amazing do you look?

LORI: Okay, brace yourselves . . . because you won't believe it

LORI: I am going to the dance 🙄

GUY: With JAKE?!?!

ANDILE: OMG!

LORI: No, not with him. With Thembi

LORI: Her boyfriend was cheating on her 😿

ANDILE: As they always do

GUY: Don't bring your crap into this Andile

LORI: What crap? What happened?

ANDILE: Well Mr. "I'm not gay" had another "I'm not gay" fling with Trevor

LORI: The saxophone player???

GUY: I am so tempted to say something about blowing a horn, but I won't!

LORI: Ha-hah! 😂 You just did!

ANDILE: Can we stop mocking my broken heart here and get back to the story please

LORI: Okay. Sorry. So Thembi broke up with the douche-bag, so we said we would go together

GUY: When is the dance?

LORI: This Friday

GUY: Interesting . . .

LORI: What?

GUY: Will Jake be there?

LORI: Probably

My phone beeped while I was texting.

LORI: Hang on, it's him

GUY: Ooooh

LORI: 🙄

JAKE: Hey

I checked Jake's message.

My heart fluttered and I felt an instant blush.

LORI: Hi

JAKE: Nice Insta post

LORI: Thanks

There was a lull in the conversation, and I watched the little typing dots start and stop over and over again. I held my breath, waiting for the message that didn't seem to come. And then when it did I felt disappointment.

JAKE: Did you see the pics from Natasha's vigil?

LORI: I was there

JAKE: You did that

JAKE: You made the whole city come together like that

LORI: You helped

JAKE: Barely . . . that was all you

LORI: Thanks

There was another lull and I could feel him wanting to say something, and me wanting to say something and neither of us saying anything and then . . .

JAKE: You look beautiful

JAKE: In your post

My heart thumped in my chest.

LORI: Thanks

JAKE: Is that for dance?

LORI: Um, sort of. I guess

JAKE: Sort of?

LORI: Well, I wasn't going to go, but Thembi broke up with her BF and so we're going together

JAKE: Oh

JAKE: So you have a date then?

LORI: Well, it's Thembi

JAKE: I thought you weren't going to go?

JAKE: I thought dances weren't your thing?

LORI: Well, I wasn't

JAKE: And now you are?

LORI: Yes

JAKE: With Thembi?

LORI: Well, yes

LORI: And you, are you going with Amber?

JAKE: NO

JAKE: What makes you think that?

LORI: You said it at Kirstenbosch

JAKE: I said she asked me. Not that I was going with her

LORI: Well, I mean, you can

JAKE: I know I can, maybe I don't want to go with her

LORI: You don't?

Another lull pushed its way into our conversation and I sat there shaking my head. What was happening? It felt like this conversation was sliding somewhere and I didn't know how to stop it. He seemed angry, the tone of his messages short and sharp. After a while he finally typed.

JAKE: I'll probably go on my own . . .

Dot, dot, dot. Again. *Crap!* I wished that somewhere out there was a guide to interpreting all these dots. What did they mean? So I did the only thing I could think of.

LORI: . . .

JAKE: ?

LORI: ?

JAKE: Huh? 🙄

LORI: Okay

I said it, although I didn't know what I was saying okay to.

JAKE: Okay?

LORI: Cool

LORI: I got to go. I'm on another chat

JAKE: Cool

LORI: Bye

I lowered my phone. That conversation had confused the hell out of me, and I felt like I needed someone to weigh in on it, so I took some screen grabs and sent them to the guys.

ANDILE: OMG, are you blind?

ANDILE: He was asking you to go with him to the dance

LORI: No he wasn't

ANDILE: Uh . . . yes he was

GUY: He was very clearly hinting. Not very well. But that's guys for you. They suck at hinting

LORI: I don't think so

LORI: Not after what happened

ANDILE: ?

LORI: We kind of kissed

ANDILE: What? Tell us

LORI: I don't know. It just happened . . .

LORI: And then I sort of ran away

GUY: Why?

LORI: IDK. IDK. I guess . . . I felt . . . IDK!

GUY: That's a lot of IDKs. Which leads me to believe you really like him?!

ANDILE: She obviously likes him

ANDILE: And now she needs to message him right back and ask him to the dance

LORI: I can't do that

GUY: Why, you're a hot, cool chick, asking a hot, cool dude to the dance—who you already kissed

LORI: IDK

GUY: Stop saying IDK

I put my phone down. I was confused. Hang on, had I just done that again? My inner insecurities screamed so loudly at me because I may have just turned down an invitation to the summer dance with Jake. *Was he even inviting me?* I reread our strange message exchange three times to see if I had missed something. But I still wasn't sure.

I took a deep breath and lowered my fingers to the phone. *I could ask him, though, right?* As friends, obviously. He could come with Thembi and me. Three friends going to a dance together. Platonic. I typed the message to him slowly, carefully choosing every single word. I read it over and over again, but just as I was about to press Send, I chickened out.

I sighed and lay back down on my bed. Clearly it was going to take more than drawing some shapes on my body and wearing a pretty dress to fix me. My confidence had waned again. I tried to grab it back, but the grains had left my fingers and were slipping away again. Why was this something that was so hard to hold on to? It was so hard to find, and when you had it, you'd think you would clutch onto it as if it was the most precious thing in the world.

48

The week sort of went by in this strange dance flurry. I hardly saw Jake, and when I did, things felt weird. I was worried that the kiss and that conversation had ruined everything between us, whatever that was anyway. Sometimes I thought I imagined all the moments of closeness with him, sometimes I didn't. But the longer we were apart, the harder it was to tell what was real and what wasn't, until I was just totally confused by it all.

My mom's reward was causing all sorts of weirdos to come forward and claim responsibility for the billboard, including one who claimed to be some kind of superhero—Cape Town's masked avenger. My dad had tried to call me several times but I didn't want to talk to him. And then suddenly, Friday was upon me and it was dance time. If you'd asked me just over a month ago whether I would actually be going to this thing, I would have said no. But so much had happened in the last month, it felt like I'd lived an entire year in this short time.

"You guys look nice," Zac said, sticking his head into my room, where Thembi and I were getting ready.

"I know." Thembi turned and looked at him.

"Are you going to be dancing? Because it's called a summer dance."

"Yes," I replied.

"You must drink lots of water," he said seriously.

"Don't worry, I will."

"I'll make sure she does," Thembi said to Zac. "Keeping hydrated is important, especially when you're as hot as us."

"Why are you hot? Do you have temperatures?"

I turned and smiled at him. "It's just an expression."

He scrunched his face up. "I hate expressions. They confuse me."

"Well, then we won't use them anymore." Thembi walked over to him. "They confuse me too. I don't know why people can't just say what they're thinking, right?"

"I think you have too much black stuff on your eyes." Zac pointed at Thembi's face before turning and walking away.

"Sorry, he's blunt," I said.

"I like it. I'm kind of blunt."

"Yup. You are."

"He's cool, and damn, he's right!" She leaned in and looked at her face closely in the mirror. "I went way too smoky." She started removing some of her eye shadow.

I laughed. I liked her. And I was glad I was going with her. Our relationship had started out as a transactional one, mainly from her side, really. She'd needed a mannequin to make a dress for, turned out I was the one she needed. But somewhere along the way, it had stopped feeling like that. We actually had so much in common: we both had a dysfunctional family, we were both artists, we both had big ambitions and dreams.

I didn't know where this was going, or whether it would grow beyond what we had now, but it felt good to have her in my life, in whatever capacity it was going to be.

The doorbell rang and I turned to Thembi. "Who could that be?" I walked downstairs and when I opened the door, tears overwhelmed me.

"Oh my God, what are you guys doing here?" We immediately fell into a group hug.

"We're taking you to the dance," they shouted at once. I ran my eyes over them. They looked dapper as hell in their suits, and Andile was wearing a bright-pink bow tie.

"How did you arrange this?"

"We have our contacts." Guy winked at me.

"What contacts?"

"You're here?" Thembi walked downstairs and I turned.

"Wait, how do you guys know each other?"

"Wow, you are even more gorgeous IRL!" Andile stepped forward.

"So are you guys," Thembi said after a little Miss Universe–style wave.

"Wait." I gestured. "What's going on here?"

"We found Thembi on Insta after we chatted and asked if we could take you guys to the dance. Thembi organized us tickets and here we are."

"And you flew here just for this?" I asked, choking back the tears now.

Guy and Andile wrapped their arms around me. "Of course," Guy said.

"Don't cry!" Thembi screeched from behind us. "Makeup!"

I pulled away, and Guy and Andile both started fanning my eyes frantically.

The four of us walked in together, in a single line, arm in arm. And it was as if our arrival had been announced on some PA system that I didn't even know existed, because as we walked in, everyone's heads turned and looked at us. Thembi turned to me.

"I've always wanted to make an entrance like this," she said with a massive smile across her face.

"Me too, babe," Andile said.

"Who hasn't!" Guy echoed the sentiment.

My eyes swept the room. The hall was completely transformed— it looked nothing like the place where I'd almost been dragged onto the stage just over a month ago. So much had happened since I'd gotten here. And in many ways, I, too, felt transformed. Maybe even more so than the hall. And that was saying a lot.

Purple velvet curtains were draped around the walls. On the stage, two huge thrones were set up against a green screen, presumably for photos. The rest of the hall was dotted with tables covered in gold and purple tablecloths; cutlery and crockery and shiny crystal glasses completed the opulent look. In the middle of all the tables was a dance floor illuminated with purple lights.

I felt an elbow in my ribs. It was Guy. "Where is he?"

"Who?" Thembi asked.

"Jake. The guy who asked her but she totally rejected."

"What? Jake asked you to the dance but you decided to come with me instead?" She looked at me with wide eyes.

"I don't know if he asked me exactly," I insisted.

Andile rolled his eyes. "Poor guy. You kiss him in the sprinklers and then leave him high and dry. Well not dry—*wet*, actually."

"You kissed him?" Thembi asked.

"Oh my God," I moaned. I really didn't want Thembi knowing all this. And certainly not right now.

"I love it," Thembi blurted out enthusiastically. "You're probably the first girl who has ever done that to him, and that makes you my hero. And Amber is going to hate you for it and that makes me love you even more."

"I thought you were friends with Amber?" I asked.

"Yeah, like a scorpion is friends with a frog."

We all turned and looked at her blankly.

"You know the story." She clicked her fingers. "Frog offers to take a scorpion across the river on its back, scorpion promises not to sting it. But does and they both drown, because *it's in his nature.*"

We all continued our blank stare and Thembi rolled her eyes. "Point is, Amber is one of those people who, given the opportunity, will sting you. And the sting seldom has anything to do with you, it's all about her. Putting others down makes her feel better about herself. It's actually quite sad. She makes people feel bad about themselves so she can feel better about herself. That's most bullies, though, isn't it?"

"And there are plenty of them," Andile said quietly, and I knew who he was thinking of. Everyone who'd teased and bullied him over the years for being a Black, gay, ballet dancer.

"Oooh! Oooh! Speaking of Amber . . . twelve o'clock," Thembi said and we all looked in the direction she was pointing.

Guy flashed her a look. "Seriously. Twelve o'clock. Are we in the army?"

Thembi flapped her hand. "Well, there. By the purple curtain."

Guy rolled his eyes. "They're all purple. What's she wearing?"

Thembi smiled. "Now that, I can do. The one in the cheap knockoff of the burgundy brocade dress that Meghan Markle wore on the red carpet, which really doesn't go with Amber's skin tone, since she has a bit of a pink undertone."

We all looked and there she was. Laughing, head thrown back in the air, gold locks tumbling down her back. And then she moved and a surprised breath escaped my lips.

"What?" Guy asked.

"Oh no," Thembi moaned. "Look away. Look away."

I tried to look away but couldn't.

"What's going on?" Andile asked.

"That's Jake," she whispered. Because it was Jake. Standing there while Amber laughed and flirted and flipped her hair, and when she reached out and touched him on the arm, a long lingering touch, I felt dizzy.

"He . . . he . . did go with her," I stuttered stupidly.

"Shit!" Guy said, grabbing my arm tightly.

I stood there frozen for a moment or two. I could feel the tension coming off the three next to me, as if they were all holding their breath to see what I was going to do. And then something miraculous happened. Vuyo came over to them, Amber slipped her arm through his, and they walked off together, leaving Jake standing there all *alone*.

"He didn't come with her," I whispered, and as if he'd heard me, his head tilted up to mine and our eyes locked across the room, *cerulean explosion*. He took a step forward and before I knew what was happening, he was walking across the room toward me. My feet moved, too, without me even consciously giving them permission to do so. We walked, getting closer and closer until we met in the middle of the dance floor.

"You look, you look—" He seemed to be struggling to get the words out as his eyes swept over me. "Beautiful."

I smiled at him.

"I thought you were coming with Thembi?" he said, looking over my shoulder.

"They're my *friends* from Joburg. They came up here to take us." I put a lot of emphasis on the word *friends*.

He smiled, as if pleased with my answer. "So . . . I've been thinking about—"

"Wait." I cut him off. "Before you say anything to me, there's something I need to say to you."

"You do?" he asked.

"I have so, so many somethings to say to you, actually." I sighed. "Soooo many."

"The floor is yours then, Lori," he said through a small chuckle.

I took a deep breath. "Okay. I'm a succulent," I said.

"A succulent?" he repeated, looking amused.

"What I mean is that once upon a time I was broken. I think I was broken a few times, actually. Had my leaves pulled off, my stem snapped and tossed away, maybe stepped on a bit, and there's this part of me that hasn't fully recovered from it yet, even though I go to therapy. I have these panic attacks and worry about things like having a stroke or drowning in air, and am so petrified of water that I haven't bathed in years . . ." I paused. "I mean, I shower, okay. I'm not, you know . . ."

"I know what you mean." Jake's voice was soft and I could see he was listening to every single word I was saying.

"But also, I think that there's this part of me that still sees me as this damaged, broken thing. And because I see myself like that, maybe I feel like I don't really deserve fixing. That maybe, I deserve to be like this and I think I've been pushing you away because of that feeling."

"Then don't push," Jake said emphatically.

I held my hand up. "Wait, there's more." I continued. "But thing is, I'm starting to grow little roots. They're really small and pink, but they're there, and they are reaching out for water and soil, and reaching for a new place to start growing. Because I want to start growing again. I deserve to start growing again, and in this really strange way, coming here to this place I thought I was going to hate has helped me. Meeting you and my new therapist and finding this voice through my art that I literally never knew I had, all that has made me the little propagating echeveria looking to put down roots."

His grin grew. "I literally have no idea what you said at the end there, but I kind of like it and I'm not sure why . . . kind of like those Grimes songs."

I smiled back at him. "I'm a bloody Grimes song!"

"You are. Brilliant and creative and once you start listening . . . you can't stop."

I felt that flutter in my stomach again, the one I felt only in the presence of Jake Jones-Evans.

"I think I know what you're trying to say, Anything But JustLori." He stepped even closer and the gap between us vanished.

"You do?"

"I think you're trying to say that you like me."

I bit my lip as the fluttering grew so big that my whole body felt like it was going to explode. I nodded. And then suddenly, I swear the heavens opened and I heard angels, because his hands slipped into mine. I looked down at them.

"I like you too. A lot," he said.

"You do? I mean . . ." I shrugged and maybe I grimaced. I didn't want that to be my reaction, but it was. "You do?"

"I don't think you see yourself like I see you."

"How do you see me?" I asked.

"I think you're beautiful. Funny. Kind. You're the most interesting person I've ever met."

"I am?" I asked, shaking my head a little. "I don't . . . I guess . . . I don't see myself like that."

"I know. And I say screw every single person in the world who made you doubt that. And especially fuck those kids who pushed you in the pool."

I bit my lip. I could feel those pesky tears that wanted to spring out and ruin my makeup. And then, the music changed. It slowed down, the lights changed, and . . .

"Want to dance?" Jake asked.

I looked around, feeling strange and self-conscious now. "Everyone is looking at us." They were probably all in shock, wondering what on earth was going on here. Why was the hottest guy in school asking someone like me to dance? They were probably wondering if they had been cast in a teen movie, the one where the once-ugly girl suddenly becomes hot just by taking her glasses off. But this wasn't a movie. This was real. And I was the star. *Barbie and Ken. Belle of the ball. All eyes on me . . .*

"Trust me," Jake whispered, "they're not looking at us. They're looking at *you*."

I glanced around again, anxiety bubbling up inside me as they all stared relentlessly, like the mirror had.

"Close your eyes," he whispered, slipping an arm around my back. "Forget them." He took my other arm and wrapped it around him. I closed my eyes and laid my head on his shoulder.

"I really, *really* like you, Lori," he whispered in my ear, his warm breath prickling against my skin and making it pebble.

"I . . . I . . . like you too," I said back to him.

I couldn't believe this was happening. In my mind a massive spotlight was now illuminating us. It was drawing even more attention to us, the kind of attention that, if I was totally honest with you, I'd wanted every single day for my entire life. This was a serious moment right here.

This was my moment. The moment that girls like me *never* got. The kind of moment that girls like me never think they deserve to get.

But I was getting it. *Right about . . . now.*

The slow music swirled around us, making it feel like the floor had spun away. Making it feel like gravity no longer existed. We floated like two ghosts above the surface, enclosed in our own magical world. A little bubble formed around us where everything, and everyone, ceased to exist. The hall melted away. The ceiling and the walls fell away, until it was just us. I pulled my head away and looked him in the eyes. *Ocean blue.* Like the sea this time. Like the waves crashing against the shore; crashing against my heart, rolling in the pit of my stomach. The purple light cast a glow across the side of his face and he was the brightest thing I'd ever seen.

"I can feel your heart beating," he whispered softly.

"Me too," I whispered back. I never wanted this moment to end. This was the moment I felt like my whole life had been building up to, without me even knowing it. I wanted to breathe this moment in, drink it down, and live in it forever, only I couldn't, because the music went off, the lights flicked on, and a voice over the PA called my name. It was the principal.

"Lori Palmer, come to my office, now."

I pulled away from Jake, and if people hadn't been staring at me before, they were certainly staring now.

49

"What's going on?" Jake asked.

And then Thembi, Guy, and Andile were also by my side asking the same question. A feeling sank into the pit of my stomach. I had no idea what was going on, but I knew it was bad when I saw the look on the principal's face. He made eye contact with me and shook his head. I looked to his left and that was when I saw Xander.

"Follow me." Mr. Du Preez's voice was demanding, and I followed him out of the hall. We walked in silence down the corridor. The only noise was my high heels clicking on the concrete, echoing down the corridor, sounding ominous. When we got to his office and walked inside, I couldn't hide my shock. My mother was there. She was standing against the wall with her arms folded, and then next to her . . . *my blood ran cold.* A policewoman.

"Sit down, please, Lori," Principal Du Preez said.

I looked at my mother. I could see she'd been crying. I looked over at Xander; he looked concerned.

"Mom, what's going on? Is everything okay? Is Zac okay?"

"Sit down please," the principal said again. His voice was firmer this time and I obeyed him. And then the policewoman walked up to the desk and slid a file across it. I looked down at it, and then back up at her. Her eyes urged me to open it and so I did.

And there I was. Grainy black and white images of me painting over my mother's billboard while wearing Jake's BWH cap.

"Where did you . . ." I started but stopped myself.

"After the reward was put out, the store owner across the road checked his security footage," the policewoman said. "We recognized the lettering on the cap immediately and came here, and that's when Mr. Brown identified you."

"Oh," I whispered.

"Oh. *Oh!* Is that all you have to say for yourself?" My mom sounded hysterical now. She walked forward and pointed down at the picture. "Why? Why would you do this to me?"

"Let's just all calm down here," Xander interrupted. "Let's all take a deep breath and talk this through calmly."

"I agree with Xander," the principal said, looking at me. "We would all just like to understand why you did this."

"Yes, Lori! *Why?*" My mom was crying now, and all I wanted to do was roll my damn eyes at her. Maybe even pull them out of my head and chuck them at her, to snap her out of this dramatic soap-opera moment she was clearly indulging in.

And now the policewoman put another file down on the desk. I flipped it open and was confronted by my other art. The crack, Rose, Natasha.

"Did you do those too?" my mother asked in a shocked voice.

"Yes." The word came out softly at first, as if I wasn't quite ready to own it yet. But the truth was, I was ready to own this. I had done this. And I didn't regret it. I stood up, pushed the chair aside, and looked my mother straight in the eye. "Yes," I said, louder this time. "I did do those. And I would do them all over again."

"Lori." My mom threw her hands in the air. "What's going on with you? Since coming to Cape Town you have been running around, disappearing at night—what has gotten into you?"

I looked at her and shook my head. I didn't know what to say to her anymore, really. No matter what I said, nothing seemed to penetrate that fake, plastic surface of hers.

I turned and looked at the police officer now, and even though my heart was pounding, I took a deep breath and pulled every last ounce of courage in the world toward me. "I know what I did was illegal, and I'm ready to face whatever the consequences are, but, you must know that I don't regret doing it at all."

The calmness in my tone almost frightened me. I was so cool and collected, like I was channeling this power from somewhere. No, not from somewhere. I was channeling the power of all those people at Natasha's vigil. Their energy was flowing through me now, just like the paintings had.

The police officer looked me up and down for a few moments, and then exhaled. "Your painting of Natasha has had the hotline ringing off the hook. We've gotten some good leads."

"I hope you find her," I said softly and then waited a while. But when she stayed silent, I couldn't take the uncertainty anymore. "So . . . what's happening to me? Am I going to be a-a-arrested?" The word stuck in my throat.

She shook her head. "No. But there's going to be a fine, and you're going to have to do some community service, and you're going to have to stop, unless you apply for the proper permits."

I nodded. Relief washed over me in bucket loads. Despite my courage, I really didn't want to go to jail for three months.

I turned to the principal and Xander. "May I go back to the dance now?"

The principal shook his head. "No. I'm afraid we're going to have to suspend you over this. I can't have pupils committing crimes, especially while wearing school clothing."

I hung my head. "I understand."

"And we'll have to ask you to leave now," the principal said, rising from his chair.

"I'm sorry," Xander added quickly from the sidelines. I looked at him and he gave me a small, encouraging smile, as if he was trying to communicate that he was on my side here, in my corner.

"Look how much trouble you've caused, Lori," my mother moaned from behind me. "When did you become such a trouble-maker? You were always such a good girl." My mom turned to the principal and Xander now. "I didn't raise her to be like this, I didn't . . ."

"Raise me?" I turned and glared at her. "*Raise me*?" I repeated, letting the question hang in the air. The tension in the room was palpable now, and the question hung in it like the smell of sulfur after a fireworks display, catching in your throat and making your eyes sting. And when my mom said nothing in response, when she didn't even open her mouth to attempt anything, I felt something happening inside me. Something big that was just fighting to get out. I took a stride toward her and in the calmest tone I could muster, I found my voice and spoke my truth.

"Mom, you haven't 'raised me' for years. Not since the divorce. You haven't been a real parent to me, or Zac, and I think it's time you acknowledge that."

Her face and lips went white and she looked around the room, shaking her head and forcing a smile as if desperately trying to keep up appearances, even though they were slipping fast with every word I spoke.

"That's not . . . it's not . . . true," she said through a big, fake grin. Default Cheshire grin. The one she always plastered across her face, no matter what she was really feeling.

"Mom, when was the last time you looked in the mirror?" I continued.

"Sorry, what?" Her fake smile faded now.

"Because I don't even recognize this person standing in front of me as my mother anymore. You have become this weird caricature of a person that I don't even know."

I heard the principal clear his throat. "Maybe now is not the time for—"

"It's never the time." I turned and cut him off. "Because she never has any time. And this time is as good as any." I turned back to my mom. "And I'm sorry Dad fell in love with someone else. I'm sorry he divorced you and blew up your perfect picket-fence life. I'm sorry you gave up your career to look after us and allow Dad to build his career and then when he got successful, he went and shared that with someone else. Someone young and beautiful. And I'm sorry that that makes you feel so insecure about the way you look that you pump toxins into your forehead and lips. And I'm sorry you feel the need to define your life with material things, and I'm sorry that you have an autistic son, and a daughter who is clearly a big, *fat* disappointment to you . . . literally. I'm *sorry*! Okay!" I paused and watched to see if any of my words had sunk in. If they'd even penetrated the surface. I wasn't sure, to be honest. I wasn't sure if my words were simply falling on deaf ears, shooting out of my mouth only to collide with some impenetrable wall and die there.

But I didn't stop. There was more to say. "Mom, you have to grow up now. I feel like I'm the only adult in the house sometimes and I am, I'm, it's . . ." And then I started crying. It was the last thing I wanted to do because it made me feel so naked and exposed, but I couldn't help it. "Sometimes I feel like I am cracking under all the pressure. I love Zac so much, I do, but I shouldn't be the one reminding you to do his OT homework at night. Sometimes I feel like my life is not mine. I feel invisible to you and Dad, and you don't care about my feelings. All you care about is yourself, being Barbara Palmer of Palm Luxury Realty. I feel forgotten, and maybe that's why I did all that stuff, Rose, Natasha." I turned to the policewoman now. "At least I could make someone else less forgotten. I could give someone else a voice, because I was voiceless." I wiped my tears and squared off in front of my mother. Her eyes were shining now, too, and I wasn't sure if it was sadness or if she was just embarrassed. We looked at each other for the longest time, the tension in the room buzzing and crackling with a static energy that felt like it was giving me short, sharp, painful shocks. And then, when it felt like the tension had to subside or it would explode the air around me, four faces appeared by the door. They were all wide-eyed and worried-looking. Jake stepped forward.

"I helped with one of the paintings! It wasn't just her," he shouted into the room.

"Jake? What are you talking about?" The principal stepped forward.

"The painting on the museum wall, of Natasha. I was there too. I also participated, so if you're punishing her, you can punish me too." He stepped into the office. And then Guy also stepped forward.

"Me too. I was also there. You can punish me too!"

And just as soon as he was finished, Thembi stepped forward too.

"Sorry, who are you?" Mr. Du Preez asked, staring at Guy.

"We're both guilty," Jake said, looking at the policewoman now.

The principal let out a loud, long sigh. "Out! All of you, out. Just leave. Get out of my office." He waved his arm in the air as if he was fed up with this whole thing. He probably was.

I looked over at the policewoman one more time, and she gave a small nod, as if concurring. So we did—we all turned and walked out.

"Where do you think you're going?" my mom asked, her voice quivering.

"I'm going with my friends," I replied.

"No, you're not. You're coming home, right now." I could see she was trying to hold on to any semblance of power she still thought she had as a parent.

I shook my head. "No, Mom, I'm not. You don't get to have this both ways. You don't get to be my mom when it's convenient for you."

And with that, I walked away.

Things I Like about Myself by Lori Palmer
I'm a good sister.
I'm a real artist (despite what Blackwell says!).

~~I, Lori Palmer, am officially good with parents!~~

I have a voice. There is power in my art.

I am brave!

I am a great kisser!

I'm a good friend (even if I don't really want to be just a friend).

My voice can start a movement!

My body is a work of art!

I have great boobs. I mean . . . AHMAZING!

I am hot!

I stand up for myself.

50

"Oh my God," Guy gasped. "Did you really do all that street art?"

I nodded.

"Why didn't you tell us? We leave you for five minutes, Lori Palmer, and you go and get yourself in trouble with the law!" Guy put his hands on my shoulders.

"That's insanely awesome that you did that," Thembi said to me.

"Thanks." I looked over at Jake. He was smiling at me.

"Sorry I also didn't step forward and claim responsibility," Andile said in a small voice. "But you know, I'm a Black male, I'd probably be the only one arrested for it. It's street art when someone like you does it, not so much when someone like me does it."

We all turned and looked at him. His words had stopped us dead. They were sad yet true, and we all fell into a moment of silence as we considered their implications.

"I'm sorry," I said to him. But what was I sorry for? *Sorry for the way the world worked?* In that case, sorry wasn't nearly a big enough word.

He shrugged. "I'm cool," he said, and then walked up to me and draped a big, protective arm over my shoulder. "I heard what you said to your mom in there. It couldn't have been easy."

"Not that she didn't totally deserve it," Guy said, also resting a hand on my shoulder.

I nodded at them both and smiled. I was okay. I had finally said what I needed to say to my mom—okay, so I hadn't imagined it happening with such a large audience. "I'm good," I said.

"*So . . .*" Andile declared loudly. "We're all dressed up, looking gorgeous and have nowhere to go, and I'm desperate to dance."

"Me too," Guy said. "Where to?"

"I know, let's go to Le Beach," Thembi suggested.

"Le Beach?" Jake widened his eyes. "We'll never get in there. It's only for celebs and VIPs."

"Lucky you guys know me then," she cooed.

"Oh yeah, and which celebrities do you know?" Andile walked up to her and put a hand on his hip, eyeballing her playfully. I looked at the two of them together and smiled; they were destined to become friends.

"I work at Simone Couture and her husband owns the club. He said I could go there anytime I wanted."

We all looked at each other. "Then what the hell are we waiting for?" Andile said.

The nightclub was like nothing I'd ever seen before. It dripped with opulence. Everything was white. Huge chandeliers that looked like crystal jellyfish hung from the ceilings. The bar was a long, glass fish tank full of tropical fish, and the bar stools were transparent plastic. We headed straight for the dance floor as a particularly bassy house track started playing. Andile and Guy began doing their choreographed dance, the one they *always* did when they hit any kind of a dance floor anywhere, and soon a crowd had gathered. The crowd laughed and clapped as they incorporated ballet into their routine (like they always did). I watched them and laughed. For Andile, ballet had been his outlet, like my art. Growing up as a gay, Black teen in rural Limpopo had been hard, and dancing was the only thing that had gotten him through it. It was also what got him out when he received a scholarship to art school. And when he danced, you could see the passion and raw emotion that poured out of him. As for Guy, he came from a theater family and it was in his blood. We were all from completely different worlds, and yet our worlds had all come together, and now we were family.

I watched as the dance turned into an unofficial dance off as others joined in and showed their best moves. I looked to my left and there was Jake, staring at me. He waved his hand at me, beckoning me to come with him as he walked backward away from the dancing. We walked through the crowd together, out of the club, and onto its private beach. It was lit up with pink and purple lights, turning the sand and water luminous. It reminded me of the bioluminescence that Jake had taken me to see. Loungers dotted the sand, and the occasional couple were lying on them, sipping cocktails.

"This way," Jake said, walking to the edge of the sea. I looked at the water and felt that cold, clammy feeling that hits me in the chest. I looked up from the water and into Jake's eyes. They were almost the same color as the sea, which made the sea feel less terrifying.

"This way." He spoke again, his voice soft and warm, like a gentle spring rain, and then he held his hand out.

I looked down at it. Big. Reassuring, and I wanted to take it. I hiked my dress up slowly. I'd already ditched the high heels—you couldn't walk on a beach with them. I took a step and stopped when I got to the water's edge. I glanced down at the small waves. They looked harmless like this, but I knew better. I knew what lurked beyond the breakers. I knew that other world intimately, that one in which you can't breathe and where you finally let go.

Let go.

The thought hit me like a wave might do. The thought that if I was out there now—falling into the water, sinking under—that this time, I would fight. I *wouldn't* let go. I would fight to breathe and live, and fight my way up to the surface with everything I had. The thought made me take a step into the water. The cool water lapped at my ankles and at first I gasped, but then it started to feel good.

I slipped my hand through Jake's as he stepped in farther.

He held my hand so tightly, and gently coaxed me in.

"Not too deep," I said nervously.

"Not too deep," he reassured me.

The water climbed over my ankle to my calf. I jumped and giggled as a small wave broke against my knee and splashed me in the face.

Jake stopped walking. "Hi, Anything But JustLori," he said.

"Hi, Jake," I replied.

We smiled at each other in the water, the music and bass

coming from the club thumping through the air. He moved closer to me and his eyes drifted down to my lips.

"There's something I didn't get to do at the dance," he said.

"What?" I asked, my eyes leaving his and also traveling down to his lips.

"This." And then he pulled me into his arms and kissed me. The music throbbed through us as the kiss started out slowly and then deepened. He took my face between his hands and I dropped my dress, letting it fall into the water below as the kiss intensified. And then his hands left my face and traveled across my shoulders and started to blaze a hot trail down my arms . . .

This was it. Don't pull away. *Don't pull away,* I told myself. Let him touch you.

His hands drifted down my arms to my fingertips, where they stopped for a while, before moving off again. And then I gasped against his lips when I felt his hands on my lower back. I wrapped my arms around his neck and allowed my body to fall into his. No one's hands had been on my body like this before—except his.

I felt a buildup of energy and pressure all over, and then millions of tiny explosions on my skin as he traced the length of my spine. And then I think I almost blacked out when his lips left mine and he trailed kisses down my neck. I laced my hands through his hair, the loose curls that were blowing slightly in the breeze, and held on tight as his lips trailed kisses back up to my chin and then to my lips again. We stopped kissing, pulled away, and looked at each other for the longest time, and then he smiled. He reached up and ran his thumb over my lip. It quivered.

"Oh my God, why didn't you say this was turning into a pool party!" We both looked back at the beach. Andile, Guy, and

Thembi—with a gold bottle of champagne in her hand—all stood there looking at us.

"Well, that's it!" Andile declared, whipping his jacket off and tossing it to the sand. Guy quickly followed suit, also tossing his jacket down. And soon they were all discarding their shoes and running into the sea. Even Thembi, who'd hiked her dress up high in one hand and had the bottle in the other.

"Best dance, ever!" Andile declared as he splashed Guy with water.

"Bastard!" Guy splashed him back, and we all laughed.

"Noooo!" I squealed as I got covered in the residual spray of water. Soon, we were all racing through the water in our fancy clothes splashing each other and laughing.

Last time I'd been in the water I'd been dying, but now, I was living in full-blown color. When we stopped racing around, Thembi held the bottle of champagne up in the air and popped the cork. The sparkling liquid shot up into the sky, and Guy tried to catch some in his mouth.

"A toast!" Thembi held the bottle out.

"What are we toasting?" Jake asked.

Thembi looked thoughtful for a moment. "To making new friends," she finally said.

Andile shot me a conspiratorial look. "To making new friends . . . *and more*."

I nudged him in the ribs and blushed.

"I'm good with that," Jake said, shooting me a very loaded look.

"Great!" Thembi held the bottle high in the air and we all shouted together.

"*To making new friends. . . and more.*"

51

News traveled quickly at BWH. Like the Cape Town wind—fast and hard, and it didn't leave a thing unturned. After my two-week suspension was over, I came back to school quite the celebrity. As I walked in heads turned and everyone stared. Suddenly, I was the most popular person at school, and everyone wanted to talk to me. Since the discovery of who Cape Town's Banksy was, my face had been splashed all over the news. I'd been interviewed on TV, for the papers, and on a radio station, and everyone wanted to know who I was and why I'd done what I'd done. I was a trending hashtag on Twitter, I was on everyone's Facebook feeds, and the international media had picked up on the story when Natasha's body had been found thanks to a lead generated by my picture. It was not the ending I'd hoped for, that anyone had hoped for, but it was an ending.

I'd gone to the funeral, expecting it to be nothing but devastating, and it was, but it was also so much more than that. Natasha's parents had come up to me and thanked me for giving them the closure they'd longed for. Rose's parents were also there—I recognized them from the news—and they, too, had come over to talk to me. So many different people had come to the funeral that the street outside the church was full. But each and every one of them had something in common; we were all united in this tragedy, putting our differences aside to acknowledge that at the core of it, we're all human. We love, we lose, we laugh, and we grieve. And not just for Natasha and Rose; we grieved together for every woman and girl who had been harmed and taken. Natasha's face had made that happen. She'd shone a light on every single missing child in the entire country, and as a result, two girls had been found alive and reunited with their families. Her death had not been in vain—her beautiful smiling face had saved two other lives, and I suppose, I'd played a small part in that. I might not have fully understood what I was doing at the time, but painting her face on that wall had been the single most important thing I'd ever done, and perhaps ever would do.

But overnight celebrity felt strange. What also felt strange was that the day I returned after my suspension, Jake and I had walked hand in hand into the school. And stranger still was how people had reacted to us. I'd expected stares and open mouths and shock. Instead, we were greeted as if it were completely normal. As if, *why wouldn't we be together*? The only person who'd treated us differently was Amber—she'd thrown some displeased stares our way and had shaken her head at us as if she was quite put out. But I didn't care, and when walking past her one day in the corridor, I decided to echo the words of a very wise woman.

"You know, Amber, sometimes us fat girls do get the hot guys."
I smiled at her as I said that, owning every single part of me as
I walked on by with a swagger—thighs still rubbing together,
ass still shaking, and boobs still doing what the hell they bloody
pleased. No one like Amber was ever going to push my head
underwater again. I had bobbed up to the surface and saved
myself. Sure, I'd had a little help on the way, but really it had been
me.

Thembi had come around every single day after school
during my suspension with class work. Sometimes we would
work together, sometimes we'd just hang out watching Netflix,
and other times we would talk for hours about everything, and
sometimes nothing at all. You know you've become friends with
someone when you can do that. Talk to them for hours about
absolutely nothing and yet still have had the best time doing it.
My community service had started—I was cleaning up streets
and parks, which was appropriate, I guess. I'd also managed to
find a part-time job in an art store a few afternoons a week to pay
for the fine.

But I'd barely spoken to my mother. We'd been passing each
other in the huge, empty house like ghosts. Barely looking at
each other, barely acknowledging the other's existence. I knew at
some stage I would need to sit down with her and talk, but then
I got an email that changed everything . . .

Dear Miss Palmer,

*We are pleased to offer you a place next year at the
Paris School of Art. As you know, some of the greatest
artists have trained here, and we feel you will be an*

excellent addition to the school. We were impressed by
your bold street art—your tone and voice as a visual
artist, as well as your voice as an activist. Art should
evoke thought and action. It should evoke change, and
that is what you have done with your work. We look
forward to welcoming you next year.

Yours sincerely,
Marine Lagarde
Head of Fine Arts, Paris School of Art

I closed my computer slowly and walked over to my window and looked out. *How did they know about me?* I rushed back to the computer and looked at the email again, and there it was. The other address that had been cc'd. I raced downstairs calling out for my mom and found her sitting at the kitchen counter, her computer also in front of her.

"Mom!" I said, out of breath from the stairs.

"I have something for you." She pushed an envelope across the counter but didn't look up at me. These were the first words we'd uttered to each other in over two weeks. "Take it," she urged, tapping her finger against the white marble.

I picked it up and peered inside. "A plane ticket?" I looked at her, and she finally met my eyes.

"Read it," she stated.

"Okay." I started reading. "'Business class, one way, Paris . . .'" I shook my head. "How did you . . . why did you . . . why was your email on the . . . ?"

"I was the one who applied for you."

"How?"

"It was easy, I just compiled a folder of all the press you received for your art, and emailed it to them."

"Wait." I waved the ticket in the air. "I thought you hated my art. I ruined your billboard. You put out a reward. You called the police, I thought . . . *why are you doing this?*"

She stood up and walked toward me. She almost touched my shoulder, but then pulled away at the last second.

"Some of the things you said to me at the dance"—she looked away as she spoke—"you were right about them. I haven't been a proper mother to you since the divorce. It's been very difficult for me, though, not that that's an excuse, but . . . I always thought your father and I would be together forever. I thought we would grow old together, and enjoy our grandchildren together and go gray and sit in rocking chairs driving you and your brother mad, together, but . . ." She tapered off, her voice shaking a little.

"Did I ever tell you how I met your dad?" she asked, forcing a small smile. I shook my head. "I almost ran him over with my car. I was pulling out of a parking space and I nearly bumped into him. He jumped out of the way and his bag of groceries went flying. Oranges rolling down the road, the milk bottles smashed, eggs broken. I got such a fright. I jumped out and started apologizing and asked if there was anything I could do to help, and you know what he said?" She looked at me and I shook my head. "He said I could take him to dinner because he didn't have anything to eat now." She gave a little laugh, as if the memory really was funny. As if the memory still meant something to her. "I thought we were going to grow old together." Her voice sounded strained and tired, and I realized that she'd never spoken to me like this before.

"But that's not your problem, though. I'm the adult. I shouldn't have allowed my feelings to affect you and Zac so much. But I did. I failed you guys." She finally looked up at me, her eyes full of tears, and my heart broke for her.

"Mom." I stepped forward. "I'm sorry." I didn't really know what I was saying sorry for—for the divorce, for Dad, for painting over her billboard, for her pain, for my pain, for Zac's autism . . . but I felt sorry. I felt so damn bloody sorry for all that we'd gone through these past four years.

A tear rolled down my cheek now as the realization hit me in the guts. I shook my head. "I can't go to Paris, Mom. Who's going to take care of Zac?"

"But haven't you always wanted to go to the best art school in the world? Isn't that your dream?"

"It is, but . . ."

"I'll take care of Zac. I'm his mother and that's *my* job. I've let you do it for far too long, too much responsibility has fallen on you."

"I can't leave him." Another tear joined the other, rolling down my cheek, carving a cool, wet line into it.

"But you also can't live your life for him," she said. Her words hit me like a ton of bricks. Right in the rib cage and it hurt like hell. There was so much truth in that statement. For the last four years I'd made Zac the center of my world. My relationship with him had become the most important relationship of my life. At times it had been one of the hardest too. But despite that, I'd poured everything into it, even if sometimes it felt like a one-way street, like pouring water into an empty well that never filled up and never gave water in return. I lived for those small in-between moments, when he let me hug him or hold his hand, when he told me I was pretty or placed his little hand on my cheek.

"It's my responsibility to parent Zac." My mom finally broke the silence. "Not yours. I haven't been doing a very good job, and I want to change that."

I looked down at the ticket in my hands, a part of me wanted to go so badly, a part of me wanted to get on that flight but . . . *Zac?*

"Zac is going to be fine," she said. "He'll adapt and you'll come home on holidays, and he's enjoying his new school and keeping busy."

"But the change to his routine will throw him so much—"

"Lori! Stop!" My mother cut me off. "You cannot live your life for him," she said again, slowly, emphasizing every single word.

And then another thought hit me. *Jake.* I took a step back.

"What?" my mom asked. She pulled a chair out at the kitchen table and sat down; I did the same.

"There's this guy," I said softly. "I think I really like him." An involuntary warm flush came over me as I said that out loud.

She looked thoughtful for a moment. "Let me give you some advice. I haven't given you much motherly advice over the last few years, so let me make up for it now."

I looked at her and waited. She looked like she was gathering her thoughts, choosing her words. "I once lost who I was because of a man. Lost my identity and lost my sense of self." She forced a small smile. "Don't do that, Lori. Go and become who you're supposed to become and if it's meant to be with him, it will be. And if it isn't, there'll always be guys lining up to be with my amazing, talented, now-famous daughter."

I hung my head because I couldn't keep it up, it was too full of thoughts. Thoughts of Jake, thoughts of Zac—but it was also full of other thoughts: thoughts of walking down the streets of Paris at night, the Eiffel Tower lit up, the Seine rushing past. I imagined jazzy music spilling out of the quaint coffee shop–lined streets. I imagined sitting in those lecture halls, the ones that the greatest artists of all time had sat in—maybe I would sit in Monet's chair—absorbing the knowledge of a hundred years that was embedded in the fabric of the place, and most of all, I imagined who I might become if I went there. Art had been my escape from the world, it had been my everything, and I owed myself the chance to see how great I could become.

I had a voice! I hadn't set out to find it on purpose; maybe it had just found me. Or maybe it had always been there, inside me, just waiting to come out. And now that it was out, it didn't want to be silenced.

I raised my head after what felt like forever and smiled slowly. "Thank you. For doing this." I said softly.

"I didn't do anything, you did. You did it when you became Cape Town's Banksy."

"You're not mad about your billboard anymore?" I asked.

"Are you kidding? Do you know how much new business I've gotten from it?"

I stopped smiling and looked at her sternly.

"Don't worry, I'm officially going to be working half days now. Since Palm Luxury Realty has exploded, I'm in the position to employ two full-time realtors who'll be running the business. But I'll remain the face of the company, obviously." She swooshed her hand around, and I smiled.

"Can I make a suggestion, then, since you're the face of the company?" I said.

"What?"

I paused, not sure if I should say this, but this was as good a time as any. "Please do yourself a favor and skip next month's

Botox, and please don't put anything in your lips again. You're perfect, just the way you are."

"Only if you promise to do something for me," she countered.

"What?"

"Never, ever, think of yourself as a disappointment to me, ever again. Ever. You've never been a disappointment to me for a single second. And if I ever made you feel like that—" she paused and looked me straight in the eye, tears welling up in hers. "If I ever made you feel *f*—"—she shook her head—"I can't even say that word, because you're too beautiful, Lori. You know the day you were born, you had this mop of bright-red curly hair, and the nurse who delivered you was so shocked she called all the other nurses because she said she'd never seen such a beautiful baby before. You were beautiful from day one, and you have grown more and more beautiful since then. And if I ever made you feel like you weren't, *aren't*, absolutely beautiful and perfect just the way you are, then I am so very, very sorry."

And then she did something that she hadn't done in ages: she reached across and pulled me into a hug. My heart felt like it was going to explode and in that moment, I realized that this was the start of us rebuilding our relationship. The relationship had been broken and damaged, and had once lain like leaves discarded in the soil, but now it was time to give it water, a little bit of sunlight, and see if we could start regrowing. So much damage had been done, and five minutes wasn't going to erase that, but this was a start.

Things I Like about Myself by Lori Palmer
I'm a good sister.
I'm a real artist (despite what Blackwell says!).

~~I, Lori Palmer, am officially good with parents!~~ I'm getting better with parents.

I have a voice. There is power in my art.

I am brave!

I am a great kisser!

I'm a good friend (even if I don't really want to be just a friend).

My voice can start a movement!

My body is a work of art!

I have great boobs. I mean . . . AHMAZING!

I am hot!

I stand up for myself.

52

I went over to Jake's house that afternoon. My heart was pulling itself in two different directions, like a rubber band that had been stretched to its breaking point. I was waiting for it to snap. I was excited to have been accepted into the most prestigious art school in the world, but I was also totally, undeniably, unequivocally in love with Jake Jones-Evans, and was feeling the loss of him, although he wasn't even gone yet. He was my first kiss, my first love, the first guy who'd seen past all my insecurities and imperfections—who'd seen me as no one had ever seen me before.

"Are you okay?" he asked as we sat on his veranda looking at the sea below.

I shook my head.

"What's wrong?" .

"I was accepted into an art school in Paris. It's the best art school in the world."

"What? That's amazing. You're amazing, so I'm not surprised, obviously." He sat forward in his chair and looked at me with those cerulean eyes that I'd come to love so much. Can you believe gold *used* to be my favorite color?

"But it's in Paris," I said softly.

He got up from his chair, walked over to my lounger, and sat down. He took my hands in his. "I always knew you were going somewhere at the end of the year."

I looked into his eyes. More than the color, I loved the way he looked at me. The wind picked up and took some red tendrils of my hair with it. He reached up and pushed the strands out of my face. "You were always going to Knysna, and I was always going to Stellenbosch. So, Paris is a bit farther than Knysna."

I forced a laugh. "A bit? It's an eleven-hour flight!"

"You'll come home on holidays?" he asked.

"Yes, I want to see Zac . . . *and you*."

"Of course you want to see me, I mean, why wouldn't you want to see me. Obviously."

I smiled at him. He reached up and wiped away a stray tear that had escaped my eye and rolled down my cheek. "Let's just have the best time together until we both have to go." He reached over and kissed me. I still didn't think I would ever get used to this—the fact that I got to kiss Jake whenever and wherever I wanted to.

"Okay," I said against his lips. Salty and soft. "Let's have the best few months ever."

And so we did.

They were filled with so much laughter and love, and believe it or not—completely cheesy but amazing—long walks on the beach. Playdates with Zac and Lisa, melting ice creams, making sandcastles sticky, the smell of coconut sunscreen and watermelon juice running down smiling faces. Evenings spent watching Netflix with him and Thembi, and other evenings spent kissing for so long that my lips were red and raw the next day. I also brought Jake into my world—we went to art shows and galleries, and found strange and curious shops that we scratched through for hours on end. Hot summer bonfires on the beach, a string of end-of-year parties, my birthday party—a surprise party that Thembi had organized and invited half of BWH to. And believe it or not, I'd enjoyed every moment of it. I felt a part of something bigger than me, and dare I say it, but I think a little BWH spirit might have seeped into my soul.

And there were quiet moments too. These were the moments I think I treasured the most. The ones where we didn't say a word to each other. The ones where we didn't need to. Where staring into each other's eyes was enough to communicate everything we both thought and felt until we both felt we needed to communicate it in a different way.

JAKE: My parents are going away with Lisa this weekend, I told them I have to stay for a water polo thing so . . .

JAKE: Want to come over?

JAKE: Pack a toothbrush 😉

53

I arrived at his house with my bag packed. I'd told my mom I was spending the night at Thembi's house, but here I was, standing by his front door, and although no words had been said, although we'd never spoken about the thing out loud, we both knew it was going to happen. Tonight. It had to. I was leaving in a few days and there had been something building between us. Getting stronger and stronger—this kind of unspoken thing that we were slowly moving toward that we could both feel. Vicki and I had spoken about it too. We'd spoken about the idea that sexuality was nothing to be afraid of or to run away from. That, when you're ready, it can be a very important and beautiful way of expressing love.

"Hi." He smiled. It was coy and cute, and I swear, he blushed.

"Hey." Equally coy and blushy and fluttery. He pulled my

overnight bag from my shoulder, like a real gentleman, and we walked to his bedroom.

"Wow. It's tidy," I said, looking around.

He shrugged, clearly trying to be casual about the whole thing, but it was anything but casual. Tidying his room was big. Tidying his room meant he'd done it for me, because he knew I was staying in his room. In his bed.

The sun was just starting to set by the time I'd arrived, and I caught the last of it through his bedroom window as it took its final bright, orange bow at the horizon and then totally disappeared. Jake came and stood next to me as I watched the sky turn a kaleidoscope of colors. He didn't say a word; instead he wrapped his arms around me and rested his head on my shoulder. I closed my eyes and took a deep breath. Taking in his smell. Soapy with hints of hair gel and a woody-smelling cologne. It was the best smell ever. It had, over the few months, become my favorite smell in the entire universe. I found it hard to imagine anything smelling this damn good. He planted a small kiss on my neck and I giggled.

"Ticklish," I said, flinching.

"That's so damn cute." He kissed me again and I laughed even louder, trying to pull away.

"Stop!" I put my hands over both sides of my neck as he came toward it with puckered lips. I squealed as he managed to pull my hand away and plant another kiss on my neck.

"Noooo." I raced to the other side of the room, Jake hot on my heels, but when he caught up to me, he didn't kiss my neck again.

"Come with me." He extended his hand and I looked down at it suspiciously.

"Are you just trying to get me to take your hand so I remove it from my neck?"

"No more neck kisses, I swear," he said seriously. I let my neck go and slipped my hand through his. I'd done this a million times before, but I still couldn't get over how perfectly they fit together. They seemed to have been designed for each other. Like a long-lost key to a treasure chest. *What were we going to find inside?* Or had we already found it? Jake and I were the treasure. The most rare and precious and beautiful thing in the world. The thing that everyone wanted, that shone so brightly it was blinding. We walked through the house onto the deck outside, and that was when I saw what he'd done. A million glowing candles. Orange and flickery and beautiful, laid around the pool and some even floating in it.

"What is this?" I asked, my voice a soft whisper.

"When those assholes pushed you in the pool all those years ago, they deprived you of something. They deprived you of that feeling of slipping into cool water on a hot day. The feeling of weightlessness when you float on your back, that feeling of cutting through the water like a fish, and I want to give that back to you before you go." He took a step toward the pool. I looked at the water, panic rising inside me again.

"We'll take it slow." He held his hand out once more.

I looked into his eyes. They were the sky and the sea and tanzanite and topaz.

"I didn't bring a bathing suit."

And then another kind of smile swept across his face. One I hadn't seen before. Sexy. Naughty. "Who says you need a bathing suit?" And with that, he peeled his clothes off, dropping them onto the deck until he was standing there in nothing but his underwear. My eyes swept over him and I almost forgot my panic for a moment as I looked at his ridiculous perfection. He looked at me in a way that urged me to do the same. To take my clothes off.

I took a deep breath. I'd learned some things about myself over the last few months, and it wasn't because I'd worn a pretty dress, or gone to Vicki, or because I was dating the hottest guy at school. I'd learned these things because I'd finally learned to shut up the bullies in my head (most of the time). I'd learned these things because I'd put in the work and had spent hours in front of the mirror with my red lip liner, exploring every part of myself. It was because I'd found my voice and my strength, and now knew that my worth was far greater than a number on the scale.

I am a work of art. My body is a masterpiece. It is a kaleidoscope of pictures and shapes that tells its own unique story. It has carried me all these years—carried me to great heights, carried me out of the lows, carried me to this moment in time, right here, right now. My body is not perfect. My body has lines and dents and wobbly bits and bits that bulge, but it's mine. I own it. It is the only one of its kind, and tonight, it is dressed in sexy, red, lacy things that make my boobs look awesome AF!

I closed my eyes, pulled my dress over my head, and dropped it to the ground. A silence followed. I swear the whole world, and everyone and everything in it, stopped. I kept my eyes closed tightly for a few moments . . . *I am a work of art.* And then I opened them and looked at Jake.

"Wow." His voice was deep and gravelly. I'd never heard it like that before. "You're gorgeous," he said softly as he looked at me. His eyes swept over my body, and I felt completely and utterly naked, even though I wasn't. He smiled that naughty smile again and then started walking backward into the pool.

"You ready?" he asked.

"As ready as I'll ever be," I said, stepping down onto the first step. The water came up just above my ankles. Jake took another step in and I followed him. This time the water came to my knees. Another step. The water lapped at my thighs now and I inhaled sharply. This was the deepest I'd been in years.

"You're okay," he said reassuringly and took another step.

I walked off the last step, and, shocked by how deep it had suddenly gotten, lost my footing. I slipped. I slipped and . . . *suddenly I was underwater again.* Instant panic. I looked up, waiting for a hand to push me back down as I came up for air, but it didn't. Instead, two hands cupped my face. Lips on my lips and then Jake was kissing me. I grabbed him as he kissed me underwater and then air filled my lungs. I could breathe. Jake was air, and with him, I could do the impossible. I could breathe underwater. We floated up to the surface together. He looked so good like this. Wet hair, water trickling down his face, lit by the soft, warm light from the candles. He pulled me closer. I felt weightless, as light as a feather, and I wrapped my legs around him. He walked deeper into the water with me. I wrapped my arms around his neck and laughed as he jumped us up and down, the water splashing around us. I felt like we were jumping on an invisible trampoline in space. No gravity. Nothing to hold us down. Nothing to keep us from flying and floating together right up into the stars and beyond.

And then he stopped. He looked me in the eye like he'd never looked at me before. He looked at me as if I were everything. As if I were the only thing that existed on this planet. Maybe even the entire universe. And when he kissed me again, we didn't stop until we climbed out and make our way to his bedroom.

54

Thembi had warned me it would be quick. Disappointing. Not like you see in the movies. But as I lay there in the morning, tangled up in his arms, the light streaming through his window, it had been anything but disappointing. It wasn't good because we'd been having sex—that was almost irrelevant. It had been good because I'd never felt closer or more connected to anyone in my life before. We spent the day in bed, talking, laughing, and, well, yes, I was no longer a virgin . . . *twice*. But this also made it so much harder to say good-bye to him that evening, knowing that in a few days' time, we would be saying good-bye for a very long time. He walked me to the front door and opened it reluctantly.

"What are you doing tomorrow?" he asked.

"I don't know yet. I want to spend some time with Zac. I want to do something really special with him, to say good-bye. I just don't know what yet."

"That would be nice. Let me know what you decide, I also want to spend some time with you."

I leaned in and kissed him. Our kisses were different this time. They had been since last night. They were the kisses that lovers gave each other. Sexier and slower and more loaded.

"I will," I said as I walked to my car and climbed in. I drove home that evening feeling this sense that everything was different. The sea looked bright and brilliant and no longer scary. The mountain looked like it probably looked to all Capetonians: beautiful and majestic. Like a lighthouse on a misty night, a safe, guiding beacon. Something to orient yourself with. Even my house, when I pulled up to it, didn't look as hideous. Maybe kitschy winged lions weren't as bad after all . . . *or maybe I was just high on dopamine.*

Things I Like about Myself by Lori Palmer
I'm a good sister.
I'm a real artist (despite what Blackwell says!).
~~I, Lori Palmer, am officially good with parents!~~ I'm getting better with parents.
I have a voice. There is power in my art.
I am brave!
I am a great kisser!
I'm a good friend (even if I don't really want to be just a friend).
My voice can start a movement!
My body is a work of art!
I have great boobs. I mean . . . AHMAZING!

I am hot!
I stand up for myself.
I am a bona fide sex goddess.

I walked through the front door and my dopamine high instantly disappeared when I saw *him* sitting in the lounge. He was helping Zac build his biggest battery in the world. My mom was sitting at the kitchen counter drinking coffee, her back turned to him, as if she was trying to block him out.

"Lori!" He rushed over and pulled me into a hug.

"Dad," I said, feeling crushed against him.

"I'm so proud of you," he said.

"For what?" I asked.

"You've been all over the news. You did those incredible paintings. You've been accepted to the best art school in the world."

"What are you doing here?"

"I couldn't let you go away without saying good-bye, poppet."

Poppet. I tried not to show emotion at this pet name. He'd always called me poppet, but this time it made me want to cry. Seeing us all in the same room together made me want to cry. Knowing that he had flown here to say good-bye to me made me want to cry.

I turned and walked away, dumping my overnight bag in the kitchen. My mom glanced down at it quickly, and when I caught her looking at it, she turned away. I could see she knew I hadn't been at Thembi's house, and when she flashed me a tiny, knowing smile, I couldn't figure out whether this was the creepiest thing ever or whether I should be touched by her apparent openness.

The rest of the evening was strange. I could see my mom was

making a huge effort to rein her emotions in as we all sat around the kitchen table sharing a pizza. This was maybe the longest time we'd been in the same room together in years, and although it felt awkward, there was something nice about it. And Zac looked so happy. He was actually smiling. My dad put Zac to sleep that night, and when he returned downstairs, my mom made herself scarce.

He sat down on the couch opposite me, wringing his hands as if he had something important to say. The tension was unbearable, so I broke it.

"So have you set a wedding date?" I asked. It came out more sarcastically than I'd hoped it would. He looked up at me. He had my eyes. Hazel. My coloring. Red hair that was looking grayer than I remembered.

"Not yet," he said softly. "I know you don't really like her, but if you got to know Maddy, you'd find out that she's not as bad as you think."

I sighed. "I don't *not* like Maddy," I said. "She's fine. She tries really hard, and is really very sweet but she's just . . . well . . ." I clutched my hands in my lap. Vicki said I needed to tell my dad how I felt, and now seemed like as good a time as any. "You had an affair with her, Dad." The words came out cold and firm, and he looked at me and nodded.

"I know," he said.

"You lied and snuck around and you weren't where you were meant to be the day Zac had his accident. When we needed you."

"I know," he whispered. I could hear the pain and shame in his voice.

"And are you sorry you did it? Are you?" I asked, my heart started beating faster now.

JO WATSON

He hung his head. "I'm sorry I had an affair, but I'm not sorry I met Maddy. I could have handled it differently, though. *Should* have handled it differently. But I didn't. I regret that."

"How long was it going on, before Mom caught you?"

He sighed. It looked like he didn't want to answer this question.

"How long, Dad? I deserve to know this."

"A year," he said.

"One year!" I shook my head and put my face in my hands. This was not what I'd imagined. A few months maybe. I looked back on that year now through a different lens. He'd lied to us for a whole year, what else was a lie? Could I trust all those times he'd said he loved me? And when we'd done things together, had he really been there, or had she always been on his mind? Coming between us like an uninvited guest. He must have known what I was thinking.

"I know I lied to you guys, but I promise that nothing else was a lie. Everything I feel for you and your brother, that isn't a lie. It was never a lie. I love you guys with all my heart."

"It's kind of hard to trust what you say, Dad. It's hard to trust your love, since you seem to have some other version of it. The kind that makes it okay to cheat on Mom and just leave us like you did."

"I'm sorry," he echoed. "I know I let you down and I'm not the man you thought I was."

"What?" My head snapped up. "Dad, you were my idol. My hero. You were the most important man in my life. I had you on a pedestal and that's what hurts the most. Not that you had an affair, but that I was forced to see you, and think about you, differently. I wasn't ready to see you like that. I'm still not."

"I'm so sorry. That breaks my heart to hear, Lori," he said quietly.

"Yeah, well that makes two of us. You didn't just break Mom's heart, you know."

We fell into a strange, long silence. I'd never been this honest with my dad before, and it wasn't as hard as I'd thought it would be.

"I hope you can see me like you used to one day again," he whispered softly. "I'm still your dad. That will never change."

"Maybe," I conceded, even though I wasn't sure that was possible. I glanced over at him and he sat up straighter in the chair.

"I've decided to fly down here every second weekend to spend time with Zac. It's not enough to only see him on holidays and half terms. It's only a two-hour flight. I'll get a little apartment here, maybe somewhere foresty, away from the beach, that way Zac can experience the best of Cape Town."

I looked up at him and forced a small smile. "That's a good idea, Dad. Zac will like that. But you must make sure you buy the same bed and carpet that he has in his room now. And the dresser. Also, the same curtains."

My dad smiled at me. "I know."

"Because you know what he's like in unfamiliar spaces."

"I know," he reiterated. "You're a great sister, you know that."

"Yes. I do know that actually," I said confidently. "I'm a bloody good sister."

His smile grew and I couldn't help it, but I allowed myself to smile back at him, too, and for a moment, wallowed in the feeling of my father's obvious love for me. I mean, I knew he loved me. And I loved him. And clearly things would never be the same between us again, and maybe that was okay on some level. Maybe we would need to find a new kind of father-daughter relationship, and that would take time. But maybe this was a small start.

"So, Paris," he said, when my smile faded.

"Yes."

"Are you nervous?" he asked.

"Yes. But excited too."

"I love Paris," he said.

"I didn't know you went there."

He laced his hands together as my mom walked into the kitchen and opened the fridge. "Your mother and I went there for our honeymoon," he said in a softer voice.

I glanced at my mom to see if she'd heard that; she had.

"Remember that little patisserie on rue Madame?" my mom asked, walking toward the lounge.

My dad chuckled. "I put on three kilos just from eating those chocolate croissants every morning."

My mom smiled now, as if she was remembering something pleasant. I looked from her to my father, shocked. They'd barely spoken to each other in years, and this—this was almost friendly.

"You'll love the jazz café on Saint-Germain," my dad added. "You have to visit."

My mom nodded. "Do you remember that bench in the park where we used to feed the pigeons?"

My dad sat up. "And the one flew into your hair."

"My hair was a lot bigger in those days." She looked at me and smiled. "A *lot* bigger. If your dad hadn't gotten it out, I'm sure it would have nested there."

We all burst out laughing, and for a second, I swear it was just like the old days. But it wasn't, and when the laughter stopped, a strange silence closed in on us. My mom and dad shared a brief look before my mom turned to walk out of the room.

"Well, I'm off to bed," she said.

"Good night, Mom," I called after her.

"Good night," my dad said. My mom stopped momentarily, as if she was about to answer back, but didn't.

As I watched her disappear, it dawned on me. In that slow walk she took up the stairs to her bedroom it all became so crystal clear. She didn't need to say a word, but I could see—for the first time ever, maybe—the depth of loneliness and aloneness she felt going to an empty bed.

My dad and I stayed up talking for another hour or so before he left to go back to his hotel. When he was gone, I walked into my room and looked around. It was strange to see it all packed up into suitcases. Mind you, I'd never really settled here properly—it was as if the universe knew this somehow. Knew that this was only a temporary stop on the way to somewhere else. I climbed into bed and my thoughts immediately drifted to Jake. Was Jake temporary too? I didn't want to think of him like that, so I distracted myself with running through the list of all the things I'd packed to make sure I hadn't missed anything. And suddenly, I remembered I had missed something.

I jumped out of bed and rushed to the little tray of succulent leaves on my windowsill. I hadn't spritzed them with water last night. I grabbed the bottle and was just about to spritz when I noticed something. I picked up one of the leaves and stared at the tip of it. There it was. So small, so tiny. The start of a bright-pink root shooting from the end. I looked down at the little leaf. Once discarded, thought to be dead, only it wasn't. It was starting to grow again. Ready for its new adventure. Ready to start its new life. And that's when it hit me, what I needed to do.

I walked out of my room toward my mother's room. I could see she wasn't asleep; light was spilling out from under her door.

I tapped my knuckles on the door softly, and opened it when I heard a faint "Come in."

"What's wrong?" she asked when she saw me.

"Nothing. I've just been thinking."

"About what?" she asked.

"Technically I'm no longer a student at BWH," I said.

"And?"

"Well, technically that means Xander is no longer my guidance counselor."

My mom looked down and shook her head.

"I'm just saying, Mom. That if you did want to . . ." I was trying to choose my words carefully now, ". . . pursue something there, it would be okay. I think you should start dating, actually. You deserve to find someone else. Someone who is going to love you and make you happy again, Mom."

She looked up at me and smiled. "I appreciate that, Lori. But I'm not sure that Xander and I are . . . well, I don't think I'll be going on another date with him."

I raised my eyebrows at her.

"He's a nice guy, but my goodness, he's very orange, isn't he?"

I laughed at this and she laughed back.

"Xander or not, you should date, Mom. You should put yourself out there. But you know, be careful and—"

"I'm not going to date for a while, Lori." She cut me off. "I need to be there for Zac now, and I think I should probably get some help with getting over the divorce first before I climb into another relationship."

I smiled at her. "I could ask my therapist for a recommendation?"

She nodded. "That would be good. Thank you."

We gave each other a small smile, and I was just about to close the door when she spoke.

"Sex!" she said awkwardly.

"What?"

"I mean, the sex talk, we've never had it and I . . . well, do we need to have it?"

"Stop!" I held my hand up. "I think I know enough about the birds and bees."

She nodded and shuffled around nervously.

"I'm pretty responsible, too, if you haven't noticed. Despite once being wanted by the police and all."

She smiled. "So you're . . . um . . . being careful?"

"*Mom!*" I shook my head. "It's way too late to be talking about this, I need to sleep, but *yes,* I'm being careful, and *no,* I'm not elaborating. Let's leave it there."

She smiled at me and shook her head. "Fine. Good night, love."

"Night, Mom." I closed the door behind me and walked back to my room feeling a small sense of relief. The kind of relief you get from knowing that you're making small steps along the right path. That you are beginning to repair things that were once broken. *But still, I wasn't going to be talking about my sex life with my mom . . .*

55

JAKE: I have an idea for what you can do with Zac today

I rolled over and reached for my phone on the side of my bed. It was only eight in the morning.

JAKE: Sorry, did I wake you?

I sat up in bed and tried to type while fighting back a huge yawn.

LORI: Kind of. But I'm awake now

LORI: What's your idea?

I climbed out of bed while Jake typed. I walked around my bedroom, opened the curtains, brushed my teeth, and got dressed all while he was still typing. I even made it down to the kitchen and was halfway through making a cup of coffee before the typing finally stopped and the message came through. And when it did, I smiled. Because this was the best idea anyone had ever had. And I couldn't think of a better way to spend time with Zac on our last day together if I tried.

We drove for an hour and ten minutes before we reached our destination. On the way, we listened to music and talked about why no one had invented flying cars yet. We rounded the last bend and as we did, they came into view for the first time. Zac leaned forward and his eyes widened. He looked like he was going to jump out of his seat with excitement—in fact, I could see he was struggling to contain his emotions as he flapped his hands in the air.

"Wind turbines!" he yelled. "Wind turbines!"

"I know," I said as I gawked at the massive steel giants that rose up into the air in front of us. Before we'd come, I'd done some reading so I could furnish him with facts that I knew he would like.

"Did you know," I started, "that they stand almost a hundred meters tall?"

"How big is that?" Zac asked.

I smiled to myself. I knew he would ask this question. "You know how tall Ponte tower in Joburg is? Well, imagine cutting Ponte in half, that's how tall they are!"

"Wooooow!" he declared. "That's tall!"

We pulled up to the gate, and just as Jake had said, someone met us there. He introduced himself as Michael, one of the technicians, and was excited to give us a tour of the facility. But he definitely wasn't as excited as my brother. Zac was like a kid in a candy store, in among the massive electricity-generating giants that turned slowly in the wind. His face was alive with excitement when Michael showed him inside the many rooms that contained more batteries and wires and knobs and switches than even Zac could handle. Zac asked a hundred questions about how the wind became electricity, how that got into your home, and into your microwave, and how the giants were built, how much they weighed, and if it was possible for him to make small ones for the beach outside his house, and if so, should he use wood and if wood, what kind of glue was best, or should he use a nail and hammer? The questions flew out of his mouth one after the other and I could see that Michael was really enjoying it. We ended the tour right underneath one of the giant turbines. Zac and I stood there and looked up. It dwarfed us. It was hard to imagine how something like this could have even been constructed. Zac looked up at it in silence, but I could see his brain was ticking away. He was probably trying to work out a million things at once while looking at it. The sun was behind us, and I looked at the ground as the massive shadows from the turbine whooshed across it.

"You know I'm leaving tomorrow to go to Paris?" I asked, my throat tightening a bit.

"Yes," he said, sounding distant and far away, as if he wasn't really listening.

"Well, you know what that means, right?"

"No," he mumbled, not really paying me much attention.

"Look at me, Zac." I moved in front of him so that I could get his attention. "Do you know what me going to Paris means?"

"That you won't be home," he replied.

"That's right, I won't be home that much. But I will come home on the holidays," I said. "And we can Skype as much as you like."

He looked at me for the longest time, and like most times, I had no idea what he was thinking.

"Who will give me my water bottle when you're gone to make

sure I don't get dehydrated?" he asked. And that was it, my heart felt like it broke into a million tiny little pieces. This wasn't his fault, though. It wasn't his fault that he couldn't express himself the way I wanted him to. And maybe that was selfish of me to expect. But I couldn't help it: I wanted him to throw his arms around me and hug me. I wanted him to tell me how much he would miss me and how much he loved me. But instead, he folded his arms over his chest and looked up at the turbine.

"Mom will give you your water bottle," I said, fighting back the tears. "I'll make sure of that."

"I only like the blue one," he said, still looking up.

"I know, I'll make sure she has the blue one."

I reached out and placed a hand on his shoulder. He shrugged it off, not angrily, but because the feeling irritated him and he was utterly engrossed in the thing in front of him.

I walked away from him a little; I didn't want him to see that I was crying now. I was crying because I would miss him so much. I was crying because I loved him more than anything, and even though I knew he loved me, I knew he would never really be able to show me that, like other people did. I was crying because I also knew that my mother had been right. I'd been living my life for him for many years now, and as hard as it would be, I needed to let go.

I needed to learn to live without him. All these years I'd thought that I had given more to Zac than he'd given to me, that I'd been the one looking after him. But in reality, I'd needed him just as much as he'd needed me, and in many ways, he'd been looking after me too.

ONE MONTH LATER

I stood in front of my mirror once more, but instead of trying on a million outfits like before, this time I was wearing whatever the hell I was wearing. The clothes that made me feel comfortable. I walked over to the window of my tiny apartment in the heart of the city and looked at the succulent leaves on the windowsill; they'd all started growing little baby plants. I picked up my bottle of water and gave them a small spray. Soon their leaves would dry up completely and fall off, and they would be ready to start their new journeys . . . *kind of like me.*

I smiled and rolled my eyes. Vicki, Vicki, Vicki, with her planty analogies that made so much sense that it was scary and kind of unnerving. She and I had continued our sessions via Zoom, although she said I was ready to face the world without her and our work together was coming to an end. But to commemorate it, and the work we'd done together, I had a surprise to show her in our next session. I looked down at my arm and rolled my sleeve up, running my fingertips over the echeveria I'd had tattooed on my forearm. It was healing nicely, but damn it had hurt!

Zac loved the tattoo, though. I'd shown him over one of our regular FaceTimes. He was now obsessed with the idea of getting a tattoo and had been drawing stars, snakes, and Egyptian symbols all over himself. He was very much obsessed with ancient Egypt and Tutankhamun now, and was currently making up his own hieroglyphic language. He's such a genius. I miss him so much, but I think me being gone has been good for him in many ways. He's learned to be a bit more independent—the other day he was so excited to tell me that he'd taken his water bottle with him all by himself, and carried it the entire time he was out. That might not sound like a lot for some, but trust me, that's huge for Zac. He's also started trying different color foods. I was so proud of him.

I was excited and nervous for my first day at university—more excited, though, especially since I'd gotten a message from Thembi the night before saying she was packing her bags and was also on the way to Paris. She'd gotten into fashion school and had finally told her parents. After a big fight, many tears, and a lot of talking about feelings, her parents had agreed she should go and follow her dreams. I was so excited to see her; I'd missed her.

I reread the message I'd gotten from Jake this morning. We'd been FaceTiming every day for hours, and at night had gotten into the habit of watching Netflix together. We were currently watching *The Sopranos*. His choice. A classic, he said. I was choosing the next show. He'd moved to Stellenbosch already, and was also starting classes soon, although water polo practice had already begun.

JAKE: Anything but JustLori, good luck for your first day, although I know you're not going to need it. You're brilliant and beautiful and everyone is going to love you, not as much as I love you tho ;)

Sometimes when I thought of Jake now, I thought of what Thembi once said to me: That maybe humans weren't meant to be with one person for the rest of their lives. Maybe we were meant to be with a person for a period of time, get what we need from them in that moment, and then move on. Sometimes this thought broke my heart. Sometimes it didn't. Sometimes the thought filled me with such happiness, because even if Jake and I weren't going to be together forever, he'd helped change me. Sure, I'd done the changing, too, but he had helped and because of that, he would always be with me in a way.

I grabbed my bag and headed for the door. On the way I picked my pill up and swallowed it with a large sip of water. I still took my pill every day—anxiety wasn't something you just got over, it wasn't something that just went away magically one day. It was a process, and I was still working on it, and that was okay.

I walked out of my apartment and into the bustling streets of Paris. Everything here was completely different than what I was used to. It was so old, so steeped in history, and everything had a story to it. There was an energy in that that was hard to describe, the feeling that you were walking through the pages of a history book every day. I walked down the small cobblestone street, past the little café that I buy Coke Zero and water from. I kept walking, until the streets got even narrower. I still can't believe people are able to parallel park their cars on roads like this! I failed my driver's license the first time on parallel parking, and the road had been twice this size.

It was bloody cold here, though, and I hugged my jacket closer. I'd had to buy a new winter wardrobe when I'd arrived because none of my "warm" South African clothes were good enough. The walk to art school took me across a bridge over the Seine; I'd been there already to register for classes and for an orientation day. And every time I walked over one of the many bridges in this city, I stopped and looked down at the water. Although the color was completely different than the sea in Cape Town, or than Jake's pool, it made me think of him and our last night together. I crossed the bridge and walked onto yet another road dotted with alfresco cafés full of stylish people sipping strong coffee and eating croissants—exactly as I'd imagined it!

I smiled to myself. I still couldn't believe I was here, even after spending a month settling in. When moving to a new city, there are things you have to get used to that you never imagined before. Like which brand of tampons you should buy when they don't have the ones you're used to. Where to buy groceries and what to buy, since nothing is in English. How to activate your new SIM card . . . what the hell to use to even get the blasted SIM card out of your phone? Settling into a new place felt daunting and exciting, all at the same time. And so far I was doing all right.

I arrived at the university and stared at the building in front of me; this was where Monet and Renoir and Degas and Delacroix and all the greatest artists had come. They had walked these very corridors, and now I was here, taking my place among the greats. I wondered if I would still feel them in the corridors, as if they had imprinted their greatness onto the walls. I hoped they had, and that I could somehow absorb just a little bit of that.

But despite that orientation day spent here, I quickly found myself lost and walking in circles, late for my first class. And when I finally found it, I rushed in and everyone turned and looked at me. That familiar prickle of anxiety stirred, but it was washed away quickly when the faces around me started to smile.

"That's her . . . the street artist . . ." I heard someone say as I walked past.

"Her work is amazing . . ."

"Sorry, I'm late," I said to the lecturer. "The signs are confusing. French!"

"Don't worry, you'll get used to reading in French soon enough."

I rushed up the stairs and slipped into the only empty seat I could find.

"Welcome to History of Art," the lecturer said as I pulled out my textbook and placed it on the table in front of me.

"Hi," I whispered to the girl sitting next to me. "I'm Lori."

"Eloise," she said with a smile. "I know who you are, everyone's been talking about you since we found out you were coming here." We exchanged brief smiles and I was just about to pull out my notebook, when I felt a strange sensation, as if someone was watching me. I turned and was immediately met by two big gray-green eyes. The eyes belonged to a guy with long blond hair wearing a black leather jacket and a paint-stained T-shirt. We held eye contact for a short while and then he smiled at me and looked away.

Wow. This was so different than my first day at BWH. And it wasn't because I was across the world in another city, it was because I was so different.

I was Lori Palmer 2.0.

And I was ready for anything.

ACKNOWLEDGMENTS

There are so many people I need to thank. *Big Boned* did not happen in a vacuum—it happened because so many people took the time to read this book and give me valuable feedback that made it better. From my agent, Louise, to all the beta readers along the way. I need to thank all my readers over at Wattpad, who kickstarted my career as an author and who've supported me since day one. Everyone at Wattpad HQ and Wattpad Books who've also been there since day one, since I wrote the opening sentence to my very first book and posted it there. A huge thank-you to my husband, who helps me come up with all the concepts for my books, and spends hours and hours with me refining the stories and characters. In many ways, he is my coauthor, and my books are all the better because of him. (Even though he's never read a single book and absolutely hates reading!) A very special thank-you needs to go to my cousin Maddy and her friends, Kyra, India, Emily, and Gabi, who gave me insight into life as a teen these days. (Since I was a teen so long ago, I won't say how long . . . .) Your input and insights were invaluable, and even some of your funny lines made it into the book.

ABOUT THE AUTHOR

Jo Watson is the award-winning author of contemporary romances for both adults and teens, including The Destination Love series and her YA debut *Big Boned*, a Publisher's Marketplace Buzz Book. A graduate of the arts and media school AFDA, Jo earned an honors degree in Live Performance and worked as a script writer, director, and producer before deciding to publish her stories on Wattpad, which catapulted her now full-time career as an author. To date, her stories have accumulated more than 50 million reads on the platform and she has become an international bestselling sensation, having sold over half-a-million books worldwide, and partnering with major publishers to bring her stories to bookshelves everywhere. She lives with her husband and son in South Africa.

To get back up,
first you have to fall.

The Opposite of Falling Apart
by Micah Good

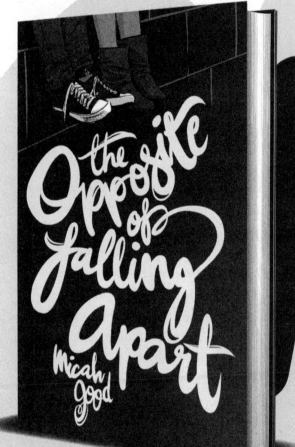

 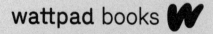

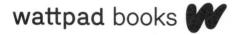

 premium

Supercharge your Wattpad experience.

Go Premium and get more from the platform you already love. Enjoy uninterrupted ad-free reading, access to bonus Coins, and exclusive, customizable colors to personalize Wattpad your way.

Try Premium **free** today.